This book belongs to...
Bernie Greaney.

© 1993 MANSELL PROMOTIONS LTD.,

Tivoli
An imprint of Gill & Macmillan Ltd
Hume Avenue
Park West
Dublin 12
with associated companies throughout the world

www.gillmacmillan.ie

© Judi Curtin 2003
0 7171 3476 8

Print origination by Red Barn Publishing
Design by Vermillion
Printed and bound by Nørhaven Paperback A/S, Denmark

A catalogue record is available for this book from
the British Library.

1 3 5 4 2

for Dan, Brian, Ellen and Annie

Nothing Great was ever
Achieved without Enthusiasm

~ ~

The Years teach Much.
Which the Days Never Know

Warmest thanks to:

Mum and Dad. My brothers and sisters. My editor,
Alison Walsh. My agent, Faith O'Grady.

Liz, for bravely agreeing to be my first reader.

And to Breeda, for lending me the newspaper that
turned out to be so significant.

ABOUT THE AUTHOR

Judi Curtin comes from Co. Cork, the setting for *Sorry,
Walter*. She studied English and German at UCC,
before training as a primary school teacher. She now
lives in Limerick with her husband and three children
and is currently working on her second novel.

Prologue

10 January

I'm thirty-four years old. I have a job and a house and all my limbs. I have a car, and a bank account which isn't quite empty. I have a television and a video and a microwave cooker. I have an ingrown toenail. I have untold riches compared to most of this world. Whole nations would kill for what I have (except, perhaps for the toenail).

But am I grateful for my good fortune?

What am I doing with these precious days of my one chance in this life?

Am I savouring my health?

Am I treasuring each breath I take?

Am I watching every glistening raindrop and every fluffy little cloud that floats gracefully past my window?

Am I giving thanks to Mother Nature, or God or Allah or Buddha or anyone greater than myself?

No.

What I'm doing on this never-to-be repeated day is contemplating the lava lamp my Auntie Mary gave me for Christmas.

Like me, the orange bubble I've been watching is boring, and rather pointless. It circulates foolishly, occasionally bumping into one of the other sad lumps that drift by, or into the glass casing. (Though the casing is probably plastic. Auntie Mary is a bit of a cheapskate.) Sometimes my bubble even joins another for a few seconds, and they cling together, briefly becoming one. Then they spring apart, their blubbery embrace over, to float alone again.

One day, someone will pull the plug on my lava lamp, and the orange lumps will drift slowly downwards, never again to move. They will end their blobby existence in a pathetic heap of saffron-coloured slime.

And no one will care.

Still, it could be worse.

At least I'm not fat or orange. And I can walk on the beach. And eat crisps.

Two packets of sour cream and onion, whenever I want.

And there's tonight. Tonight could be the night that will change my life forever.

Chapter One

11 January

My name is Maeve and I'm a writer.

I know I'm a writer, because Walter told me so last night, and he should know, he's an expert. He tossed his red curls out of his eyes, placed his thin, freckled hand on my head, and declared solemnly, 'Maeve, you are a writer.'

I suppose I shouldn't get too carried away, because he did the same to all the other sad souls in his creative writing class. There was some nervous giggling, but it soon died under Walter's disappointed, myopic gaze around his students. And, let's be clear on this, no one laughed too much because we all desperately wanted to believe him. Each one of us wanted to be the lucky individual who would, some day, prove him right.

For many years, when I was young and foolish, any time I read an exquisite poem, or a great novel, I found myself wishing that I could use words to create something, anything as fine. I have always wanted to write truly glittering prose, using language to impress, to shock, to teach, and to make lots of easy money.

Only trouble is, I never wrote anything.

Of course there were a few tortured, introspective poems when I was a teenager, and a couple of diaries, but not much else. The real stumbling block never changed; if I was having a wild, wonderful, exciting life, I had no time for writing, and if I were deadly bored and miserable, then my writing would reflect this, and read like the memoirs of Moaning Lisa. The few snippets I did get around to writing were so pathetic and whingy, I had to shred them before dumping them, lest I cause a mass suicide amongst our notoriously nosy bin men.

Then I reached thirty and realised that Keats had written his great works, died and been buried four years by the time he was my age. I knew at that stage it was time to give up my writing ambitions, or at least put them on the furthest back burner, saving them for my retirement, just in case it turned out that I was too arthritic for golf or too senile for bridge.

Honestly. I had decided to forget the whole thing. It was passé. Finito. Not on the agenda. But that was before my mum waded in. It's all her fault that I found myself in that draughty, cold classroom last night, subjecting myself to Walter's light touch and his false hopes.

Don't get me wrong though; my mum doesn't really care if I ever write anything. She doesn't want me to be

4

the next Maeve Binchy. She doesn't dream of going shopping for a fancy hat with feathers, and a lemon-coloured suit with matching handbag, so she can proudly watch her precious, talented daughter accepting the next Booker Prize.

No, my poor mum's ambitions for me are humbler than that; she just won't give up her feeble hope that one day I'll meet a nice man and settle down.

Mum tries hard to be subtle, but I can still see through her. (To be honest, a blind man could see through her – in the dark.) Every Christmas, since it began to dawn on her that I was a nearly hopeless case as far as marriage is concerned, Mum has bought me a set of night classes at the local technical school. Very kind of her, you might think, and so it is. However, it has become clear over the years that her choice of subject is greatly influenced by the number of male students that she thinks will be in the class. There's no aromatherapy or flower arranging or dressmaking for me. Anything remotely girlie or feminine is out of the question. No. It's been woodwork, metalwork, car maintenance, and DIY. I attend the classes dutifully, showing up on wet and windy winter nights, for the required ten weeks, but I haven't the heart to tell Mum that she's really wasting her money. Well, I suppose some of the classes have been interesting and I have a nice collection of shelves and plant holders, and an impressive wrought-iron poker for my troubles, but Mum still doesn't realise that, regardless of subject, all of the classes are full of women. Men are either off having wonderful lives, or else sitting at home watching sport on the television. (Well actually, I'm not sure where all the men are, but I know by now that they're not down at my local tech trying to improve themselves on Wednesday nights in January.)

This year Mum chose creative writing, perhaps hoping that I would meet a deep, arty, intellectual man, with whom I could glide off into a dreamy, metaphor-laden sunset. Or indeed, any man with a pensionable job and a heartbeat would do really. And if push came to shove, she'd skip the job and settle for the heartbeat. Just anyone at all would be fine by her, so she could at last answer in the positive when her nasty, nosy, so-called friends ask, 'How's your Maeve? Has she met a nice man yet?'

Mum made it her business to nab me this morning, when I dropped over to get a loan of her iron. (If iron-repairing classes are run in our area, my mum obviously doesn't know about them.) She sat me down with a nice cup of tea, and a plate of chocolate Kimberleys. She parked herself opposite me, blocking my escape, and fiddled with the lid of the china sugar bowl, while making small talk about nothing at all. I wasn't fooled when eventually she asked in her ever-so-casual, premeditated way, 'How was your writing class?'

What could I say? I couldn't tell her that the wonderful, dreamed-of men, her possible saviours, and mine, weren't there. I couldn't tell her that the class was full of sad, bored housewives, all planning to write witty articles for magazines, chronicling the daily activities of their darling children. I couldn't tell her that she'd failed yet again, and that perhaps she needed a new strategy. I couldn't tell her that it might be time to give up, and acknowledge the fact that her daughter is a spinster, and likely to stay that way.

I tried the non-committal approach first.

'Well, Mum, the class was fine, thanks. Could you pass the milk, please?'

'*Fine, thanks,* she says. I'm a lot wiser now, aren't I? Was it interesting? Did you write anything? Did you get any homework? Some poetry would be nice. Are you going to write some poetry? Or perhaps you could do a short story for the parish newsletter. Did you see the rubbish they printed last week? Sure they'd print anything at all.'

'Thanks, Mum. Thanks a lot for that vote of confidence in my writing ability.'

'Ah, Maeve, don't be so touchy. You know well what I mean. Don't you remember when you were little how you always wanted to be a writer? Well, this could be your big chance.'

'No, Mum. I don't think the parish newsletter is for me. That's not exactly what I used to dream of when I was little.'

'It would be a start though, wouldn't it? You can't expect to sit down and write a best-selling novel off the top of your head. Still that's not really the issue is it, anyway? Isn't the idea of the class just to get you out of the house? To get you to meet some new people. Tell me, was there anyone interesting in the class?'

About average for Mum. Forty-seven seconds to get to the point. It was time for some diversionary tactics.

'Well, the teacher was very interesting. His name is Walter, would you believe? I didn't think anyone was really called that. He's weird-looking. Kind of scattered, with straggly, gingery hair and a long, wispy beard. He was wearing little gold-rimmed glasses, but I think they were there for image-enhancement rather than vision improvement. Mind you, there was a dirty, scummy film on the lenses so they'd be quite useless in either case.'

'Maeve. How many times have I told you, you can't judge a book by the cover? The poor fella was probably in a hurry to get out for the class, and had no time to clean his glasses. I don't know why they always put on the classes at half-seven. Sure it's much too early. Auntie Helen and I were going to do bridge classes last year, but we gave up on the idea in the end. By the time I have Daddy's tea ready, and the wash-up done, and the J-cloths soaked, it's nearly eight o'clock.'

'Well, Mum, I think just for once you could leave the J-cloths unsoaked, if you really wanted to do the bridge classes. Meaningful life is possible you know, even when the cloths haven't had their daily soaking.'

'That's not the point and you know it. The people

8

who set up these classes obviously don't cook real food. I know their type. They shove any old rubbish into the microwave and call it dinner. Then they eat in front of the telly. It's easy for the likes of them to be ready at half-seven. And they make no allowances at all for people like me. For people who like to do things properly. We can go sing for all they care. That's why the crime rate has gone up so fast you know. It's all selfishness nowadays. Everyone wants to do things their own sweet way, with no thought for the old ways. And I always say, if the old ways were so bad, how come they lasted so long?'

'Probably because people were afraid of change,' I suggested tentatively. I am always slightly wary of interrupting Mum in mid-flight. She can be unpredictable at the best of times, and a nudge in the wrong direction could be disastrous.

'That's not it at all. Old ways are best. Take baking, for instance. For years and years we creamed the butter and sugar first. Then these fancy chefs come on the telly, and tell us it's all wrong, That Jamie Olivier fella, with his "bung it in" and his "that's just pukka", what does he know? And what kind of a word is pukka?'

'Apparently it's an Indian word meaning genuine.'

'You know everything, don't you, smarty pants.'

'You asked me, so I just told you what pukka means.'

'It was a rhetorical question, actually. And since you're so smart, tell me this; did anyone ever eat a cake that Jamie fella made? I doubt it. Like rocks I bet. They just jazz them up so they look good for the camera, then as soon as the lights go out they throw them in the bin. You can't get a light cake unless you cream the butter and sugar first. And what's his girlfriend doing in the show? I bet she's not even a chef. Poor old Gay Byrne got into awful trouble for letting Kathleen do a few voiceovers on the Late, Late, and he only trying to make a few honest bob, after the terrible way his so-called friend treated him. And as for that Nigella one. She has no time to cream butter and sugar 'cause she spends all her time putting on her make-up, and adjusting her tights. Pornography is her game, not cookery. It wouldn't have been allowed twenty years ago. Then half her show is given over to her so-called friends arriving for dinner. Friends my eye. They're only actors. There was a guy in her dining room last week, and I'd swear I saw him propping up the bar in the Rovers Return the next night. They fill them up with drink so they won't taste the food. I'm no fool. I know what they're at.'

Mum rambled on, as she does, and I didn't interrupt. I wasn't reminding her of her briefly forgotten crusade. I wasn't going to be the one to tell her that she was meant to be finding out about the potential husbands in my creative writing class. As she rambled, I nodded occasionally and mused about Walter. He fits the stereotype of a writer perfectly. In the unlikely event of one of his pupils ever succeeding in writing a novel, he couldn't figure in it. He'd require far too much suspension of disbelief. He is too predictable to be true.

I spent the entire class watching him in amazement. He waved his thin, freckled hands around a lot (when he wasn't using them to anoint us), and he enthused about the joy of writing, the wonders of the imagination. He told us about the muse that might one day land on each of our shoulders and whisper wonderful, dreamy secrets, tickling our ears with its scented breath. It was hard to concentrate on the muse's scented breath, though, as my nostrils filled with the scent of wet overcoat emanating from the lady in front of me. Anyway, even though I might have been moved by all of this ten years ago, now I felt old and jaded, and I didn't really care any more. I didn't want to be rude though, and while I didn't feel inspired by his enthusiasm, I did feel a bit embarrassed and guilty and so I agreed to write something for next week.

One serious-looking woman, with the imprint of her apron strings still clearly visible on her wrinkled neck (either that, or she was engaged in a little light bondage before coming to class) raised her hand. She bravely asked the question the rest of us were afraid to enunciate. 'What will we write about?'

Walter (surely he made that name up) gave the answer he must have learned in his first class at creative-writing-teacher training college. 'Write about what you know.'

That's settled it then. I'm going to write about something I know very well: a subject very near and dear to my heart. I'm going to write about myself.

I suppose I'm going to end up writing a diary, which is really a bit sad. You see, I won't have anything terribly exciting to relate. I'm not going to be writing about death-defying skydiving leaps or passionate romances, or tear-inducing tragedies. I won't be writing about million-pound deals, or incredible betting scams. There won't be any handsome doctors falling for shy young nurses. There won't be any tall, dark men with rugged good looks and cleft chins. The beautiful, scornful women, tossing manes of golden hair, will be absent too. There won't be sex, or much shopping either, unless I decide to write about my sad trips to the supermarket, buying meals for one, and the small cans of baked beans.

No. I'm just getting a feel for writing, after years of writing nothing more creative than end-of-term school reports. (Now that I think of it though, they need to be creative in their own way, as I struggle to find a way to say, 'your child is a complete menace,' without giving offence.)

Walter will be very pleased with me. I've bought a lovely new hard-backed notebook with pretty pink and mauve flowers on the cover. I've taken out the fountain pen that I got for my sixteenth birthday, and filled it up with deep black ink. I'm going to write a little every day. I'm going to be the perfect student, with pages and pages of neat, if unexciting, writing to present to my mentor every Wednesday night.

And so what if no one ever reads my work? So what if someone finds my little notebook a few weeks after my funeral, and tosses it unread into a bonfire, along with my other treasured possessions; the little scraps of paper, and photographs that mean so much to me, and would mean nothing at all to an outsider? It may singe first and then burn slowly at the edges, the flames licking onwards, towards the centre, first eating up the pink and mauve flowers, and then my precious, carefully thought-out words. Afterwards some happily married strangers might turn away, well-satisfied, ready to clean and paint my little home, and make it theirs, alienating my ghost, leaving me homeless forever.

See. I said it in the beginning. When I'm fed up and miserable I'll be very prolific. I'll produce miles and miles and miles of sad, depressing words.

Walter, you've a lot to answer for!

Chapter Two

This is it.

My writing career has been reborn.

My recently anointed head is full of marvellous ideas.

My pen is full of ink.

My flowery notebook is full of blank pages.

My stomach is full of the toasted cheese and tomato sandwiches I made in an effort to put off the brave new beginning.

A little profile to get me started. Walter says we should set the scene in the opening chapters of our novels, gradually introducing the characters, dropping snippets of information, tiny teasers to keep the reader interested. (I'm not writing a novel, but I can't tell him that. I couldn't bear the look of disappointed distress that I know would wash over his gaunt, freckled face.) Anyway, his way sounds like very hard work, so I am going for the less subtle approach, and if the reader (in the unlikely event of there ever being one) loses interest, well, so be it. Indulge me. I'm new to this entire writing lark. Maybe I'll get better as I go along.

> *Name:* Maeve Hurley.
>
> *Age:* Thirty-four.
>
> *Sex:* None recently.
>
> *Background:* Second of three children. No great family traumas or skeletons. Well brought up by loving parents. Brother and sister both happily married. Seven sweet little nephews and nieces who love their Auntie Maeve.
>
> *Appearance:* A difficult one this. I'll give you the basics — brown hair, brown eyes, average height, average build. I'm sure you're not any wiser now though. It's difficult to look at one's own appearance, and give an honest appraisal. Twenty years ago I used to look in the mirror and see if I could see spots, or blackheads; now it's wrinkles that catch my eye. Those and grey hairs of course. If I had done something wonderful with my life, I suppose I could live with the grey hairs, but as it is, I feel that my life hasn't yet got going; it's too soon to be showing signs of age. I'm not ready for all that.
>
> If it's any help, I suppose I should mention that I'm probably rather nondescript in appearance. I've decided that by watching how people respond when they first meet me. They

neither recoil in horror, nor give me that eager, animated attention I've seen beautiful women receive. It could be worse I suppose. Then again, it could be better.

Oh dear. I think I've just got a bit carried away. Sorry, Walter, I'll try to keep to the point.

Occupation: Teacher in nice, ordinary primary school near Cork.

Reason for taking this nice job in nice ordinary primary school near Cork: To save up for wild exciting trip around the world.

Reason for not having been on wild exciting trip around the world: Traumatic break-up with boyfriend who was to have been fellow-traveller.

Years that have passed since this happened: Ten.

Reason I haven't got off my behind and gone without him: Despite my best intentions, I never got around to it.

Number of men I have been out with since traumatic break-up: Fifteen. (Yes, I'm such a sad person I've kept count, and I've even included one guy I went for a casual cup of coffee with, after a union meeting. Oh and one guy, whose name I forget, that I drunkenly snogged on New Year's Eve three years ago.)

Number of men I've been out with more than twice since aforementioned traumatic break-up: None.

Reason I cannot maintain relationships: Despite my best efforts, all the men I meet have to measure up to the rat who left me because he wasn't ready to get serious, and who married a year later and is now wonderfully happy with his wife and three perfect children.

So there you have it. As promised, I didn't go for the subtle approach, but I've got the basics in. (Let's ignore the fact that I have probably just copied the style of the last novel I read – let's call it admiration, not plagiarism.) That's me according to me. Trouble is, I don't know if I'm a good judge of character, especially my own. I may have unwittingly left out the one crucial detail that would encapsulate my personality, revealing all in a few carefully chosen words. Did I tell the truth or did I lie? Can I possibly be as ordinary as the person I have just described? Could anyone be as ordinary as that? Or, indeed, is everyone, thus being by definition, ordinary? Did I just neglect to mention that I am a world champion at synchronised swimming, or a pioneering scientist, or a convicted murderess?

Then again, perhaps the truth will seep through my words, whether I like it or not. Perhaps my writing is like a cracked bowl: porous, ugly and useless.

That's tough, non-existent reader; you'll never know.

If you want the truth, read the Bible.

If you want fiction, read the Cork city bus timetable.

If you're not quite sure what you want, and have lots of spare time . . . read on.

Chapter Three

Creative writing class tomorrow, so I'd better write some more. Can't let Mum and Walter and the housewives down. Can't give up while my sight is still clear and my middle finger unblistered. Can't abandon my writing career without even having refilled my fountain pen.

We just went back to school today after the Christmas holidays. We were two weeks late because the pipes burst, and the plumbing was in such a state that it took the poor long-suffering plumbers this long to get it sorted. I will spare you the gory details, because, believe me, you don't want to know what the little darlings had managed to stuff down plugholes, and flush down toilets. I will say though, that the plumbers, in one cistern alone, found three soggy packets of sandwiches (one cheese, one ham and one unidentifiable), two oranges, assorted crayons and pencils, and a disintegrating pack of rude playing cards. And I thought my job was hard!

Now that it's nearly February though, it was even more embarrassing than usual to be returning to my classroom to see the Christmas decorations still droopily adorning the walls and ceiling. The paper chains, cardboard Santas with cotton wool beards, and the lopsided stars with varying numbers of sagging points, hung defiantly from the ceiling, swaying in the draught from the rattly windows. They seemed to accuse me, as they dangled there – 'You're a bad teacher, you should be on page fifty-six of the maths book by now, not pulling down last year's rubbish at the beginning of this bright New Year.'

I'm beyond help really, imagining myself being put down by a blotchy, red Santa with a body made from the inside of a toilet roll.

The kids were happy, though. All keen to tell the world what Santa brought them. Two spoilt little articles got PlayStations complete with a large selection of mindless, violent, anti-social games, bought by so-called loving parents. Most of the others got the usual mix of sensible, practical presents and total rubbish which will clog up their homes until their frustrated mothers will dump it all in the bin while I am distracting the little darlings by revising their six times tables. Again.

My Christmas presents are all neatly stacked on the shelf in my living room, just to the left of the fireplace. Every year I like to keep them there for a while, partly because it makes me feel good that so many people buy me presents. (Though that's a bit pathetic as in our school it's practically compulsory for each child to give their teacher a 'token of their appreciation' at Christmas time, which gives me an automatic thirty gifts by the twentieth of December. And presents from family don't count, as they're hardly optional either.) Anyway, I like to look through my pile of treats every now and then, before they assimilate themselves into my life, or find their way into a charity shop, to continue their lives in a never-ending circle of purchase and rejection.

My aunt gave me a spoon-rest once. It was made of fine white china, decorated all around the edge with deep-blue forget-me-nots. It was inoffensive, I suppose, and pretty enough. I'd say it was even expensive, but I ask you, a spoon-rest? Had she never heard of saucers?

I know everyone has different tastes, but there are certain things in this world that nobody could possibly want. I always thought foot spas were a joke. I thought they were made-up booby prizes for daytime quiz shows. I didn't think they really existed until another auntie gave me one for Christmas. (I'm Irish. I get to have lots of aunties.) Am I that pathetic that she honestly thinks I would like to sit alone in my living room, bathing my feet in barely bubbling water in a silly blue and white plastic dish? Does she think my life is so empty that I would dance home from school, singing, 'Yesss!! Life is so wonderful. Tonight I'll have

21

a foot spa.' Does she think I get through my lonely days by dreaming of happy evenings of wet floors and wrinkled feet?

If I were ever fool enough to feel the need to use my foot spa, this is what I'd have to do. First I'd have to spend half an hour dismantling the box, separating the polystyrene sections and the countless plastic bags, unwinding those resilient little black wire ties, resisting the urge to eat the little white sachets of 'do not eat' gel. Then I'd have to read the instructions, (which come in a seventy page book, one page of which is in English). Next I'd have to remove a plug from some underused electrical appliance, attach it to the foot spa, re-boil the kettle... No, my life isn't that meaningless, thank you very much Auntie Helen. I can always watch QVC if I get that desperate to fill a few hours. Or I could iron my tea towels. Or I could write a sonnet sequence.

Foot spa, be warned. Your days in my house are numbered.

You've probably heard enough about my Christmas presents, so I'm going to tell you a little about the staff of my school, Castlelough Primary, established (according to the grey stone over the front door) in 1931. Walter says we should observe real people, watching their little quirks of character, but not write openly about them, lest we be sued when we are published. This drew girlish titters from the housewives, (who are no longer girls), but I ignored it, as my work is going to be tossed unread on the bonfire etc. etc. I alone can tell the truth.

Mr Flynn, the principal, teaches fifth and sixth classes. I don't know how old he is, but I figure he must be close to retirement age. He's the old-style school master. Big into mental maths and Irish grammar. Not so hot on project work and 'that old arty stuff', which he only teaches under protest when he knows the inspector is due for his brief annual visit. (It doesn't matter, really, as the inspector doesn't appear to be interested. As far as I can see he only comes for a chat about GAA, and the free cup of coffee, and the Mikado biscuits that Mr Flynn seems to think he would like. We all jump to attention anyway, and show our best sides for the duration of his stay. We feel a bit nervous while he's there, but only because it's expected of us.)

Mr Flynn is very strict, but the children love him, as he has a gentle way about him, and a fine sense of humour. He regularly bores the pants off them though, droning on and on, but they don't seem to mind. Sometimes I pass their room, and it seems as if the children have learned the art of group reverie, gazing into space, completely ignoring their teacher. If any of his pupils graduate to become commuters on London Transport, they'll fit in perfectly – looking straight ahead, showing no awareness of their surroundings, the living dead on wheels.

Mr Flynn (I can't call him William, even after all these years) never comes up with wild ambitious schemes of change, like some school principals do. He likes everything to run along smoothly, predictably. He doesn't interfere much in what goes on in the other classrooms. I suppose he figures that if there was a major problem, he'd hear about it, and if not, then we're better left alone.

That suits me fine. I teach third and fourth classes, and have done since I started work here eleven years ago. It's that sort of school, you find your own special niche, and you stay there. Forever. That's life for you. Here today – still here tomorrow.

I cover the basics adequately, but prefer to spend my time doing the more interesting peripheral subjects. I can do this without guilt, as I know that when they move on, Mr Flynn, regardless of what I have done, will spend his time drilling the children on facts and figures. I enjoy the children. I love to listen to their little stories, seeing the innocence under their superficial sophistication, searching for what is hidden under the worldly-wise ways learned from television and adult pop songs. I love to see their childish pride when they master something new like knitting, or multiplication, or spelling, or making paper aeroplanes. It's such a shame they have to grow up and become people.

Pat, who teaches first and second classes, is a brilliant teacher, and the kids get on great with him. Sometimes, though, it seems that he's just putting in the time between premier league matches on Sky

Sports. He knows that no one else on the staff finds soccer to be the most riveting topic of conversation, but he's so wrapped up in his precious Manchester United, he can't help telling us all about them, at length, after each of their winning matches. The children in his class, whether they like it or not, do extensive projects on soccer and their maths problems are all about the area of soccer pitches and the complexities of goal difference. When it's time for art, they draw pictures of soccer matches, or design flamboyant jerseys for imaginary Italian soccer teams. When Pat divides the children into groups for reading, he names each group after a premier league team, careful never to give offence by naming the weakest group after the poor losers who are facing relegation.

It wouldn't be for me, but perhaps Pat has the perfect marriage. He and his two soccer-mad sons watch telly all night, and his wife is free to go out to play bridge every evening, winning cup after cup. Perhaps she's trying to impress them but I suspect they're not interested. They only care about the sort of cups won by eleven sweaty men in shorts and trendy haircuts, who marry supermodels and get involved in widely reported bar brawls. I think they're probably glad that she doesn't stay home vying for the remote control, trying to watch *ER* or the news, when they could be following the fortunes of the Romanian second division, or whatever it is they watch on the odd night when there's no English soccer on. Pat is the classic Irish male, and proud of it, and he's raising two fine sons to follow in his old-fashioned footsteps.

Since I've got this far, I'd better continue down to the infants class, and Theresa.

Where should I start?

I know that if I really got going, I could fill lots of flowery-covered notebooks with descriptions of the great Theresa.

I hate her, really. She's twenty-two, and has been on the staff for two years. Though I liked Mrs Lynch, Theresa's predecessor, I had been looking forward to some new blood, a new face in the staff room, some new topics of conversation to liven up our coffee break on wet November days. Then Theresa arrived, and I began to wonder if there was any way to tempt Mrs Lynch out of retirement; any sob story I could make up that would persuade her to come back and deliver us.

Theresa is prim and proper and smug. She can sing and dance and act and sew and speak four languages. When she was in training college, she won the medal for the best student in her year. Every year. She plays the tin whistle, and has medals for camogie. She's a member of the Saint Vincent de Paul Society, and the Legion of Mary. She's good at everything. If she went to Thailand, she'd probably be good at the rude things the girls do with bananas and bottle openers.

I bet she was a model child. I doubt very much if she ever picked her nose or used bad language, or hid her unwanted broccoli in her trouser pockets. I'm sure she always said 'please' and 'thank you,' and 'excuse me from the table'. She probably even wore her days-of-the-week knickers on the correct days.

She's the perfect teacher. Her notes are always up to date, her class is always happy and occupied, her work could never be faulted. She invariably takes down her Christmas decorations on the day of the holidays. She puts away her Christmas wallcharts for next year, (on the shelf in her chart press labelled – 'seasonal events, Christmas, Halloween etc'), and then lays out the work for the first day of the new term on her desk, all ready for January.

She dresses in clothes my mother would reject as being too old-fashioned; all tweed skirts, woolly tights, sensible shoes and silky blouses with bows at the neck. She always wears her hair tied back in a ponytail, and she only owns three scrunchies: one brown, one navy and one bottle green. She will never be accused of flamboyance, our Theresa.

Theresa, as she often reminds us, is engaged to be married. Her fiancé, Michael, is also a teacher, in another nice ordinary primary school a few miles away. They've been going out together since they met in the first year of teacher training college, and got engaged on the day of their graduation. They're not getting married for two more years though, as they 'don't want to rush things'. They're saving for a nice deposit on a nice house, and have a joint bank account for that purpose.

Theresa ignores me most of the time. I think she despises me because I'm different to her and that's fine by me. The feeling's mutual. Mostly I just ignore her back, but sometimes I can't resist baiting her. I don't know why I bother though, as I never get a decent reaction. Occasionally, on a Monday morning, I ask if she and Michael have been on a dirty weekend together. She never rises to the bait, though. She just flicks her dull grey eyes towards the ceiling, shakes her head in an irritating, patronising fashion, and returns to her knitting.

I forgot to mention that, didn't I? Theresa spends her coffee breaks knitting jumpers for Michael. He must have hundreds of them stashed away. Arans, Fair-Isles, striped and plain ones. He picks her up after school every day, ('having two cars would be such a waste'), and each day he wears a different one of Theresa's works of art, afraid, I suppose, to wear anything else. They're all knitted in thick, thick wool, which must irritate his poor spotty neck terribly. Theresa doesn't notice this though, and knits away furiously, as if she has something to prove.

I even hate the way Theresa walks. She puts her head slightly down, and strides along swinging her arms like an over-enthusiastic army sergeant. She never strolls or ambles; she walks with a purpose, with the heels of her sensible shoes making little thudding noises as they firmly strike the ground. Theresa knows where she's going, and you can be sure she will get there, which I suppose is the real reason for the hatred I feel for her.

That's it. That's our staff. Wonderful bunch, don't you think?

Wouldn't you wake in the morning with joy in your heart at the prospect of spending hours in their company?

Wouldn't you skip in the doorway, rushing for your first glimpse of their dear faces?

Wouldn't you hang on their every word, savouring each precious syllable?

No?

Me neither.

And yet, something drags me in to that school, day after day after day. I haven't missed a day in nine years. I know I'd get away with the odd pretend-sick day, curled up in my warm bed with hot drinks and the newspaper, but I don't try.

Perhaps I am filled with a sense of duty.

Perhaps I wouldn't like to let the children down.

Perhaps I would feel guilty about defrauding the Department of Education.

Perhaps I know I might never go back if I were to escape for a few precious hours.

And what would I do with my life then?

Chapter Four

24 January

I've been very bold.

Walter doesn't collect our work, like I collect the children's copies at school. He just gives us his watery (Waltery?) gaze and suggests that we might like to select a little piece of our week's work, a snippet to share with our fellow writers. That's all very well in theory. In fact, the housewives vie to be the first to read out their drivel, spouting forth until even Walter can't take any more and begs for someone else to be allowed to read. But, for me, this writing lark's becoming more than a mere exercise, more than just a few words to keep Walter happy. Suddenly it seems that everything I've written is too personal to share with the housewives.

And besides, what if one of them knew Theresa?

So while I was waiting for Walter to arrive this evening, I scribbled out a meaningless poem. It was in a stream-of-consciousness style, or maybe torrent-of-consciousness would be more accurate. I got a bit carried away and produced two pages of utter garbage. When my turn for sharing came around, I read it aloud, and the housewives muttered amongst themselves, wondering if I was a hidden genius, or just totally nuts. Walter probably learned in creative-writing-teacher training college, that he should find something positive to say about every piece of work presented to him, but it was clear he was in difficulty. He stood with one hand in the pocket of his fawn corduroy jacket, and the other stroking his hairy chin, racking his brains.

'Hmm. Hmm. That was very interesting, Maeve. Most interesting indeed. There's a lot of stimulating imagery in there. I can tell you've worked very hard on this piece.'

I shrugged and did my best to look like someone who works hard on pieces of poetry.

My response must have been appropriate, because Walter continued. 'Now Maeve, a few small questions for you to ponder. Do you think metaphor works here, or should you have reverted to simile in the third stanza? You end with a rather daring use of assonance, can you justify this in the context of your poem? What do you think is the crucial image?'

I tried hard to look as if I knew what he was talking about. I pursed my lips and nodded pensively.

'Well, Walter, I'm not quite sure actually.'

31

Walter kindly decided to help me answer this difficult question. 'To me, the image of the crumpled eiderdown is just a little jaded. The seventies poets beat that particular image to death. I find the mauvely dripping wisteria and the burnt lasagne to be much stronger threads. Which of those is closer to your heart? Which one feels so right that it almost hurts?'

This was worse than I had feared. I put my head down and muttered something non-committal.

'Now, Maeve, don't be shy. We're all friends here. Aren't we?' There was a silent chorus of nodding housewife heads. 'Pick one image and tell us how it came to you. Did you strive for it or did your muse drop it unannounced, like a single soft snowflake on a winter's day?'

I could see that I would not be allowed to escape. It was clear that Walter was going to hound me with his flowery histrionics until I co-operated. I took a deep breath. 'OK, then. The burnt lasagne. It came to me because when I was writing this poem I could see a dirty lasagne dish soaking in the sink.'

One housewife began a chortle, but stifled it under Walter's steely glare.

'Yes, Maeve. That's good. Don't ever be afraid of the ordinary. It's important to see poetry in the mundane. Now, would you like to tell us in a few words what your poem really means to you?'

'Sorry, Walter,' I answered brightly. 'It's a bit personal.'

Walter tried not to look too relieved, and moved quickly on.

'Thank you, Maeve. Now, Annie, I can see you are itching to share your work with us.'

Annie gave a simpering little smile that might have suited her if she had tried it thirty years earlier.

'Thank you, Walter. My poem is called "Persuading Peter to Eat". It's about my son, Peter, who will be three in July. The twenty-fifth. He was three weeks premature. He gave us a few frights, but he's fine now, thank God. His bowels. . .'

Walter interrupted. 'Yes Annie, background information can be critical in understanding a work of literature, but let's not get bogged down, shall we?'

Annie gave a small, slighted toss of her head, and began to read.

'Peter, sweet Peter.
I love you as much as I wish you loved your
    food.
I love you as much as I wish you loved
    mashed potatoes.
And lamb chops.
Even chips would be OK.
The oven kind.
Organic cornflakes. . .'

Annie went on to read four pages of dull verse about the pros and cons of various breakfast cereals, before ending mid-sentence, frantically flipping from sheet to

loose sheet, mystified as to where to go next. Walter
dived into the silence, just a second too late, as there
erupted amongst Annie's peers an animated discussion
about weaning, food fads and the difficulty in getting
toddlers to eat. One lady left her seat, tiptoed over to
me and gave me a little household hint for removing
burnt-on lasagne from Pyrex dishes. Walter began to
look a little distressed, as he knew he had lost them, so
he declared the class to be over, though I knew there
was ten minutes left. He loped off disconsolately, and I
left too, leaving the strains of 'my Jason just won't eat
his veg,' echoing bleakly in the deserted corridor.

*

Did I write about my Christmas present to myself yet? I
had some money saved to buy a new table and chairs
for my kitchen, and I went as far as going to look at
some in one of those huge furniture warehouses that
have sprung up on every entrance to the city. I found a
few I liked, and a few I could afford, and one set that I
could both afford and live with. Then I looked around
me, and noticed that all of my fellow-shoppers were
young couples, arguing good-naturedly over prices and
colours, or discussing how many they could seat for a
dinner party or whether their baby's booster seat
would fit onto a particular chair. One loud couple
cornered a timid-looking salesman, stridently
demanding instructions for removing dried porridge
from the woven straw seat of a large carver.

All of a sudden, I felt like an outsider, alienated in the gloomy, draughty expanse of the warehouse. I had no business in a furniture shop. My scruffy old red-Formica-topped kitchen table is only used in the morning as I force down a virtuous bowl of muesli and a mug of hot tea. I eat my other meals from my knee, in front of the television. Suddenly I realised that I was buying this furniture in a pathetic effort to belong to a different world, to be a different person.

As if a fancy new table and chairs could make me fit in!

I'm afraid that would take a bit more than a few sticks of varnished light oak, and some tasteful paisley-patterned cushions, all on special offer at €499.99. (Delivery included.)

In a rare flash of inspiration and impulsiveness I decided to spend my precious savings on a computer. I rushed out, and predictably, there was a computer superstore next door (and, you've guessed it, a carpet warehouse next to that). A lucky young salesman, with short, gelled hair, a cheap pinstriped suit, and a smarmy manner didn't even have to try, as I bought the first machine he showed me. It was delivered the next day, and I haven't looked back since.

I'm having great fun on the Internet, wandering around, wide-eyed and impressed, like a gormless stranger in a foreign country. I feel sorry for the poor encyclopaedia salesmen, trying to peddle their wares in a world that has the World Wide Web in it. How can they compete with the information that's out there, swirling over our heads in some electronic netherworld, waiting for us to tap in?

Since I got my ugly grey machine, I've found out lots of things I never knew, and to be honest, lots of things I never needed to know. For example, a flyer came with my post one day, trying to sell me some patio plants. One was a miniature peach tree called 'Bonanza', which sounded very nice, but then it would, they wanted me to pay €29.95 for it. I looked it up in my many gardening books, but none mentioned it. Then I remembered my trusty friend, the Internet. Carefully, I keyed in 'Bonanza', and then, so as not to get all of the sites devoted to 1960s TV serials, I added 'peaches'. I'm not quite sure how, but suddenly my screen was full of sites called things like 'Asian Babes' and 'Hot Japanese Schoolgirls'. Purely in the interest of improving my computer knowledge, I clicked on a few, and found half-revealed tantalising pictures, and little boxes urging me to type in my credit card details. They assured me with great pride that I wouldn't be billed, but they wanted the details just to prove that I was over 18. Now, I might be a simple Irish girl, but I'm not quite that naïve. I don't really fancy having to phone my credit card company asking them not to pay the account called 'kinky lesbo sex', as I didn't really mean to subscribe. I'm sure they've heard it, and rejected it all before.

A lot of the time I am a little lost in my surfing, lost

in space so to speak. It's a nice kind of lost. I'm not going anywhere in particular anyway, and sometimes I stumble across some unexpectedly interesting places, places I wasn't looking for, but places I'm glad I found. Yesterday I came across a site dedicated to home exchanges, and I clicked in. Home exchanging is the kind of thing teachers do, like buying a Ford Fiesta when they get their first job, or playing the tin whistle in an Aran sweater or sending home-made cards at Christmas. This site sowed some seeds in my mind, as I feel I deserve a nice long faraway holiday this summer, but can't really afford it. It would be nice to spend a few weeks in America without having to cough up serious money for a large, scary, impersonal hotel. A villa on the beach at Santa Monica would be much more my style.

I will look into this a bit further next week. Now I must get ready to go out jarring with my best friend, Maria. (See Walter. I can do it. See how I casually slipped this new character in.)

Maria and I have been friends since college. We studied together, travelled together, got drunk together and cried on each other's shoulders. Many times. Maria had the unhappy knack of getting involved with men who treated her badly. She became used to being two-timed, ignored and cruelly dumped. I could never understand how such a nice girl seemed to attract every scumbag in the Northern Hemisphere. She began to expect bad treatment, so much so, that when Joe came along and treated her with basic respect and decency, she didn't quite know how to react. She kept waiting for him to change into a cruel rat, as if a cruel alter ego was lurking in the shadows of Joe's big, open personality, waiting for its chance to pounce, and destroy the dreams she was afraid to dream. It took quite a while for her to realise that this wasn't going to happen. Luckily she had sense enough to marry Joe, and they are blissfully happy. She doesn't cry any more.

I was afraid our relationship would not survive Maria's marriage but I was wrong. Joe, Maria and I get on great, and I often socialise with them, or join them at home for meals. Occasionally though, I feel the need to step back and give them some space, as I worry that they would be jumping on top of each other, having mad passionate sex on the kitchen table if I weren't there. (I'm not married you see, so I don't really know what goes on. What I know of marriage comes from the two extremes of my parents' affectionate, but jaded union, and the marriages from hell that are regularly portrayed on Channel 4. I'm not exactly an expert.) It can be difficult. Sometimes, after a pleasant dinner at Maria and Joe's, I feel a bit in the way, but if I said this, they would protest vehemently, so I have to invent reasons to leave, pretending I have other great diversions. Politeness requires such a lot of lying! The truth is always the same though; I keep one eye on my watch for the entire evening, and then leave reluctantly to return to my own, dark, empty home.

Every Thursday night, Maria and I head off to town to drink and talk girlie talk, just like we always did. Joe pretends to sneer at us. 'Off to talk about your insides again girls?' he asks each week. We just make rude gestures to him, but not too rude, as we need him to collect us from the pub and drive us home. This is kind of him, as their wonderful, rambling home in Carrigaline is a few miles from mine, but he says he doesn't mind, and I appreciate the opportunity to enjoy a few drinks without having to worry about driving home. I love those nights with Maria, and I find myself saving up anecdotes during the week, rehearsing them in my head, ready to share with her. She could go on a quiz show, and have as her specialist topic – 'Why Maeve hates Theresa' or 'Everything that is boring about Castlelough Primary School.' Maria is perfect; she's a good listener and a good friend.

That's why I don't mind the fact that she's my only friend.

I also have my family.

And anyway I was never one of life's social butterflies.

And I quite like being on my own.

I'll just try not to dwell on the summer a few years ago when Maria and Joe went to Australia for two months. That summer passed in a haze of emptiness and isolation. I was bereft in a way no normal person should be, just because her friend has gone on the trip of a lifetime. I waited for Maria's funny, chatty postcards with an impatience that could not be natural. And, when she came home, I was half-shy of meeting her again, afraid that she would observe my relief at her return, and be frightened by my need.

What if Maria went to live in Australia forever?

Or if we fell out?

Or if she died?

I suppose I could become a nun. There'd always be someone to talk to in the convent. I'd never be alone again.

Even if I wanted to.

I'd have to take a vow of poverty.

And I'd have no sex. It would be just like now.

With prayers.

And a black dress. And black looks really awful on me. It makes me look as if I'm dead.

Which might not be inappropriate.

There would be tea with the parish priest. Or with the bishop on special occasions.

I'd get to live in a half-empty, draughty convent.

I'd have to pretend to enjoy the religious programmes on TV. I couldn't laugh if *Father Ted* got switched on by accident.

There'd be sniggers from haughty, knowing school-girls.

And institution food. Boiled cabbage. Lumpy custard. Semolina.

Gammon steaks.

Oh, dear. Maybe I'd better just be nice to Maria, and

make sure she keeps taking vitamin supplements and drinking green tea.

And perhaps I should try to make a few new friends, just in case.

Chapter Five

Wherever did they find Walter?

And why don't they put him back there?

Ten minutes before the end of last week's class Walter raised his arm for silence. He waited with noble patience, while one housewife picked up the scattered contents of her pencil case, including a pencil parer, which managed to roll the entire length of the classroom, ending up in the farthest, dustiest corner. He tapped his foot with remarkable equanimity while another woman undid and then redid her elaborate, greying bun. Finally, he folded his corduroy-clad arms, and intoned one single word.

'Home.'

After a brief pause he repeated himself.

'Home.'

For one joyous moment I thought he meant for us to go home, but unfortunately I was wrong. Walter had just started his usual scene-setting for the upcoming week's work.

'Great writing does not need exotic locations. No. Great poetry comes from the heart, and as we all know, home is where the heart is. Or to put it another way, there's no place like home.'

I feared we were going to be burdened with a litany of clichés about the home, but Walter suddenly veered to another course and began to recite 'The Old Woman of the Roads'. Now that is a classic poem, and I have nothing against classic poems, but in this case it was a mistake. The housewives began a sing-song accompaniment to Walter's recitation, and when he stopped after the second verse, they continued, right to the bitter end, to the last word of the fifth verse, all in unison, all without feeling, no doubt dragged back in time to tedious poetry classes of their schooldays. Walter knew better than to interrupt, so he waited in silence, picking at his left thumbnail until they were finished.

'I see you all learned that by heart, and that you all have very long memories. Now, what does home mean to us?'

This was becoming a familiar exercise. The obedient housewives began to call out words and phrases, and Walter scrawled them onto the blackboard using purple chalk.

'Security.'

'Peace.'

'Safe and warm.'

'Sanctuary.'

When everyone else had offered something, Walter turned on me with the intense look I was beginning to dread. I decided to play the game, and muttered feebly, 'Bricks and mortar.'

'Well done, Maeve. Good creative thinking. We need the concrete as well as the nebulous. We don't want to get too airy fairy, do we?'

'No, Walter, I suppose we don't.'

Walter drew a series of elaborate squiggles around the words on the blackboard, and turned to us in triumph. 'Now, ladies. For next week please do some creative writing on the topic of 'home'. As usual, find a quiet corner so your muse won't be afraid to appear. We know how timid muses are, don't we? And we don't like frightened muses, do we? Frightened muses are silent, aren't they? And is a silent muse any good at all, at all?'

His docile pupils nodded and shook their heads where appropriate. Some silly women were even painstakingly copying down the meaningless scrawl from the blackboard.

Walter continued. 'Don't forget. You must write from the heart. Poetry, prose, it doesn't matter at all, just let the words flow, and we can share the results next week.'

He hesitated. 'Class dismissed.'

The housewives and I packed our belongings and left.

Home. That's fine by me; it's time I set the scene for my life. A sense of place is important. And, anyway,

I've already written about most of the people I know, and I'm not very good at making people up. The housewives won't get to hear any of this though. I've prepared a small dissertation for them, about a wild cavewoman living on a deserted island. Of course the island can't be deserted if the wild cavewoman is living on it, but that doesn't matter. They never listen to me anyway, so they won't notice. They've relegated me to the role of token oddball in the class, and I'm quite enjoying playing to their expectations. Walter doesn't know what to make of me, so he just tries hard not to engage me, as he attempts to find different, noncommittal words to describe the waffle I read to him each week. It's a bit mean of me to treat him so, but he's getting paid: he might as well earn his money.

Now to the real business: my home.

For a long time I imagined that I would set up home with Paddy, my erstwhile beloved boyfriend. I pictured a romantic little cottage with roses around the door, and a white picket fence, all modern conveniences inside, and a few golden-haired children playing in the sunshine outside, but, as you know, that didn't work out. After that I just lived at home, with my long-suffering mum and dad. When I got to the age of twenty-five, though, it was faintly embarrassing to be still there, with no prospect of ever leaving. Then I gradually became aware that Mum and Dad didn't like to go out in the evenings, leaving me alone, as if they still needed to baby-sit me, as if I had to be kept company all the time. That was a little unfair on them, even though I didn't ask for or expect such treatment. I found myself developing a childish charade, pretending to them that I had plans to go out, just so they'd go out, and once they were gone, I'd curl up by the fire with a book, and one of Dad's beers.

That was another thing. I never got to do the shopping or the cooking or the washing. Mum and Dad shared willingly, but it was always their food, their house. I never did the grown-up jobs. Sometimes I dried the dishes, or swept the floor, but that was about it; the same tasks I started doing when I was nine. I paid a token few pounds towards my keep, but otherwise I lived there like a parasitical aged teenager, from whom there was no escape.

I began half-heartedly to look for a home of my own, not because I wanted to leave, but because I felt it wasn't right to stay any longer. After six months I found the perfect place.

Do you know the small, quiet road that runs along the coast between Myrtleville and Fountainstown? The one that's lined with those dark green, sticky hedges with the pink flowers that smell so sweet in summer, reminding me of long, happy childhood days. The road that will ultimately collapse into the sea as a result of coastal erosion or be swamped when global warming raises our seas up around us. That's where I found my dream home. It's an old cottage, used for many years as a summerhouse, but it's well constructed and cosy. What really sold it to me was the quaint wooden veranda in the front, with the pretty white railings around it. I could picture myself in a swinging seat like the Waltons used to have, swaying gently, gazing out at the quiet ocean.

My brother, Sean, came to see the house with me that first day, and he assured me that he would help me to do it up. When, after months of waiting, the house was finally mine, he kept his promise. He helped me a lot, and we spent many companionable weekend afternoons, scrubbing and painting and varnishing. Then, as evening fell, we'd relax over a beer for a chat, pleased with ourselves after an honest few hours' work. Much as I liked his company though, I always chased him home after one beer, as I didn't want to upset his wife, Eimear. She would have been right to be upset. It wasn't really fair of Sean to leave her alone, with all of their household jobs undone, while he spent the day with me, so I always made sure he got home at a decent time. Leaving me alone again. Naturally.

There's nothing incestuous about the relationship between Sean and me, but I often think that I could live very happily with someone like him. He's easy-going, and fun, and he tolerates my little foibles and oddities without pandering to them. He laughs at me, and jollies me along when I'm fed up, but never patronises me. Unfortunately, he's probably just one of a kind, and he's my brother.

Anyway, back to the house. It's got two bedrooms at the back of the house, both small, but just big enough to accommodate a wardrobe and a double bed. (Though why I need a double bed, I'm not quite sure, as I've never shared it with anyone.) The kitchen is also small, but perfectly adequate. I don't have big dinner parties, and when people visit me, they tend to bring their own food with them, I can't think why. The bathroom is wood panelled, with lots of shelves for me to dust when I get bored, and lots of little places to store the thirty fancy soap sets I get from my pupils each Christmas. Then there's just the living and dining area which takes up the front of the house. I have a huge floppy couch, covered with a brightly patterned throw and lots of mismatched cushions, offensive to the sensitive eye, but incredibly comfortable. One of the windows has a padded window seat, and when it's too cold to sit on the veranda (yes, I got the swinging seat), I sit here with my feet up, reading and relaxing. I have an open fire, and I spend many cosy afternoons on my own, stoking the fire, drinking lots of caffeine-rich drinks and admiring the view.

In this world where there's so much disease and death and violence and pain and hardship, wouldn't it be selfish of any girl to want more than I have?

Sometimes I'm a selfish girl.

Still, I'm not all bad. I do weekly penance for my sin of selfishness. I've just got back from creative writing class.

I know a lot about homes now.

Three of the housewives arrived in a chattering huddle. Two of them seemed to be pushing the third ahead of them. This lady is a shy, twittery creature, with faded hair and a nice range of floral tents that she uses as dresses. (What is she thinking when she buys these vile creations? Does she select a voluminous garment from a sagging clothes rail, skip into the fitting room, lower the offending item over her actually not that large frame, and cinch it in at the waist with a belt or a guy rope or something. Does she look in the mirror and say, 'Oh yes, this twenty yards of orange and pink flower-bed would really suit me. Quite becoming indeed. And think how handy it would be if I needed to go on an unexpected camping trip.')

One of her cohorts, a thin-faced old crone, spoke authoritatively to me. 'Sheila has a great poem this week.'

Tent-lady looked as if her shyness was going to envelop her completely and make her implode in a blushing, simpering heap.

Her other friend, a pale lady with frightening dyed-black hair, nodded. 'Yes. We know Walter will love it. It's short, but very succinct.'

Thin-face seemed to like that word. 'Yes, succinct. It's very succinct. Walter will be very impressed.'

Raven-hair played the trump card. 'It rhymes too. Not like some so-called poetry we've heard recently. Walter says rhyme can often be underrated.'

49

She looked at me combatively as she spoke. It suddenly dawned on me that these ladies seemed to be vying with me, as if Walter's praise were a prize to be fought over, a trophy to be held aloft and worshipped.

Just then Walter came in, and before he could speak, Thin-face jumped up, and squealed. 'Oh, Walter, just wait until you hear Sheila's poem. You are going to love it. It's full of images. It's very succinct.'

Walter looked rather discomfited. Clearly, he could wait until he heard Sheila's offering. Equally clearly, that would not be wise, as Thin-face and Raven-hair were already heaving their friend to her feet. After lots of throat-clearing, and tent-adjusting, Sheila began.

> 'Homes
> To the Romans, Rome is home.
> To the Turks, homes have domes.
> Dolphins swim in foamy homes.
> Wriggly worms like loamy homes.
> Gnomes have tiny, tidy homes.
> I will never roam,
> From my home.
> The End.'

Hello? When is she going to read the marvellous poem?

Tent-lady sat down, and put her head in her hands. The blush had spread to her ears and neck.

Can you die of shyness?

There followed a series of mind-numbingly boring

accounts of warm, happy homes. There were thirteen poems. Each writer had imaginatively rhymed *home* with *roam*. I was tempted to do a bit of roaming myself.

Across the foam to Rome, if necessary.

That wasn't allowed though. Walter insisted on hearing my dissertation about the cavewoman on the deserted island. It prompted a lot of nudging and tutting on the part of the housewives. As predicted, none of them seemed to notice the contradiction of an inhabited deserted island. Unusually, Walter didn't notice either. I'm a bit disappointed in him. Still, I suppose he has an excuse. He was obviously still reeling from Sheila's poem.

Poor Walter.

Poor, poor Walter.

Chapter Six

I had a really awful day at work today. A blanket of drizzle spent the day resting on the townland of Castlelough, so the children got no chance to run around the schoolyard, fighting and screaming and biting and kicking and exercising their basic instincts. Whenever this happens they are incredibly difficult by the afternoon, wild and restless and all but impossible to teach.

Paul, the bane of my life, suffers more than most. He's an adorable child, clear-skinned, black-haired, with huge, almost black eyes. He tries very hard, but I think it is impossible for him to sit still. The best he can manage, on a very good day, is a sort of agitated jigging around in his seat. The rest of the time, he wanders around the classroom, with no ill intent, but nonetheless causing rows by bumping into tables and upsetting work. When corrected, he always has the same reaction – he clamps his hand over his mouth, letting his beautiful eyes shine out at me, and mutters,

'Oops, sorry Miss.' He goes straight back to his place, but inevitably, five minutes later, he's moved on again, causing more trouble. Deep down, I'm very fond of him, but I have to admit that when he's absent, my classroom is a much more peaceful and productive place.

Paul was at school today (why do the wild children never seem to get sick?), so by eleven o'clock, I badly needed a caffeine fix. It was Mr Flynn's turn to parade the corridors, trying to prevent fatalities, so I was condemned to a quarter of an hour with Pat and Theresa. Manchester United won last night, and I tried not to yawn as Pat used up three of my precious fifteen minutes describing the winning goal. Yet again I regretted the fact that I didn't put Pat straight years ago. You see, unfortunately, I let it be known some years back that I enjoyed watching the World Cup matches. Also unfortunately, Pat didn't realise that that did not necessarily mean that I enjoyed soccer. No, I just cared who won the World Cup. I watched matches, wildly cheering for the underdogs, for the small teams, from countries I'd never heard of, who never won anything. I loved to see the arrogant nations being beaten, watching the self-important superstars tossing their long, sleek, dark hair, as they slunk from the pitch, clearly unused to defeat. I came into the staff room in the mornings saying things like, 'Great news, Cameroon won last night.' Pat would immediately respond with an analysis of how the game went, and I foolishly failed to mention that I didn't really care about anything except the result. I should have spelled it out – 'I cannot bear soccer. I don't care about the offside rule, the onside rule, any rule in fact.' I didn't though, and as a result, Pat directs a lot of his obsessed talk in my direction.

Maybe it wouldn't have made any difference anyway. In a small staff like ours, it is most unlikely that one would find someone with common interests, and since people like Pat and Theresa feel the need to share their views without any regard to the interests of their listeners, they'd probably waffle on regardless.

So, this morning, Pat told me about the match, Theresa told Pat about the housing estate where she and Michael would like to buy a house, Mr Flynn popped in for five minutes and told us all about a new Irish grammar book, and I sat there silently, watching the drizzle streaming down inside and outside our dodgy windows, wishing I was somewhere, anywhere else.

I made it through the day, and spent a cursory few minutes tidying the room after the children had left, picking up stray scraps of paper, erasers, crusts of bread and what looked like the entire contents of Paul's schoolbag. I wondered idly how his poor mother would react when he arrived home minus all of his copies, his pencil case and his homework notebook. Then, bored by this idle wondering, I made my own escape. It's funny, when I was a child, trapped in a boring classroom, gazing out the window, envying the passing clouds their freedom, it never occurred to me that the teacher was probably even more desperate than I was to get out, and get on with her own life.

If she had a life.

I left the school, waving a false cheery wave at Theresa and Michael, who were just pulling out of our parking area, and went to my own home, my refuge. I lit the coal fire, made a cup of strong, strong coffee, and sat down with a Snickers bar. Yes, I know that is almost obscene, but a girl needs her treats, and I felt that I had earned it. I spent a happy half-hour poking at and stoking the fire. I like the way the hot coals disintegrate when I touch them with the poker, sending forth a warming and attractive shower of red sparks.

I think I'd have made a good cave man. I could have had the job of keeping the fire alight, and would very happily have sat there all year round, wrapped in a nice cosy bearskin, thinking ancient, wise thoughts, prodding at the embers every now and then, ensuring the survival of my tribe. Knowing my luck though, I'd probably have got the job of skinning the animals, something I couldn't manage now with the best of sharp knives, and I suspect it might have been a touch more difficult back then with nothing more sophisticated than a scrap of sharp stone.

Or I might have got the job of protecting my people, standing alone using a pointy stick to defend myself against howling packs of marauding wolves.

After a while of these pointless thoughts, yet more minutes of lost life, the computer beckoned, and as usual, I responded. I found myself keying in 'home exchange' and was rewarded with a long, long list of sites. Most needed subscriptions before they would disclose their secrets, but then I found one, 'Home Exchangers Unlimited', which was different. Once the many boxes had filled with garish colours, I could see bold red letters jigging across the screen like wayward line-dancers, 'Register Free'. This was an offer too good to refuse. I filled in an endless list of questions like, 'affiliations of interest, ages of participating children, and area of home in square metres'. (I had to guess the last one, as I really didn't have a clue, so I hope I haven't represented my house as either a grand palace or a particularly small coal shed.)

Then I got a chance to describe my home in a few lines.

This is what I wrote: 'My home is a two bedroomed cottage, overlooking the sea, between Myrtleville and Fountainstown, Co. Cork. There are many beaches and seaside walks in this area. The bright lights of Cork City are less than thirty minutes away. My home, though small, is well equipped, and I have put a lot of effort into decorating it since I bought it some years ago. It stands on a quarter of an acre, with flowers and shrubs in the front and a sort of rambling vegetable garden at the back. If an exchanger were prepared to water the vegetables while I'm away, they would be amply rewarded with fresh produce for their meals. I would be happy to provide more details to anyone who might be interested in exchanging with me this summer.'

One more click and it was gone.

Somewhere.

I trust An Post, in a way that I don't yet trust my computer. When I use snail mail, I just seal the envelope, lick the nasty-tasting stamp and drop my letter into the rectangular slot. I don't stand forlornly at the post box, wondering if my missive will arrive safely. No, I just post and forget. Then, if I happen to see the postman driving past my house, I don't think, 'Oh no, he's got a letter for me and isn't delivering it.' I just accept that no one has written to me and that the junk mail producers have decided to give me a rare day off.

One day maybe I will click and forget, but not yet. If I get no response to my home exchange entry, I'll never know why. I don't know if there's a way to tell if my message arrived. It could be trapped forever in cyberspace, aimlessly knocking at the doors of every server in the world, always denied entry, but unable to find its way back to me, to tell me about my failure.

Then again, it might be that people don't really want to spend their precious holidays in a house the size of a small coal shed. Time will tell.

I decided to check my messages, a rather pathetic task as I've only ever got one, and that was from my server, spelling out all the do's and don'ts of e-commerce. Still, I live in hope (and write in clichés it seems). I clicked once on 'send and receive'. Magic! There was a little blue '1' in brackets next to my inbox. I've arrived! I can do it! The message was from Home Exchangers Unlimited acknowledging my application and welcoming me aboard.

I have to be honest and say that I sat and smiled at my computer for a long time.

Is it possible to feel real emotion for an unattractive grey plastic box with lots of confusing wires in the back, and rows of little green lights on the front, that beeps loudly at the most unexpected times?

If that is possible, is it only for particularly pathetic people, or do normal people fall in love with clever pieces of plastic too?

Why do I ponder these useless things?

Will my life ever be so meaningful that I will be too busy for such stuff?

I fear not.

Chapter Seven

Walter likes the traditional approach to selecting subjects for our creativity. Maybe he's afraid of what we'll produce if he gives us a controversial subject; fearful of unleashing passions that he could not restrain in class, demons that would rampage wildly around the shabby corridors of the school, bouncing on the mottled grey floor tiles, hiding in the noisy metal lockers and leaping out at the most inopportune moments.

Walter doesn't realise, though, that whatever topic he assigns us, the housewives will still write about their homes and their families. They have their own agenda, and will use gentle subversion to get what they want. They will always find a way of twisting things so their precious darlings take centre stage.

This week Walter has asked us to write, 'a short piece about love'. We've got to read it out tonight, and I can't wait. I know the housewives will have an assortment of pieces about their baby's first smile, home-made Valentine cards and the devotion they feel for their plodding husbands.

My piece is a beauty. It's a verse in nearly rhyming couplets, all about my love for a fictional pet. It begins,

> 'Some people wouldn't care a fig,
> About my black pot-bellied pig.
> I don't care though, what they say,
> I love my darling anyway.
> He's named like Mr Stardust, Ziggy,
> Oh how I love my cute black piggy.'

I wrote it this morning, during coffee break, and it took me nearly fifteen minutes. That's not bad, because it's got eighty-three lines. I know that means I got mixed up somewhere and one couplet must be a singlet, or a triplet, but it doesn't matter. The housewives have stopped even pretending to listen to my work, and Walter, rather meanly looks bored when I first open my mouth. I hope he's religious. Then he can count his time with me as a credit off his time in Purgatory. Now that I think of it, I've spent a lot of time with Theresa. That will surely count for something in a future life.

Anyway, this is what I really wrote about love. I wrote it at the weekend, sitting in my little window seat, curled up in a cosy fleece blanket, occasionally gazing out at the grey sky and the grey sea. The tragic heroine, all alone.

*

Paddy.

We met in Germany one summer, when I was working in a gherkin factory for the holidays. My job entailed watching shiny wet gherkins rolling past on a conveyor belt, and I had to pick out any bad ones and fling them into an unreasonably large skip in the corner. It doesn't sound too arduous, but when you realise that gherkin farmers in Germany must be very conscientious, and days, even weeks could go by without a bad gherkin appearing, you'll understand that it wasn't exactly a fulfilling way of spending one's summer holidays. Ten hours a day I spent at this belt, and at night, when I went to bed, the belt kept rolling, with endless images of unblemished gherkins streaming past my tired, closed eyes.

Then Paddy came along, and the gherkins faded away and ceased to haunt my nights. In fact, I stood at the conveyor belt by day and saw no gherkins either, no good ones and no bad ones. I just gazed stupidly into space, and saw Paddy, with his casual air and his faded-denim shirt. I usually fell for odd types; strange-looking misfits playing made-up French songs on sticker-covered guitars, or intellectual, aloof types quoting Sartre and Camus. Paddy was different. He was like the boy next door. Just scruffy enough to qualify as a student, just clean-cut enough to impress my mother. My mother loved him too – until he ditched me. Then he became public enemy number one, for hurting her precious daughter.

We went out together for four years. I was young, but I wanted no one else. I went out and had fun with my friends (I had lots of friends back then and I'm not quite sure where they all went), but I felt no need to play the field. Paddy was enough for me. They were happy years. I was in no rush to get married, I was fine as things were, but Paddy began to run scared. Friends began to marry off in front of our eyes, and though I put no pressure on him, Paddy felt pressure from somewhere. One night, as he walked me home after what I thought had been a great evening in the pub, he blurted it out with no warning preamble. 'I want to finish things between us.' We sat on a bench in the little park near my home, and talked for hours. My shock turned first to anger, then tears. I'm ashamed to say I begged.

I grovelled and betrayed every one of my independent, feminist ideals. I tearfully asked what had become of our plan to travel the world together. He shrugged, muttering that it was just a fantasy. 'You know we'd never have got around to it, Maeve. It was just one of those things. It was only a dream.' He waved his hand in the air, waving away my plans and my hopes. I offered all kinds of compromise, but he held firm. 'I'm too young,' he kept saying, 'I don't want to settle down.' When I wept and insisted that I wasn't ready to settle down either, he just replied that in that case we were going nowhere, and were better off apart. That didn't make much sense, but by then I was weary from crying, and I went home, unable to argue any more. I spent the next days in a kind of hazy half-world. I struggled through the days and cried every night, and soon there were no tears left. Paddy left town suddenly, and I heard that he moved to America a few weeks later. I haven't seen him since.

Once, about two months after he left me, he wrote, and I ripped the letter open excitedly. It was full of waffle though, all designed to assuage his guilt. Platitudes tumbled off the page, 'It's all for the best', 'You were too good for me', 'You'll meet someone better than me', etc., etc. The letter went on for three pages (Paddy knew a lot of platitudes), and in temper I shredded it. I tossed the pieces dramatically out of my bedroom window. They were picked up by a sudden gust of wind and then dropped suddenly, fluttering to rest all over the next-door hedge. They lingered there for weeks, wet and soggy, taunting me by their very existence, though I never found the energy to go and remove them. One day I looked and they were gone.

Like Paddy.

For a long time I harboured the hope that one day the doorbell would ring and he'd be there, with open arms, crying and saying what a mistake he'd made. I wondered how long I would have to pretend not to want him, before graciously forgiving him, and planning the rest of our lives together. Of course, he never came, and then thirteen months after the split, a well-meaning acquaintance told me that my commitment-shy ex-boyfriend had just got married in New York to a Japanese girl he'd met six months previously. I was glad she told me, as it finally put paid to my ill-founded hopes of old age with Paddy and I could at last stop playing the romantic reunion scene in my head.

Yes, Walter, I can almost feel the slightly sour warmth of your breath on my ear, and the weight of your impertinent hand on my left shoulder, as I imagine you leaning over my right, criticising my work, in that insidious way that irritates me so. 'Tut, tut, Maeve. I think you can do better than this. It's not very original, is it? This is the plot of a hundred films.'

I know, Walter. It is. But, do you know what? It's not original, but it's the way it happened. When I was crying over Paddy, it was no consolation to know that all over the world, hot tears were being shed over similar betrayals. It didn't ease my pain to know that somewhere, in an intense dry heat, beautiful girls were sitting on riverbanks, combing their hair, and weeping over lost loves. Or that in high rise buildings from Moscow to Hong Kong, women lay on rumpled beds and stared at cracked, white ceilings, crying and waiting for phone calls that never came.

It doesn't have to be original to hurt, you know.

They say that women forget the pain of childbirth. I'll probably never get the chance to find out. I know I will never forget the pain I felt back then, when all hope was finally gone, and I had to try to hold my head high and face into a life that would not be shared with Paddy. I never had real, concrete plans for a life together, just vague, happy imaginings, and then these evaporated, leaving nothing there to console me. There was a wide, gaping space in my life, and I have never since managed to fill it. Other things just sort of edged their way in, and I learned to live without Paddy, but it was never the same. The special joy was gone from my life, just as, no matter what I did, the beautiful grainy brown sheen faded from the conkers I hoarded every autumn when I was a child. I used to wrap them carefully in soft white tissues, fold them up in my old baby blanket and hide them in a little box under my bed. When I returned to them some weeks later, they were still round and brown and hard with crisp white centres. In many respects they were unchanged, but they were no longer the treasures I loved, and I tossed them carelessly into the bin. Worthless rubbish.

Time of course, as it does, healed the hurt, and I wouldn't take a present of Paddy now, in the unlikely event of him ever reappearing. Still though, he's always there, lurking in the back of my mind, distorting my view of other men. I know that when I knew him, we were young and foolish and irresponsible, while any men I meet now all have jobs and houses and cars and overdrafts. And wrinkles. And paunches. They probably have piles too, though I tend not to discuss that kind of thing with casual acquaintances. The men I meet now can't, on a whim, set off hitch-hiking around

America, or go stamping on grapes in sunny, picturesque villages in Bordeaux, and nor, indeed, can I.

Nevertheless, I compare in my head, and everyone I meet seems too serious, too grown up. Their every little fault becomes magnified and they get rejected without a fair hearing, without any hearing at all. I can't shake myself free of Paddy, and as a result, no one else will do.

Only my mother really still tries, and I don't imagine she'll ever give up. She sees it as her one remaining mission in life, to get me a man. I don't know if she's read Jane Austen, but I expect she'd have liked Mrs Bennet. They'd have a lot in common. My poor faithful mum will probably be eyeing the diggers of her grave, from up above, checking to see if any would make a likely mate for me.

Sometimes I think the arrival of a man on the scene would mess up my cosy little life, so I don't consciously try very hard. Other times though, as I lie in my bed, when the meagre traffic sounds have ended for the night, and when the creaking of the floorboards in protest at the heating being turned off has ceased, and there's a break in the wail of the wind off the sea, there's a faint little noise in the corner of my brain. It's not loud, but it's persistent. It beats in time with my heart. It's the famous, often written about, biological clock, whispering insidiously in my ear, reminding me ever so gently, 'Do something soon or die a lonely, childless spinster, missed by no one except the meals on wheels lady and a few mangy cats.'

I don't even like cats, but I get the general idea. There's a lot of loneliness ahead for a single girl with only one friend.

I think of Paddy and how his leaving me changed my life. I don't cry though. I just feel empty inside, like an abandoned, scraggly nest, after the young birds have flown on to a glorious new life in the sun.

What would you say to that, housewives?

That would make you sit up and listen.

That would quieten you for once.

That would silence your mindless meanderings.

If I were ever foolish enough to share it with you.

Chapter Eight

It's like Christmas every day.

I rush home from work, throw my bag and coat in the corner, plug in the kettle, turn on the computer, click on the Internet, listen to twenty-nine seconds of hissing and beeping and finally touch 'send and receive'. Every evening it's the same. The lovely sentence appears, 'Receiving list of messages from server.' At that stage I always run back to the kitchen, make the coffee and when I return there's a beautiful blue number next to my inbox. Usually it's quite a big number: eight, nine, and last night ten. They all have the same preface – 're: the home you registered with Home Exchangers Unlimited.' Greedily I scroll through them looking at the senders' names, wondering who they are. Then I check each one, watching the tiny envelope icons open, savouring the excitement, enjoying the anticipation. I've started to keep my atlas next to the computer, as I need it to find out where most of the offered places are. Geography was never my best subject, though I've come along a lot in the past few days. I've had offers from places that I'd just heard about in songs, like Chattanooga, Amarillo and Scarborough. I don't know that I should base my holiday around a song though. I have to reject most of the offers immediately, as they are totally unsuitable. I don't really want to spend my precious holidays alone in Oklahoma or Idaho, though I'm sure they too have their own special charms. I've put a few possible offers on hold, but I'm waiting for the big one, the one that really grabs me, the one that feels right. I have no idea where that could be, but I'm sure I'll know it when I see it.

My friends and colleagues have not exactly met my idea of a home exchange with total approval. I try not to talk about personal stuff in the staffroom, but I let this particular gem slip, in a rare unguarded moment, and unfortunately everyone seemed to be present and conscious. Mr Flynn, in his fatherly way, is totally against it.

'It's a bit risky for a girl like you, isn't it? There are too many wild hooligans out there, waiting to take advantage of young innocents.'

(I wonder what it is he means when he says, 'a girl like you.' Does he mean a stunning beauty, source of temptation to holy monks, or just a gormless imbecile, too thick to be allowed abroad alone?)

'Why don't you get a summer job teaching Irish in the Gaeltacht? Wouldn't that be a bit more in your line?'

Pat nodded his head in agreement. 'I did that for three summers in a row before I got married. It was great crack altogether. We used to get brilliant games going between the boys in the afternoons. We were meant to be playing GAA, of course, but we played soccer anyway. The lads preferred it. And why wouldn't they? If ever there was an inspector in the vicinity the boys just picked up the ball and pretended they were playing Gaelic football. 'Twas mighty crack altogether. There were no televisions in the houses, but it didn't matter, as there were no English matches on in the summer back then. Strange, that. I wonder what the players did with themselves? Wouldn't you love to know, Maeve, how Steve Heighway and Kevin Keegan and the lads spent their summers?'

'I wouldn't actually, Pat. Funnily enough, I find that I can sleep soundly in my bed at night without the need to rack my brains about what your ageing idols did in the long hot summer of 1976.'

One of the few great things about Pat is that it is impossible to insult him. He just shrugged mildly, ignoring my attempt at a putdown, and returned to his paper.

Mr Flynn continued as if the soccer aside had never happened. 'You'd be dead safe there, in your own country. You could go to a few céilí's and you might even find a nice young man. A teacher. Or a guard. A farmer maybe. A bit of romance would be just the thing for you. You don't want to be spending the rest of your life on your own. Do you? Too much independence is a bad thing, I always say. Would you like me to have a word with the inspector? He could easily fix you up with a place.'

I thought I could see the traces of a mean smirk appearing on Theresa's thin lips. If Mr Flynn wasn't so gentle and well-meaning, I'd have told him what I really thought of his idea, but I hadn't the heart, so I fudged the issue as usual.

'I'll look into it next week, Mr Flynn. I promise.'

Theresa looked up from her Fair-Isle chart to offer her putdown. 'Ugh. I wouldn't do a house swap. I wouldn't want strangers tramping about my house, touching my things, sleeping in my bed.'

I stopped myself from saying that I'd rather sleep in Mr Flynn's smelly dog's house than in her bed, and turned back to Pat in desperation.

'What do you think, Pat? Isn't a house swap a great idea?'

Unusually for Pat, he had an opinion. He raised his eyes from the sports page of *The Examiner*, and dived in to the fray. 'Well, Maeve. I wouldn't do it if I were you. Anything could happen. You could be raped, cut up, murdered and sold in to the white slave trade.'

Interesting sequence. I hope his lesson plans are more carefully worked out.

The raised voices in the schoolyard outside brought the conversation to an end, but I know I will have Michael's opinion to look forward to, once Theresa shares the concept with him – 'We discuss everything. It's an important part of our relationship. Secrets can be very divisive.' Puke. Where does she get these sickly notions?

I don't dare to mention my wonderful travel plans to my parents. They would fret and be anxious about me for months, long before I even picked a destination or bought a flight ticket. If nothing comes of these plans, I'd hate to think of all their wasted worry, so I'll leave them in the dark for a while. It'll be time enough to tell them when I know for sure that I'm going.

Sean came over on Saturday to put up some shelves (I'm a real helpless female, aren't I?), so I ran the idea by him. I was a bit shy of mentioning it, as I was half-afraid of what he would say, so I waited until he had both hands occupied holding a shelf in place, and a mouth full of screws, preventing impulsive speech.

'Sean, I was sort of thinking of doing a house swap this summer. I've looked it up on the Internet. There are loads of agencies that help people to set up deals. All kinds of people do it. I could have a month in America just for the price of the flights. It would be a bit of a laugh.'

When Sean had spat out the last screw and could finally speak, he wasn't overly enthusiastic either. 'I don't know, Mae. I don't like the idea of you on your own in a strange house. You could end up in a very rough neighbourhood. You'd be relying on the good will and honesty of strangers. It could be a bit dodgy.'

'Ah Sean, I'd be fine. I'm a grown adult. I could be murdered in my own bed anyway. I could be mugged on Patrick Street in the morning. I could die of boredom here one Saturday night, and no one would notice. Nowhere is completely safe, and I have to have a life.'

Sean spoke soothingly. 'I know Mae. Of course you have to have a life, but it's stupid to take unnecessary risks. Why don't you stay in a hotel if you must go to America? A hotel would offer some small level of security. There would be other people around, and they couldn't all be crazy, drug-deranged muggers and murderers. Do you need a loan for a few months?'

Typical, kind Sean. He'd lend me money, even though he knew that doing so would very likely cause trouble between him and Eimear. Sean's opinion matters a lot more to me than a hundred of Theresa's or Pat's or Mr Flynn's, so I was a bit disappointed, though not entirely surprised by his reaction. For the first time, I began to have doubts, but I don't like to admit defeat. I've just decided to see what offers come up and plan from there. Half of me is afraid to go alone, but I don't have many options. People aren't exactly queuing up begging me to go on holidays with them.

Still though, I would die rather than go on an official 'singles' holiday. I couldn't admit to the world at large that I have no friends except one married girl

73

who loves her husband. I couldn't get on a bus outside some foreign airport, blink in the hot sun, and eye up a group of equally desperate strangers, wondering if one of them could be the answer to all my hopes and dreams.

I know for sure that I couldn't do this, because I tried it once. I arrived at a welcome meeting in a tacky Greek resort, to be met by a group of people who looked too much like me for comfort. One poor guy, Robert, wore an eager smile, a T-shirt with the slogan, 'Laugh and the world laughs with you' and brown socks under his open-toed sandals. He was clearly so desperate that he no longer tried to hide it. I spent the entire fortnight in the company of a shy girl from Westmeath with whom I had nothing at all in common except a shared desire to avoid Robert's clammy clutches.

No, I'd sooner stay at home than do that again. I'm just going to wait and see. I need something to look forward to.

*

Creative writing class was due last night. Only three to go. I'll miss old Walter, much as I miss an itchy scab when it falls from an old cut. He's irritating, but I'm kind of getting used to him in my life. He wasn't there though. There was just a hand-written note pinned to the little hammered glass window in the classroom door.

'Walter is unwell. Classes are suspended until after Easter. Sorry for the inconveniense.'

No, that's not my spelling mistake. I hope it wasn't the English teacher who wrote that. The housewives were very disappointed. They got in a little huddle, and I heard them planning to find an unlocked classroom, so they could share their works of genius. They didn't invite me to join them, and though I despise everything they stand for, I was still hurt. I trailed through the near-deserted school, noticing how shabby and neglected it looked, with the paintwork scuffed and peeling and the cold tiled floors marked by years of studded boots.

I drove away in a mood that is becoming worryingly familiar. I felt alienated, apart and alone. (If I were typing this on my word processor, I could use the thesaurus and find lots more synonyms to describe my isolation.) I'll look on the bright side though; the cancelled class gave me a few more hours on the computer when I got home. I think I'm becoming an anorak. I've even got an offer to exchange homes for Easter. That seems a bit too soon. Now that I am beginning to have doubts about the whole exchange business, I don't want to rush in to anything.

I'm starting to sound like Theresa with this new cautious approach to life. She and Michael are going on a pilgrimage for their Easter holidays. I should probably show some religious tolerance, but I find it hard to see the point. They'll walk barefoot on sharp rocks, stay without sleep for two days, say lots of public prayers and dine splendidly on pilgrimage soup (boiling water with pepper and salt added).

It seems to me that if they really want to do some good for their souls, they could spend a few hours scrubbing the tiles in the boys' toilets at school. Don't the boys' dads teach them any target practice? Do they spray the walls at home like they do at school? Sometimes, when I dare to go in to the toilets, they are in such a state that I wonder if any wee at all makes it into the bowl. Once, I was tempted to throw a penny into the toilet and urge the boys to aim at it, but in these suspicious days I'd probably be accused of some distorted kind of abuse, so I abandoned the plan.

Anyway, the result is that the toilets are so smelly that even the undiscerning six-year-olds are beginning to complain. Theresa and Michael could clean for hours in virtuous, self-denying pain. For added points, they could work barefoot or wearing ankle and wrist weights. I'd be happy to oblige by swiping their backs with twiggy sticks while they worked. (That sounds a bit perverted – maybe that's why I've got no friends.)

I'm going to spend my holidays digging the garden and sowing the first lettuce, peas and onion sets.

Surely all that decent honest labour will be good for my soul.

Chapter Nine

Like most teachers, I've only ever been to school, college and then back to school again. (I don't think the gherkin factory counts.) This leaves me with a terrible ignorance of other jobs. There are whole sections of commerce and industry that are a complete mystery to me.

I mean, what does an actuary do?

What is a loss-adjuster?

How does a quantity surveyor spend his days?

What exactly does a fitter fit?

Anyway, I've no idea what it is that Joe does for a living. I know it's something to do with engineering, and that he designs things, but beyond that I'm a bit lost. For all I know, he could be designing nuclear bombs, or then again, he could be just trying to redesign the wiggly bit of metal that joins the toilet handle to the ballcock.

Yes, Walter, I can hear your endless tutting in the background. It's OK though, this information is actually leading somewhere.

You see, Maria called over the other day, and when we were settled with our cups of coffee and Mars bars, she gave me the good news that Joe has just got a big promotion. I was delighted for them both.

'That's great, Maria. Will he get a pay-rise? Will he be driving us to the pub in a Mercedes every Thursday night?'

'Fat chance. You know he'd never sell his precious Beetle.'

'Yes, I suppose that's true. I couldn't really see him in any other car. Will he have to work longer hours?'

'Well, it doesn't seem too bad. He'll get quite a significant pay-rise, and it seems there won't be that much extra working time. It's all to do with responsibility and productivity. I'm not quite sure how they figure these things out.'

'Sounds good to me. He must be thrilled.'

'He is. There's just one small thing. He's got to go on a training course for a month. In Texas.'

'What a bummer! Still, a month isn't that long, and we can have some mighty sessions. You can stay here if you like. You can drown your sorrows and I can drown my ulcers.'

'That's the thing. Joe's got to go away in July, and you won't even be here. You'll be off in some palace of a house, sipping gin by the swimming pool.'

I suddenly felt the beginning of a wonderful warm glow, an unusual feeling for me when alcohol wasn't involved.

'I'm sure I could arrange a palace big enough for two. If you wanted.'

Maria smiled her big smile. 'Are you sure, Maeve? Would you mind if I went on holidays with you? I'd hate to be here on my own while Joe is away.'

'You big eejit, you know I'd love it. It would be like the old days. We'd have a ball. And at least now that you're happily married, I won't have to beat you up to stop you going off with every pathetic waster who spins you a sob story.'

Maria gave a snort of laughter. 'Do you remember that guy in Mykonos? The windsurfing instructor?'

'How could I forget him with his endless whine? "Maria, you are so sexy. I think I love you. Just buy me one more glass of ouzo, and I will take you home to meet my mama."'

'Oh my God, wasn't he just dreadful? Still, I shook him off in the end. And anyway, you weren't exactly perfect yourself. Who fell for the guy who operated the motorboat to Paradise Beach? Who insisted on taking that particular boat ride four times a day? For two weeks? And he was a complete slime-ball.'

'True. But I was young and foolish back then. We're much older and wiser now. It'll be fantastic. Joe can go off to his old training course happy in the knowledge that you'll be safe with me.'

'Indeed. Now turn on that Internet. We've got a holiday to plan.'

Liberated and independent though I try to be, holidaying alone can be a bit lonely, and daunting. I've done it before, and quite enjoyed it. I've seen some great places and met some interesting people. I usually get a nice golden suntan. I can say 'tummy-bug' in five different languages. There have been times though, when I've sat alone on foreign beaches and felt an unhappiness that frightened me with its intensity, leaving me shaken. (Not stirred.)

Maria coming puts a whole new slant on things though. The world is ours for the taking, and we spend happy hours sitting with an open atlas, open minds and an open bottle of red wine, taking turns to close our eyes and stick a pin onto a possible holiday destination. Then we collapse with squeals of childish laughter, when we look to see that we've pinpointed a jungle in Uganda, or even worse, a field in Ballybofey.

We've surfed the exchange website and made offers to places as diverse as Bali and Brooklyn. None of these have replied positively yet, but the unsolicited offers are still pouring in. There are two that sound particularly promising. One of these is in Santa Barbara and the other is in Vancouver. I have to be honest and admit that I had to look both these places up in the atlas, to find out exactly where they are, as I had only the vaguest idea. Now, however, I am very well informed, having studied the tourist office info on the Net. I've even read their local newspapers, pleased to see that neither reports too many muggings or drive-by shootings, though there's been an investigation into a dodgy planning application in Vancouver and a spate of dognappings in Santa Barbara.

E-mail is a funny old business. I've exchanged messages several times with both prospective swappers, and we have developed a familiarity unusual between total strangers. Suddenly it seems as if communication by letter is terribly formal and old fashioned.

Santa Barbara is the home of Chuck and Darlene, and I confess that at first I was convinced I was dealing with fictional characters sporting made-up names. They appear to be genuine though. They are both in their fifties, just retired (lucky them), and keen to see the world by exchanging for twelve consecutive months. They have shared with me, a stranger, the details of Chuck's prostate surgery, Darlene's fear of heights, and their joint grief at the death of Sweetheart, their pet poodle.

I, who have never met or spoken to them, who have never set foot on their continent, know that they have buried their former pet under an avocado tree in their garden, and that they plan to put up a pink marble heart-shaped plaque reading, 'Goodnight Sweetheart'.

Maybe they're not genuine after all. I didn't think anyone could be that loopy. Mind you, it would almost be worth swapping with them, just to see Sweetheart's final resting place. I hope Chuck and Darlene take some comfort from the fact that Sweetheart is safe under the avocado tree, and not in danger from the dognappers.

Charlie in Vancouver is a little more reticent, so I don't yet know anything about his medical history or his views on genetically modified food. I do know though that he's a college lecturer in physics, divorced, and planning to travel with his nine-year-old son, Todd. His apartment sounds nice; small, but close to the city. He also wants to exchange his Chevy Tahoe for my Fiesta, for the duration of the swap. This didn't bother me until I found a picture of one (guess where), and realised that it closely resembles the huge trucks that drive up unpaved mountains, and deliberately crash into each other, on some sad programme on satellite TV. This is somewhat intimidating to someone who backed out of a recent deal to buy a Ford Escort on the basis that it was too big and would be too difficult to park. (I know. That's a really girlie, unliberated attitude, but there it is. I can't embrace every facet of feminism all on my own. Try as I might, I can't carry all the placards for the female half of the human race.)

We have had both these offers on hold for a week now, but Charlie is keen to get a definite answer. He's too polite to say why, so I just have to guess.

Maybe his ex-wife is snapping at his heels, and he needs something certain to keep her at bay.

Maybe he's on the run because of the dodgy planning deals.

Or maybe he's one of those wonderfully decisive executive types who makes up his mind and just wants to get on with it.

My sneaking fear is that I'll come to an arrangement with someone, and immediately afterwards get the offer of a lifetime that I'll have to turn down. Darlene and Chuck don't seem to be under any pressure, but I've e-mailed both parties to let them know that I'll give them a final answer by this day next week.

Maria and I plan to spend a full night drinking and discussing it (we seem to think better when under the influence of alcohol). Then, when we are suitably sozzled, we will formally select a destination, by writing each place name on a scrap of paper, scrunching them up, and getting Joe to select one at random.

Decisions. I hate them.

Chapter Ten

Bad news.

Chuck's piles have prolapsed.

Yes, he has shared this with me, and most likely with a few hundred sad, swarthy computer hackers in anoraks. He's on a waiting list for surgery, but it seems their health service isn't perfect either, so he probably won't be able to travel until August. Maria only wants to travel in July, because that's when Joe will be away, so we've sent Chuckie a musical get-well e-card (honestly, I must have too much time on my hands), and abandoned all hope of Santa Barbara. Now at least we don't have to make a decision, which suits me fine.

I've been in touch with Charlie again, and after a bit of to-ing and fro-ing we have come to an agreement to exchange for the complete month of July, Chevy Tahoe included. I'm still a bit suspicious of electronic communications, so I'm glad that the exchange agency requires us to exchange real bits of paper, with real signatures in real ink. I've sent mine off, confidently dropping it into the post box in Carrigaline, and I expect Charlie's any day. Maria and I have provisionally booked our flights, Cork-Heathrow-Vancouver. Roll on July.

I'm really enjoying my Easter holidays. Now I know that my summer holidays are going to be so busy, I feel I can be a complete slob now. I read late into the night and I sleep late every morning. When I get up, I make a rasher sandwich (one of the great joys of life) and eat it in my dressing gown, while watching endless, repetitive daytime chat shows, or freak shows as they should more accurately be called.

'My teenage daughter is pregnant with my lover's father's baby.'

'I've cheated on my husband forty-three times, but he still loves me.'

'I've pulled out my hair by the roots to knit underpants for my boyfriend.'

OK, so I made the last one up, but you get the picture. They almost get as bad as that. All programmes come complete with rabble-rousing presenter (big hair compulsory) and self-righteous, arm-waving, accusatory audience. There are very few silences, pointed or otherwise, but many pointed fingers. While I'm not unduly religious, I feel they could all benefit from a quick read of the part of the Bible about casting the first stone. As it is, the audience is practically queuing up to castigate the poor public victims, displayed in all their twisted glory, for the entertainment of the equally twisted masses.

Sometimes, for a bit of a change, I listen to the radio instead. This being Irish radio, it's a little more restrained. You know the type of programmes that are on in the daytime; some nice, undemanding, easy listening music, and lots of phone-ins, giving the common people a voice. I know that listening to them is a bit sad, but phoning in is even sadder. People feel the need to have a say, and by God, they are going to have it, regardless of whether their opinion could possibly be of any interest to anyone else, apart from their mothers, neighbours and 'everyone who knows me'.

One of the hot topics this week was broccoli. We are meant to care what Mary in Mullingar and Deirdre in Durrow think about how much broccoli stalk they have to pay for in their local supermarket. Women (and I'm afraid to say, it's always women) went live on air to describe the underhand ways they have found to remove the stalk from their broccoli before weighing it.

What happened to the good old days when dishonesty was something to hide? Now it's seen as something to be proud of, something to be shouted from the rooftops and aired on the airwaves. Now people phone up, vying with each other to be the most dishonest of all. And this a good Catholic country!

Eventually, even I tire of this presentation of modern life at its best, so I then put on my old denims, a scruffy blue fleece jacket and my yellow wellies, for a few hours of happy pottering in the vegetable patch. (Incidentally, I bought those wellies in Germany many years ago, the summer I met Paddy, back in the days when every German under the age of thirty had yellow wellies, and sported an 'Atomkraft, Nein Danke' sticker on their car windscreens. But that's neither here nor there.)

My Dad loves gardening, and passed this on to me. However, where he always prides himself on growing the biggest and best of everything, winning regular prizes in his garden club, I have taken a slightly different line. I like to grow organically, and it shows. I could only enter competitions if they invent some new categories, like, 'Least eaten by slugs.' Or, 'Not too badly affected by potato blight. Considering.'

Still, I try. I have spent many dark, wet evenings, torch in one hand, old teaspoon in the other, hunting down slimy invaders, enjoying catching them in the act of eating my precious greens. I then take pleasure in dropping them into a jar of boiling salted water, before returning to catch their unsuspecting friends and family, who probably thought their dear departed friend had just stepped behind a lettuce for a wee.

Sometimes I wonder though. Last year I sent away to a specialist seed store for an exotic variety of lettuce seed. (When I later worked out the cost, I realised that for the same price I could have bought fifteen ready-grown lettuces in Dunnes Stores.) I sowed my precious, expensive seeds in small green trays made out of recycled plastic, dropping them one by one into their bed of organic peat-free compost. I nursed them through their early weeks, misting them ever so gently with filtered water each morning before I went to work. I hardened them off gradually, carrying them in and out of doors depending on the weather, protecting them from every cold wind or heavy rainfall. Only after weeks of anxious shilly-shallying did I reluctantly plant them out in a sheltered spot just outside my kitchen window.

Next morning, as I waited for the kettle to boil for my tea, I glanced out the kitchen window to see how my babies were doing. There they were – gone. Those vicious slimy slugs had done their worst. They had left their filthy, slippery calling cards, but of my precious baby lettuces there was no trace. Not one leaf was left to show that they had ever been there. That night I rounded up scores of the usual suspects, but I know well that hundreds more lurked beneath the soil, waiting their chance to slimily foil my gardening plans.

I think that, given enough time and financial incentives, I could grow to love all God's creatures; except for slugs and Theresa. That's not too bad. Is it?

I often tell people that I love gardening, and how surprised they would be if they saw my garden. Most of the year it's a pathetic sight: shrubs overgrown, reaching wildly for the sky, or collapsed in a flailing mess; grass bumpy, weedy and yellow; paths scarred with dandelions and stray grass. However, in late summer, I take real pride in picking peas, beans, tomatoes and sweetcorn. (All the vegetables that my slimy enemies seem to scorn.) I go out with my little wicker basket and fill it up, feeling that for once in my life, I have produced something real and tangible, something useful.

I grow, therefore I am, sort of thing.

A few hours in the garden each afternoon justifies my existence this Easter, so I can then spend the rest of the day at leisure. I drink lots of coffee, read, stroll on the beach or wander around town, window shopping. I dismiss all of the new summer clothes on display, even though the colours are so bright and welcome after the drabness of winter, telling myself I'll be buying much better for half-nothing in Vancouver.

I also get time to read the Sunday papers, every one of them. I buy them faithfully all year round, feeling some irrational fear that I'll miss something if I don't. Usually though, I just flick through them, skimming through the headlines, ignoring many articles, half-reading the rest. Then I dump the lot in the bin on Saturday, in a big crumpled heap, in preparation for the next onslaught.

This week has been different though. I've read everything except the appointments page and the sports section. (I know Pat will bring me up to date next week if I miss some wonderful story about a transfer in the Latvian schoolboy league.) This week I've even had time to read the lonely hearts columns on the back pages of the magazine section. Yes, I know, it's not lonely hearts any more, it's 'encounters', or 'personal notices', or the impersonal 'classifieds', but we all know the truth – it's for sad, lonely people like me, who can't meet a mate any other way.

Someone smarter than me should do a study some time, on the content of these ads, and how the male version differs from the female one. The men are often so arrogant and particular, I find myself clutching the page in temper, glad that these people are lonely, and in no doubt as to how that state has come about. Even their mothers couldn't love some of these guys.

I'll give you an example from last Sunday: 'Handsome fifty-year-old male, successful, good company, and happy, seeks perfect partner.' (Yeah right, as my fourth class boys would say. If you're so handsome and successful and nice to be with, why aren't you beating women off your doorstep?) It continues, 'Must be aged twenty to thirty, slim, blonde and beautiful with no ties.' This is typical. They lay down the law about looks, body size and age, as if they are selecting from a menu, with no consideration for real people, who may, of course be slightly flawed. 'No ties', is of course adspeak for, 'I don't want any squawky, snotty children getting in the way of my manly ardour.'

The women who advertise are, in general, a little less demanding, ready to settle for less. They look for qualities like kindness, gentleness or SOH. (For the uninitiated, SOH means sense of humour, though I confess that at first I thought it stood for 'straight or homosexual', and wondered how these poor women could be so desperate that even sexual orientation didn't matter.) These women tend not to have particular requirements concerning looks or age, unambitiously seeking 'someone to make me happy,' or 'someone to cuddle on a cold night.'

One poor unfortunate must be really losing hope. She wants a man – 'looks unimportant, preferably under seventy, a brain would be nice.' Poor girl, she'll probably get no replies, as her desperation screams out from the page, audible even through the pretended cynicism, and the last thing a desperate man wants is an even more desperate woman. She's just wasted €14.10 per line. (Plus VAT).

Even in my worst, dark moments, I would never for a moment consider using the personal columns in an effort to find a partner for life. I know this, because I went on a blind date once. It was set up by a girl I was sort of friendly with about seven years ago. We met for coffee one day, and she spent quite some time talking about her cousin, Patrick who had just come back from Africa. I couldn't figure out why she kept going on about him, and it took a while for me to realise that what she was doing was trying to sell me the idea of him as a boyfriend. By the time the truth dawned, and I desperately tried to backtrack, it was too late. I had agreed to meet him for a drink.

We met in a small bar, where we spent what must have been the longest ninety minutes of my life.

My so-called friend had neglected to tell me that Patrick was what my granny used to call a spoiled priest. I had no problem with this, but unfortunately he did. He spoke at length about his failed vocation, and the reasons for it. It seemed to be something to do his feelings for the tribeswomen who formed part of his flock in a remote village in Africa. I had no problem with this either, but, guess what? He did. He told me at length how he felt when he saw them performing their traditional dances. As he described their traditional, skimpy dresses, little flecks of spittle were gathering on his lips. He was practically foaming at the mouth. He edged closer to me on the seat and grabbed my hand as he described the climax of one particular dance. I could see beads of sweat forming on his brow and a muscle under his left eye began to twitch. I began to fear that the dance wasn't the only thing that was about to climax, and I suddenly remembered an urgent appointment elsewhere.

I've been blind drunk a number of times since, but that night I realised that blind dates were not for me.

Anyway, I digress again. I had a great day today, even without 'that special someone to share the good things in life with'. It's the last day of the holidays, and I am already checking the calendar to see when the next day off is. I got up even later than usual, and watched the soaps for even longer. Maria called, and we went for a walk. It rained after about five minutes, so we retired to our local pub. There we spent three happy hours, huddled over the coal fire, drinking lager and eating Taytos (another of life's great pleasures), while we discussed the wonderful time we are going to have this summer.

Eimear has taken the children to stay with her mother in Limerick, so Sean came over for the evening. I know I'm probably being over-sensitive, but I can enjoy his company without guilt when I know Eimear isn't around. He arrived with a wonderful, greasy Chinese takeaway, which we ate from our laps, washing it down with our favourite red wine, a strong Rioja, 'punch-in-the-face wine' as Sean calls it.

We had a grand chat, most of it about Vancouver, as Sean is now a big fan of the trip since he discovered that Maria is coming. After Sean left at around ten, I shoved the dirty dishes into a dark corner of the kitchen, binned the takeaway bags, and got back into my nightclothes, though it felt as if I had just taken them off. I wrapped myself in my duvet, and I began to write.

I'm really enjoying this writing lark. All this baring of my soul. This real stuff, not the garbage that Walter has come to expect. He's due back tomorrow night, and I don't like to disappoint him. I'm sure it was the thought of my creative efforts that got him through his recent illness, so I'll have to find a few seconds to produce some writing about 'happiness'.

I can feel a sonnet coming on.

Chapter Eleven

Happiness.

I read out my humble offering, and for the first time ever, the housewives listened approvingly, nodding their heads, as if they were just about to say the same themselves. When I was finished, they all simpered in my direction, and made worrying, happy, hissy little noises. Walter was particularly impressed.

'That's very promising, Maeve. I like it.'

'Er, thanks, Walter.'

'I have to be honest, Maeve. It's the best work you've ever shared with us.'

'Oh, I don't know,' I said airily.

'No, really, Maeve. That imagery is quite mature. Very evocative. You should try to write more like this.'

I began to wonder guiltily what the penalty for plagiarism might be, but I suppose the real author, Ellen O'Doherty, won't mind. She's only eight and a half, one of my third class pupils who wrote the poem during free writing time this morning. I must get her to write some more to cover the next two weeks, and then Walter and I will be free of each other forever.

Paul was absent today. He's in hospital, under observation, having swallowed one of his father's contact lenses. The class spent a happy half-hour making him get well cards. We seem to spend a lot of time doing that, writing get-well cards for Paul. We've already had to do it twice. The first was after he broke his leg skateboarding down the stairs, and the one before this was after he did himself an injury while trying to use the family's pet terriers and his baby sister's buggy to re-enact a Victorian polar expedition. His lovely, gentle, long-suffering parents must have come under suspicion in the hospital by now, but anyone who spends more than ten minutes in Paul's company would surely see the truth; with a child like Paul, the best a parent can aim for is damage limitation. It must be hard on them living under the pressure of knowing that someone is keeping count of every bump, bruise, scrape and stitch.

I'm sorry for Paul of course, but I couldn't waste this chance. Without him, the classroom was a haven of peaceful activity, and I rushed to get lots of work done before his return.

Poor Paul. Maybe when he grows up he'll get a job as a presenter on one of those manic TV programmes that make me feel so old and crabby. You know the ones. They are usually on late on weekend nights. The camp presenter dances around in a shiny suit, shouting to be heard over a background of loud rock music, and then, as if your senses aren't confused enough, snippets of written information scroll across the bottom of the screen, defying you to catch everything that is going on.

In a fantastic new development, it seems that you can now buy televisions that show two different channels, side by side, at the same time. Wonderful – two camp, shiny-suited presenters dancing around, etc., etc., etc.

Mind you, Paul is probably admirably suited for the world we now live in. Maybe I'm the one who is moving at the wrong pace. I know that makes me sound so old, but I think life is moving too fast for me.

Do you remember those cute ride-on cars and engines we used to beg our parents to let us ride on when we were little children? On the rare occasion when I could persuade my mother to part with the few required coins, I sat, rapt, entranced by the gentle swaying motion, thrilled by the pure joy of it all. Recently though, I brought Darragh, Sean's youngest child, to town, and he, without much difficulty, persuaded me to pay for one of these supermarket rides. He popped in the fifty-cent piece, and the movement commenced. So far, so good. Just like it used to be in the olden days when I was a child.

No longer is the child expected to be satisfied with this though. Darragh was bombarded with flashing lights and electronic beeps, coming from a console in front of the steering wheel. Gradually it began to dawn on me that he was also supposed to play a letter matching game, keying in answers as he swayed. I could only shake my head in wonder, irritated beyond words by the incessant refrain, 'Sorry, try again.' Poor Darragh, not alone was his little three-year-old brain being swamped by excess information, he was also unable to appreciate what should have been one of the great pleasures of the occasion – the joy of smug gloating, lording it over passing children who looked on in envy.

I digress. I must ask Walter if digressions are good or bad. He won't know of course, as I'm beginning to realise that he doesn't know much at all about writing, but he'll be flattered that I asked him, and he'll spill out a suitably waffly answer.

Unfortunately, Theresa returned safe and sound from Lough Derg, and the religious experience didn't seem to require a vow of silence. She positively gushed. 'It was so marvellous. So real. So spiritual. It wasn't hard at all. I think you get a special kind of strength. Some people fell asleep during the vigil, so Michael and I woke them up. Michael and I never fell asleep. We kept ourselves awake by discussing our future together.' I'd have thought that would have prompted instant slumber, but decided not to mention it. Anyway, no one got a chance to say anything as she spouted forth. 'The soup didn't taste that bad. Well it did, but we didn't mind. And the stones weren't that hard. Well they were quite hard, but you get used to them after the first hour. And the people we met were so nice. So sincere.' As she added the last bit, she seemed to be eyeing me in particular. But that's not fair. I am sincere. I am sincere in my hatred of Theresa and all she stands for. Pompous old cow.

I have a recurring nightmare, in which Mr Flynn resigns and Theresa's Michael gets his job. Now that would be a scenario of horror. If I had to face those two together every day, I would surely take to my bed, never to rise again; legitimately too sick to go to work.

Other news from the staff room: Man. United are doing well, and are in line for a double. Yawn. Mr Flynn and his wife can't decide whether to change their car or go on a holiday this summer. I urged him to go for the holiday. *Carpe diem*, and all that, but he just looked at me kindly, as if to say, 'What could a slip of a girl like you know?' He's an old gentleman, and if he knew half of what I got up to in my student days, he'd probably die of the shock. Anyway, now that I've told him I'll have company on my trip to Vancouver, he's all for it. 'When you come back you can teach the class all about Canada. It will be great for their geography. The inspectors will be very impressed.' I suppose he's right, but I don't want to see my trip as a teaching exercise. I'm not going all the way out there to impress a few middle-aged men in grey suits, and I certainly don't want to think about September, before I even go on my holiday.

Mum and Dad also think the Canada trip is a great idea. Mum's always encouraging me to 'settle down' and she says she'd like me to be more like my sister Niamh, a contented wife and mother. However, she got a kind of absent, wistful look when I told her, and I wonder, as I often have before, if she hasn't found marriage to be a bit restrictive, and whether deep down, she envies me my freedom. I wonder if she's being a little dishonest, urging me into a state which may not have brought her the happiness she'd anticipated.

Anyway, how free am I? Most of my daytime hours are spent with Theresa, Pat, Mr Flynn and thirty youngsters to whom I am a benign dinosaur. The evenings and weekends I often spend alone. I am not unhappy, just vaguely discontented, and I'm not quite sure what it is I want from life.

Still, I don't feel like grappling with the bigger picture right now. *ER* is on in ten minutes and I'm going to make a cup of milky cocoa before it starts. I'll need it to calm me down at the sight of all those bodies.

And that's just the doctors.

Chapter Twelve

Tonight was my last night with Walter. In some strange way, I'll miss him. He really enjoyed my final recitation, a short, witty piece entitled 'Endings', penned by nine-year-old Kevin, for his homework last Tuesday evening.

The housewives have great plans. They are going to publish a compilation of their best work. 'Best' is a funny word though. Does it imply that some of it is going to be good? I hope not, because any of their work that I've heard was really, really awful. It will probably be like those things people sell door to door. You know those times the bell rings as you're about to sit down to dinner, or just as one of those handsome ER doctors is about to invent a daring new procedure to save the life of a mother of ten? You rush out, hoping it's a social caller, deflated beyond words to find an earnest-looking pair trying to flog their works of art.

These books invariably have a light green cardboard cover with an arty line drawing. The drawing is usually slightly off-centre, wandering through the crooked staples towards the back cover, though probably not deliberately so. Inside, there's lots of waffle, in a large decorative font, double-spaced so it will look like more than it really is. Also tradition dictates that this waffle must be typed on a word processor which does not seem to be equipped with a spell-check facility.

The housewives haven't asked me to contribute, I can't think why. After all, they really liked my recent work. I've got lots of suitable titles for them – 'Life with the little brats', 'Dreary dross' or 'Head lice and worms: wildlife our children bring home'. The possibilities seem endless, but as I said, I'm not invited. I'm not one of them. I don't want to be one of them, but it would be nice to be asked all the same.

When the time came to leave this evening, I tried to sneak out without being seen. No chance though. Walter stepped nimbly between the door and me, blocking my escape. For what seemed like an eternity, he looked at me intently with his washed-out, greyish eyes. He took my hand in his and gave it a limp shake (surprising really, with all the hand-waving he does, I'd have thought his wrist muscles would be stronger).

'Thank you, Maeve. It's been wonderful teaching you.'

'Er, thanks Walter. It's been a pleasure for me too.'

'Really Maeve. You should be proud of yourself. You've come on so well.'

'Thanks. I did my best, I suppose.'

'Now, Maeve, be fair to yourself. It was more than that. Not everyone can raise their game the way you did over the last few months. I've watched your work mature. You've come on in leaps and bounds. Well done.'

'Well. You know how it is.'

This was getting embarrassing, and, short of pushing him out of the way and making a bolt for the door, I had no idea how to stop the flood of Walter's gushing words.

'May I speak plainly, Maeve?'

I shrugged. What could I say?

'Your early work was quite immature. Dare I say, even childish. And for a while I suspected that you weren't taking your writing at all seriously.'

He shook his finger in my face, as if chiding a small child. 'For a while I thought you were toying with us, Maeve.'

I tried to look horrified at the prospect of toying with Walter and the housewives. I must have succeeded in this endeavour, as Walter changed tack.

'But as the months have passed by you have blossomed. The change is quite remarkable. You have grown into an intuitive writer. A writer of feeling. A writer of depth.'

The housewives were still huddled together in the doorway and they were beginning to look a bit jealous and mutinous. I looked at Walter, and for one horrible moment I feared that he knew about my plagiarism, and that he was just winding me up, pretending to be impressed by my writing skills. Then I got sense and realised that such intuition was beyond him. I wasn't taking any chances though. The housewives were beginning to look dangerous. Decisive action was necessary.

I firmly removed the hand he had been holding all this time, and waved it gaily in the air.

'Thank you so much, Walter. You've taught me so much. You've changed my life.'

That silenced even him, and I brushed past the open-mouthed housewives and made my escape.

Roll on next January. I wonder what delightful class my mum will find for me next? Maybe I've gone through all the locality has to offer, and I'll have to backtrack, revisiting some of my erstwhile teachers, who thought they were free of me forever. Teachers who breathed premature sighs of relief at my departure. Teachers who thought it was safe to go back into the classroom.

Watch out, Walter, I'll be back!

I've got the piece of paper from Charlie. Real paper and real ink. He signed it with a predictable, academic-type, illegible scrawl. He also printed his name underneath, in neat precise letters – Charlie Kerr.

I wonder what he's like, this man who's entrusting us with his home and his car. This man who will be living in my house for a month. In a modern world where there's so much dishonesty, and broccoli stealing, this home swapping is a real act of faith in human nature. I hope my faith isn't misplaced. Now that I've got the piece of paper pinned to the notice board in the kitchen (next to the out-of-date washing powder vouchers), I know I'm going. Our flights have been confirmed, and deposits paid. At last it seems real. Maria and I are going to Vancouver. This is the most exciting thing I've done in years. We are going to have a ball. It's going to be the holiday of a lifetime. I am looking forward to it so much. I am going to be a good person, so I will deserve it. I am going to keep my teaching notes fully up to date, and I'm going to write all new ones, not just copy last year's. I am going to listen attentively to Pat's talk of soccer. I am going to try very hard to stay awake while doing so. I am going to talk Irish grammar and long division with Mr Flynn. I am going to be nice to Theresa (well, maybe that's a bit extreme. I'll just try not to mock her too much).

It's official. I am a good person, and I'm going to Vancouver on my holidays!

Well, maybe I need not be that good. Nice things can also happen to bad people. There was a boy who sat next to me in primary school who was horrible. He picked his nose and ate it. All day long. The other boys called him 'Greenfingers'. He stole the eraser in the shape of a troll that Santa brought me. Then he lied to the teacher and said I'd promised it to him for letting me kiss him on his ear. She believed him, and I wasn't allowed to do cookery that afternoon. And we were making toffee crumble.

Now he has his own big factory and he drives around in a red Jaguar.

I think I can safely skip being nice to Theresa.

Well no. I'm not taking any chances. I'll stick to indifference.

Just to be on the safe side.

Chapter Thirteen

14 June

Being good has been so boring. It mustn't be in my nature. I think some inbred, bitchy part of me needs to snipe at Theresa, and I'm afraid that if I don't give in and do it soon, I will explode into a sick, jeering tornado, whizzing through the staffroom, sparing no one.

Still, my virtue is paying off. My teaching notes are written up to the end of term (only two more weeks), my pupils are happy, my house is tidy, and my lettuces are thriving, growing fresh and strong, all ready for the first slug onslaught. The weeds are doing very nicely too. Wouldn't life be just marvellous if slugs ate the weeds? They could multiply happily, and not live in fear of my nightly torchlight processions of death. They could fill themselves up on dandelions and bindweed, and sleep soundly, with no fear. Why is life never as simple as that?

My house is always quite tidy anyway, but I have used the imminent arrival of Charlie and Todd as a spur to do the really thorough jobs like cleaning under the beds and sorting out cupboards. I've cleaned the skirting boards, and vacuumed the cobwebs from the ceilings. I've dusted the pictures, and scrubbed the kitchen cupboard doors. I've removed the dried up peas which seem to think that the space underneath the microwave is their spiritual home.

I suppose Charlie will use my room, as it's the biggest and nicest, so I am going to remove all of the girlie stuff like tampons, bras and Immac, in case he's a shy sort of guy. (Anyway, I'm a shy sort of girl, and I don't fancy him looking at that stuff.) I've locked away personal items like letters and photographs, and I've given my only valued china, a bowl my Granny used to own, to Sean to mind, just in case Todd decides to play baseball indoors.

Do Canadians play baseball?

Some of the home exchange websites have recommended sending a photo of yourself to your exchange partner. On some of the sites, non-members can even access pictures – family groups, smiling at the world; grinning at strangers from Bombay to Ballybunion. They are all dressed in their best, grouped in such a way as to show both themselves and their home to best advantage. I look at them in idle moments, wondering if they are all leaning against a gaping crack in the house wall, or if they are standing in such a strange pose in order to block the view of the oil refinery next door. I look at the wholesome teenagers, wondering if the arms casually held behind their bodies are adorned with tattoos of snakes or naked women. The pictures are taken from such a distance that I cannot easily determine whether nose rings, eyebrow rings or tongue studs have been hastily removed. Do the all-American baseball caps hide mohican haircuts, or dreadlocks? It's not that I'd object to these things of course – I'm a free-thinking modern girl; it's just that these families all look suspiciously like the Brady Bunch. They must be hiding something. Could it be that these home-exchangers are really the families from hell, who have found a website, 'photographs of trustworthy-looking families' and downloaded a selection of images to fool us?

I have no notion of sending my picture to strangers, but in an unfair, sneaky kind of way, I would love to get one of Charlie and Todd. I know they could be serial axe murderers, or professional thieves, and that this would not necessarily reveal itself in a photograph, but for some strange reason, what I really fear is that they will be fat and dirty. I have a dreadful picture in my mind, of two huge wobbly bodies, clad in polyester shorts and brightly coloured shirts, with the fabric damp and staining under their arms. I see them stopping at the Coke and crisps machine in the airport, and emptying it in seconds, before weighing down my precious little car with themselves, seven suitcases and countless large bags full of cookies and candy.

Then I picture my living room. I can see Charlie and

108

Todd, dirty feet up on the couch, watching TV, eating greasy chips (sorry, fries), wiping their fingers on my cushions, and spilling their fizzy drinks on my nice clean throws. I see them beached amidst a days-old mound of papers and used cans. I worry that they will turn my neat, clean home into a smelly, filthy tip.

I think I'll try to persuade Sean to spy on them, and let me know what they're like. He can find an excuse to call, and peep over their shoulders into the living room. Then if they have wrecked my house, he can let me know, and I can reciprocate, sevenfold. I could leave a few raw chickens under the beds on a hot day! That wouldn't be much consolation though — my house would still be a wreck, and if they were that slobbish, they probably wouldn't notice if their own was similarly destroyed.

Anyway, all the exchange agencies assure me that damage to houses is rare, and that exchanging has to be entered into with a spirit of trust. I don't know you Charlie, I'll never meet you, but I'm trying to trust you Charlie, I really am.

You can be fat – I don't have a problem with that. I'm not really all that prejudiced, and I'll understand if you and your son have an inherited metabolic disorder, but please don't be dirty.

Charlie sent me an e-mail the other day. It was nice to have the contact with him, but unfortunately he didn't mention whether he's a dirty slob.

Dear Maeve,

Thanks for the paperwork you sent me. Todd and I are very much looking forward to our vacation in Cork. What kind of car is a Fiesta? We don't have them here. Is it big? You'll just love the Tahoe. It's a Chevy. Do you have Chevies in Ireland? Will the weather be warm? Do we need to bring sweaters? Which terminal in Cork airport will the car be in? Is the beach at Myrtleville good for surfing? Do you like boats? My friend has a boat you can use if you like. You could cruise around the harbour. Please let me know if there's anything I can do to help you before you arrive in Canada.

Regards,

Charlie

Oh, dear. This is what I felt like writing in reply:

Dear Charlie,

You eejit. No, a Fiesta is not big. It would probably fit into the boot of your precious Tahoe. And there'd still be plenty of room for a few hundred crates of carbonated drinks. And a couple of boxes of crisps. No, we don't have Chevies. We respect the environment over here, and don't drive those awful gas-guzzlers. The weather will probably be freezing. And wet. As well as sweaters, bring fleeces, hats, gloves, scarves, wellies and raincoats. I'll ignore the question about Cork airport as it's so pathetic. No, the beach at Myrtleville isn't good for surfing. The waves are so timid that a small ant couldn't surf on them. Yes, I love boats. Looking at them, that is. Letting me sail one would be about as wise as asking a few friendly slugs to keep an eye on your lettuces while you pop down to the shops for cornflakes.

Regards, Maeve

P.S. Are you a fat slob?

Of course, as I'm such a nice girl, and as I want to keep this guy on my side, I didn't send that particular message. What I did write was this:

Dear Charlie,

Thanks for your message. Fiestas are made by Ford. (Did you know that Henry Ford was from Cork?) They aren't very big. We don't have Chevies, but I've seen them on the television. You might need one or two sweaters, and bring a light raincoat, in case of showers. Cork airport is probably smaller than what you are used to. It has only one terminal, and you won't have any problem finding the car. (Your local supermarket parking lot is probably bigger

than the one in Cork airport.) Myrtleville isn't exactly a surfing beach. It's more a toddlers-with-buckets-and-spades kind of beach. I love boats, but wouldn't feel quite competent to sail one around Vancouver Harbour. Maria and I are looking forward to our trip too.
Regards, Maeve

An hour later, Charlie's reply appeared in my inbox.

Dear Maeve,
Sorry. Did I sound very ignorant? I haven't been to Europe before, and am not quite sure what I should expect. I forgot to ask if you keep pigs in the kitchen and poultry in the parlour. Don't worry though, the culture shock will be good for us arrogant Canadians. I am certain I will love Cork. And that you will love Vancouver.
Regards again,
Charlie

Hmmm. Interesting. I like a man who's got a sense of humour.

I like a man who's not afraid to admit when he's wrong.

Well, actually, I've never met one of those.

But I'm sure I'd like him if I did.

Pity I won't ever meet you, Charlie. I'm sure you aren't all bad.

Chapter Fourteen

I don't subscribe to the popularly held view that the two best things about being a teacher are July and August, but I am human. I'm not programmed to love work the way robots and computers and Theresa are. I am a normal person and I am free to rejoice that at last, at long, long last, the holidays are here.

If I were a less inhibited person I'd be jumping around, singing, dancing and doing cartwheels.

If I could sing and dance and do cartwheels I suppose I wouldn't be a teacher, but never mind. In my own quiet, understated kind of way, I am very, very happy.

I am free of work for two wonderful months. My fourth class have been despatched into Mr Flynn's capable care, and my third class are the new fourth, big and proud.

I have taught Paul for two long and eventful years, and have somehow managed to keep him free of schooltime accidents, the first teacher ever to have done so. In many ways I will miss him. I like his spirit and his innocent charm, but I am glad to be handing the responsibility for him to someone else. Next year it will be lovely to chat to him in the yard at playtime, enjoying his good humour, and his irrepressible exuberance. Then I can watch in peace as he joins someone else's line, and trails clumsily into someone else's classroom, where he can ruin someone else's carefully planned lessons and raise someone else's blood pressure to levels that could not possibly be healthy.

For nine precious, wonderful weeks I won't have to listen to Theresa's gushing anecdotes about her darling Michael. I won't have to put up with her forced sighing whenever I speak, or the endless click click of her knitting needles. I won't have to endure Mr Flynn's well-intentioned pontificating, or his kind dismissal of me. The premier league is over for the year, but no doubt Pat will find some soccer action to fill the time until the new season. I'm just glad I won't be around to share it with him; he will just have to find another helpless victim and bore them to death.

Perhaps my colleagues look on this sojourn away from me with equal delight, savouring the days they won't have to spend with me, but I don't really care.

With some lingering virtue, I have cleaned out my desk, and given back all of the erasers, Star Wars figures, comics, and Pokemon cards that I have confiscated during the year. Tears were once shed over these items, but it's funny how many remain unclaimed. Fads have moved on, and precious treasures have become worthless. Mind you, some of these treasures might have been worth more if I hadn't let a packet of Mentholyptus sweets melt all over them, but it wasn't my fault. Honest. I just put them there in October when I had a nasty throat infection. Then I turned my back, and they dissolved quietly, gathering paper clips, plastic beads and pencil shavings as they slid slowly into a sticky, glutinous heap.

Anyway, they are such a lovely shade of purple; the front right corner of my desk drawer is almost a work of art. Advertising executives in London have paid tens of thousands of pounds for less.

I have untangled elastic bands, and removed thumbtacks and pieces of Lego from large dirty lumps of Blu-tack. I have sharpened pencils and stored them carefully in old baby-milk tins. I have sorted out my store cupboards, and labelled the shelves on my chart press. I have taken my pictures and charts down from the walls, and torn up the dog-eared, tatty-looking ones, so I will be forced to make new ones next year.

I have attacked the nature table, and I have binned the crumbling, dusty honeycomb that has adorned it for the past five years. I have returned the appendix clips, which some child thought should have pride of place. (Were they a health risk? Oh dear, it's too late to worry about that now as they've been there since the second week of September.) The robin's nest that showered the area with twigs and dirt every time it was touched was discreetly dumped.

What smart alec thought the 'nature table' was such a wonderful concept? It might have seemed like a good idea at the time, but really? Did they think it through properly? Whoever it was has condemned the youth of Ireland to forever associating nature with dust, decay, dirt, wizened conkers and school milk. (Some law seems to decree that when the milk arrives in the classroom, it is invariably placed on a corner of the nature table to spend a few hours warming up before lunch.)

But do I care?

No. I do not plan to think of tepid milk or nature tables for a very long time.

My last job was to clean the art corner. Paul helped me so my job was very easy. I just let him loose for twenty minutes and then I could dump the lot without guilt, as he had rendered everything useless.

My classroom is now a dirt and clutter-free zone. It is labelled and organised to within an inch of its life.

Horror of horrors. Now that I've stopped mocking Theresa, I've become her.

In the last few minutes before home time, as the children chewed happily on the sweets I'd given them as an end of year treat, I looked out the window at the waiting mothers in the schoolyard. (I know I should be politically correct and refer to parents, but the reality isn't politically correct. There are countless mothers, and just one father, a bigshot businessman who spends months at a time in America, and has just appeared for the first time since Christmas.) The mothers stood in little groups, leaning on buggies, or holding tight to little toddler hands. In the main they were poorly dressed. There were no power suits or little black dresses. It was mostly jeans and fleeces and tracksuits. There was even one horrific shell suit to be seen, but maybe the wearer was only doing it for a bet.

For these women, their work is never done. They didn't get holidays today like I did. There's always a nappy to change, a shoelace to tie, a green nose to wipe, a mop of hair to search for wildlife. These women have no careers and no independence. They probably haven't finished a cup of tea or a sentence in many years. While I wouldn't swap with them, part of me is deeply envious of what they have. Their children run towards them, full of the joys of summer holiday freedom, and they leave in little straggly bunches, making arrangements for sleepovers and parties and trips to the beach.

They are never alone.

But why am I whinging? It just shows how ungrateful I can be. Tomorrow I leave on the trip of a lifetime, and I've got a lot to be happy about.

Anyway, I'm not even sure I want to be more like those badly dressed mums; it's probably just that I want to be less like me.

My house has never been so clean. Everything is tidy, and all surfaces sparkle and shine. There was a lingering scent of bleach, so I've sprinkled some lavender oil around in an effort to make the place less institutionalised-smelling. I've had my car serviced, and I've vacuumed it for the first time ever. The vacuum cleaner doesn't work any more now, and I've no time to get it fixed, but anyway, if Charlie is the slob I fear, that won't matter to him.

There was a moment of panic yesterday after I tried for the first time ever to do a thorough clean of the oven. I had broken all my rules and purchased a can of very strong, very environmentally unfriendly oven cleaner. I sprayed it on liberally, and retired to the back garden, half-choked by foul-smelling fumes that caught in my throat and made me cough. I waited the required thirty minutes, and then returned to mop up the collapsed foam, and the greasy debris that lay on the floor of the oven. To my horror, I found twelve perfectly-shaped, black, crumbly discs amongst the slop. I dabbed them dry, and lay them on a sheet of kitchen paper, wondering what toxic agent could possibly have been in the spray that would dislodge parts of the surface of the oven. Sean dropped in just then, and I told him of the tragedy, and asked whether he thought they were vital components. He examined one carefully, turning it around in his hand, and holding it up to the light.

I was impatiently worried. 'Sean, tell me what I've done to my oven. Can it be fixed? How can I go to Vancouver leaving poor Charlie with a broken oven?'

He gave a wry smile. 'I don't know, Maeve. It could be serious.'

'Please, Sean. How bad is it? Can you fix it?'

'How many of these did you find?'

'Twelve. Look, I have them all.' I held out the kitchen paper, with its crumbly contents.

Sean took the paper from my hands, and rubbed his chin reflectively. 'Hmm, Maeve. Twelve is a lot. I've never seen an oven this bad.'

To my amazement, he crumpled the paper and tossed it and the crushed black discs into the bin behind him. I was horrified.

'Sean! Why'd you do that? We'll never fix it now.'

He gave a low, mocking laugh. 'Ah, Maeve. They weren't exactly vital components. Your oven might even work better without them.'

I was scrabbling in the bin to see if any could be saved. 'That's crazy, Sean. If they weren't vital, why were they in my oven all this time?'

He grinned. 'Because, my dear sister, they fell off the last pepperoni pizza you cooked, that's why.'

Oops.

I have cut the grass, and pulled up the worst of the weeds in the front garden. The vegetable patch is as weed-free as an organic area can be, and the vegetables are positively glowing with health and goodness. They almost look happy.

I have left post-it notes everywhere, describing the

119

operation of everything that operates. I have left my e-mail password for Charlie, and he's giving me his, so we can contact each other if necessary, without running up huge telephone bills. I have left a long list of emergency telephone numbers, doctor, dentist, car repairman and so on.

I have everything packed for my holiday, not too much, just what I can carry myself, so I have lots of room in my suitcase for anything I'll want to buy in Canada. (Yes, I've reached that time of life; I travel with a suitcase instead of a scruffy rucksack.) I have my passport and tickets and travel insurance and health insurance and exchange agreement all ready in my newly sorted-out handbag, which is strangely light now that I have removed things like the receipt for knickers I bought in Dunnes last November, and the recipe for salt dough I got on a summer course two years ago. Everything is so clean and tidy and nice, it almost seems a pity to leave.

Almost.

I've walked the beach a few times, trying to see it with a stranger's eye, hoping Charlie and Todd will like it. I've driven around picking out scenic spots that might interest them, and I've walked slowly down Patrick Street, hoping they'll be impressed with its undoubted charm, impressed enough not to notice the litter, and the slight seediness creeping into some parts. I've tried to describe some of the different, quirky things that give Cork its character. I've listed the old family shops and the independent ones that have sprung up over the past years, hoping my guests won't spend their time in the faceless chainstores that adorn every town in this island. I've optimistically recommended lots of good shops and restaurants, though I know that by the time Charlie gets here, half of them will have been closed down and turned into mobile phone warehouses.

I've written lots of ideas for things to do, things that might interest Todd, but I know I might be wasting my time. I can accept the possibility that they might be shallow touristy types who will just want to kiss the Blarney stone, visit the Lakes of Killarney, take a day trip to Dublin and then say that they've 'done Ireland'.

But what is it to me?

They can spend their holiday in Cork airport for all I care.

Tomorrow Maria and I fly to London, where we will stay with her cousin for one last night of European debauchery, and then it's Vancouver, here we come!

Chapter Fifteen

Here we are on board flight number something or other, Heathrow to Vancouver, and we are taxiing towards the runway. The velvet-voiced pilot has politely welcomed me on board. I am securely buckled into my seat. My seat back and tabletop are suitably secured in an upright position for take off.

I don't have a laptop computer or a GameBoy or a mobile phone, but if I had, I would have dutifully turned them off. I have watched the air hostess trying not to look too bored as she wrestled with the life-jacket and oxygen mask during the safety demonstration. I know that I should never inflate my life-jacket while still inside the aircraft. I have carefully read the safety chart from the seat pocket in front of me, I have located the nearest emergency exit, and I have tried not to think too hard about what possible use all this will be to me in the event that we crash into a mountain.

There was one genuine moment of panic that wasn't covered in the safety demonstration. It happened before the aircraft doors were even closed. Maria and I were safely ensconced in our seats when an earth mother type, all dangly earrings, flowery trousers and open sandals advanced down the aisle towards us. I kid you not, the largish infant tied to her front with a fringed shawl, was breastfeeding as her mother walked along, with two more scruffy-looking toddlers of indeterminate sex scurrying along in her wake. They were laden with half-closed canvas bags, full no doubt, of tofu, brown rice and incense sticks. One toddler clutched a torn cellophane bag, and left a trail of sesame sticks in its wake. The other, the smaller and dirtier of the two, with tear-streaked face and green runny nose, was chewing their boarding cards. A sleekly well-groomed air hostess who I trust is well paid for what she has to put up with, gently removed what was left unchewed, and directed the family a few rows behind us. A second after they passed, my nostrils were assailed with the intermingled odours of onions and musk, and the unmistakable ammonia smell of not recently changed wet nappy. I breathed a heartfelt sigh of relief and couldn't resist a smug look back to where a poor unfortunate man in a clean navy suit was looking quite unwell at the prospect of ten hours in the company of these charming people.

We had a marvellous time in London last night. You know the feeling. The great first night of a holiday. All the work and preparation is done, and the panic of,

'Have I packed my Ladyshave? Did I put in my bikini? Did I turn off the gas?' is all behind you, as now that you've left home, there's no point in remembering what you've forgotten, as it's too late to do anything about it anyway. As for my usual worries as to whether I locked the house and emptied the breadbin, they don't count this time, as sometime around now Charlie will be letting himself in, and filling the breadbin with sliced pans of stodgy white bread, and loading the fridge with fizzy drinks and ice-cream and burgers. Now that my holiday has started, I've stopped being concerned about the house, and don't really care what happens while I'm away. They can do their worst, and I'll worry about it when I get back.

Maria's cousin, Donal, was most hospitable. He met us at the airport, gave us five minutes in his flat to drop our bags, wash our faces and catch our breath, and then he took us on a lightning tour of all the pubs in his neighbourhood. For a small neighbourhood there were lots of pubs. Most were dark and gloomy, with no great atmosphere, but that didn't matter to us, as we were in such good form. Donal smiled at us like a benign old man, as we chattered excitedly about all we would see and do while we were away.

Maria was slightly tipsy and was boring Donal with her plans for shopping in Vancouver, when I cut her off.

'For God's sake, Maria. Give Donal a break. I bet he's not interested in shopping.'

Maria stopped her monologue, and Donal gave me a grateful grin. 'Come on girls. It's time for food anyway. And I know the perfect place.'

Maria gave me a cross look, but decided not to sulk. 'Great, Donal. Are you going to show us a nice cool bistro? Or maybe an Indian?'

I interrupted her. 'No, Maria. Wouldn't Thai be nice? Remember that great Thai meal we had in Dublin last year?'

'Oh yeah, that was delicious. I can still taste that spicy sauce. Are there any nice Thai restaurants around here, Donal?'

Donal looked shocked. 'No, Maria. That wouldn't be the thing at all. You need to be prepared for your holidays, and you're not going to Thailand, are you? You need to practise. I thought we'd go to McDonalds.'

It was my turn to be shocked. 'Tell me you're not serious, Donal. Please.'

Maria was less polite. 'Forget it Donal. Just 'cause we still live in Cork, it doesn't mean we are totally unsophisticated. Our culinary tastes are a touch above Happy Meals and strawberry milkshakes. And anyway, we're going to Canada, not America.'

Donal scoffed. 'Hah, I bet there's the occasional McDonalds in Canada too. Anyway, I know you Maria. You can pretend all you like. I know how partial you are to a cheeseburger, and I bet Maeve's the same.'

He looked at me, waiting for an answer. He was right, of course. I held my hands up in a gesture of surrender. 'OK, OK, I admit it. I have eaten the odd cheeseburger, and I'm not totally indifferent to hot caramel sundaes.'

Maria looked as if I had betrayed her, but still she said, 'Right Donal, you win. Lead us to the golden arches. And I want extra nuts on my caramel sundae.'

He patted her arm in a mock patronising manner. 'That's the girl. At last you've seen sense. And anyway, look on the bright side. At least it will be fast. There's a few more pubs I'd like to show you.'

Maria grinned and patted his arm back. 'Now you're talking, Donal. Lead on.'

Donal treated us to all we could eat, and we continued on our pub tour of Earl's Court, drinking happily until closing time.

We returned to Donal's flat, for coffee and more chat, though we retired earlyish as we didn't fancy being both hungover and tired for our long flight. Even though he's a bit of a slob, I was touched to see that Donal had made an effort and his two tiny spare beds had spotlessly clean, darned sheets. (Thank God for the Irish Mammy.) And while the bathroom wasn't exactly clean, he had at least tried, by squirting some bleach inside the stained toilet bowl. I slept a peaceful sleep, dreaming of beaches and glistening water and caramel sundaes.

*

And now we're en route. On the plane, in the air. On our way at last. I'm writing now, because it's too soon for food or a film or sleep, and, let's face it, there's not a lot else to do on a plane, unless you've brought a sexual partner. Then, if you have the neck to squash into the toilet together, in full view of twenty rows of bored passengers, and if you're thin enough to be able to close those silly concertina doors once you're in, and if you trust the flimsy lock, and if you're sure the smoke alarm isn't a camera as well, and if after all that you fancy having sex with your behind wedged against a small, cold, stainless steel sink labelled, 'For the comfort of other passengers, please wipe after use', well then, you're welcome to it.

As none of this applies to me, I'd better stick to my scribbling. I have great intentions. I'm going to dutifully take out my notebook and pen every single night. Charlie's apartment will be a hive of literary industry. I plan to write lots and lots, to have a record of the trip, more fuel for my posthumous bonfire.

And if I don't write a word, you'll know I'm having a ball.

Chapter Sixteen

I brought a copy of Charlie's entry in Home Exchangers Unlimited with me, so I could be suitably outraged if it turned out that he had misrepresented his home. It reads as follows: '*Small, two-bedroomed apartment in downtown Vancouver. Well located, with good views of English Bay. All mod cons.*'

Charlie could not be accused of lying, but he is certainly guilty of underselling his home. OK, so it is small, but it's all we need in terms of accommodation. He neglected to mention, however, that it has a large balcony, which boasts, not good, but absolutely spectacular views. Just below us, (well, fifteen floors below us to be exact) is a beach which seems to stretch for miles along the bay. The bay itself is beautiful, with a mountainous area beyond it, which I think might be Vancouver Island. All around us, to the sides and behind, are skyscrapers, but please don't picture a grim, smoggy, industrial backdrop. These skyscrapers seem to be made predominately of a bluish-green glass, and they are truly beautiful to behold.

Maria and I arrived a few hours ago, having got a taxi from the airport. (Charlie had wanted to leave his car at the valet parking section of the airport for me to collect and drive here, but I begged him not to. I'll grapple with the driving later, not now, not on our first day; not while my brain is twisted from jetlag and excitement. And three glasses of complimentary red wine.)

We struggled out of the lift, tired and cross after our journey, tried five keys in the lock before finding the right one, and then stepped into a wonderful, bright, airy living room. Double doors with closed blinds led to the balcony, and we found the key on the fourth attempt. We dropped our suitcases and duty-free shopping bags, stepped out and were transfixed. Two inviting lay-back deckchairs begged for contact with our denim-clad bottoms, so we obliged, and sat there speechless for I don't know how long. Boats chugged in and out of the bay, cyclists and inline skaters zigzagged along the cycle path beneath us, and a warm, loving sun caressed our tired faces as we sat there trying to take in the beauty that lay spread out at our feet.

Maria broke the silence. 'How could Charlie leave this place, even for a few weeks?'

I sighed. 'I don't know. How does he even go to work in the morning, leaving all this behind?'

'If he's sitting here in the evening enjoying a cold drink, how does he bring himself to go in for a wee?'

I giggled. 'Maybe he doesn't. Maybe he has a potty.'

Maria joined in my giggling. 'Maybe he uses an empty beer bottle, or the ground.'

I checked the corners of the balcony but could see no telltale urine stains. I reclined my deckchair even further, and closed my eyes. 'I wonder what he's like?'

'Mmm. Who cares? I'd forgive him anything, since he has this great place.'

'Good point. And I wonder what Todd is like?'

'Who cares?'

'I wonder if it's cold here in winter.'

'Who cares?'

'I wonder if it's raining in Myrtleville?'

'Who cares?'

Clearly Maria wasn't in the mood for lengthy discussion. I knew how to stir her though.

'I wonder if there's any food in the freezer?'

She jumped up, almost collapsing her seat with the speed of her movement. 'Oh yes. I need food. Remember I didn't eat any of that plastic and cardboard stuff that passed for food on the plane. I wonder did good old Charlie leave us anything nice.'

Good old Charlie certainly did. He had left only one post-it note, compared to the thirty-six I'd left for him, but his was on the freezer, and contained only three words – 'Please eat everything.'

Good old Charlie indeed. The freezer was a small one, part of the refrigerator, but it was carefully and methodically filled with all kinds of wonderful treats –

ready-to-heat meals, garlic bread, frozen cakes and pastries, and something I'd only read about in books – Ben and Jerry's ice cream. We each selected a meal, and while they were revolving on the glass disc of the microwave, we checked out the other rooms.

Everything in the apartment was spotlessly clean, making me feel guilty about the bad thoughts I'd had about Charlie being a dirty slob. Also, pessimist that I am, it made me worry that we will have to work very hard so it will be just as clean when we leave.

I'm so sad, aren't I? I'm picturing the day we leave before I've even had time to unpack, or to take my crumpled boarding pass out of my jeans pocket. Jetlag hasn't had time to kick in properly and already I'm planning my departure.

That's the trouble with travel – you can traverse vast oceans and snowy mountains but you can't leave yourself behind. My personality has tagged along uninvited. It is still snapping at my heels like a badly trained puppy dog, reminding me of its presence, never, even for a second, allowing me to forget that it is there.

The bedrooms were small and bright. They were sparsely furnished, and I don't mean to be sexist, but it was clear a man had decorated them. Everything was painted a pale yellow, with all soft furnishings in a bland sort of oatmealy colour. There were very few adornments anywhere. Obviously, Charlie was as

131

concerned with our sensibilities as I had been with his, and there was no sign of male occupation, even in the larger room, the one I took to be Charlie's. There were no razors, no boxer shorts lying around, no socks behind the door, no athlete's foot powder, no pin-up girls on the wall. There were no condom wrappers in the bin, no toenail clippings under the bed. In fact, there was little sign of any type of occupation. It was like an impersonal hotel room, with just a few books on the shelves as a hint that anyone lived here. Then I opened a cupboard in the hallway. Charlie it seems had packed all of his and Todd's belongings into boxes, and they were stacked to the roof of this smallish, walk-in space. Whether this was done to make life easy for us, or to protect his things from us, I have no idea.

The only personal items that had been left were some photographs of a boy I presume to be Todd, which still hung on the wall of the larger bedroom. There were ten of them, randomly but carefully arranged. Todd as a baby. Todd toddling barefoot on the beach. Todd in a school uniform. Todd wielding a baseball bat. Todd on a boat.

He wasn't particularly handsome, this stranger's child, but he beamed out of each picture, with a happy, smiling, open face. All the photographs were in similar frames, made of a dull silvery metal, prompting me to think that they were all selected and framed at the same time, probably when Charlie and his nameless wife separated. I pictured a sad little scenario, as a heartbroken Charlie packed his belongings, watched over by a thin, shrewish wife, checking that he didn't take anything he shouldn't, while an innocent Todd slept peacefully, unaware that his beloved father was leaving, and that family life as he knew it was ending, while he dreamed his innocent dreams of warm milk and Barney videos.

I don't know why I'm taking the man's part in this drama of people unknown to me. Maybe he left her, pregnant and weak, while he went off with his big-busted, brassy, teenaged lover. Maybe he beat her or terrorised her psychologically. Maybe he's obsessed with cleanliness and order, and impossible to live with.

I don't know, maybe I'm just siding with him because he owns this wonderful apartment, and I'm staying in it for a month.

Then again, it could be the thought of the ice-cream, and the chicken tikka.

Whatever the reason, until convinced otherwise, I'm on Charlie's side.

Anyway, this pointless little reverie was interrupted by the sharp beep of the microwave, so I dashed into the kitchen, collected my chicken tikka, gave Maria her chicken jalfrezi, grabbed two forks and we retired to the balcony to eat from the packages (and I was afraid that Charlie was a slob). We washed down this little feast with some of Charlie's beer, which we promised to replace, and then indulged in a little selection from the five cartons of Ben and Jerry's that Charlie had so thoughtfully supplied. We were tired, but we sat for quite a while, a little woozy from the beer, too lazy to rise and unpack, reluctant to do anything but sit and admire and be happy.

All of a sudden, my horizons have narrowed. I have no more interest in visiting the many wonderful places I read about on the Vancouver tourist website before I left home. I can live without those. I would be quite content to stay here for all of my holidays. We could eat Charlie's food, and then when the freezer was empty we could phone for takeaways. Surely the local liquor store would deliver, especially if we order enough. The Tahoe could stay in the underground garage enjoying the nice rest that I'm sure it deserves. This balcony with its view is all I need. I could sit here quite happily every evening for a month, sipping strong red wine and watching the sun go down on English Bay.

Charlie, I don't know you.

I'll never know you.

But I love you.

Chapter Seventeen

Maria and I have been on holidays together many times, and we are the perfect travelling companions. We have similar interests, and neither of us is fanatical about any activity that might threaten to dominate a trip. Neither of us is likely to insist that we climb sheer mountains, or clamber into dark, damp caves, or dive deep in murky, uncharted waters. We both like to tour a little, eat and drink a little (well, OK, drink a lot), sunbathe a little and shop a little. Nothing too slobbish, but nothing too cultured or highbrow or energetic either.

We've been here for nearly two weeks now, and are having a very laid back, easy kind of a holiday.

We've wandered into town most days, sauntered around the shops, marvelled at how cheap everything is, had regular breaks for sandwiches and strong black coffee, and then wandered back to the beach in front of our apartment. There we've spent a happy few hours working hard on our tans, and sipping Coke. We've spent quite a bit of time dozing, using jetlag as a prolonged excuse for hourly sessions of shut-eye. Other times, we've occupied ourselves by reading fat bestsellers, with lime-green covers and titles in raised gold script.

Strangely, all these books seem to be written by women I'd like to be, about women I'd like to be. Happy people happily rattling off happy tales about happy people.

Why don't whingers ever write popular novels?

Perhaps the answer to that question is so obvious, it's better left unsaid.

It's fun watching the other sunbathers. We found ourselves sitting on a patch of sand next to a young woman the first day. She was somewhere in her twenties, tall and slim. Except for her chest of course. There was nothing slim about that. When this girl lay down on her back, her boobs didn't flatten and sink like the rest of ours do. They stood firm and proud, attracting, no, demanding, attention. Her long sleek hair was a golden-blonde colour, and she was nearly dressed in a very, very tight red swimsuit. No one who has ever seen *Baywatch* could avoid the obvious comparisons. The strange thing was, she wasn't at all pretty. Her perfect nose didn't suit her face, her lips were thin, and her eyes were small; a dullish grey colour that reminded me of Theresa. The fact that those boobs could not have been natural, that her hair was clearly dyed, and that her nose was suspiciously manufactured-looking (page twenty-seven of 'Pick your new Nose'), didn't stop the ogling men and boys who trailed in a constant gawping stream along the sand in front of where she lay. Some of these nonchalant passers-by almost had their tongues hanging out as they sidled along, in a strange crab-like gait, surely designed to allow maximum viewing time for each sally past. They didn't seem to notice that Maria, for example was ten times prettier, with her large clear eyes and her perfect unadulterated smile.

Men are so shallow! This mass ogling confirmed something I have always suspected – the poor things are easily fooled. I have a sneaking suspicion that I could pay for a boob job for my 85-year-old granny, give her a long blonde wig, sit her on a park bench, and she would get lots of attention from every breathing male pensioner in the county.

I suppose there's a consolation in there for me. I could always go under the surgeon's knife, and it would be easy to grow and dye my hair. It would be interesting to see if these external changes would alter the course of my life.

I don't want to spend the rest of my days looking like Barbie though.

I don't want her plastered-on smile, her permanently surprised look.

I don't want to model myself on twelve inches of false pink plastic idealism.

And I certainly don't fancy the poncy Ken as my partner in life.

Speaking of partners in life, there was an interesting guy on the beach the other day. OK, so I admit I'm not supposed to be on the lookout for a man, but even when you are not specifically window-shopping, occasionally something interesting catches your eye. That's allowed. Isn't it?

This guy was quite eye-catching indeed. He was sitting in Barbie's place. (I suppose this was vacant as she's checked into a plastic surgery clinic for a further pitched battle with Mother Nature.)

Maria saw him first, as we arrived and settled ourselves on what we now thought of as our own private patch of sand.

'Look, Mae. Quick. Look what the last wave just washed up.'

I spread out Charlie's beach towel and gave a casual glance in the direction Maria had indicated. I was impressed.

'Wow. Can he possibly be real?'

'Nah. Doubt it. He's probably a plastic dummy from Baywatch. I bet they use them to save spending money on extras.'

'Do you think extras on Baywatch get paid? I thought they'd do it for the glory.'

'Don't know. Maybe they just get expenses. Pocket money for sunscreen and blonde hair dye and boob jobs.'

'Who cares anyway? Look at that guy. He's so cool.'

'Maeve, you cannot be serious. He's a freak, a

138

throwback. He's a mirage left over from the seventies. His real self is now a balding grandad with varicose veins and knotty hands.'

'Maria, you are so prejudiced. Just because he's a little different, you're dismissing him. I don't care what you say, I still think he's nice. He's the best-looking guy I've seen in months. Not counting your Joe, of course.'

'Please Maeve, tell me you're joking. He's pathetic. Theresa's Michael has more sex appeal.'

'How do you know? You've never even met Michael.'

'I know, but having seen this guy, I figure Michael must be sexier. God, Maeve. My grandad's sexier than this guy.'

I gave a pretend huffy toss of my head and settled down to read, with my book carefully angled to give me an uninterrupted view of Interesting Guy.

He looked as if he'd just arrived in a cloud of foam, fresh from a Californian surfing movie. Bleached blond hair of course, in wild waves to his shoulders, with a few stray locks dangling over his eyes. Even with the yards of sand, and the stray locks of hair that came between us, I could see that his eyes were a bright, bright blue. I didn't like to stare, but his body was just perfect. Long and lean and tanned. He was wearing faded denim cut-offs, and a relaxed semi-smile. He looked as if he could conquer the world if only he weren't so busy chilling out. He was sitting on his tattered canvas backpack, and staring intently out to sea, as if awaiting the arrival of a beautiful girl to share his life.

'Hey, I'm here, over here,' I shouted.

Just kidding.

I sat and gazed in silent wonder.

Fortunately, Beautiful Girl didn't show up, and I spent a happy hour watching this vision, and flicking pages occasionally, so just in case he was paying attention, he'd think I was actually reading.

Eventually, he stood up, and put on a snow-white T-shirt he took from his backpack. I half-expected him to walk across the waves and vanish into the horizon. But no, it seems he was mortal after all, or, if not, clearly he wasn't in the mood for wave-walking. Luckily we were on his path from the beach, and he walked tantalisingly close to us. I boldly raised my eyes towards him, and he flashed me a perfect white smile as he sauntered past.

He could be paid millions for advertising tooth-paste.

But what am I saying? He was so perfect he could be used to advertise anything. Shampoo, exercise regimes, sun lotion, fast cars, peat briquettes, disposable nappies. Whatever you want to advertise, you could use this guy to do it. One look at this guy and consumers would surrender and buy anything.

Even foot spas and spoon rests.

When he was safely gone, I rolled onto my back and gave a little sigh of satisfaction. Just looking at this guy had given me pleasure. I looked towards Maria to see her exaggeratedly rolling her eyes heavenwards. 'You never learn, do you, Maeve?'

I could think of plenty of witty ripostes to this comment, but the day was so nice, and I felt so good that I decided, just this once, to spare us the aggravation.

I closed my eyes and dreamed on.

Yesterday we felt a bit guilty at all this inactivity, realising that if we just wanted to slob out in the sunshine, we could have done it much less expensively in Spain. So, filled with a sudden burst of energy, we took ourselves along to Stanley Park, as advised by the tourist brochures that Charlie had kindly left for us. There were streets full of cycle hire shops, and we carefully selected one because it offered a ten percent discount to voucher holders (thanks, Charlie). We stood outside for a while and watched in wonder as a never-ending stream of humanity passed through. Teenagers, wrinkly grannies, cuddly babies, smoochy couples, tough toddlers, you name it, they were there hiring some form of wheels. They left on varying combinations of skates, mountain bikes, racers, and baby seats. The cutest of all were the little baby-sized trailers, towed by proud mums and dads on wobbly bikes, with tiny helmeted offspring clapping and grinning from behind mesh safety sides.

We toyed with the idea of renting skates, but when we saw ultra confident nine- and ten-year-olds speeding ahead of their parents, we felt a little out of our depth, so we decided on top of the range, multi-speed mountain bikes. These were a bit more sophisticated than I was used to, as I hadn't cycled since I retired the trusty green Triumph 20 that had transported me to and from secondary school for six years. Maria was even worse, whispering to me that her last bike was an orange Chopper. We didn't like to admit this though, so we succumbed easily to the persuasive enthusiasm of the salesman, afraid that he would discover the sad truth.

We donned our compulsory helmets and set off bravely, trying to look as if we knew what we were doing. I did my best not to wobble too much while we could still be seen by the ultra-confident, smirking Australian guy who had done the deal with us. I needn't have worried though; it's true what they say – you can't forget how to ride a bike, and shortly we were whizzing along with the best of them, enjoying the warm breeze on our faces, feeling like children again.

The done thing, according to the tourist literature, is to travel along the sea wall surrounding the park, a distance of about six miles. The ever efficient and farsighted Canadians ensured that motor traffic travelled inside the park, leaving the best views for slower travellers like us. The path was one way, and carefully split in two, one side for pedestrians, and one for wheeled travellers like us. They know how to do things, these Canadians.

I remember when I was a schoolgirl, it was a great treat to be allowed to stay up until television closed down for the night. (Yes, there was once a time when television stopped, and it seemed that some great being in Dublin was telling the country that it was time for bed.) I loved to linger till the last possible second, dragging out the moments, waiting until the screen went black. Just before that, the national anthem was played, and it was always accompanied by film of a stream, with sunlight dancing and sparkling on the rippled surface of the water, seeming like magic to my unsophisticated eyes. (Yes, Walter, this story is leading somewhere. It's not a complete red herring.)

The point is that I had never seen that trick of the light in real life, until now that is. As we cycled through Stanley Park, the water, always on our right, caught rays of light and glistened, fascinating me with its endless, changing movement.

There were benches strewn along the way. As it was all so scenic, there were no 'scenic spots' and the bench erectors were probably just told, 'toss them down anywhere', so they did.

Every few hundred yards, we stopped to sit down, not because we were tired, but because we wanted to savour the beauty, to make it last, just as one nibbles rich Belgian chocolates, rather than wolfing them down greedily.

Every now and then we came across a piece of sculpture at the path's edge, or balanced on a convenient rock by the shore. Each one a remarkable work, beautifully placed. The locals, mostly on skates, whizzed by in tight tops and shiny black cycle shorts, many trailing panting dogs on leads. They travelled mostly in small groups, chatting or listening to music on headsets, seemingly oblivious to the views that had for once silenced Maria and myself. I found myself silently resolving to never allow familiarity to blind me to such beauty. Yet another promise to myself that I probably won't keep. (That makes three thousand, two hundred and forty-six.)

Even with all the stops, we still finished the cycle all too quickly, and though neither of us had cycled for years, we didn't feel tired or saddle sore. It was still early, and we couldn't face giving up the bikes so soon, so we agreed to go around again. More adventurous souls might have tried to find another cycle route, as there must have been many more, but boring people that we are, we went for the route we knew, and already loved. As Maria said, 'How could any other path be as nice as the one we've done? We don't want to waste our precious time on a lesser route.' We had already 'wasted' lots of precious time lying on one small beachtowel-shaped patch of sand in front of our apartment but I didn't mention it. I knew what she meant. Some people enthuse about treks through Kathmandu, or daring climbs up the Matterhorn, but for me, the cycle around Stanley Park sea wall must be up there with the great trips of the world, something that everyone should do once.

So what if it's so easy that I did it twice?

In the same day.

Without even getting breathless.

Without breaking into a sweat.

So what if it didn't require two years planning, three wealthy sponsors, six teams of Sherpas and lots of dried food and tinfoil sleeping bags?

And lots of very strange toilet arrangements?

That's what's so nice about it – it's accessible. Even for people like me.

On the second circuit, we stopped only twice, both times for food. First we had hot dogs from a path-side vendor. (In Canada, even the vendors inspire confidence, selling appetising food from squeaky-clean carts, which bore very little resemblance to the rusty grey ones that sprout like poisonous mushrooms around every parochial dogfight in Ireland.) These perfect hot dogs we ate on a small little beach, imaginatively titled, 'second beach'. Despite the size of the city, and the fact that the weather was a perfect mid-twenties sort of temperature, there were only about twenty people scattered around the sand. In most cities, this place would be crowded beyond reason, with people vying to find space to fully spread out their towels, trying to find a place where it would be possible to stretch out their feet without inserting their toes into someone else's ham and cheese sandwiches. Each family would then guard their precious patch with a viciousness incompatible with the fact that they were ostensibly there to relax and enjoy themselves.

No crowds on second beach though, and no fighting. There were too many other beaches, with more than enough space for everyone.

Not for the first time since arriving in Canada, I found myself wondering at the inequalities in nature. Some poor countries have to contend with deserts and drought and pestilence and flies, with very little in the line of beauty to distract the unfortunate long-suffering inhabitants. Here though, nature seemed wasteful, extravagant, tossing beauty upon beauty, one natural resource upon another. I picture a benign god, creating Canada, lovingly shaping and colouring it, taking time to get the finishing touches right, and then, when it was too late, realising that there was little left in the paint box for everyone else. As a result, what was left had to be shared, with some countries doing very badly in the divvy up.

I sat on that heavenly beach for forty-five minutes, and found myself wondering all kinds of things, including whether all this sunshine and beauty is turning me into a raving loony.

And whether I would ever see that handsome blond guy again.

We finished our hot dogs, and slowly pedalled a little further along the way. Once again we had to wheel our bikes through the children's area, where squealing tots ran backwards and forwards through sprays and jets of water. There was even a kids' dryer, like a little car wash, where the children stepped in, and were blown dry by whooshes of hot air, before returning to the water to do it all over again.

A little further on, we stopped once more and enjoyed some ice-creams with double chocolate topping, as we lay contentedly in the shade of a huge oak tree.

I'm not one of life's martyrs, but I especially love being on holidays, where I need no excuse for complete self-indulgence. It has long been a catchword of our trips, as Maria and I egg each other on, with any hint of sensible reticence blown away by the simple words, 'Who cares? We're on our 'olidays.'

We finished our second circuit rather too quickly, and reluctantly returned our bikes, enthusing to the cycle shop assistants about how wonderful it had been. They smiled politely, but were probably bored by yet more tourists getting carried away by a simple bike ride.

They didn't understand, you see. Cork is a city of quite considerable charm, and I love it, but I wouldn't cycle there to save my life. In fact, by not cycling there I probably am saving my life. If someone were to cycle there, they'd have to contend with horrendous traffic (no cycle lanes to speak of), sickening exhaust fumes, and the sudden shrieks of the Echo boys, which would surely frighten any unsuspecting cyclist into steering under the wheels of the next passing sugar beet lorry.

No, I'm afraid I'll do a few more two-wheel trips while I'm here, and then I'll have to abandon my bicycle clips for another twenty years.

That was a great day, but still looming over me was the dreaded Chevy Tahoe. I half-heartedly tried to persuade Maria that we should show some concern for the environment and cycle everywhere, but, sensibly, she was having none of it. I've been to the underground car park to look at the frightful vehicle, and was not pleased with what I saw. It's huge and shiny, and clearly well cared for. I would have been happier if it had a few dents and dinges, just in case I had a mishap, but no chance; it looked as if it had been towed there, straight from the dealer's showrooms, with ne'er a scratch nor a scrape to be seen. I'd be as comfortable driving a school bus or an articulated lorry back home. I am nervous enough about driving, but the prospect of driving this monstrous machine, in a strange country, with new driving rules and on the wrong side of the road, takes me to new heights of apprehension.

Maria, unusually for her, has taken a tough stance, and issued a firm ultimatum. 'If you don't get your act together, and drive me around this wonderful country, I'm going on strike. I'll just sit on the beach, and read rubbish every hour of every day until it's time to go home.'

It's easy for her to be so tough. She's not named on the car exchange agreement, and isn't insured to drive the beast. I know she's right though. It's an awful waste not to use the car, and while I know she's not serious about the threat, I've made up my mind: tomorrow I'm going to drive. After all, how difficult could it be? I've watched gum-chewing, baby-faced seventeen-year-olds, and frail, bespectacled grannies driving bigger machines without appearing to find it a problem.

Still, I have promised myself (number three thousand, two hundred and forty-seven) that if I ever find myself in a similar situation, I'm not going to be the named driver. Someone else can have the honour, and I can sit back, put my feet up on the dashboard, give orders, and nag.

And that's bad news. I could nag for Ireland.

Chapter Eighteen

I've done it.

I've driven the monster and lived to tell the tale.

What I really wanted to do that morning was saunter down to the beach, casual like, and wait to see if Blond Guy would show his beautiful, suntanned face. Maria wouldn't hear of it though, so a few days ago, bright, but not too early, we descended together to the bowels of this building; to the grey concrete underworld that could be anywhere. I expected any minute to hear the screech of brakes, and to see large saloon cars hurling themselves around corners, and bouncing ostentatiously over ramps in a movie car chase, but as it happened, all remained silent and normal.

Unsettlingly so.

There was to be no backing out, but there was lots of reversing. I opened the doors using the remote control keyring, which was in itself a novelty for me. With difficulty we climbed up to the front seats, wondering if perhaps there should be a ladder to assist our ascent. Then Maria had to climb all the way down again to direct me out. Something suddenly dawned on her, and, for the first time she began to look worried.

'Have you ever driven an automatic car?'

'Well, sort of.'

'Maeve, don't mess with me. What do you mean by sort of? Have you, or haven't you ever driven an automatic car?'

'Can I count Sean's remote-controlled one?'

'Maeve!!'

'OK, OK. Can I count the go-karts in Tramore?'

'No.'

'Well then, the truth is I've never before driven an automatic car.'

'Thanks a lot. Now you tell me.'

'You never asked before.' I looked at her innocently, and put the key in the ignition.

'Stop, Maeve, stop. Don't turn that key. Don't do anything foolish.'

I grinned. 'OK, I promise. Hey, Maria, let's not bother with this old car. It's bad for the environment anyway. Why don't we just walk to the beach? There's a guy there I urgently need to make mad passionate love to.'

'No way. We're intelligent girls. We can work this out. Get out the instruction manual.'

Luckily, since this was Canada, the instruction manual didn't give me any credit for prior knowledge, so I read how to start, stop and reverse. I got plenty of practice at the latter, as I edged out ever so slowly, to hear a now very nervous Maria bellowing, 'No. Maeve. Stop. You're too close. Mind the mirror. Try again.'

After several efforts I managed it, and after quite a few circuits of the car park in search of the exit, I drove proudly out into the welcoming sunshine.

Fortunately, Canadian drivers are ever so courteous, so they didn't look too cross as I hesitated at every junction, and edged my way around their city. No one beeped impatiently, or overtook aggressively when I lingered a little at traffic lights. No one shot me threatening looks when I froze momentarily in the middle of a busy four-lane street. Canadian drivers are so polite I didn't even see anyone picking their nose.

'Where are we going?' I asked, when after twenty minutes I finally had the confidence to speak and drive at the same time. We giggled together at this strange omission. I had been so nervous about the driving that it had become an end in itself, and we had no destination. I kept driving aimlessly, quite enjoying myself now, while Maria flicked through the maps that Charlie had left in the glove compartment.

'Let's go to Whistler.'

'That's miles away, isn't it? Why don't we just go to the nearest shopping mall? I'd love a caramel sundae. Or a latté. A latté would be nice.'

'No, Maeve. You're not escaping that easily. Anyway, I'm sure they've got caramel sundaes and lattés in Whistler too.'

'Come on, Maria, you've made your point. I've driven the beast. Let's go to the beach.'

'No'

'God, Maria, you're being a right bully.'

She smiled sweetly. 'I know. Come on, Maeve, don't be a chicken. Drive us to Whistler. It's only about three quarters of an inch from here on this map. That can't be far.'

I was too busy driving to see the exact scale of the map she was waving nonchalantly in the air, and since Maria rarely puts me wrong, I decided to go with her idea.

As usual, she was right, and we arrived in Whistler within a few hours. On the way we had decided to make it an overnight trip, so we made a small detour to a concrete mall to buy toothbrushes and clean underclothes. We bought a twin-pack of toothbrushes (free toothpaste included), and a four-pack of knickers between us. Oh the joys of girlie friendship.

The bully allowed me ten minutes for a latté too, so it wasn't all bad.

Whistler is a ski resort which is open all year round, finding attractions to draw visitors to fill the summer hotel rooms. It's a picturesque little town, all wooden chalets with asymmetrical roofs, and window boxes overflowing with brightly coloured flowers. The streets are neatly cobbled with stones of a nice, uniform size, and every now and then we walked past a little bubbly fountain, soothing our ears with its undemanding tinkly sound. The streets in the centre are closed to motor traffic, and seemed exclusively populated by relaxed, aimlessly sauntering tourists. The sun shone, not too hot, just warm enough to allow us to sit outside and drink coffee, but not so warm as to deter us from our plans to indulge in a little undemanding hill strolling. For all the world, Whistler could have been an alpine town magically polished up, neatened at the edges, and transported here, a little treat for the already pampered Vancouverites.

We ended up staying two nights (lucky we had those spare knickers), and we had a marvellous few days, egging each other on to partake of all kinds of activities which cannot possibly have been safe. We went white-water rafting, solemnly donning all the available safety equipment, as if a helmet and a lifejacket and ten minutes tuition could be of use to us, as we hurtled down a raging torrent of a river on an inflatable yellow rubber dinghy, not unlike the one we used to play on as children on the ripples we called waves on Fountainstown beach.

Flushed by the success of the white-water trip (by success I don't mean that we learned a wonderful new paddling technique, just that we were alive at the end of the expedition), we decided to go on an ATV trip (all terrain vehicle to the uninitiated). This involved driving big, unwieldy vehicles with balloon-like tyres up steep gravelly slopes, and then speeding downwards into muddy pits, while, to add to the torture, hired hands in spattered green boiler suits sprayed us with pressure hoses.

How do they think of these things? Do they sit around and say, 'Let's think of something really dirty and tiring, that can justify charging lots of money and will leave the tourists aching and covered in sticky, brown, Whistler muck.' Still, I shouldn't be so churlish; we loved it, shrieking with the others in the group, and only the lack of time stopped us joining another group the next day.

In Whistler, even walking has its own risks. Everywhere we went we were warned to be aware of bears. Bears! For God's sake. Where I was raised, a stroll in the woods might lead to a rain-soaking, or a few midge bites, or at worst, a meeting with some boring old neighbours who'd want to stop for a chat, so it was difficult to get my head around the idea that around the next tree might lurk a man-eating giant.

The safety advice we read was not very reassuring. 'If you come across a bear, don't scream or run.' Very sensible I'm sure, but could we do that? Could we stand there and hope that the total stranger, who sat in a nice safe bear-free room and wrote this, knew what he was talking about? He covered himself nicely by pointing out that every meeting with a bear was different, as they are unpredictable animals. Could we be sure that the bears read the pamphlets? Could we stand there, not screaming or running, and determine whether it was a curious bear, a surprised bear, or just one that wanted to eat us as fast as possible? We were not encouraged when we read that bears can run faster than racehorses, and climb almost as well as monkeys. Playing dead was frequently encouraged, but that wasn't so tempting when we read the final proviso – 'If the attack continues for more than several minutes, consider fighting back.' Great. No screaming, no running, just play dead, and then after enduring a five-minute assault, fight this creature. What would we do, give it a Chinese burn, pinch it, or perhaps call it names? Hurt its feelings? Poke it in the eye with our sunglasses? Squirt suncream in its face?

Then, the final insult. A small addition, at the end of all the other dire warnings, just in case we weren't intimidated enough. 'There is some evidence that bears are attracted by the scent of menstruating women.' And guess what?

Luckily, neither our retention of the safety information, nor our courage was put to the test, and after an exciting few days, we returned home, to our real home overlooking English Bay. There we spent yet another long, happy evening, bare feet propped on the balcony railings, sipping chilled white wine, and surveying 'our view'.

I got so much information from Home Exchangers Unlimited when I finalised the deal with Charlie.

I got hints on cleaning, on how many sheets and towels to leave, what food to stock up on, and what to tell the neighbours. I got advice on phone calls, and car mileage, and electricity usage, and breakages and insurance. I thought every eventuality was covered.

Now I realise they forgot one thing.

Has it ever happened that an exchanger has returned home to find that their exchange partner refuses to leave?

I can envisage chaining myself to the railings of Charlie's balcony, to avoid going back home.

I was born too late to be a suffragette, but I can still use their well-tried methods to get my own way.

How will I ever be able to leave this wonderful place to return to my lonely, grey home?

You'll have to rewrite the booklet, Home Exchangers Unlimited.

Chapter Nineteen

Decided to turn on Charlie's computer for the first time this morning. He had left his password, and fortunately his computer works just like mine. (Maybe they all do. I'm too much of a technophobe to know these things.) I went straight to the mailbox and found a list of unread messages. I didn't feel it was prying to read them, as they could of course have been from Charlie to me.

While I was at it, I decided to have a sneaky look at his old messages. I didn't feel too guilty as I presume he's been rooting around in my private electronic world, too. Anyway, for some strange reason, snooping around electronic correspondence doesn't seem quite as bad as opening real envelopes and reading someone else's paper letters.

Charlie keeps a very untidy inbox, all full of ancient messages and junk mail. Little rat! All the time he was courting me and my little house by the sea, sharing the joys of Vancouver with me, he was following up a deal with a couple in Donegal. The fact that I didn't tell him about my overtures to Darlene and Chuck doesn't make me feel less betrayed. Still though, by the time I'd carefully read every message in his inbox, it became clear that the Donegal people were still interested up to the end of the correspondence, but he rejected them in my favour.

You poor Donegal people. I wonder where you are now?

There was a big line of messages from Melinda, who, it appears, is Charlie's ex-wife. She doesn't appeal to me. She sounds very smug and superior, and lots of her sentences start – 'Toby and I think. . .' Now I know Toby could be her pet dog, but it is more likely that he is Charlie's successor in her affections and, if so, it's a bit mean to talk about him so much, especially when he seems to hold opinions on Todd, Charlie's son. 'Toby and I think that Todd would prefer a vacation in Hawaii, rather than in Ireland. Isn't it very wet there?' or 'Toby and I think that Todd should take up piano lessons.' 'Toby and I think that Todd should change schools.' I couldn't resist reading Charlie's replies (well he should have deleted them if they were all that personal) and they were all very mild and nonconfrontational, stating his own view and paying no attention at all to what Toby and Melinda think. Fair play to him.

There was one message for me, from Charlie. Now that he's in my house, and I in his, we can be quite familiar, and he has abandoned the semi-formal language he used to use when e-mailing me.

> Dear Maeve,
> Wow. I love your home. Thanks for clearing the pigs from the kitchen. That view from the terrace is fantastic. We have eaten some of your lettuce and onions. Very good. Slugs were attacking so we put down some poison pellets. (Just kidding. Looks like you don't hold with that kind of stuff.) Todd and I are doing lots of swimming and walking and just hanging out. We have been to Galway and the Burren. Cork City is great. Your vacuum cleaner hose was blocked but I have managed to fix it. Don't you guys have waste disposal units in your sinks? Sure hope you and your friend are having a good time in my place. Please eat all the food. I hope you like ice cream and Indian food. It's kinda hard to shop for strangers. Did you find the beer? Have a great holiday. We are.
> Best wishes,
> Charlie and Todd

Suddenly, I don't care if Charlie is a lazy slob. I don't care if my precious house is awash with empty Coke cans and greasy takeaway bags. I love his home and his city, and his style of e-mailing and I'm prepared to forgive him anything.

I sent him back a message in a similar vein; then I showered in his shower, dried myself with his towel, ate his food in his kitchen, locked up his apartment and went to the beach for another wonderful day.

And was it a wonderful day!!!

Maria and I decided that walking back to the apartment for lunch was eating too much into our precious relaxing time, so we agreed to bring a picnic with us. It didn't take us long to pack. We found a cool-box in Charlie's kitchen, and we filled this with chilled beer, crisps and a large selection of sandwiches. (Cheese, ham, and ham and cheese.)

Shortly after we had settled ourselves on the beach for the morning, Interesting Guy appeared and he settled himself down quite near us. As before, he was clad in cut-off shorts and a white T-shirt, and he carried the same rucksack, from which he produced a huge, fluffy white towel. He casually arranged his towel on the sand, and casually arranged his perfect body on top of it. Then, without as much as a glance in our direction, he tossed his perfect hair, closed his perfect eyes and slept for two hours.

Luckily my trashy novel didn't require too much attention as it's funny how much attention I needed for the sleeping Adonis adorning the sand ten feet away from me. Any time Maria caught me looking in his direction she made mock vomiting motions, but I bravely ignored her and maintained my vigil.

Eventually my tummy and I got bored and I sat up and opened the cool-box. Maria awoke from her slumber, and we helped ourselves to beer and sandwiches. From the corner of my eye I detected a movement from Interesting Guy. He sat up, and he turned, ever so languidly, towards us. He spoke in a wonderful Vancouver accent.

'Hi, girls. You are Irish, aren't you?'

My mouth was full of ham and cheese sandwich, so I nodded in what I hoped was an interested manner.

'I bet you hear this all the time, but my grandmother was Irish. She came from County Tipperary. Her name was Ryan.'

Clearly Maria was doing her haughty 'I'm not getting involved' act, so I swallowed the last of my sandwich and responded.

'Well, there are a lot of Ryans in Tipperary.'

This didn't appear to bother IG. He smiled and shrugged and gazed out to sea. I struggled to find something marvellously witty to say, but failed dismally. I heard my words pop out and hang pathetically in the warm air between us.

'Are you from around here yourself?'

Even this didn't scare him off, and to my amazement, he skilfully scooted his towel in our direction, and ended up sitting right next to us.

'Yes. I'm from Vancouver. I live near the university. Do you know it?'

Part of me wanted to pretend to be a marvellously

162

intelligent woman who always hung out at the university in strange towns. But I'm a very poor bluffer, so I shook my head, trying to convey my deep regret at such an oversight.

'Perhaps I could show it to you some time.'

Maria was pointedly looking at her book, but I could see her eyes widen at this comment. I didn't know what to say. I found myself blushing stupidly, and lost for words. I reached for another beer to hide my embarrassment, and found myself offering it to IG. I was rewarded with a glowing smile, as he accepted without hesitation. Though I could sense Maria's disapproval, I offered him a cheese sandwich (just in case he was a vegetarian), and again he accepted gratefully.

Maria's book must have been very interesting, because she remained engrossed in it for the next half hour. IG and I chatted about nothing at all, in a vaguely casual-flirty kind of manner. We finished the beers, sandwiches and crisps, and relaxed into a companionable silence. Suddenly he jumped to his feet.

'What time is it?'

'Five to three.'

'Oh. I have an appointment. I should be gone.'

He stuffed his towel rather inelegantly into his backpack, and flung it casually over his shoulders. He took a few steps away, and then turned back to us.

'Have you girls been to Wreck Beach yet?'

It was kind of him to say 'girls' as Maria had

completely ignored him all the time he was there, and was continuing to do so.

Clearly she wasn't going to answer, so I replied. I had never even heard of Wreck Beach, but didn't like to admit it.

'No actually. We haven't had time to go there yet. I believe it's great. We might go there soon.'

IG smiled his easy smile.

'That's cool. I was thinking of going there tomorrow. Would you like to come with me?'

It was unclear whether 'you' meant Maria and me, or just me. It didn't really matter anyway, as I had a feeling that invited or not, nothing would persuade Maria to go anywhere with this guy. I broke with thirty-four years of tradition and made a snap decision.

'That sounds great. Let's go tomorrow.'

'Cool. I'll be here at eleven, and we can go then.'

I grinned foolishly at him, and he sauntered off towards the road.

Maria waited until he was well gone before she spoke.

'I take it you're joking?'

I played innocent. 'Joking about what?'

'Please don't tell me you plan to go to this Wreck Beach place with that eejit tomorrow.'

'I do actually.'

'For God's sake, Maeve. He's a complete waster. "My granny was from Tipperary." Did you ever hear anything so lacking in originality? And did you see how he rushed over when you produced the beer?'

'He was just being friendly.'

'Thirsty, you mean. And it looks as if he was hungry too. He scoffed a huge bag of crisps all on his own. And did you see how many sandwiches he ate? I could have done with another few.'

'Why didn't you climb down off your high horse and ask for one then?'

She grinned ruefully. 'Sorry. Was I really rude?'

'Yes, you were.'

'It's just that he's so pathetic. You don't even know his name, do you?'

'No, but I call him IG – Interesting Guy.'

'Huh. BB would be more like it – Beach Bum.'

'Very funny, Maria. I don't want to marry him and bear his children, you know. I just want a bit of a laugh. Anyway, you spend your life telling me I should be more daring, that I should take the odd chance. You say I think too much. Well this time I'm not thinking at all. I'm going to meet him and go to Wreck Beach with him.'

'How are you going to travel? I bet he hasn't got a flashy motor.'

'This is Canada. Everyone has a car. Anyway, even if he hasn't got wheels, I can take the Tahoe. Would you like to come?'

'No thanks.'

'Fine then, I'll go on my own.'

'Please do. I need to wash my hair anyway.'

We weren't our usual chatty selves for the rest of the afternoon, but for once I didn't care. Maria could play the goody-goody all she liked; I was going to live a little. Maria read her endless book, as I lay on the sand and dreamed of a long, happy future with IG.

When we got back to the apartment that evening I could see that Maria was still cross with me, and while she had no proper cause, I didn't feel like a serious row, so I offered to microwave the dinner while she relaxed on the balcony with a beer. Maria responded to my peace offering by volunteering to look up Wreck Beach in the guidebooks.

It occurred to me that perhaps one of the important ingredients in a successful friendship is the wisdom to see which particular battles should be fought to the end, and which should be left to die a quiet, unheralded death.

When I arrived on the balcony shortly afterwards with our dinner on a tray, Maria had already tidied up the guidebooks. She seemed very happy.

'I found Wreck Beach. It's not far at all. It looks interesting.'

'Great. Are you sure you won't come?'

'Thanks but no thanks. You go and have a ball with BB. I'll just chill out here. But, Maeve?'

'Yes?'

'Have some fun but don't do anything stupid.

Joking apart, you don't know this guy. Don't go back to his place, whatever you do. Stay in public. Stay on neutral ground. Or bring him back here if you must.'

Clearly Maria has read the warnings that go with the personal ads in the Sunday papers. I promised to be careful, and we let the subject drop in favour of a silent, but not unfriendly, devouring of our food and drink.

Chapter Twenty

This morning, I took an extra long shower, double-conditioned my hair, and made sure to wear clean shorts and T-shirt for my hot date with IG. It was reassuring that he didn't seem to be the type who would expect snappy dressing from his date. I was quite confident that clean and casual would be the order of the day.

After repeated safety warnings from Maria, I set off for my rendezvous, slightly nervous but with a nice unfamiliar buzz of anticipation.

IG arrived right on the dot of eleven. He held out his hand in a formal gesture.

'Let me introduce myself. I'm Wesley. My friends call me Wes.'

I took his hand and shook it. It was firm and warm. Slightly dry-skinned too, but I suppose you can't have everything.

'I'm Maeve.'

'Nice to meet you, Maeve. Now that we are acquainted, shall we go? I have wheels.'

We walked up to the road, and he led me to a shiny clean, very large motorbike.

Oh dear.

I was torn between fear at the thought of travelling on this machine, and relief that Maria had decided not to come. It was beginning to look as if she wasn't invited after all.

Wes handed me a crash helmet, donned one himself, and we climbed aboard. I tried not to look as if this were my first time on a motorbike. (A guy in college once gave me a lift into town on his Honda 50, but somehow that wasn't quite the same.)

Wes started the engine and we set off. I was absolutely terrified, but it was nice to have the excuse to cling tightly to his lean, sinewy back, as we lurched around corners and raced up quiet streets. After a few minutes I was beginning to enjoy myself, but unfortunately by then we were there.

Wes parked the bike, and locked the helmets to it. I tried unsuccessfully to rearrange my windblown hair, as we walked towards a narrow path leading downhill. There was a large sign at the top of the path, and even from a distance I could read the large heading – FREE BEACH.

Hoping that my instinct was wrong I casually turned to Wes.

'What exactly is a "free beach", Wes?'

He looked surprised. 'You know, free. You surely know what a free beach is.'

'Er, no. Not exactly.'

He shook his blond head in rather patronising wonder at my ignorance. 'It means you're free to wear whatever you like.'

'Oh.'

Wes strolled on, obviously not seeing any necessity for further explanation.

I had to know. 'Or perhaps, not wear anything?'

'Yeah, that's it. Most people don't wear anything.'

I gave a slightly hysterical giggle.

Wes stopped walking and turned to me. 'You don't have a problem with that, do you?'

I gave a vague expansive gesture with my arms. 'No, of course not. That's fine. Absolutely fine. Free beaches — I just love them.'

Oh dear. What on earth had I let myself in for?

Now, I'm no prude (as all prudes seem to start their protests), but I feel I'm a bit long in the tooth for nudist beaches. Good Irish Catholic though I am, I spent a few happy weeks in Greece as a student, and mostly went topless on the beach. Then once, in a fit of youthful daring, Maria and I briefly bared all on a crowded beach in Mykonos. No one honoured us with a second glance, as everyone else was naked too, but we were pleased with how sophisticated and modern it made us feel. I have to admit that even back then I didn't feel really comfortable until I was safely back in my skimpy blue and white striped bikini.

That was then, though, a lifetime ago. I was only

170

nineteen, deeply tanned, and conscious that, while no model, I was slim enough, and my flesh was firm and untouched by cellulite. The arrogance of youth (which I only recognised after it was gone) was still with me back then. Now though, I feel I have spread out a bit. I have one nasty varicose vein on the back of my left leg, and orange peel thighs, and there are parts of my body that have not seen the sun in more years than I care to remember. It's not that I'm shy, you understand, it's just that I feel it would be an affront to the other beach users to expose every bit of my white, ageing body to their unsuspecting eyes.

And besides, how on earth could I sit down with this guy that I'd just met, and calmly remove all of my clothing as if it were something I did every day?

Sorry.

Nudity and sex are too closely entangled in my narrow emotional psyche.

Would he strip off too?

Would he pull off his shorts, absentmindedly scratch his testicles, and set off for a swim?

Oh, dear, oh dear.

I was beginning to wish that I'd listened to Maria and stayed at home.

Wes led the way down the steep stepped track. It seems that here naturism and fitness are meant to go together. We had to walk for what seemed like hours, through a shady, but oppressively warm, wooded area. As we walked, I watched people walking uphill towards us, pleased to see that they weren't too weird or extreme looking. They were all wearing clothes too, which was strangely reassuring. They didn't look as if they were just leaving for a spot of light lunch after a wild open-air orgy. But then is this kind of thing always obvious to the naked (!!) eye?

Eventually the path emerged from the woods, and we stepped, hot and breathless, into what seemed like a time warp. I turned and looked back along the path we had travelled, half-expecting it to have vanished into a damp, streaming mist, marooning us on an island floating forever in the past. We walked a few yards away from the track, dropped our bags on a convenient log, and sat down. The naturist code, which was displayed on a board at the edge of the woods, says it's rude to stare, but it was hard not to.

The huge beach was packed. From every side came the idle strumming of guitars, and jingling noises as if from wind chimes, with occasional bursts of a muted repetitive chanting sound.

I found my eyes drawn to a trail along the centre of the beach, which had been kept clear. This was the path for an endless stream of naked traders. In a bizarre touch, most of them wore bum bags, but as if not to cause offence by being modest, these were carefully turned to the side, hiding nothing. Also, most of the traders, though obviously keen to free themselves from the tyranny of clothes, didn't seem to have a problem with jewellery, as they wore tons of the stuff. Leather cords and beads adorned wrists, necks, ankles and midriffs. Nipples, ears, noses, mouths and brows bore multiple piercings, and I tried not to stare at my first view of something I had thought could not really exist – a penis ring. Now that must be a sore thing. Still I suppose if men never have to endure childbirth they will have to look elsewhere for sources of unbearable pain.

The traders walked slowly, strolling along in the warm sunshine. Both males and females were invariably long-haired, with deep brown tans, unspoiled by even the faintest trace of white marks from bikinis or trunks. They carried their wares in boxes on their shoulders, and, in keeping with the laid back air of the place, they spoke rather than called their wares. They were selling hot drinks, cold drinks, pizzas, and beads. One dark-haired beautiful boy of about eighteen, called softly as he walked by, 'Mushrooms. Fresh and strong.' Even I was not naïve enough to think he meant the innocent kind I sometimes pick in the field behind my house in Cork, and use to make thick, comforting soup. And I suspect if anyone ever did use these particular fungi to make soup, they'd end up far too chilled out to do the washing up.

I sat in quiet wonder, thinking how very far this place was from the innocent green fields of Myrtleville.

One girl, skinny and sinewy, declared as she went by, 'Buy a cocktail and get a free massage.' To my great regret, she got no takers, at least not in our part of the beach, so I'll never be quite sure what exactly was on offer. Would she and some strawberry daiquiri purchaser skip off hand in hand for a half-hour of ecstasy in the privacy of the woods, or would she just give their bare shoulders a cursory rub with her strong, tattooed hands? Yet another mystery. One of the many things in life I'll never find out.

Wes took off his T-shirt and interrupted my open-mouthed wonder. 'Cool place, isn't it? This is my favourite beach in the whole world.'

'Yes, you're right. It's very nice indeed.'

I couldn't think of anything sensible or smart to say. While I was racking my brains for some other conversational gem, Wes was unzipping his shorts. He took them off, and then casually removed the white underpants he wore underneath. For a moment, I didn't know where to look, or what to say.

When I dared to look closer, I could see that he was rather well-endowed, but I was too embarrassed to enjoy this observation.

Wes carefully folded his clothes and put them in his backpack. Then he sat on the log beside me.

'Well, Maeve from Cork, how about a swim?'

I was wearing my prim, one-piece, blue and black striped Speedo swimsuit under my outer clothes, and I had no intention of removing it. (If I'd been wearing a bikini, I might possibly, just possibly, have taken the top off. I wasn't though, and somehow I didn't think it would be the business to prance around Wreck Beach amongst all these ever so cool people with the top of my one-piece drooping around my midriff. How sad would that be?) If I harboured any vague thoughts of being naked with this guy, I had sort of thought it would be a rather more intimate affair, in a dimly lit bedroom, not in the harsh light of this beach with three hundred witnesses.

I took off my sandals, shorts and T-shirt, and brazened it out.

'Ok, Wes. Let's swim.'

'Are you keeping your swimsuit on?'

I smiled a wry smile, trying to convey without words my deep regret at the situation. I tried to look as if there was nothing I desired more than to stand naked on this beach in front of three hundred naked strangers. And a naked blond guy I fancied like mad.

'Unfortunately I'd better. I got bad sunburn last week. I need to be careful.'

He shrugged. 'Suit yourself.'

'Swimsuit myself, even?'

It was the first half-witty thing I'd thought of since we met, but evidently it was lost on Wes. He gave me a bemused look, and led the way to the water.

After a bracing swim, we returned to our place on the sand. I wrapped myself in my towel and sat down. Wes produced his snow-white towel again. (Clearly someone in his house likes washing.) He sat beside me, and ever so gently, he used the corner of his towel to smooth my eyebrows — an intimate gesture that left me strangely moved. Then he rubbed suncream on my back, an experience I didn't want to end as his strong fingers smoothed and caressed my skin. I lay on my towel and gave myself up to the sensuous experience, and I found myself thinking that perhaps I would be happy to bear this guy's children and live happily ever after with him. When I was ninety he could rub Deep Heat into my arthritic back, and I'd think I was in Heaven.

When the suncream ritual was finished, I felt I should offer to apply cream to his back. He refused my offer, saying his skin was used to the sun. Whew. Rubbing his back would have been fine, but in the absence of a swimsuit demarcation line, wherever would I have stopped?

Wes spread his towel next to mine, and lay beside me. I closed my eyes and luxuriated in the happiness of the moment. We chatted in an idle, lazy manner, about nothing in particular.

After a while, Wes stretched over and began to rub my neck, and then my shoulder, in an easy, unthreatening kind of way. I wasn't quite sure if I should reciprocate, so I compromised, and rubbed my fingers along his golden-brown arm. A rather pathetic gesture I suppose, but it was the best I could manage in the circumstances. After a short while his caresses ceased, and I found, to my disappointment, that Wes was asleep, with a dreamy half-smile on his lips.

I was restless, and didn't feel like a snooze, so I sat up for a while and was entertained by the stream of humanity walking barefoot and bare-bottomed across my line of vision. After a while, I began to feel a little apart as I resolutely kept my swimsuit on, but not so much as to tempt me to take it off.

Before long Wes stirred from his slumber. He sat up and draped his arm over my shoulder as if it were the most natural thing in the world. He gave my neck a little nuzzle with his face and whispered in a soft dreamy voice. 'I'm famished. Do you fancy a pizza?'

I was hungry too, but for some irrational reason I wasn't too happy about buying a pepperoni and pineapple pizza from one of the naked men passing by.

Where would the world be without shy Irish Catholics, full of old-fashioned inhibition and repressed sexuality?

'Why don't we go somewhere else for it? I'm feeling a little hot. I'd like to eat in the shade.'

This was fine with Wes, so we each put on whatever clothes we had earlier removed. Wes chivalrously carried my backpack tucked inside his larger one, as we trekked slowly back up through the shady woods. I stopped for a moment when we reached the road. I needed to catch my breath, and to shake off the strange feeling that I had somehow intruded on a parallel universe that was incredibly different to the one I usually inhabited. I half expected to look at my watch and see that no time at all had passed since we left.

After a few minutes of watching normal, clothed people driving past in normal cars, on normal everyday business, I regained my normal confused demeanour.

We donned our helmets again and rode to get a pizza from a small takeaway restaurant near Charlie's apartment. I'm quite sure that the insolent-looking adolescent who served us had a penis and pubic hair, but we didn't have to look at it so it wasn't an issue. There was no fleshy appendage bobbing around in front of us, flapping against his thighs as the youth keyed our order into the cash register. When he turned to shout our order through the metal shelving dividing us from the kitchen, we didn't have to look at his naked buttocks, or his spotty back.

Wes took the box containing our pizza (pineapple and pepperoni on my half, tuna and sweetcorn on his), and selected drinks from the cooler. I reached for my purse in my shorts pocket, and after a brief demur on his part, I paid for our purchases.

We took our food outside and ate it on a park bench. We washed the food down with ice-cold Coke, watching the world skate past us, lithe and young and carefree.

As I gathered our rubbish and put it in a nearby bin, Wes suddenly remembered another urgent appointment. He gave me a chaste kiss on the cheek, then a rather more intimate one on the lips. He drew away and I thought he was going to vanish without another word. Unusually for me, I called it wrong. He flicked a stray lock of hair from his eyes and asked easily, 'Could we do this again, Maeve, do you think? I'd very much like to see you again.'

I tried not to sound too eager, as I responded eagerly, 'Yes, I'd love that. Let's meet again.'

He pulled a mobile phone from his pocket. 'Can I call you? I have rather a busy schedule at the moment.'

He had the relaxed air of someone who never had a busy schedule in his life, but I figured he just did yoga or crystal hugging or something to keep the stress at bay. I called out the number of Charlie's telephone. Wes keyed it into his phone, touched me lightly on the nose with his finger, and then he left.

I sat for a while on the park bench, thinking about his strong hands rubbing my back, and the gentle way he nuzzled my neck. I thought how nice it would be to see him again, if only for an innocent holiday dalliance. No commitment needed – just lots of nice nuzzling and rubbing.

It was only when I got up to leave that I realised that Wes had left with my backpack still tucked inside his.

And with Sean's good camera I'd borrowed for my trip.

And my watch, which I'd removed on the beach to protect it from the sand.

And a hundred dollars I'd zipped into the side pocket of the bag, for emergencies.

How lucky that he had taken my number!

Imagine how embarrassed he'd be if he discovered that he'd taken my bag and had no idea how to get it back to me.

I'm looking forward to chastising him for his careless oversight.

Luckily Maria was home when I got back to the apartment, as I had forgotten to bring keys in my rush out to meet Wes. She met me with a big grin, and all at once the truth dawned on me.

'You knew it was a nudist beach, didn't you?'

She smiled a supercilious smile. 'I knew that wouldn't be an issue for a liberated girl like you.'

'You rat! I nearly died. Can you imagine how I felt when he began to strip off?'

She giggled. 'Well. Was he worth it?'

'I don't know. I was too embarrassed.'

'And did he get to see every inch of your pale Irish skin?'

'Well, I wanted to expose all, but I couldn't because of that awful sunburn I got the other day.'

'Oh, you big cheat. You're such a prude.'

'Come on Maria, be honest. What would you have done? Would you have gaily bared all?'

She had the good grace not to answer.

'Why didn't you tell me it was a nude beach?'

'Serves you right for going off with strangers. Anyway, did you have a good time?'

'Great, thanks, not that you care.'

Maria sat me down with a cup of coffee, and dragged out all the details of my day. I felt too happy to be bothered by her open dislike of Wes. We both laughed loud and long at my reluctance to buy food from the naked vendors. When I got to the part about Wes leaving with my backpack, she looked wary.

'Oh Maeve. I don't like the sound of that.'

'Don't be silly. It was just a mistake. He's going to ring me. He'll bring it back, I know.'

Maria looked doubtful, but said nothing more on the subject.

I'm not worried though. I'm sure he'll ring.

Maria hadn't spent the day in complete slobbishness. She'd gone to the food market on Granville Island and brought back bags full of wonderful fresh food for our dinner. While I relaxed on the balcony after my hard day at the sand-face, she prepared the dinner. She produced a fine meal of steak, asparagus, boiled baby potatoes, and an enormous salad of organic leaves. This we washed down with lots of beer and a bottle of fine red wine, and lots of laughs about Irish prudes.

Life's not so bad, after all.

Chapter Twenty-one

Joe and Maria live a balanced life together, enjoying each other's company, but yet not smothering each other. They have lots in common, but they each have plenty of outside interests also. They have fun and they share a sense of humour that oils the wheels of their relationship. (Is it obvious that I have kind of a crush on them as a couple; my ideal marriage scenario? They probably aren't perfect, though I have not yet managed to see any flaws in their union. Admittedly I haven't looked very hard, but why should I? I like the idea of perfection.)

Despite her independence though, I can tell by the wistful look in Maria's eyes that she's beginning to miss Joe. Her calls to him in the evenings are becoming longer, and while she doesn't complain, it's clear from her slightly subdued manner after speaking to him, that she's lonely. The other day Joe telephoned with the news that his course is likely to be extended for a few weeks, and that he has no choice but to stay until it is completed. Poor Maria cannot bear the thought of being at home without him for so long, so she's decided to see if she can change her flight tickets, so that she can fly down to Texas to spend some time with him, and to fly back to Cork from there.

I have no real problem about travelling alone. I've done it many times, and have never felt in the least bit threatened or afraid. I can cope with the impossibly long check-in queues, and the dodgy food, and the airless departure lounges. I can even cope with the spiteful luggage carousel that spits out everyone's suitcases except for mine. I have held my head high as two hundred strangers smirkingly watched my grey Dunnes Stores knickers peeping out through a tear in my cheap suitcase.

But I don't really relish the idea of ending this marvellous trip by flying on my own into Cork, returning alone to my unexciting, uneventful life. I'm beginning to regret not arranging to stay longer.

I wonder if Darlene and Chuck are still available to exchange for the month of August? How long can it take to unprolapse some piles? I might try e-mailing them, just to see what would happen, just to postpone my return. Then they could get to clean up Charlie's drink cans and takeaway rubbish.

After all, I don't have to go back to work until the first week of September, so why hurry home? There's nothing there that cannot wait.

I'm not going all the way back there just to water some thirsty vegetables and to cut the lawn. Something tells me that the mountain of junk mail can wait another few weeks for me to deal with it. The man who sells me a lottery ticket once a month might manage without my custom just this once. And if my Tesco vouchers go out of date before I get back, well I suppose I can live with that too.

I got a letter from Mum this morning. Another reason not to go home. I'm thirty-four years of age, and she writes to me as if I'm a ten-year-old away from home on her first sleepover.

Dear Maeve,

I hope you are well. Daddy and I are fine. I have a bad old 'flu though, and Daddy has been constipated since last Tuesday. It could be worse though. Did I tell you when you rang that Daddy's hip has been acting up again? It's still bad.

We went to Kerry last week to spend a few days with Sean and Eimear on their holidays. Imagine she expects Sean to cook the dinner every second night, even though he's meant to be on his holidays! Of course, just between you and me, neither of them could boil an egg properly anyway. Most nights they just microwave some old processed thing from the supermarket. I hope you are cooking properly, and making lots of stews. Be sure to eat lots of vegetables. Don't let yourself get run-down.

Whatever you do, don't eat any of those doner kebab things. There was an article in The Examiner about them the other day. I won't repeat it, but trust your dear old mother and keep well away from them.

You know Mrs Carey down the road? She got knocked down yesterday on the way home from Mass. She'd have died in a state of grace, but she only sprained her wrist.

I must go now and get the tea. Remember Maeve, don't take lifts from strangers, and don't go off with any of those hippy types you usually go for. You know Mrs Byrne who lives two doors down? She's gone to live with her daughter, and her house was sold last week. A very nice chappie has been to see it twice. I think he has bought it. He's about your age. There's no sign of a wife. We'll ask him over for tea when you get home. Just to be neighbourly.

Daddy says hello.

Love from Mum

PS. Be sure to eat lots of fruit. Especially apples.

No 'hippy types'. I'll have to dump Wes then.

Not.

Mind you, he hasn't called me since our trip to Wreck Beach, which was nearly a week ago. Something tells me he will call. Blind faith, I suppose.

Maria is wrong to doubt him. I don't often acknowledge this, but the truth is that since she met Joe her taste has become a little conservative. Before Joe, she'd have encouraged me to have a laugh with Wes, and would even have been on the lookout for a similar model for herself. Now she's made a cosy little camp for herself on the moral high ground.

I don't care anyway. I like it here in the moral lowlands. I fancy Wes very much, and if there's any hope of spending the time with him, I'll happily cancel my flights too, and find a way of staying here for another few weeks.

Maria and I are going to the beach this afternoon for a few hours. Maybe I'll get really lucky, and Wes will be there. Who knows?

Midnight. Very happy.

I've had the most beautiful day. For the first time in many years, I am very seriously attracted to someone who isn't a film star or a pop idol or a happily married father of seven.

Someone I've actually spoken to.

Someone I've kissed.

With tongues.

I'm alone in my bed, but it doesn't matter. I feel a warm glow in the air around me, and I love it.

Let me explain.

When Maria and I arrived on the beach this

afternoon, we took up residence on our usual patch. There was no sign of Wes. I hid my disappointment, and settled down for a snooze. Just when I was in that dreamy, half-awake, half-asleep state that is so pleasant, I heard Maria give a contemptuous sigh.

'Oh dear, Maeve. Wake up and see what the tide has washed up yet again.'

I sat up to see Wes ambling towards us, with my backpack over his shoulder. I shot Maria a quick look of triumph, and smiled a broad smile at Wes. He gave a quick nod in Maria's direction, and then sat on the edge of my towel. He kissed me lightly on the cheek.

'Maeve from Cork. Great to see you. I took your pack by mistake. I haven't had a chance to call you. Were you worried? Did you think you would never see me or your pack again?'

I looked him straight in the eye. 'No, Wes. I knew you'd bring it back. I wasn't worried at all.'

Maria had the good grace to look a little sheepish, but she said nothing. Wes took my hand in his, and fixed his blue eyes on mine. I could feel funny fluttery movements in my belly.

'So, Maeve. How've you been? What's been happening?'

I gave a vague shrug. 'Oh, you know Wes. Nothing much. We've been living the quiet life. How about you?'

'I've been rather busy actually. Important business deal going down. It was touch and go for a while, but it seems to be OK now.'

I looked at his tanned body lolling on the towel next to me, and found it very difficult to picture this man in a suit and tie, negotiating business deals. Still, Canada is very different to Ireland. Things are a lot more casual here. Maybe Wes has a real high-powered job that he works at for days at a time, and then he's free to slip back into beach-mode to recharge his batteries. Unfortunately, he wasn't volunteering the nature of his business, and I felt it rude to ask.

Even though Wes had proven his honesty, it was clear from the turn of Maria's lips that she wasn't happy to see him. She began to pack up her things.

'You know guys, I think I'll go for a walk. I'll see you in the apartment later. Bye, Maeve. Bye, Wes.'

I waved goodbye, and for once in my life, I was glad to see the back of her. Her disapproval was written all over her face, spoiling her normal pleasant demeanour, almost spoiling my pleasure in Wes's company.

I lay face down on my towel, and Wes edged close to me, lining his long legs up next to mine.

I tried the artful girlie thing I'm not usually very good at.

'Wes, is my back getting sunburnt?'

He knew the appropriate response and I got five minutes of luxurious touch, as he spent much more time than was necessary rubbing coconut-scented cream into my grateful skin. It would have been quite perfect except for the fact that I had to work hard to stop myself purring like a contented cat at each stroke of his strong hands.

I suppose we spent a few hours on the beach. It was hard to keep track of time, as we chatted and exchanged innocent but sensuous touches. Gradually the air became cooler, and people began to pack up and leave, gathering together their towels and their bags and their tired children. I lay there next to Wes, wondering desperately if there was any possible way of clutching at each precious moment, pinning it down and reshaping it so it wouldn't end. Eventually Wes stretched languorously, making me fear that he was going to announce another urgent appointment.

'Looks like it's time to leave, Maeve. It's getting rather chilly. Why don't we go get something to eat?'

A picture flashed into my mind of the two of us, hand in hand in a trendy bistro-type restaurant. Wes was gazing into my eyes in the flattering candlelight, and whispering sweet promises of tomorrow, begging me to stay in Vancouver for just a few more weeks. I was being coy, and demurring, but the look of desolation on the dream-Wes's face persuaded me to change my mind. The dream-me was rewarded with a winning smile, and a deep, passionate kiss, interrupted only by Wes waving at the waiter to bring his best champagne.

Unfortunately, the real Wes had different ideas.

'Any food back at your place?'

I tried not to look too disappointed, as the romantic bistro evaporated in front of my eyes.

Maybe Wes doesn't like restaurants. Maybe he has to do a lot of wining and dining as part of his business, and prefers not to eat out when he's off duty. Maybe he gives all of his money to charity and can't afford to eat out, but is too much of a gentleman to allow me to buy him food for a second time.

Anyway, I knew there were a few stray ready-meals left in Charlie's freezer, and I could trust Maria to make herself scarce if necessary, so I firmly banished the dream of the candlelit restaurant and answered brightly.

'Sure, Wes. We've got plenty of food. Let's go for it.'

When we got to the apartment there was a note from Maria saying that she'd gone to bed with a headache. I peeped in to her room, but she appeared to be asleep, so I quietly closed her door, and returned to Wes. He had let himself onto the balcony and was reclining in the last rays of late-evening sun. He put out his arm and drew me to him.

'Cool place this, Maeve. You got lucky.'

'I sure did, Wes. I sure did,' I murmured, thinking happily that getting the apartment was only the least of my good luck.

I'd have been quite content to sit there on his knee for the entire evening with no more thought of food, but I suddenly recalled one of Mum's clichéd sayings about men's hearts and their stomachs, and I reluctantly removed myself to the kitchen to microwave our dinner.

Wes followed me and began to root around the cupboards in search of wine. He produced a bottle that looked rather expensive to my uneducated eye.

'Way to go, Maeve. Let's drink this.'

'I don't know, Wes. That could be one of Charlie's special bottles. It looks as if he's kind of into wine. There's a bottle here that Maria and I bought. Why don't we drink that?'

'No, Maeve. I know this wine. It's good. Don't worry. I'll bring a bottle to replace it next time I'm here.'

The mention of there being a next time was so nice and reassuring that I abandoned my doubts and handed him the corkscrew.

We ate on the balcony, and when we were finished, Wes carried in the plates and rubbish and tidied the kitchen. I felt a funny warm glow as I sat there, knowing that he was looking after me. He returned with coffees and a fleecy blanket, which he kindly wrapped around my chilly shoulders. He edged his deckchair right next to mine, and sat beside me. He stroked my face, and whispered nice things, which I am sure would sound very trite if I were to record them here. I inclined my head onto his shoulder and after a while we lapsed into a companionable silence. I sat there thinking that if only I were able, I would gladly freeze the moment, and spend the rest of my days on that balcony with my head on Wes's shoulder.

Unfortunately, Wes had different ideas. He drained the last of his cold coffee and got up.

'Gotta go.'

I hoped he meant that he had to go to the toilet, but I wasn't really sure. How embarrassing if I led him to the toilet when what he really wanted was to go home. I followed him into the living room, and was intensely disappointed when he walked towards the hall door. I was rather unsure about what I should say or do, so we just stood there for a few moments, half-acknowledging each other like strangers at a bus stop. In the end, I felt a bit foolish and I half-heartedly reached for the latch. Wes took my arm, interrupting the movement. Then he embraced me. He gathered a fistful of my hair and held it tightly, almost, but not quite, hurting me. He kissed me deeply and passionately. I clung to him, savouring the salty, alcohol smell, and the pressure of his thin body against mine. Parts of him that I hadn't seen since that day on Wreck Beach pressed urgently against my body. I was wondering if I dared to lead him towards my bedroom. Panicky thoughts of condoms and AIDS ran through my mind. For a bizarre moment a picture of Mr Flynn's disapproving face flashed unbidden into my mind. I pushed Mr Flynn firmly out of my thoughts, but just as I wondered if I really had the courage to say, 'come to bed,' in my huskiest voice, Wes pulled away.

'It's been great, Maeve, but I need to go.'

Definitely not the toilet this time.

I tried to hide my disappointment.

How could he do this?

I wanted to grab him, and kiss him again, but I

didn't want him to think me a shameless hussy, when it was clear that he was so remarkably well-controlled.

We never discussed religion. Perhaps he belongs to one of those strict sects that outlaws sex before marriage. (Of course, so do I, but that's not quite the same, is it?)

I tried to look demure. 'I've enjoyed myself too, Wes.'

He draped his arms lightly on my shoulders and put his face close to mine. A pleasant waft of garlic, alcohol and spice warmed my face.

'I have to see you again, Maeve from Cork. Please say I can see you again.'

I resisted the urge to press my body against his. I kept the demure look firmly in place, though my flushed cheeks surely betrayed my real feelings.

'That would be lovely. I'd love that.'

'I still have a few meetings lined up. I have your number. I'll call you soon. Real soon.'

He touched my nose with his finger, just as he did when he was leaving me before. Then he opened the door and was gone.

And here I am.

I was afraid that I would never feel this way about anyone again. I close my eyes and I see his face. I see his clear blue eyes. I see the tiny scar on his chin. I see his perfect teeth. I hear his slow, deep laugh, and his slightly drawling accent.

Wes is the guy for me.

I'm a bit disappointed that he made no serious advances on my body.

Maybe he was just showing respect.

After all, we have only just met.

Maybe he was embarrassed about Maria being in the apartment.

Oh God, I hope he fancies me the way I fancy him!

Maybe we'll go to his place next time and make sweet music together.

Very sweet music indeed.

All night long.

I've always known the truth.

I'm a simple girl, and it takes very little to make me happy.

Chapter Twenty-two

Something really weird has happened.

I won't write about it yet though. I'll get around to it in a minute. Walter always says suspense is important in a novel.

Maria went to the travel agent this morning and had no difficulty in rearranging her flights. She is now officially going to Texas. I can't help feeling envious, but I feel bad about it, as Maria is being so considerate. She's constantly asking if I mind, and whether I can possibly forgive her for abandoning me, as she calls it.

Every morning we have the same conversation. It goes like this.

'Maeve, are you sure you don't mind me going to Texas?'

'Yes, Maria, I'm quite sure.'

'Really though. You're not just saying that?'

'Really Maria, I'm not just saying it.'

'Honestly?'

'Yes, Maria. I honestly don't mind you going to Texas.'

'You don't think I'm abandoning you?'

'No, Maria, I don't think you're abandoning me. Are you squeezing the orange juice this morning?'

'Yes, I'll do it now. Do you hate me for being so selfish?'

'No, Maria, you're not being selfish.'

And so on. And on. And on.

She even, kind person that she is, invited me to travel with her, and spend a few weeks with herself and Joe. Now, I might be fed up and lonely, but I'm not so desperate as to want to muscle in on her precious time with Joe. The awful thing is, I know it's not an empty offer, made from guilt. Maria is one of the most honest people I know, and I believe her when she tells me that she'd like me to travel with her. I know that Joe would welcome me too, but I need him to know that Maria and I are not joined at the hip. I'd hate him to ever feel that by marrying Maria, he has somehow saddled himself with me also. I don't want him to think that I squeezed past the ushers and sneaked up the aisle when his back was turned and somehow inveigled myself into his marriage vows.

Anyway, whatever the state of Joe's marriage vows, the bottom line is that I have to stop moaning and pretend to Maria that I'm keen to get back home. I'm pretending to be deliriously happy at the prospect of getting back to whatever lettuces have survived the slugs, back to my peas and my sweetcorn and my ornamental gourds. I have to tell her that I just can't wait to get back to my garden and my own little house by the sea.

Of course, Maria is not stupid, and she isn't fooled for a moment, but what can she do in the face of my obdurate insistence that I'll be fine?

Half the problem is that there's been no word from Wes. I keep hoping that there will be a knock on the door, and he'll appear in all his golden glory, but we've had no callers except the pizza delivery man. Maria and I haven't talked much about Wes, even though I'd love to be able to explain to her how wonderful he is. Last night, however, she did broach the subject.

'Mae, you shouldn't get your hopes up. I don't think he's going to ring.'

'He will. I know he will.'

'It's been days and days. He'd have phoned by now. Just put it down to experience.'

'Well, I told you. He's busy.'

'Busy at what? He doesn't look like a busy kind of guy. What does he do?'

'Oh, God, Maria. You are beginning to sound just like my mum. Who cares what he does? I know it's not going to be a lasting relationship, I don't need to see details of his life insurance or his pension plans. But I like him, and I'd like to see him again before I leave. What's so wrong in that?'

'Nothing at all. I just don't want to see you hurt. There's something not quite right about that guy. Do you think he might be a drug dealer?'

'Maria! How could you think such a thing?'

'Sorry, Maeve. Maybe I shouldn't have said that. It's just that he doesn't look honest.'

'What do you know? You said I'd never see my backpack again, and you were wrong about that.'

'Well, did you check the contents?'

That was a bit of a worry, actually. When Wes left that night I went to unpack the bag, and found my watch and Sean's camera untouched inside. There was no sign, however, of the hundred dollars in the zipped pocket. I frantically checked every compartment, but it definitely wasn't there.

Could it have fallen out when we were on Wreck Beach?

Could Wes have put the backpack down somewhere, and had the money been stolen then?

Could I have taken the money out before that day, and put it somewhere else?

I couldn't discuss this with Maria, as I'm quite sure what she would think. She would blame Wes and nothing would shake her in this belief. But why would he steal from me? And if he were to steal from me, why would he return with my bag? Did he think he could bluff his way out of trouble if I missed the money while he was there?

No, that's foolish talk. I know he didn't steal from

me, and when I see him again I'll ask him if he happened to see the hundred dollars at any stage. We can work this out.

He'd better hurry up and call though. I have only four days left until my flight home.

Anyway, I haven't got around to telling you about the really weird thing yet.

Walter said to be sure to allow plenty of suspense in a long piece, giving it time to build up slowly, but I think I got a bit carried away.

When we arrived home from the beach this evening we checked the telephone messages, as we always do. Each time I secretly hope that there will be a message from Wes, but they always seem to be junk calls offering to sell us water filters and life insurance and membership of health clubs. This time though, there was a message for me. It was from Charlie. It was very strange as, even though I'd written to him many times, slept in his bed, peed in his toilet and driven his car, I'd never before heard his voice. It was deep and friendly, and strong on the Vancouver accent that I was growing to love. His message was strange though. He'd sent me a copy of his itinerary months ago, and I thought I knew his plans. On Saturday, he was to lock up my house, drive my car to the airport in Cork, fly here and collect his car, which I was to leave at the airport on this side for him.

It was very simple. We'd pass each other out, thousands of miles over the vast snowy expanses of

Greenland. Then we'd each reclaim our vehicles and our homes and our lives and there would be an end to it.

The telephone message was a surprise, to say the least.

'Hi Maeve. It's Charlie. I know this sounds a bit crazy. I've had to change my plans. I'll call you in the morning, and I'll probably see you later on. Don't wor...'

Then, cruelly, for some unknown reason, the tape stops. That same tape has managed to record long minutes of salesmen extolling the virtues of their reclining orthopaedic chairs, but now, when it mattered, it let us down badly. We replayed it a few times, but were no wiser. It didn't manage to flip itself onto another explanatory side, putting our minds at rest.

What was Charlie thinking of?

Had he returned to Vancouver too early?

Were we going to meet him?

Was he coming here?

That was never in the plan.

Was he going to evict us?

Had the neighbours phoned him to complain about us?

(We had done nothing complaint-worthy, as far as we knew, but you can never tell for sure. Perhaps we had breached some unbreachable apartment rule. Perhaps I ran over the concierge's scabby cat when I was reversing the Tahoe.)

Or was there a terrible problem with my house?

Had he flooded it?

Had he managed to knock or burn it down?

Had he been deported for using my home as a base for neo-nazi gatherings?

I could think of lots of possible explanations for Charlie's strange half-message, but they were all bad, and we had no way of knowing what had really happened.

Action was better than inaction. (Well, maybe not better, but at least it made us feel less helpless.) After a brief panicked discussion, I raced to the liquor store to replace all the beer we had drunk. In a moment of disloyalty to Wes I bought a bottle of wine that looked sort of like the one he and I had drunk. While I was gone Maria began a whirlwind sweep of the apartment, cleaning, dusting and mopping, and dumping the oceans of glossy brochures we'd acquired over the happy, lazy weeks when Charlie wasn't coming back.

It is looking as if the end of our trip is going to be quite eventful.

If I don't write any more, you'll end up wondering if a crazy Charlie came round and shot us dead, in bursts of insane indiscriminate gunfire.

Or perhaps we were duped, and our innocent jaunts around Vancouver in the Tahoe turned into drug-running expeditions, for which we will be jailed for the rest of our natural lives, without access to paper and pens.

Or should I look on the bright side?

Maybe I won't write because Wes and I will be living on a remote desert island raising a clutch of wild but beautiful children.

Or maybe I'll just get bored of writing, and finish here, petering off in a final submission to apath. . .

Chapter Twenty-three

Things aren't so bad after all.

Well maybe they are. I'm still writing.

This pen spews forth waffle faster than Paul wrecks classrooms.

Faster than I jump to conclusions about strangers.

Faster than a drunk vomits diced carrots.

Charlie telephoned first thing in the morning. Most mornings up to this we'd have been asleep at that time, slatternly creatures that we had become, but his call of yesterday had us worried. As a result we were up and dressed bright and early, afraid he'd arrive on the doorstep, let himself in (as was his right), and find us still tucked up in bed.

He was apologetic as he explained. It seems that Melinda and Toby were worried about Todd being too jetlagged to go to summer camp, and they pressurised Charlie into returning a few days early to give him time to recover. I was dismissing Charlie as a total wimp for giving in to that kind of pressure, when he saved himself by admitting sheepishly, 'They're right actually. I made the flight reservations without checking the dates of Todd's camp, and since then I've been very worried about his ability to canoe, and mountain bike, and abseil in safety while suffering the effects of a ten-hour flight and multiple changes of time zones. I was kinda glad they pushed the issue, so I could give in without admitting I was wrong.'

I was only half listening as I was starting to worry about the next few nights and the possible repercussions of this unforeseen overlap.

It could be like a divorce, and surely one divorce was enough for Charlie.

Who would get to use the apartment?

Could we possibly share the Tahoe?

Who would have custody of the freezer? (Though as the freezer was empty except for the revolting green pistachio ice-cream and the prawn curry that neither Maria nor I could face, this would be no big deal.)

Charlie must have heard the manic panic in my voice, and he rushed to explain that he was staying at a friend's place, and had no desire to reclaim either his home or his car (for some reason he didn't mention the freezer). However, he said that he'd like to drop by to pick up some clean clothes, and other odd items that he needed. We could hardly refuse him entry to his own home, so he finished by saying, 'OK then. See you in fifteen minutes.'

Maria had done a good job of scrubbing the night

before, but we still drove ourselves into a frenzy, cleaning up our breakfast things, making our beds and shoving our toiletries into the bathroom cupboard, hoping that he wouldn't open it to be showered with our girlie bits and pieces. I foolishly mopped the kitchen floor, which stubbornly refused to dry, gleaming accusingly, traitorous witness to our last-minute efforts.

The buzzer went, and for a brief, foolish moment I dreamed that I would open the door to find Wes there, smiling and apologetic.

No such luck though.

Maria and I went to open the door together, a gesture of solidarity in what could have been an embarrassing encounter. You see, for all its trust, the exchange agreement was quite impersonal. It was all about business and personal gain. At no stage did I ever expect to meet this guy, and I didn't really want to. I just wished he'd stay away and leave us in peace to get on with the last few days of our holidays.

Too late for that though. We tentatively pulled the door open, and there stood Charlie in the hallway, politely waiting for us two strangers to invite him into his own home.

He was smallish, bearded, wearing delicate, gold-rimmed glasses, which unfortunately made me think of the dreaded Walter. His hair made me think of Wes, but only because it was so different to his, tightly curled and neat rather than long and flowing.

Charlie wore the not very trendy, but unremarkable attire of blue jeans with a faded check shirt and new white runners. He smiled winningly, a friendly, open smile, as Maria and I gestured not very confidently towards the living area. He stepped in and I closed the door behind him. Then I turned and looked over his shoulder, and saw with horror a long line of empty beer bottles, and last night's takeaway bags adorning the table on the balcony. If Charlie noticed these, he was kind enough not to comment, or even to look too surprised.

Charlie sat down on one of his oatmeal-coloured armchairs and I wondered desperately if it was right to offer him a cup of his own coffee. Maria decided it was, and meanly rushed off to the kitchen to prepare it, leaving me with this total stranger, not knowing quite what I should say or do. I perched awkwardly on the edge of the sofa, and then tried to unobtrusively slide onto the seat, afraid that he'd think we didn't respect his furniture.

Charlie was more at ease though, and he won me over by telling me in great detail how he loved my home, what a marvellous time he'd had, and how he couldn't wait to go back to see more of Ireland. 'That was my only consolation as I left,' he said. 'I'm sure to go back again. As soon as possible.'

Maria returned with the coffee, and we busied ourselves with the pouring and stirring and passing of cups and milk. I offered around a plate of the walnut biscuits I'd bought as a present for my Auntie Helen. We had, as it happened, plenty to say to each other, as we told him about the highlights of our trip, and he related the best of his to us.

I was still a bit worried about arrangements for the next few days, and it must have shown on my face.

Charlie was completely reassuring.

'Please, Maeve, once I leave this morning, act as if I'm still in Cork.'

I wish you were still there, I meanly said to myself.

'I wish I was still there,' he said.

At least I could be shut of the Tahoe. 'You'll want the Tahoe back at least, won't you, Charlie?'

'No, it's cool. My friend says I can use his car, and that suits me fine.'

Maria was cautiously polite. 'Are you sure, Charlie?'

Charlie smiled easily. 'Please, girls, believe me. It's cool. My friend is away until September. Don't change your schedule in any way. Stay here, use the car. Act like I never came back.'

After all my fears about meeting Charlie, I was pleased to see that he had a lovely, easy manner, and wasn't at all intimidating. Mind you, I must admit that once it was clear he wasn't going to either evict us, or move in with us, I didn't care in the least what he was like. For all I cared he could have had seventeen different personality disorders, and a few highly contagious diseases, once we were free to use his apartment for a few more days. The fact that he was nice, and apparently healthy in mind and body, was an unnecessary bonus.

After half an hour of easy chit-chat, Charlie ate Auntie Helen's last biscuit, drained his coffee, collected his belongings and left, promising to give us a call again before we went home.

There was a strange feeling of anti-climax, as Maria and I sat and surveyed the empty coffee cups. Now that Charlie was back, it seemed for sure that our holiday was over. In a funny kind of way Charlie's reappearance made me feel certain that I wouldn't see Wes again. I felt as if there was no point in planning any more outings. Maria and I should just resign ourselves to leaving, empty the wardrobes, do our packing and get on with the business of departure. I sat at the table, and ran my finger around the rim of Charlie's best jug, too fed up to get on out to make the most of our time, too fed up even to clear away the dishes.

We sat there dejectedly for quite a while, chins in hands, when the phone rang, interrupting our inactivity. I snatched at the receiver with wild hope.

Could it be Wes, begging to see me?

Could it be possible that I would get to spend more time with him?

Could I have more of his wonderful gentle touches and his fierce kisses?

Could it possibly be him?

208

I suppose it could, but it wasn't. It was Charlie again, and luckily he didn't appear to notice my curt greeting. He got straight to the point.

'Can I run this idea by you, Maeve? Todd's gone to Melinda's. I don't feel like cooking. How about if you and Maria come out for dinner with me tonight? I know a great place. Do me a favour and save me from a terrible takeout, and a night in front of the TV.'

I hesitated, but Maria, who has marvellous hearing, nodded enthusiastically, encouraging me to accept. She probably figured that the only thing worse than a night out with Charlie and a grumpy me, was a night out with a grumpy me and no Charlie to fill the inevitable black silences.

Charlie agreed to pick us up at eight, and we hung up.

'It'll be fun,' Maria declared before I could protest. 'We should go out and see the town by night. Charlie can escort us, and show us the hotspots. It will be nice to have a native to guide us. We should take advantage of this opportunity.'

I wasn't so sure. Thirty minutes in Charlie's company over coffee was fine, but I worried about an entire evening with him. I feared he would be deadly boring, all talk about his feelings, and his divorce, his beloved son and his dreary students.

And what if Wes showed up in the meantime and asked me out?

Would Maria be happy to go with Charlie on her own?

I doubted it, but it was too late to do anything about it now, so I grudgingly didn't complain.

We spent the afternoon on the beach, though I couldn't really enjoy myself, as I spent the time in a fruitless scanning of the area for Wes. The beach was full of golden-haired men, but none of them was Wes. Every time one of his almost-clones walked by, my hopes were raised, only to plummet suddenly when the sad truth dawned. If I could get a cardiac readout of the afternoon, it would surely look like a child's drawing of perfectly symmetrical hills and vales. Up and down with sad predictability.

In the end I was happy when Maria suggested going home early to shower and change. It's sad to say that the idea of a night out on the town was a novelty to us. We giggled as we wondered if Charlie would expect us to greet him with big hair and brown foundation. Did he think we'd be attired for the night in gold boob tubes and shiny flared trousers? In fact, as our holiday wardrobe was exclusively casual, the only concession we could make to the occasion was to wear canvas trousers instead of jeans, and deck shoes instead of our usual runners.

I made a special effort and used some of Maria's concealer to hide the spot that was in the process of erupting on my hitherto-unblemished chin. (Though I'm not quite sure why I bothered. Why did I care if this guy knew I had a spot? And anyway, he's a college lecturer. He must be faced every morning with a sea of spotty adolescent visages. Angry red and green eruptions must be his everyday lot. He's surely used to it.)

We both splashed on some of the sweet, expensive perfume that Maria had bought in the duty-free on the way out, and that was that. We were not exactly the height of sophistication, but he'd have to live with that. Neither of us even wore proper make-up. Just perfume for special occasions, and of course concealer for the spots that didn't seem to know quite how old we were.

That simple look might have been admirable when we were twenty, but now it's probably just a bit sad, as time takes its inevitable cruel toll on us, and nature could do with a bit of a helping hand. At this late stage, though, it would be like a betrayal, if one of us suddenly took to paint and powder for the first time.

No. Maria and I are woolly jumper and traditional music types, and no one could change that, especially not a bespectacled, bearded Canadian stranger who, for better or worse, was having the pleasure of our company for the evening.

Chapter Twenty-four

Charlie arrived, as I expected he would, on the dot of eight o'clock.

Is ours the only culture that considers it rude to arrive at an appointed time?

Wouldn't life be easier if eight o'clock meant exactly that, and not a vague, arbitrary moment somewhere between half past eight and nine?

Or ten o'clock if drink was involved?

It was an instant point in Charlie's favour that he was dressed in a similar manner to ourselves. No slick suit. No tie. No highly polished black shoes. No shiny, oily hair clinging to his scalp. No fat gold medallion, and no chunky rings on his little finger.

He was wearing navy canvas trousers, an open-necked shirt, and hooked on one finger, over his shoulder, was a grey, ribbed cotton jumper. (OK. So the shirt did have a designer logo on the breast pocket, but we can overlook that. It was very small and very discreet, and perhaps he was only trying to impress us.

Or maybe he shops in outlet malls where only the most expensive items are logo-free.) Anyway, except for that minor slip, Charlie fitted our dress style exactly; smart casual as I like to think it might be called.

Of course, Charlie's clothes were hideously over the top compared to anything I'd ever seen Wes in. But I suppose I shouldn't quibble.

I didn't just spend a month in Wes's flat.

And Wes never took me out to dinner.

And besides I spent one afternoon with Wes during which he was completely naked all the time.

Oh dear. I shouldn't go there.

I don't want to see Charlie naked.

Ever.

Charlie declined our polite invitation to come in.

'Vancouver awaits. We can't hang around my apartment. We must go experience.'

He gestured towards the hallway with a mock bow and a flourish, and Maria and I stepped out, ready for the night, trying not to catch each other's eye, trying to keep down the nervous sniggers which threatened to bubble over into the balmy evening air.

We had a marvellous night. Charlie was great company. He was relaxed, and still determined to act as if he was on holidays. 'I'm not due back for a few more days. I'm still on vacation. That's official. I have to have fun. I need to get cracked, as you guys say.' Laughingly Maria corrected him, assuring him that while we might like to have some craic, we certainly didn't want to be cracked.

We went for a pre-dinner drink in a quiet, understated bar which Maria and I had managed to walk past every day for three weeks without noticing. The drink turned into two, helping us to lose the slight awkwardness which existed between us, the feeling that we had to be on our best, slightly stilted, behaviour. By the time I was finished my second bottle of beer, it was as if we had known each other all our lives. I'd have been happy to stay there all evening, stocking up on crisps and dry roasted peanuts if the hunger pangs got too much for me, but Charlie had gone to the trouble of reserving a restaurant table for us, and it would have been rude of us not to go there with him. Besides, I didn't want him to think we were drunken slobs. The fact that he might have been quite correct in this opinion was beside the point. We had just met him after all, and were entitled to be thought of as nice girls.

Charlie led the way down a few narrow pedestrian streets, to a tiny Italian restaurant, which he swore was the best in town. I had my doubts. It was very kitschy-looking, with raffia bottles arranged on the windowsills, raffia bottles suspended from the ceiling, and yet more raffia bottles, wax encrusted, holding the candles which flickered precariously, dripping streams of hot wax onto our red and white checked table cloth.

The food was superb though. It bore no resemblance at all to the food in my local Italian restaurant in Cork, which was a very good thing. We ate crisp fresh salad, several varieties of pasta, with tomato sauce and chicken, and slice upon slice of crisp yet drippingly buttered garlic bread. Charlie recommended the house special dessert, which was a heart-attack-inducing mound of cream and fruit on a light spongy base. Maria and I dived unceremoniously at the shared dessert, attacking it greedily with our spoons. This seemed to please Charlie, who muttered something about it being nice to be with people who were not afraid to eat. Immediately I thought of Melinda, deciding that she must have been anorexic, picking at her food and counting calories and lettuce leaves.

Then again, maybe Charlie was just trying to make conversation.

We washed down our meal with rather a lot of Chianti, and lingered over cups of strong black coffee, which were constantly refilled by a handsome, smiling waiter in an impossibly white starched shirt. When the bill came, Charlie chivalrously offered to pay, but like a true gentleman, he didn't argue when Maria and I insisted on chipping in for our share. (Much later that night though, I found the money for our share tucked into the inside pocket of my jacket. I figured that Charlie must have slipped it in there when Maria and I were on one of our many giggly trips to the toilets).

We then moved on to another drinking establishment, another quiet little gem that Charlie knew. Where I'm afraid to say that we drank serious amounts of alcohol. We all three got to the wonderful stage of inebriation where we thought we were constantly witty and original, though to any impartial, sober bystander we probably just looked jarred. Indeed a group of city girls with impeccable make-up, and well-tailored power suits looked askance at us, haughtily staring whenever our volume became too loud. But I was beyond caring by then, and I just sniggered childishly in their direction whenever I managed to make eye contact with one of them.

Maria, Charlie and I were having a ball. We spent a long time discussing complete garbage, loudly disputing pointless points. Every now and then one of us would slap our hand to our forehead and declare in mock horror, 'I'm cracked.' Then we would giggle hysterically, as if this were the funniest thing anyone had ever said. We had reached that lovely stage, hard to achieve and harder to maintain; not blind drunk, just happy and pleased with ourselves, pleased with the world. Not caring about tomorrow.

Or yesterday.

Or the supercilious observers in the corner.

Charlie must have had a partitioned-off section of his brain that was immune to alcohol, as he had the wisdom to call a halt at some early hour of the morning.

'I like you guys. You're great. I want to get you back home while you still seem to like me. Then we can do this again.'

By this time, Maria and I were so laid back that we'd have drunkenly agreed to anything, and we docilely followed as he led us on the short walk home.

We took the elevator, and Maria thought it was incredibly funny to push the button for every floor, so the journey upwards took quite a while. I didn't think it was quite so funny as I urgently needed to make contact with Charlie's varnished-pine toilet seat. We tried to whisper as we approached the apartment door, but past experience has shown me that drunken whispers can be a bit deceptive, so I hope Charlie's neighbours can find it in their hearts to forgive him for the strains of, 'if you're oirish, come into the parlour,' which must surely have penetrated their slumbers.

Once again, Charlie refused to come in, but left us, each propping up one side of his front door, promising to return tomorrow, 'for more craic'. I hope the neighbours didn't call the drug squad.

Maria and I sat in the kitchen for a while and chatted.

'He's nice, isn't he Maeve?'

'Mmm. Good craic. He's cracked.'

We giggled for quite a while at this very unfunny joke.

Maria leaned across the table towards me in a conspiratorial manner.

'No, Maeve. I mean nice. Really nice. Don't you think he's quite fanciable?'

I was drifting off a bit, and my concentration wasn't that great. 'Who's fanciable? Wes? I know that. I fancy him like mad.'

'No, Maeve, I mean Charlie. Isn't he. . . you know, dishy, hunky, a bit of all right? Good for a quick cuddle on a breezy Vancouver night?'

I was shocked. 'Maria! That's awful. You can't fancy him. What about Joe?'

She gave a big, boozy sigh. 'Oh you eejit. I don't fancy him. I thought perhaps you might. He's kind of cute, don't you think?'

'No Maria. Actually I don't think he's cute at all. He's nice. Not cute. Wes is cute. Charlie is nice.'

Maria gave a drunken grumble. 'Wes, Wes, Wes. Give it a rest, Maeve. I'm sick of it. Wes is a waster. Charlie is charming.'

'No Maria. Wes is wonderful. Charlie is. . .'

I couldn't think of another 'ch' word to describe Charlie. Maria must have had less to drink than me, as she continued the game in triumph. 'Wes is woeful. Charlie is champion.'

I finished the conversation with some drunken wisdom. 'Maria, Wes is the guy for me. Perhaps I'm not the girl for him, but such is life. Love hurts.'

Luckily, nothing, not even love, hurts that much when you are as drunk as I was, so I made my way to bed, giggling and muttering as I went. 'Wes is wonderful. Wes is wild. Wes won my heart on a warm Wednesday.'

I lay in bed, sleepily grateful that I'd managed to stop drinking eventually, and that I hadn't drunk enough to make the ceiling spin horribly as it sometimes did, threatening to lurch me out onto the floor if I didn't grip the bed tightly with both hands. As I lay there, almost asleep, I found myself, instead of seeing Charlie's return as the end of our holiday, wishing that we could have seen more of him. We'd had a memorable night. Charlie was good for us. Maria and I had been rather unadventurous in our socialising. Except for Wes, we'd had no real contact with anyone in Vancouver, and unfortunately, I didn't have half enough contact with him.

My last thought before I drifted off into tipsy slumbers was that I had foolishly wasted a great opportunity for a wild, exciting holiday. This night out with Charlie had been much more fun than all those evenings I spent sitting on the balcony with Maria, waiting in vain for Wes to ring, talking endless girlie talk, watching the golden sun do its nightly disappearing act.

When I finally slept, my slumbers were haunted by a bizarre dream in which Charlie with Wes's face, and Wes with Charlie's face were both pursuing me around a desert island surrounded by menacing sharks. All the while I could hear Maria's voice in the background, taunting me.

'See, Maeve. I told you so.'

Chapter Twenty-five

Our second-last full day.

We awoke late of course, but it must have been good quality alcohol that Charlie had searched out, as we had no raging hangovers. I actually felt quite healthy, all things considered, as I sat on the balcony in my nightdress, sipping fresh orange juice that Maria had kindly squeezed for us with Charlie's ultra-modern chrome citrus press. I surveyed the view, which was by now like an old friend, but none the less precious for all that. It had rained during the night, but now the air was fresh and clear, and the sun was already warm. The harbour was as busy as ever, with merry, brightly sailed little boats bobbing along in the wake of larger, commercial boats. The thought of my own home, with a pleasant enough view in its own understated way, did nothing to console me at the thought of leaving this wonderful place. There had been mutterings on the news a few days ago about a possible air traffic controllers' strike, and I had a little glimmer of hope that perhaps I would not be able to travel, but now it seemed that all was fine, and nothing could impede my journey home.

Except Wes of course. If he appeared out of the blue and invited me to stay on longer, I'd be sorely tempted. I'd find somewhere to stay so I could live out my romantic dream for another few weeks. Dream on, Maeve.

Maria and I had agreed to do all the shopping that we hadn't got around to before, so, even though I felt no enthusiasm at all, I showered and dressed, and prepared for an assault on the best that Canada's shopping malls could offer, and to be fair, they had a lot to offer.

First, it was difficult to decide which of the many malls to go to, as according to our guidebook, all had a huge selection of shops and restaurants. In the end, we made our choice based on location, going to one that we had passed previously, and that we knew we could find easily again. The summer sales were in full swing, with much of the merchandise already down to half price. I am not one of life's shoppers, and began to regret this, as I wandered amongst the rails of designer label jeans and T-shirts, all of which were far cheaper than anything at home. I bought a few pairs of jeans, a sweatshirt and a wind chime for my porch – not bad by my standards.

Then I had to go through the ritual of buying presents for the aunties. My dad has three sisters, and I have locked myself into the foolish tradition of bringing them back presents from my holidays. I don't know if they actually compare notes, but nevertheless I have to be very careful. Everything has to be seen to be equal. There would be no point in me buying my Auntie Helen a silk scarf for half nothing in a sale, if Auntie Mary is going to be eyeing it enviously, and wondering why she only got a Granville Island key-ring and a bag of saltwater taffy. I had bought each aunt a box of walnut biscuits already, but as Charlie had demolished one box, the other two were now useless. (I'll just have to eat them myself in the interest of peace between the aunties.)

In the end I decided to buy each auntie a small brass model of a totem pole. They were cheap tourist tat of course, but the aunties like that kind of thing. Well at least that's what they say every year when I present them with more tacky rubbish, and if they are lying, well they need to be punished for their dishonesty.

I always bring something home for my parents too. Dad is easy, I just get him a bottle of whiskey in the duty-free shop on the way home. Mum is more difficult. I know what she would really like. There's one thing that would make her very happy indeed. She'd love a postcard from me saying,

> Dear Mum,
> Having a great time. Just met a wonderful man. He's a farmer on holidays from

Ballinhassig. He has a hundred acres, a milk
quota, and a cut stone farmhouse. We plan
to get married in the spring.
Love,
Maeve

Obviously, I can't deliver on that particular wish, so
Mum will have to settle for the cut-price silk scarf, in
fashionable shades of moss and aubergine.

Maria was a little more adventurous in her shopping.
She knew that she would be spending a few more weeks
in this part of the world, before facing back to a grey
Irish autumn, so she splashed out on two floaty, flowery
dresses. It is so unusual to see her in anything but jeans
that I could not but sigh in wonder when she sailed out
of the dressing room. She was beautifully tanned and
healthy-looking, showing off the first of the dresses, a
mauve and blue one, to perfection. I felt an unusual
pang of jealousy, as a picture sailed unbidden into my
mind, of Maria, barefoot, arm in arm with Joe, walking
on the sand. (Is Texas on the coast? Are there beaches
there?) Anyway, in my mind's picture she's walking on
golden sand, with a gentle wind blowing her hair and
aforementioned floaty dress, smiling and laughing with
Joe, and gazing into his clear eyes: perfect for a
shampoo or a tampon commercial.

I feel really mean on the odd occasions when I am
jealous of Maria. She is a true, good friend, and I
should be glad she is happy, but I am only human, and

jealousy seems to be part of the deal. It goes along with greed, and sloth and all those other deadly sins that I learned in catechism lessons many years ago.

Worn out from our efforts, we decided to take a food break. We had a long, lazy lunch, in a great hall, which was surrounded by every manner of takeaway counter, with a communal eating area in the middle. I selected a hot and spicy chicken stir-fry, which was delicious, while Maria equally enjoyed her lasagne and salad. After several coffees and some sinful chocolate cake we set off again, Maria to buy a few more supplies for her trip to Texas, and me to select presents for my nephews and nieces. It's great being an auntie. (It's being a niece that I find so difficult.) I can buy marvellously politically incorrect, television driven toys, which the children love, leaving the parents to buy the 'educational' ones which litter the playroom floors, never played with, always trodden on. This time, I selected Barbie dolls in pink frilly dresses (so much for being a feminist) for the girls, and vicious-looking *Star Wars* figures for the boys.

Then it was time for more coffee and cakes (since we're on vacation), before struggling back to the car, feeling like real shoppers for a change, with bulging carrier bags and slim purses.

We made our way back to the apartment with no real plans for the evening. It looked like it was going to be one more night on the balcony, and that suited me fine. There was a telephone message from Charlie though.

'Hi guys. Sorry about last night. I got a bit out of it. It must have been something I ate. How about we go out again tonight, for a respectable evening. A bit of culture? I'll drop by at seven-thirty, and if you're not there, that's cool, I'll understand. Bye.'

As I said, we had no plans, and we had had such a good time last night, we decided to give him another opportunity to entertain us. And anyway, there will be plenty of sunsets to watch when I get home. One every evening to be precise. Canada doesn't have a monopoly on sunsets. And if I can't even see the sun, because of mist or rain, well I've got an imagination, haven't I?

We were ready on time, each of us dressed in our same smart casual clothes, as Maria had decided to save her dresses for Texas and Joe, and I possessed nothing else except denims, which might not meet the dress code for the cultured evening Charlie had in store. I was beginning to regret my limited wardrobe, but short of pulling down the curtains and making myself a dress, there wasn't much I could do about it.

Charlie arrived on time again, looking a bit sheepish. It began to dawn on me how the culture difference was manifesting itself. For us, going out with a virtual stranger, getting jarred and having a ball was quite acceptable, something to brag about in fact; for Charlie, it was as if he had breached some hidden code of etiquette, and he was quite embarrassed by it. He was relieved to see that we took it so lightly, brushing off his apologies with laughing denial.

'I took the liberty of reserving some tickets for a show, I hope you don't mind.'

I minded quite a bit as it happened. I fancied another wild night, not a demure evening at the theatre, but it would have been churlish to refuse, in the circumstances. So Maria and I feigned enthusiasm, and we set off.

I could not have been more wrong in my expectations. We walked the short distance to Stanley Park, and then Charlie led the way to 'The theatre under the stars'. It was perfect. A small open-air theatre set in a clearing amongst some woods. An amateur company was performing 'West Side Story'. They played their hearts out, singing and dancing like pros. I sat transfixed, the balmy air on my face, the muted city sounds just audible in the quiet moments, thinking that nothing could ever be so perfect again.

When the show ended, the audience, predominantly tourists by the look of them, filed out silently. I saw more than one person discreetly dabbing their eyes as they went. I couldn't speak, and was glad that Charlie and Maria were similarly afflicted. Perhaps it was the setting. I have a funny feeling that the same show transported to the parish hall in Carrigaline would not be quite so moving.

We picked our way along a narrow path, half-lit by a perfect crescent moon. We had walked to the edge of the park in silence, when Charlie suddenly dropped on one knee in front of Maria, narrowly avoiding tripping her up, as he had taken her by surprise. Then he sang in a surprisingly pleasant voice, 'Maria, I've just met a girl called Maria.' There was a moment's silence, and Charlie began to look embarrassed, wondering if he had made a complete eejit of himself. Maria saved him though, by singing loudly in her truly tuneless voice, 'How do you solve a problem called Maria?' Desperate not to be outdone, I countered with a high, warbling version of 'Ave Maria'. The three of us skitted with laughter, pleased with our good spirits. It was the perfect break to our mood, as it doesn't do to be too solemn for too long, and after all, we were on our holidays.

Maria and I insisted that we stand Charlie dinner, as he had treated us yesterday, and he accepted graciously, sheepishly promising not to sneak the money back to us when we weren't looking. He suggested a Chinese restaurant, which, like everything else, turned out to be only a short walk away from his apartment. Poor Charlie. I wonder how he coped in my house, where nothing was a short walk away except for the sea, and the fields. Oh, and of course there was the ice-cream van on the beach, when the sun shone. And the mobile library on Thursday mornings at ten.

The restaurant turned out to be excellent, and we wined and dined healthily, almost, but not quite reaching the stage of inebriation that we had achieved last night. Perhaps that was because we spent so much time rolling things in pancakes, dipping things in spicy sauces, and dabbling our fingers in warm, lemon-scented water, that we had less time for pouring wine down our greedy gullets.

After our meal, chivalrous as ever, Charlie walked us home, refusing yet again to come in. We stood in the doorway, not needing it to hold us up this time, smiling as we watched Charlie amble along the corridor, whistling softly, 'Maria, I just met a girl called Maria.'

A sudden, sick thought rushed into my pleasantly addled head. What if Charlie fancies Maria? Is he being so nice to us just so he can get her in the sack? Is he desperately wondering how he can get rid of me so he can have his wicked way with Maria? Is he going home to dream rude dreams about her? And what if she fancies Charlie? She laughs a lot when he is around. She's already admitted that she thinks he's cute. Where does all of this leave Joe? Am I the only thing between him and the divorce courts? Can I save their marriage all on my own?

I reassured myself madly, telling myself how ridiculous I was being. Maria loves Joe and would never be unfaithful to him. Charlie is just being nice and friendly. It's his way. He's a friendly kind of guy. Nevertheless, as Maria and I had a last beer together before bed, I spent the time talking about Texas, and Joe; willing her to love him, as I know in my heart she loves him.

And later, when I lay sleepless in bed, I stared at the flawless white ceiling, and wondered why it was that I couldn't find it in my heart to love anyone at all.

Except Wes the Waster.

And what good is he to me?

Chapter Twenty-six

Our very last day today.

I awoke to the usual sunshine, and the memory of last night's fears about betrayal and marriage break-ups. In the pleasant light of day, those fears seemed rather ridiculous, and I was ever so relieved that I hadn't shared them with Maria. She would have been horrified. And rightly so.

Charlie is becoming more familiar. This morning, without even ringing first to warn us, he arrived at the front door, politely knocking rather than letting himself in with his key. Still, the knock on the door prompted panic, as we could think of no one else it could possibly be (except of course for Wes, and even I was beginning to accept that I'd seen the last of him.) The trouble was, Maria and I were still swanning around in the flimsy garments we used as nightwear. We were not suitably attired for receiving guests, to say the least, as we are not the sophisticated breed of people who could comfortably entertain in their pyjamas.

Maria struggled into grubby jeans and a T-shirt that she had left adorning one of the kitchen worktops yesterday. (We were at the stage of our holiday when washing clothes seemed like too much hard work.) My dirty clothes were hidden under the bed where I'd shoved them the day Charlie arrived, so I flung myself dramatically into my bedroom, to dress at a more leisurely pace, in the cleanest of my not very clean clothes. Maria let Charlie in and slipped into the role that seemed to be becoming hers – maker of Charlie's coffee in his own house. I joined them a minute later, trying hard not to look as if I was just dressed, but failing no doubt.

Charlie was as affable as ever, slouching comfortably on the sofa, right on the cushion that harboured a nest of my socks and knickers that had been airing on the balcony chairs the day he arrived. 'You guys probably have plans, but if not, I'd be happy to take you to see some more of Vancouver. You know, a kind of send-off treat.' Maria and I looked at each other. We had thought of cycling around Stanley Park one last time, but had made no definite plans for this. Going with Charlie sounded like a good idea to me, but I didn't like to agree, just in case Maria didn't want it. Years of close friendship have helped our non-verbal communication, and I spotted the very slight inclination of her head, indicating that it was fine by her. 'That sounds great, Charlie. Let's go for it.' I could see that he was pleased by my answer, and I felt a small wave of pity for him. Clearly he would have liked to be spending these days with his son, but of course Todd was off having his quality visit with Melinda and Toby, and therefore unavailable.

'How about Capilano?' was Charlie's suggestion. 'It's full of tourists, but still a great place. And you two are tourists after all.' We'd read about it but hadn't been there, so we readily agreed. It was so easy to let someone else make the decisions for a change. It was even better when that person knew his way around, lessening the danger of the best part of the day being spent on endless three-point turns, and reversing around corners. Charlie could save us from hours of pointless discussions with the people who always materialise when you are lost. You know the ones. The people who for some reason cannot distinguish left from right, and seem to be blissfully unaware of that sad fact, as they gesture wildly with their right hand, while declaring confidently, 'Go left, then left again.'

'Ok then. Let's roll,' suggested Charlie, full of the enthusiasm that I was really beginning to like about him. I began to smirk at the thought of poor Maria who still wore short, pink gingham pyjamas under her clothes, and I began to wonder how we could ask for some time in private so we could dress ourselves properly. Perceptive Charlie spotted our momentary hesitation, and apologised. 'How thoughtless of me. You guys need a few minutes to get yourselves together. Will I drive?' When we nodded together, he continued. 'You take your time. I'll go and wait in the Tahoe.' He sauntered off, and we rushed to ready ourselves. I took the opportunity to rescue my underclothes from under the sofa cushion, and throw them into my suitcase. I had a horrible fear that if I left them I might forget about them altogether, and that Charlie would discover them weeks or months from now, pulling them out while searching for loose change or a lost comb.

Charlie was incredibly relaxed and easy-going, and we knew he wouldn't be staring pointedly at his watch, and impatiently drumming his fingers on the steering wheel when we arrived, but we didn't want to take advantage of this, so we surpassed ourselves and were ready in record time.

Ten minutes later we drove out of the car park, and I slouched back in my seat, glad to be free of the responsibility of driving; glad Charlie wouldn't have to witness the lurching starts in which I specialised.

We drove through Stanley Park, which wasn't that exciting, as the best views were obscured, available only to non-motorised travellers, but we were amply rewarded when we crossed the spectacular Lion's Gate Bridge. It was difficult to decide where to look, as there were great views on both left and right, so I dithered as usual, turning my head quickly from side to side, trying to see everything. I was afraid that I would miss something wonderful, but I ended up by not giving myself time to see anything properly, and everything passed in a hazy blur. Story of my life, I suppose.

The suspension bridge in Capilano was great. Scary enough to cross, but worth it as we stopped in the middle, and stood, gently swaying, looking down at the waters raging far below. There were nature trails on the far side, and as Charlie was familiar with them, we set off on a gentle hike through the cool woods.

For the first time since we'd arrived in Canada, I became aware of mosquitoes, buzzing around my almost bare, shorts-clad legs. Organised person that I am though (eat your heart out, Theresa), I produced my unopened bottle of all-natural mosquito repellent, turning my nose up at the chemical variety that Charlie produced from his trendy leather backpack. Maria loyally used mine and we made a great show of spraying it on liberally, sniffing enthusiastically at its natural lemony scent. Twenty minutes later, the sad truth became clear – my all natural insect repellent was perfect in every way except for one – it didn't repel insects. After I'd been viciously bitten for the tenth time, Charlie, decent enough not to gloat, gave me some toxic chemical soup, which did the trick, protecting me for the rest of the walk.

The day passed in happy, gentle activity. Charlie knew great places to go; little hidden lakes, tiny villages off the tourist track, and he was the perfect guide, not boring us with facts and figures, just giving us quick insights, giving each place an interesting angle. The only downside to the day was my own fault. My terrible habit of not enjoying the present, reared its ugly head again, and I couldn't stop myself from marking out the hours to myself.

'This time tomorrow I'll be leaving for the airport.'

'At this time, I'll be two hours into the flight.'

And so on.

And on.

It's a terrible affliction to be the kind of person who ruins the present by worrying about a future that cannot be changed.

Though of course Charlie didn't know me well, it would have been difficult not to notice my sporadic morose silences, and my discontented expression, which would have stopped a hundred clocks, and turned gallons of milk sour. Maria, who knows me so well, obviously noticed, but said nothing.

Sometime in the late afternoon, the three of us sat on a rustic little bench, on a path by a sparkling, babbling stream, somewhere in North Vancouver. I've no idea where exactly we were, as I had abandoned myself to Charlie's guiding, happily agreeing with whatever he suggested, as everything he suggested was so agreeable. I was pleased too, to be free of the worry about finding my way home again, as I knew we could rely on Charlie to escort us back.

I watched the sun glistening on the water, highlighting one area and then, in fickle notion, leaving that for another little chosen spot. The gentle breeze blew the small branches over my head, and in my sick fashion, I pictured them laughing at me, and waving goodbye. (I think perhaps I watched the forest scene in *Snow White* a few times too many.)

Charlie interrupted my sad, mad musings, gently probing. 'You don't relish the thought of tomorrow do you, Maeve?' Then in a moment of insight he asked, 'What is so bad? Is it the thought of leaving here or the thought of being back home?'

How could I answer that six-marker? How could I tell this stranger, kind though he was, how I felt? I wasn't even sure how I felt anyway. It was just that the thought of a month of long days at home, and long bright evenings, with nothing particular to do, filled me with emptiness. (I know that doesn't make sense, but it's exactly how I felt, full of emptiness.) I could see no bright light, nothing to entice me back. I had nothing to look forward to. I scuffled my feet on the leafy compost under the bench, and didn't reply.

Charlie spoke tentatively. 'You know, Todd is away at camp for the next four weeks, and my friend isn't due back until September. I can stay at his place, and you're welcome to use mine until you have to get back for work. Why don't you prolong your holiday for a while?' Maria, on my other side, was silent, pretending not to be paying attention, but I could tell by the way that she abruptly stopped stripping the veins from a large leaf, that she was, as they say, all ears.

What could I say? I knew it was a genuine offer, and

I felt that for some reason Charlie really wanted me to accept, but I couldn't seize the moment. The philosophy of *Carpe Diem* was never my forté. A million reasons to say no leapt into my head, and they all clamoured noisily around in my brain, begging to be uttered, doing their obstreperous best to obscure the big reason that I should say yes. Because of course I should have said yes. I needed to take a chance, I needed to live a little, to be a bit daring. I needed to act more like a healthy young woman, and less like a timid, ailing granny. I needed to be brave.

So, of course, I heard a cold, wimpish voice coming from my mouth saying, 'No, Charlie. I couldn't possibly do that. You need your home. I've booked my flight. Thank you for offering, but I have to go.'

Charlie shrugged, stretching his tanned arms upwards towards the trees, which had suddenly ceased their whispering, as if afraid of missing any part of this riveting conversation. He spoke gently. 'It's your choice. You're welcome to stay. I have a buddy at the airport. A hot shot. He can fix anything. He could change your flight if that's your biggest problem. He could get you a seat on any flight you wish. Stay a week. A month. It's up to you.'

I remained silent. I didn't know how to react, what to say to him. I picked at the nail of my index finger. Charlie closed the subject, 'You decide. Think about it tonight. I can fix it for you in the morning if you want. Let me know then.'

Chapter Twenty-seven

We decided to eat together one last time, though I had no enthusiasm, no interest. I didn't care what I ate or who I ate it with.

I'd have been happy to eat a takeaway in front of the television.

Or to have no dinner, and go to bed early.

What was the point in going out?

I was fed up and sorry for myself. I was sorry that I was leaving, sorry that I fell for stupid Wes, and cross that I couldn't be brave and agree to accept Charlie's kind offer to stay.

Poor Maria. Even though she is always endlessly patient with me in my morose moments, she was probably glad at the prospect of having Charlie around to lighten the atmosphere. I'm sure she was dreaming happily of a month in Texas, hundreds of miles away from me and my thunderous looks and black moods.

Charlie dropped us home, and we agreed to meet in an hour in a small bar, just up the street. Maria and I went in to the apartment, and I flopped on the couch, determined to sulk, though I'd no real reason.

Maria, who knew me so well, and never teased me about men, couldn't stay silent. 'He fancies you, you know. It's written all over his face every time he looks at you. He's nice too. Very nice. You could do an awful lot worse.'

I was genuinely taken aback. I'd never for a moment entertained the notion that Charlie might like me. To me it just wasn't an issue. Not on the agenda.

And me? I liked him a lot. He was genuine, warm and funny. He was smart and kind and gentle. That was it though. I felt nothing extra about him. There was no magic sparkle. No buzz. I suppose, to be honest, what I'm saying is that I just didn't fancy him. There was no sexual attraction. I felt he'd be a great friend, but nothing more.

(Wes, now, he could be more than a friend. Much more. I'd happily sparkle and buzz with him. But what good was that to me? I hadn't heard from him since the night he ate in the apartment. He couldn't be that busy, so presumably he just wasn't interested. In fact, I'm beginning to wonder why he bothered with me at all.)

When I told Maria the sad truth about my feelings for Charlie, she was kind enough not to scoff, but I could tell she wasn't impressed. 'You read too much. You've warped your brain by reading too many romantic novels.' She was completely wrong in this, as I never read romantic fiction, but I knew what she meant so I let it pass, and she continued. 'Life's not like that. It's not all about hearts and flowers and violins. First you're supposed to like the guy. Then you're supposed to learn how to love him. You always mix this up. You expect too much. You expect some trendy lefty Adonis like bloody Wes to sweep you off your feet, and whisk you off into the sunset to live happily ever after. That's not how it happens. Just face up to it, Maeve. Wes was nothing, and that fool Paddy is never coming back. You'll never be twenty again, and it will never be like that again.'

When she dragged Paddy's name into it, I gave her an even blacker look, though I had no energy to reply. Maria took a deep breath and continued in a softer tone. 'Why don't you stay? Don't go back to your ivory tower by the sea. Stay here and see how it goes. Then in a few weeks, when you go back you'll have work to distract you, and it won't seem so bad. You're your own worst enemy. Give yourself a chance to be happy. Don't ruin your own life.'

She hesitated for a moment, as if afraid that she'd said too much. Then, I suppose figuring that there was no going back, she finished her speech with a final flourish. 'You won't be vowing eternal love. You don't have to marry Charlie and live with him until you're ninety. Just be nice to him and see what happens.'

I was shocked into an uncharacteristic silence. Maria wasn't given to lengthy speeches. And as I mentioned, she never pushed me with regard to men.

She knew it was a delicate subject, and even though she didn't as a rule avoid delicate subjects, this was one that she instinctively shied away from. She was right too. It was just too sensitive, and I suspect that our relationship would have suffered if she tried too often to come close to something I hadn't yet come to terms with myself.

I had a sudden flashback to an occasion some years ago, when my mother somehow discovered that I'd been out with a man a few times, and then refused his further invitations. She had become quite agitated, losing her normal calm demeanour, forgetting to take the scenic route to the point of her speech. She snapped quite brusquely at me, 'That's typical of you, Maeve. You spend your life looking for Mr Perfect and you won't accept that maybe Mr Alright will have to do.'

I was horrified. For the first time I felt as if my mother were trying to sell me short. She was telling me to accept something other than the best. I was too upset to argue with her, but that night I cried bitter tears on Sean's shoulder, and when that was sodden, he went home and I cried more into my pillow, soaking the cover I'd embroidered by hand in domestic science class in my first year in secondary school.

Now, I couldn't believe my ears, Maria was telling me something similar, albeit less bluntly, since she was more of a diplomat than my mother. I found myself going on the defensive, resorting to the sad ploy of numbering the reasons she was wrong and I was right.

'One: I don't think Charlie fancies me. You're imagining it. He's just being nice. Two: I don't fancy him. Whatever you say about hearts and flowers, I know how I feel, and I don't feel for our friend Charlie. I feel for Bloody Wes as you call him, but that's not much good to me, is it? Three: if I stay just to use Charlie's flat, and without seeing him, I'll be bored on my own, without you, so I may as well go home and be bored in my own home where I'm used to it, and I know my way around. Four:. . .' I was getting agitated now and upset and couldn't think of a number four reason. I could feel hot tears welling up. Maria, conciliatory as always, tried to pull back. 'I'm sorry, Mae. I didn't mean to upset you. I just want you to be happy. I'd like to see you stay, but if you don't want to, that's your choice. Go home. Do whatever you think is best.'

Then she giggled, 'He really does fancy you though. Believe me.'

I shook my head, still not believing her, but her giggling was contagious, and we laughed together. After all, whether it's true or not, it's nice to be told that someone likes you. Nice to think that you might be deserving of affection.

We discussed it at length, calmly and coolly, with Maria being very careful not to step over the unspoken demarcation line. In the end, while we agreed that it would be possible for me to stay, regardless of any feelings Charlie might or might not have for me, I decided that without him and Maria, I'd be at a bit of a loss. However, if I stayed on the basis that I'd be spending my time with him, I could well end up deeply involved in something I didn't want to be involved in, and things could become very complicated. After all, Charlie was still a virtual stranger. Either way, I couldn't see how it was right for me to stay, and even though I desperately wanted to be daring and free, I knew that I'd leave in the morning, just as I'd always planned.

So don't hold your breath, non-existent reader, it doesn't look as if there's going to be a happy ending. I don't think this particular story will end up with the heroine riding off into the sunset with her handsome Canadian lover. My final words will not be written to the pealing of wedding bells. The last pages will not be sprinkled with confetti, and scented with orange blossom. It's not turning out to be that kind of a story. Sorry.

I decided to make the best of it, and enjoy this, my last night in Vancouver. I stood up to go for a shower, and realised with a shock that we were meant to be meeting Charlie in ten minutes. There was a mad scramble as Maria and I raced to shower and dress, and we dashed along to our rendezvous, only a few minutes late, arriving breathless and laughing.

Charlie was there waiting, and he quickly ordered the first of our evening's drinks. We were a quiet, almost morose lot, so we didn't delay in the bar, and moved quickly on to a nearby restaurant.

After we had finished our main courses, Maria suddenly rose from the table.

'You know guys, I have a dreadful headache, I think I'll go home.'

I jumped up too. 'That's fine. It's time we all went. We have an early start.'

Maria was unusually adamant. 'No, I'll be OK. You two stay for coffee and dessert. I'll see you later.'

I reluctantly sat down, and then Charlie jumped up. 'Maria, you can't walk home alone. I'll see you home and then come back here for coffee with Maeve.'

I jumped up again. 'That's crazy. Why don't we all just go home? We can have coffee in the apartment.'

Maria and Charlie exchanged a look and they both sat down again. Maria spoke with a sigh. 'OK, let's not fuss. We'll just have coffee here then.'

Well, at least that was settled.

We sat for a few moments in silence, and then, it was as if Charlie suddenly remembered the last step in the strange jumping up and down ritual we had been enacting. He rose one last time, and spoke with authority. 'No, Maria. I can see you're tired. It's not a problem. I'll see you home, and come back here for coffee with Maeve.' He was ushering her towards the door as he spoke. 'I'll be back in ten minutes, Maeve. Please order me the sticky toffee pudding and a latté.'

Maria gave me an inscrutable smile, and then they were gone.

This was very strange. Maria wasn't usually a

schemer, but could this be a crude attempt at throwing myself and Charlie together? Was she having one last go at matchmaking, despite our earlier conversation? Or even worse, was Charlie scheming for the opportunity to get Maria on her own? Was he going to take the long way home, chivalrously throw his jacket over her bare shoulders, and then declare undying love for her as they strolled in the moonlight?

I'm not very good at this relationship lark. I never seem to know what's going on. I always manage to miss the point. All kinds of crazy possibilities were jostling around in my brain. I sat there in utter confusion, barely noticing the young waitress bringing the desserts and coffees I had somehow found the presence of mind to order.

Before long Charlie was back, slipping quietly into the chair facing mine. He was rather flushed-looking, but I had to admit, if his object had been a declaration of undying love for Maria, he'd been very quick about it.

He busied himself with his dessert and coffee, while I wondered what to say. In the end, he spoke first.

He took a deep breath and gave a little speech. Something about the way he spoke made me feel he'd been rehearsing what he had to say.

'Maeve, I want you to know that my offer of the apartment for the next few weeks was sincere. It would please me very much if you decide to stay, but you don't have to feel that I'm a necessary part of the package. If you want to stay and let me entertain you and show you my city, that's great. I'd be happy to oblige. If, though, you'd just like to use the apartment, and do your own thing, and leave the key under the mat when you go, that's fine too. I don't want to put pressure on you. Decide in your own time. Do whatever is right for you. Let me know in the morning, and I can call my buddy about rescheduling your flight.'

He stopped there, looking a little bit shy. Clearly he'd used up all of his rehearsed words. I was touched by his obvious sincerity, and by how vulnerable he looked, and one half of me wanted to cry out, 'Yes. I'll stay. Let's give it a try. Let's be friends and then see what happens.'

Underneath, though, was a deeper, darker me, one that was afraid of becoming involved, one that flashed an unwanted picture of Paddy, my first love, in front of me. This deep, dark me was whispering insidiously, 'Don't do it. Don't stay. Remember what happened before. Go home. Go to your own house where you'll be safe and no one can ever hurt you.'

I could see clearly what was happening. I'm not blind to my own weaknesses. I know that I am terribly afraid of becoming involved with anyone. I know I stay aloof in order to avoid being hurt again, but that knowledge doesn't help me. I probably only allowed myself to fall for Wes because I knew in my heart that nothing would ever come of it. But what can I do? I can't, on a whim, shed my personality. I'm a product of my past. I'm stuck with it. I'd love to be a different person but I can't.

Despite his protestations to the contrary, I could see that Charlie was waiting for an answer, but I couldn't help him out. I gave a thin little smile, 'I really don't know what to say. Can I tell you in the morning?' I felt like I was dismissing him, the way I used to dismiss Walter whenever he asked probing questions about my work. But Charlie is too nice and too sincere to be treated like Walter, so I felt doubly bad.

I was using my long-handled teaspoon to scoop out the last creamy drops from my latté when Charlie spoke again.

'Maeve, I have to say one more thing.'

I raised my head, surprised by his serious tone. Something told me he wasn't going to launch into a conversation about the weather, or the price of eggs. He continued, 'You know, Maeve, I don't usually rush into things like this. I'm a cautious kind of guy. But if I don't speak now, you'll be gone in the morning and I'll never get the opportunity again.'

I was embarrassed, and looked back to my drink, scraping urgently at the creamy residue. Charlie pulled his chair closer to the table, and clasped my hand with both of his, stilling the frantic movements. He didn't speak for a moment, but held my hand tightly. I found myself looking into his eyes, somehow compelled, despite myself. For a second I thought he was going to kiss me. We sat like this. No one spoke. Charlie leaned ever so slightly closer. Perhaps he saw the panic in my eyes, or perhaps he just got sense, but at the last moment he pulled back. He spoke in the husky voice they use in the movies when the handsome hero is declaring undying love for the heroine. Charlie didn't look like a hero though, with his glasses a little askew, and a fleck of creamy latté foam on his beard.

'Maeve. I've just met you, but I can't account for how I feel. It's as though I have known you forever. You make me laugh. You make me feel good.'

He stopped, and took his hands from mine. My hand felt suddenly cold, without the warmth of his.

Charlie took off his glasses. He began to clean them with the corner of the tablecloth in a distracted, agitated manner. I could see his freckled eyelids and the two red oval-shaped marks his glasses had left on the bridge of his nose. I wondered should I say something light and witty, so we could forget this was happening. I wondered was this a good time to say goodnight and leave. Charlie replaced his glasses, took a deep breath and spoke softly. 'God, Maeve, I have to say it. You most likely think I'm crazy, but I think I'm falling in love with you.'

Oh, dear. It was turning out like a movie all right. A bad movie. And it certainly wasn't going to have a happy ending.

'Charlie, I don't know what to say. You're. . .'

He gave a wry smile, and raised his hand to stop my flow of panicked words. 'It's OK, Maeve. Don't answer. I guess I shouldn't have said anything. I just didn't want you to leave without telling you the truth. You can still use the apartment, I won't bother you. I won't come near you if that's what you wish. Keep the Tahoe too, if you like.'

Life is so stupid. Why couldn't it have been Wes there opposite me, flicking his blond fringe out of his eyes, and declaring undying love?

And what about poor Charlie? He deserves better. He's a fine, decent person. Why did he have to choose a scared, dry fool like me to fall for?

I spoke sincerely. 'Charlie, I think you are the kindest man I have ever met.'

Charlie gave a soft sigh. He finished his coffee, and walked me home in silence.

Chapter Twenty-eight

31 July

I'm a sick, self-hating person.

Some people get involved in terrible, abusive relationships, living with people who demolish their self-esteem on a daily basis, but I don't need to do that, do I? No, I can do it all myself. I can beat myself up and make my own life a misery, with no help from anyone, independent in this as in everything else.

For some reason, Walter has come to mind, admonishing me silently, as he sometimes does while I'm writing. 'Set the scene. Don't make your reader struggle to know where you are, and what you are about. Tell them.'

Oh, please shut up, Walter. Give me a rest. I'm sick of your endless carping and fault-finding. I'm tired of your pitiful non-stop bleating in my ear. I'm well able to see my own faults, thank you very much. I don't need you to put me down. I can do it myself.

I'm on a plane, leaving Vancouver. I'm alone, as

usual, though there are hundreds of people strapped in with me in this long red and white metal tube. I hate myself. Did I mention that already? Tough.

Six hours later.

I'm still on the plane. I've had a few hours sleep, and I've given my neighbour enough angry looks to ensure that he won't try to strike up a conversation with me, or probably with anyone else, ever.

Maybe a few years of therapy will help him to lose the cowed look he has gradually developed since he was unfortunate enough to be shown to the seat next to mine. Another poor victim of the great aeroplane seat lottery.

This morning was awful. Maria was excited at the prospect of seeing Joe again, and readied herself eagerly, humming as she packed the last of her belongings, carefully folding her new dresses to avoid creasing them. I just threw my things in any old way, not really caring if I ever saw any of them again.

We tidied the last few things from the kitchen, and surveyed the apartment, confident that it was almost as sparkly clean as when we arrived, four long weeks ago. I checked under all the beds and cushions making sure we were not unintentionally leaving Charlie a few reminders of our sojourn in his home. In a strange way I felt as if I were leaving my home, with all the insecurity that implies.

Maria took a final photograph from the balcony, though I refused to stand into it, as I didn't want to scare some poor unsuspecting photo lab technician with my black glare.

Charlie arrived to drive us to the airport, chivalrously carrying the heaviest of our bags into the lift, across the car park, and into the back of the Tahoe. I was embarrassed about last night, unable to look him in the eye. He didn't mention anything about the possibility of me staying on in his apartment, and I was beginning to wonder if he had forgotten that I hadn't given him an answer. Had he forgotten everything except for my unspoken rejection of his love?

Then, when we were all strapped in, and just as he was about to turn the key in the ignition, he turned to me and said, 'Can I take the presence of your bags in the trunk of my car as an indication that you are leaving?' I nodded. A nasty part of myself felt like crying out, 'It was you who put them there anyway. You can have some of the blame. It's not entirely my fault, Mr smug would-be benefactor.' That would have been quite unfair though, so I resisted.

I had no excuse, no reason to give him that would lend urgency to my departure. I couldn't pretend to have pressing engagements in Cork. I wasn't able to make it easy for him or for me. I didn't know myself why I was leaving, so how could I explain it to Charlie?

He gave a tight little smile. 'OK. Let's go. You've got planes to catch.'

As we were using the same airline, Maria and I were able to check in together. We selected what appeared to be the shortest of the very long queues, and then stood for an hour watching the other queues whizz past us. The old man directly in front of us spent ten full minutes arguing with the perky blonde check-in girl. He was adamant that his oversized holdall classified as hand luggage, and she was equally adamant that it didn't. He then proceeded to unpack it, carefully spreading his belongings on the tiles in front of us. He rearranged his trousers and books and repacked them, as if that would somehow make his bag lighter. When this didn't work, and the harassed girl threatened to call security, he reluctantly allowed his bag to be labelled and roughly shoved along the access way, to slide bumpily along the conveyor belt. He gazed after it sadly, savouring the last glimpse, as if it were a dear friend that he might never see again. Mind you, airport statistics suggest that might not be an unreasonable fear.

When we were finally checked in, we joined Charlie for a coffee. My last chance this holiday to have a latté with caramel. The only sweetness in a bleak day.

We sat in silence. Charlie wore a rather cross expression which was terribly at odds with his normal pleasant demeanour. Maria fiddled with her boarding card, aimlessly removing the shiny slip from its cardboard cover, and replacing it upside down. I hadn't told her about Charlie's declaration of love. I knew that if she knew that, she'd be even crosser with me. And anyway, as I wasn't staying, what was the point? She looked rather resigned and weary. I couldn't blame her. Perhaps this was the last straw for her. Had I finally pushed her to the limit with my dark nature and endless moaning?

Would she arrive in Texas, hug Joe and spend the next four weeks telling him how much she hated me? Would the sad teacher with only one friend now be the even sadder teacher with no friends at all?

I sipped my coffee and sulked.

Why should I be the one to make everything all right?

Who should I apologise to?

And what for?

I was too pathetic to know what to do.

And do you know what? I'm so pathetic that, as I sat there, I found myself scanning the passing faces, in a sick hope that Wes might appear. He knew the date of my departure, and though I knew in my heart he wouldn't show up, part of me kept hoping. I could picture him running towards me, pushing his way through indignant crowds, hugging me and laughing. How Maria would stare, as he'd plausibly explain why he hadn't called me again. She'd shake her head as he held my hand and produced the hundred dollars his dishonest flatmate had 'borrowed'. I would happily agree to Wes's plea to stay in Vancouver for another month with him. Charlie would understand. He'd give a generous smile, and he would graciously use his influence to change my flight date. We would all hug like happy, civilised adults, and then I'd set off for a month of bliss with my golden lover.

And after a month of bliss, sure anything could happen, couldn't it?

Unfortunately, the only blond heads to cross my line of vision were in a pack of Scandinavian boy scouts, all, for some reason imitating the Swedish chef from the Muppet Show.

I toyed with my coffee and sulked some more.

My plane was the first to leave. I was glad when the time came for me to go. Maria and Charlie walked me to the final limit, the glass cubicle where I had to show my boarding card, and beyond which they could not pass. Maria had a few hours to wait for her flight so she had decided to stay land-side with Charlie for another while. I had a few minutes to spare, but there wasn't a lot to say. There was no point in lingering. It was preferable to spend the last few minutes of my holiday wandering aimlessly in the duty-free shop, rather than hanging around in the awkward silence that hovered between us. Maria gave me a long hug, and wished me a safe journey. I could see that she was disappointed in me, but she wisely said nothing. Charlie began to shake my hand formally, and then changed his mind and hugged me instead. A big, strong, bear hug, short but tight. We said our goodbyes, and wished each other well. I handed my ticket to the faceless uniformed person at the desk, and crossed the great divide. I walked to the first turn, and looked back for a final wave, but Maria and Charlie were gone.

So now, here I am, travelling home at a cruising speed of several hundred miles per hour. Several hundred miles per hour too fast. The in-flight movie is half over. You know the type they show on aeroplanes. Like Walter, airlines don't like to risk emotion. As a result the films they select are rather limited. Nothing too scary. Nothing too sad. Nothing too funny. Usually a 'romantic comedy', undemanding and totally forgettable, generally starring some famous but have-been actors. Sometimes I think that perhaps the airlines of the world only have one movie, and they show it over and over, year after year, hoping that no one will ever notice, as it is so bland.

Bland. Now there's a nice word. And it brings me around nicely to the food.

I've just eaten my meal. The highlight of my trip. Not. I'm sure you know the kind. The flight attendants smile their practised smile and offer the choice – beef or chicken. You don't wonder which will be the nicest; you just try to figure out which will be the least awful, craning your neck to see what your fellow-travellers have chosen, wondering if perhaps by some miracle one of the options will be edible. I chose the beef, and it was truly awful. It reminded me of the food with which my misguided parents fed me on our first trip abroad, when

I was thirteen. We went camping in Brittany, a great adventure in those days. There we were, August, in a fertile agricultural area, with the finest of fresh produce bursting from the ground all around us. There were fields of sweetcorn and artichokes stretching for miles. Plump, healthy chickens scrabbled and clucked in every farmyard. Fat, bright-eyed fish flopped around every picturesque fishing harbour, begging to be caught and eaten. But in the midst of all this plenty, what were we, the Hurley family from Cork, eating? I'll tell you. We were eating canned stews and Spam, bought in Dunnes Stores, and carried all the way from Ireland. The contents of these cans were carefully dispensed into our only saucepan, where they got to sit for forty minutes until they were half-heated by our tiny blue gas cooker. I suppose it wasn't all bad. After forty minutes waiting we were all famished and would have eaten anything. We often found ourselves squabbling, God help us, over the last pink, over-processed morsels. Once, Sean and I didn't speak for a whole day, because I felt he got a thicker slice of Spam than I did.

This fine fare we washed down with water purified by tiny blue tablets, added by my careful mum. They certainly worked – the water tasted so bad that no one drank more than a token sip, and thus we were at no risk of the deadly unmentionable foreign diseases which terrified my poor parents.

Anyway, some things never change. Here I am, twenty years on, eating similar food, but at least this time, I can deaden the taste with my personal, complimentary, very small bottle of cheap and nasty red wine. (Though I don't know why, when I've paid seven hundred Euro for the privilege of sitting here, they have the nerve to call anything 'complimentary'.)

Along with the stew and the wine, my tray contained five other fiddly plastic capsules, each offering another tasteless little gem. There was a dry bread roll, insipid, whitish and blobby, a heavily salted cracker with some plastic cheese, and a brightly coloured concoction that may have been a portion of trifle. This last was adorned with lots of red, red cherries and a small hillock of puffed-up artificial cream. After lifting the plastic covers and revealing these wonders, I lost hope, and so will never know what the two unopened ones contained. I spent some time idly musing (a lot of my life seems to be spent in idle musing), wondering whether the airline chefs have an annual competition to see who can offer the least appetising food in the least environmentally friendly packaging.

After the ordeal of the food, I sat back and people watched. There was a little boy close by, and though I watched him for several minutes, I never saw him raise his head from his hand-held computer game. He was pressing buttons with one hand, and using the other to feed himself from his plastic tray. Occasionally he gave a small sigh, or a little animal grunt of glee, but otherwise there wasn't much sign of intelligent life. All this time he was watched by his adoring mother, who smiled indulgently at the top of his head and apparently thought that this was normal behaviour.

Across the aisle sat a really lovey dovey couple, all hugs and kisses, who ate from each other's plates and drank from each other's glasses, as if there were no longer a clear boundary between them. The girl was young and beautiful, with slim tanned feet curled up underneath her. Her toenails were painted a deep maroon colour, and just above her left ankle I glimpsed a tattoo of a tiny blue bird. Her lover was dark and handsome in a sultry, sensuous, Lawrence of Arabia kind of a way. (Or was Lawrence of Arabia blond? Or am I just obsessed with blond men?) They sat shoulder to shoulder, and seemed totally unaware of their surroundings, absorbed as they were in each other. I wasn't close enough to decipher any of their conversation, but it involved lots of whispers, and little giggles. Every now and then he gently stroked her neck, and she responded by inclining her head towards him, touching his cheek with hers. I was sickened, but am honest enough to admit that naked jealousy may have played a part in this reaction. I found myself humming the refrain to a song I heard years ago.

'Keep young and beautiful.
It's your duty to be beautiful.
Keep young and beautiful,
If you want to be loved.'

Still, sick-making though the young couple were, it could have been worse. At least the earth mother and her brood from my outward journey hadn't reappeared. But how could they? No doubt they are by now firmly ensconced in a commune, hugging trees, eating brown rice and chanting meaningful mantras to passing frogs and lizards. Well anyway, commune or not, I'm relieved that they haven't come along to share their bodily odours with me one more time. Been there. Done that. Bought the gas mask.

All this time, while I was thinking these bad thoughts about people I've never spoken to, one hard-working flight attendant worked doggedly. All his colleagues had disappeared, perhaps to have mad passionate sex in the toilets for all I know. Or maybe they were chatting up the captain, distracting him from his important job of flying me home safely. Anyway, this one guy, the one who was still working, was young so I suppose that's why he got no rest. He, poor man, had the job of parading the aisles, holding aloft different items, which it seems we could have if we beckoned him. First it was hot towels, then more 'complimentary' cheap wine, and finally mineral water, before beginning the circle again with more hot towels. I suppose it wouldn't have been correct to cry his wares aloud, so he just pointed with his free hand, and wore all the time, as if to encourage us, a plastered-on smile, that had somehow changed, by the time of his third circuit, into a leer.

Everyone else in my field of vision is even more boring than those I've just described, so I give up. I'm going to sleep, and when I wake, I should be closer to Ireland than Canada, and my holiday will be officially over.

Keep young and beautiful.

I was young once, but I never was beautiful.

Everyone gets to be young. The beauty part is reserved for a select few.

No sultry vision of a lover was ever going to stroke my neck, and caress my eyes with his.

(Except for Wes, and it doesn't count if he's only doing it for a free meal and the chance to nick my emergency cash.)

No man that I could truly love would ever love me back.

I think that I was picked out at birth, and marked with an invisible but indelible mark.

The sad one.

The lonely one.

What chance did I ever have?

Chapter Twenty-nine

30 August

I've been home for four weeks now. It hasn't exactly been a barrel of laughs.

Mum and Dad were pleased to see me of course. They met me at the airport when I got back. I was glad they were there. Mum hugged me and kissed me, and Dad punched me lightly on the shoulder, the way dads on television do. They asked about my trip. I gave them a quick, edited version, telling them all the things I knew they'd like to hear, skipping the daredevil bits in Whistler, as even in retrospect I knew that would frighten them. And of course there was no mention of Wes. Mum would have scoffed. She'd have been right, but that wouldn't have made it any less hurtful.

Charlie was also airbrushed out of my version of my holidays. If I told Mum that this kind, decent, sane, healthy, employed man fell in love with me, and that I rejected him, I'd never hear the end of it. She'd harp back to him whenever she got vexed at me. Like nuclear waste, this sad story was best encased in concrete and buried for ten thousand years.

Much safer for everyone that way.

Sean had kindly collected my car from the airport and taken it for a badly needed service, and I was relieved at this, as I was too tired to drive. I strapped myself into the back seat of Dad's car, just as I used to when I was a little girl, and listened to the familiar squabbling.

Dad eased himself into the driver's seat, pulled the car keys from his anorak pocket, and held his hand expectantly towards Mum. 'Can I have the car park ticket please, dear?'

'No, Daddy. You have it.'

'I remember quite clearly. I handed it to you.'

'Yes, you did. But I didn't bring my handbag so I gave it back to you.'

Dad heaved himself up from his seat, and produced his wallet from his back trouser pocket. Then he made a big show of emptying the contents onto his knee. He rifled through them and then turned towards me in triumph. 'See, Maeve, I was right again. No ticket. Your poor mum is getting very absent-minded in her old age. I always said we shouldn't be using those aluminium saucepans.'

Mum grunted in a patronising manner. 'It must be in your jacket pocket, then.'

Dad dutifully patted, and then searched each of the

many pockets of his anorak, producing as he did so, a charming selection of little boy rubbish, such as elastic bands, pieces of string, and even, God help us all, a conker. (The last was a bit worrying as this year's conkers are not yet ripe, suggesting that my poor dad has been carrying that particular, shrivelled one around in his left top pocket for most of a year.) No car park ticket appeared though, and Dad gave another little crow of triumph. 'Now dear, that settles it. You must have it. Hand it over.'

Things were beginning to look dangerous. I suspected that even if Mum found that she had the ticket now, she wouldn't produce it, and that she'd risk a penalty payment, rather than admit to being wrong.

'Daddy. I told you already I don't have the ticket. Where would I have put it? My handbag is at home in the airing cupboard, behind the good pink bath towels. There have been dreadful muggings all over this city. If I carry my handbag I might as well tell every criminal for miles around that I want them to have my money. I might as well start handing it out as soon as I step outside the front door. They're all on drugs you know. Crazy from drugs the whole lot of them. They'd knife you as soon as look at you. Or use a syringe. God be with the days when a syringe was just something that might save your life. Nowadays one stab of a syringe and you're as good as dead. If I got one touch from one of those crazy guys' needles, I'd start picking out the hymns for my funeral Mass. "Ave Maria" is always nice. I'd like something by Daniel O'Donnell too, but I suppose it wouldn't be allowed. That Father O'Dwyer is very old-fashioned. If he had his way we'd all be wearing mantillas to Mass again. Mind you, mantillas always suited me. My poor mother, God rest her soul, always said that I looked quite sophisticated with my mantilla on. Not like that Josie Whelan. She always looked like a trollop, my mother used to say, no matter what she wore. I had a lovely black mantilla once. Real lace. I won it for handwriting at school. I always got top marks for handwriting. Sister Perpetua said I had the best handwriting she'd ever seen.'

While Mum reminisced about her former glories as handwriting champion, I could see Dad furtively remove the car park ticket from inside his glasses case, and we drove towards the exit. Mum was gracious in his defeat, and contented herself with a few bickers and aggrieved grunts. She generally won this type of argument, so it was no novelty to her, and she didn't feel the need for serious gloating. Dad drove down the wide sweep of the, oh so familiar, airport hill, and I got my first glimpse of Cork City spread out beneath us. The glimpse that used to thrill me in the old days when I was happy to be home. How I loved that view when I was returning from long trips working abroad when I was a student. Even though the city was usually shrouded in mist or haze, and everything wore a greyish tinge, it was home, and I was always glad to be back. Happy days.

Without consultation, Dad drove me to their house

for a meal. I wouldn't have refused anyway. I needed some loving care, and Mum and Dad are good at that type of thing.

In small doses.

Any more than that and their care becomes cloying, making me feel cross and sick.

Much as I feel after too many caramel lattés.

Not that I'll be having any of them for a while. Lattés haven't quite made it onto the menu of the pubs and coffee shops in my area. It's tea or coffee in the places I frequent, with the most sophisticated rising to decaf.

Poor Mum can't seem to shake off the notion that I don't eat well on holidays, and always thinks I need a course of renutrition on my return. It's as if 'foreign food', which seems OK for everyone except the few million people stranded on our dear green island, isn't quite good enough for her precious daughter.

Unfortunately, my mum has another notion that she can't shake off. This notion made it hard to be enthusiastic when she hugged me again in the hallway, closed the door behind me and said, 'Of course you must be starving. I bet you haven't had a decent meal in weeks. I've cooked your favourite.'

OK, so shepherd's pie was my favourite meal once. But that was when I was seven, and that was a long time ago. My tastes have matured a little since then. In the intervening years I've discovered pesto and olives and ricotta and sundried tomatoes. Harissa and passata have made their way into my store cupboards. (And stayed there, as I'm not quite sure what to do with them.) I have a chorizo sausage in my fridge. It celebrates its second birthday next week. Maybe it will invite the unopened box of arborio rice to its party.

Poor Mum has never in her life cooked a meal that doesn't have carrots or onions in it somewhere. She thinks spaghetti bolognaise is a daring, avant-garde kind of dish to serve. She has never bought any cheese except cheddar or easi-singles in her entire life, and she still makes lemon meringue pie for special guests. (Mind you, that's so old it's probably back in fashion again. And maybe it's cool again to wash it down with Babycham. God help us.) It was nice to be pampered though. Whatever Mum's faults, I know she loves me unconditionally, and who else in this world would do that? Sometimes I take my parents' love for granted. Maybe that's my job though, since I'm their child. They love me and I find fault with them. It's the way the world works.

I sat at the kitchen table and submitted to Mum's fussing, letting her undemanding flow of chat about friends and relatives wash over me like a warm stream. For all my mental bitching, the shepherd's pie was great. It was warm and comforting and just what I needed. I even had seconds, and still had room for a large slice of lemon meringue pie that was produced with a theatrical flourish.

When Mum suggested that I stay the night, I readily agreed. I was tired and jetlagged, and sorry for myself.

I threw myself into my old single bed, in the room I had shared with Niamh for seventeen years. It hadn't been redecorated since I left home, and it was comforting to lie there examining the details in the blue flower-patterned wallpaper that had witnessed my teenage dreams. I found the familiar flawed spot where two petals joined, giving the impression of a broadly smiling cherub. I found the corner over the wardrobe that had a slight damp stain from an old attic leak. I found the faintly pencilled 'P' for Paddy, which I boldly wrote after one particularly romantic night out together. I curled up under the pale blue quilt that was like a dear old friend, and I slept.

Next morning, Mum cooked porridge for my breakfast, topping it with a dab of butter, which melted at once, leaving a puddle of gold floating on the surface. She squeezed fresh orange juice for me, prompting Dad to raise his eyes from *The Examiner*, and comment mildly, 'I'd have liked some of that myself.' Mum replied equally mildly, 'Then get some for yourself. Maeve needs it after her holidays. That foreign food has no vitamins. They store it in huge fridges under the ground until there's not one scrap of goodness left in it at all.' Dad grunted and looked back at his paper; he didn't want orange juice badly enough to leave his armchair and get it for himself.

I finished my porridge and fiddled idly with the fridge magnets in the shape of churches that I had brought from Greece thirteen years ago. I felt no desire to leave. It frightened me when I realised that I was half-tempted to stay longer in this safe, undemanding haven. Listening to their good-natured banter, being half-ignored, like the child I felt myself to be.

After a while though, it came. Mum had held it back valiantly, but in the end she could resist no longer. The dreaded question popped out, just as it always did, as reliable in its annual recurrence as Puck Fair or the Dingle regatta.

'Tell me, Maeve. Did you meet any nice men while you were away?' I know she can't help herself, and is desperate on my account, so it was a bit mean of me to reply, 'Yes. I met lots actually but they were all gay,' knowing it would silence her.

Mum didn't acknowledge my answer. She just tightened her lips and went to the sink to wash the porridge pot. I could tell by her posture that she was cross with me. I knew it was time to leave.

My car was still in the garage and, despite Dad's protestations, I walked the short distance to pick it up. I could call later for the suitcase full of grubby clothes. Knowing Mum, she would probably have my things washed and ironed if I left them there long enough, but for once that was no great treat. After all, I hadn't a whole lot to do in the next weeks, and I didn't particularly want someone else muscling in on the precious few tasks that were available to me.

I needed the walk, and I was glad of the excuse to

leave, without having to go straight home. After I collected the car (how small and light it suddenly seemed), I went to the supermarket, and bought a few essential items of food. Then I drove back to Mum and Dad's to collect my suitcase, thus depriving my socks and knickers of their one chance in life to be ironed. Mum had got over her earlier pique, so I went in for another cup of tea. I knew it was just a temporary truce though. Mum would find another opportunity, and 'the question' would be asked over and over until it was answered to her satisfaction. For now we were friends though, and I left with a portion of shepherd's pie for my dinner, and a slice of lemon meringue pie that would feed a hungry family of four.

When I could think of no more delaying tactics, I drove home slowly, not thinking about the route, just taking the familiar turns automatically. I pulled up in my small gravel driveway, and climbed out of the car. It was a lovely day, and the sea glistened in the mid-morning sun.

I fumbled with the keys that were momentarily unfamiliar, and let myself in to my home. It was a strange feeling, knowing that Charlie and Todd were the last to have been here, in my little house. The place was spotless. Everything was sparkling, just as I left it. There was a note on the table, propped up on the empty milk jug. I rushed to open it, but it was brief and impersonal. I remembered with a start that Charlie and I had never met when he wrote it.

'Hi Maeve. Just a note to tell you that we have had a marvellous time in your home. We hope you enjoyed Vancouver. Perhaps we will have met by the time you read this. If not, thanks again. Charlie and Todd.'

I was strangely disappointed, though it was hard to say why. What was I expecting him to say? What else could he have said? What could he possibly have written to a stranger? 'You have a lovely home and must be a wonderful person.' 'I feel we could make beautiful music together.' 'I've scoured your photo albums, and read your letters and I think I might love you.' Get real, Maeve.

A little touch of nostalgia stopped me from crumpling the note and tossing it into the sink, so I propped it on the mantelpiece, against a little bronze statue of a crying child.

Charlie had gathered any mail that arrived in my absence, and arranged it in a neat pile on the kitchen worktop. I flicked quickly through it without any great interest. Nothing very exciting, mostly money-off vouchers for butter, and great deals on photograph developing. The stub of my pay-cheque, which had gone directly to the bank and was already spent. A note from the dentist saying that he hadn't had the pleasure of my company for six months. A reminder from my insurance company that my insurance is up at the end of the month. There were postcards from

Niamh and Sean, both enjoying family holidays in the Irish countryside, both expressing the thought that my holiday would be much more exciting than theirs. Huh.

I unpacked, and threw most of my clothes into the washing machine, scattering grains of golden Canadian sand all over the floor Charlie had mopped clean. I emptied out my handbag, and realised that, as usual, most of what I was carrying around on my shoulder was actually waste paper – airline ticket stubs, flight boarding cards, Canadian car parking receipts, and ticket stubs from various Vancouver attractions. There were also a few stray Canadian coins that hadn't found their way into the plastic sphere at the airport, to be donated to local charities, and of course my passport, ready to idle away a few more lonely months or years in the dark of my bedroom drawer.

That was it. Twenty minutes after returning home, I'd done all the jobs I needed to do. Four weeks to the new school term, and I had no idea how I would fill them. Wonderful, Maeve. I turned down Charlie's generous offer, and now I was sitting, utterly bored, with nothing to do and no one to do it with.

I could clean my house. Except it was already cleaned to the limit.

I could weed the vegetable patch, but a quick glance out the window showed that Charlie had already done that.

I could go for a walk.

From here to Donegal.

I could read *War and Peace*.

Three times.

I could learn Russian and read it in the original.

I could just sit in my window seat, on the imprint in the cushions made by Charlie's bottom, and wait crossly for the time to pass.

The weeks passed by somehow, as of course they always do, whether I am happy or not. I did lots of gardening, and already much of the vegetable plot is dug and manured, ready for next spring. The weather has been lovely, and I've spent a lot of time on the beach, sitting on my own, catching up on the reading I was too busy for in Vancouver. I've swum a lot and walked a lot and eaten a lot. I've watched the ER reruns on Sky One.

I've spent the required afternoon at each of the aunties' houses, drinking cup after cup of weak, milky tea, not daring to say, 'No, Auntie Mary. I don't feel like tea today. Do you have any latté with caramel?' I've listened to their little clucking noises of insincere pleasure, as they unwrapped their ornamental totem poles, and pretended to wonder how they managed to live so long without such precious treasures.

I've spent a lot of evenings with Sean or my parents, and a lot on my own, sitting on my veranda, reading and sipping cold beer. These have all been perfectly pleasant activities, it's just that they haven't been very exciting, and I've become even more discontented than usual.

About a week ago I got a letter from Charlie. He enclosed some photographs he'd taken on our day out together. There were a few of Maria and myself, tanned and laughing, and one of the three of us, taken by an obliging passing Japanese tourist. I remember it well; the man had fussed over the pose, worrying about backlight, and asking how to turn on the fill-in flash. By the time he felt ready to shoot, Charlie, Maria and I are wearing rather forced smiles, wishing he'd be less particular, and realising we'd have been better to ask someone who wasn't wearing three fancy-looking cameras slung over his shoulders.

I put the photos on the mantelpiece, and went to make myself a cup of coffee. As soon as the coffee was ready, I took the letter out on to the veranda, balanced the coffee on the white railings (a fine art, mastered painfully over many years of scalding errors) and flung myself into my swinging seat. I adjusted my designer sunglasses (outlet store, Vancouver) and settled down for a good read. Not.

> Dear Maeve,
> I hope you had a safe journey home, and that you have happy memories of your time in Vancouver. I am now quite settled back here, and am enjoying the last weeks of my

vacation from the university. Todd's summer camp was very successful, and except for a bruised shin he appears to be uninjured.

How are your vegetables? I watered them before I left, but the weather forecast was for lots of sun, so I hope they didn't suffer too much from drought. Your zucchini were most likely grown into marrows by the time you got home.

Did I mention when I met you that Todd accidentally broke one of your green mugs? I tried lots of stores but had to settle for a similar mug in a slightly darker shade of green. I hope the difference is not too obvious.

I'm enclosing some photographs from the day trip we did with Maria. Do you remember that crazy Japanese guy? He was a riot.

Well, it was nice to have met you and Maria, and I hope you go on to do many successful home swaps. I have many fond memories of my time in Cork.

Regards,

Charlie

All very nice.

All very impersonal.

It was like the letters I used to write to penfriends when I was a teenager; nothing to say, and all said in one carefully written page. Stretched to the limit, with big wide margins and large spaces between the lines.

I don't know why I was disappointed that there was no mention of that last night in Vancouver. The night he told me he loved me. I don't love him. I couldn't love him, so why did I feel slightly cheated by his casual words? Just vanity, I suppose. Vanity and desperation could be a dangerous mix. Lucky I came home when I did.

Maria and Joe came back a few days ago. They invited me over for dinner last night. I went a little shyly, as I felt guilty about the almost row I'd had with Maria, which we'd never really resolved. I'd just got a few chatty postcards from Texas, and otherwise we hadn't been in touch. I feared that the incident would hang in the air between us.

I shouldn't have worried though. Maria rushed out to greet me as soon as she heard my car in the drive. She hugged me and apologised. 'I'm sorry, Maeve. I shouldn't have hassled you that day in Vancouver. It was none of my business and I should have kept quiet.'

'No, Maria. It's fine.'

'I don't know what came over me. I just couldn't stop myself.'

'Maria, it's fine. Really.'

'Can we forget I ever spoke?'

'Of course we can. You meant well. And anyway, it was half my fault. I shouldn't be so sensitive.'

She gave a sly smile. 'Do you think you're sensitive?'

I lied blatantly. 'Me sensitive? Nah. I'm tough as nails.'

We looked at each other for a moment, and then finished my sentence together.

'Not!'

We laughed and hugged again.

'Honestly, Maria, let's just forget it. It never happened.'

Maria smiled and said tentatively, 'OK, I promise. We'll forget it. But before we do, I need to say one thing. Charlie really did like you. When you left on the plane that day, I could see it. He was really sorry to see you go. We watched your plane take off, and he was like a little lost puppy dog watching you fly away.' She hesitated and eyed me carefully, to see if I was going to react badly again, but I showed no emotion. 'I just thought I should tell you. For the record.'

Oh dear. I wasn't planning on telling Maria about what Charlie had said on that last night in Vancouver, but a sudden fear came to me that perhaps he had confided in her, in those few hours they had together before her flight. Did he plead his case in an effort to get her even more on his side? That would have made her doubly cross at me. Still, she didn't seem cross any more, and I didn't want to argue with her again, as that was an argument that was going nowhere. Some things are just too complicated. Instead I just shrugged, and we went in for our meal.

We were having Joe's tried-and-tested speciality, lasagne, garlic bread and salad. (Forget milk quotas, and civil service jobs. I want a man who can cook.) As we ate, Joe entertained us with stories of the tutors on his course, and the clichés that filled the course manual, having great fun in exaggerating the easily mocked accent of the Deep South. The evening passed quickly. It was great to have Joe and Maria back, as I'd missed them more than I'd realised. I left feeling better than I had for weeks, happy in the knowledge that Maria and I were friends, and that next week we'd be back to our regular girlie night out.

Now, I need to do some serious late night reading. It's my last chance for this luxury, because tomorrow is my last morning lie-in. Then it's back to the old routine of work.

I can't wait.

Oh yes, I forgot. Something has been niggling me since I came home from Maria and Joe's house. They were unusually lovey-dovey to each other, even for them, and once or twice I caught them exchanging looks that I couldn't interpret. At first I thought that perhaps they'd done some soppy marriage vow renewal lark in Texas. Then, I realised that Maria had no pre-dinner drink or after-dinner drink, and just sipped a half glass of wine while we ate. That's not the Maria I know and love. Maybe she's trying to get pregnant, and cautious girl that she is, she's avoiding alcohol.

Or maybe she's already pregnant, after her romantic sojourn in Texas.

Then again maybe she's just getting over a tummy bug.

Or perhaps she's decided that as she's my only friend she needs to start taking better care of her health.

Chapter Thirty

First day's teaching over. Only one hundred and eighty-two more to go until the summer holidays. That's kind of cynical, isn't it? All the doting parents put their precious darlings in my care, and that's how I react. After only five and a half hours, I'm counting the days until I'm free of them.

Well, really, it wasn't that bad. I have a nice group this year. I know half of them from last year, and the new half are so happy to be promoted at last, after two years in their previous classroom, that they are touching in their eagerness to please me. They are probably relieved that the first day is over, and I haven't mentioned soccer yet.

Most of the children have smart new uniforms, and those who didn't had their old ones cleaned and pressed to within an inch of their lives. One poor girl, the youngest of five sisters, had a skirt that was shiny from wear, and a jumper with transparent elbows. Both were spotlessly clean, and she walked in to the classroom with her shiny, pig-tailed head held high.

The children's faces are tanned, and polished looking, as everyone makes a special effort on the first morning. I know that tomorrow half of them will turn up with traces of milk and cereal around their mouths, and unkempt hair. Within a week the suntans will be fading, revealing greyish skin ready for the long winter ahead.

The bright new schoolbags are bursting with new pencil cases, new lunchboxes and new schoolbooks carefully covered with clear sticky film. Some of the sticky film isn't even wrinkled and bubbly.

I listened attentively to each child's tale of their holidays. Some described trips abroad, some described day trips around here, some innocently invented impossibly exotic voyages in an effort to impress me. I listened to the carefully repeated plotlines of every film that played in Cork during the months of July and August. I heard about a new baby sister, a new baby brother, a new puppy, a new car and a dead granny. We stacked the textbooks in the cupboard, and left them in high neat piles, waiting their turn to be used. I said a quick prayer of thanks that I'd cleaned the cupboards in June. We wrote some holiday stories, and did some simple undemanding maths, all in an effort to ease the children, and me, gently into this new world of work, after the freedom of the holidays.

Nothing could ease me gently into the staffroom. I lingered in my classroom for a few minutes during our first break, and then found a tiny flicker of masochism that made me join my dear colleagues. It is frightening how much the same the staffroom was, as if Mr Flynn, Pat and Theresa hadn't left for the holidays at all, but just remained in suspended animation, waiting for September to arrive, waiting for me to come back for more punishment. Small details had changed of course, but nothing of any magnitude. The dodgy kettle has at last been replaced. Someone cleaned the windows while I was away. There's a new year planner pinned to the noticeboard, so whenever I want I can mentally tick off the days, wishing my life away.

Pat was still wearing the navy V-necked jumper he wore all of last year. And the grey pants that look like an overgrown version of the boys' school uniform. As usual he was reading the sports pages of *The Examiner*. As usual, he thought it necessary to share some juicy titbits with me.

'Guess what, Maeve. Man. United are negotiating with Barcelona for a new striker. The deal is nearly done.'

'Great, Pat.'

'Yeah, isn't it? He might be here in time for the Arsenal match. Wouldn't it be mighty altogether?'

'Great, Pat.'

'Still. Even if he misses Highbury, they say he'll surely make the first Champions League match. That's what it's all about this season. The European matches are mostly on Wednesdays. I'll let you know when the first one is on.'

'Great, Pat.'

Pat returned to his paper, happy that he had made my day with his generous sharing of football knowledge. Oh dear, I can let my eyes glaze over as often as I like, I can think rude thoughts and smile, but still Pat will tell me about the soccer. That will never change.

Mr Flynn and his wife decided to change their car instead of having a holiday, so they just took day trips in the locality, enjoying picnics on the fine days. Not terribly exciting, of course, but they enjoyed themselves, and I know that as the term rolls slowly on, I'll get to hear every single dreary detail. By Halloween I will know the price of a cup of tea in Ballycotton, and the name of a good place to buy four-ply knitting wool in Skibbereen. Today's virtual visit was to Clonakilty.

'Were you ever in Clonakilty, Maeve?'

I smiled politely, feigning interest. 'Just once, Mr Flynn. It was years ago. My friend Maria and I went there one time on a camping holiday.'

'Maureen and I had a lovely lunch in Clonakilty one day in August. Bacon and cabbage. Three thick slices of bacon each. And lovely spuds. Balls of flour they were. Six euro only. And they threw in a free cup of tea. Did you and your friend eat in any nice restaurants when you were there that time?'

'Yes. We found a few nice places all right.' (We were saving our money for drink, so we lived on crisps and bananas. The only time we saw the inside of a restaurant was when we sneaked in to use the toilets.)

Mr Flynn nodded in a roguish man-of-the-world kind of way. 'The pubs are nice too, aren't they?'

'Yes, Mr Flynn. Maria and I saw some lovely pubs while we were there.' (We went on a pub crawl one night, visiting eleven of them before we got too drunk to count.)

'Those little side streets are so quaint. Tourists must love them.'

'I bet they do, Mr Flynn.' (I hope no tourist ever dared to go down the one where Maria and I hid to avoid some drunken locals she'd been chatting up in one of the pubs we'd visited. We were there for ages, and in the end we both had to have an emergency wee behind some already smelly dustbins.)

'Mind you, it's quite a compact little town. You'd walk through it in ten minutes.'

God this conversation was hard work. 'Yes, you're right, Mr Flynn. It is quite small.' (It didn't seem very small that night as we staggered around for what felt like hours, trying to remember where we'd pitched our tent.)

'And that monument in the square. A fine piece of work altogether.'

'Yes, Maria and I loved that monument too.'

'Wasn't it put up in memory of one of the United Irishmen? What was his name again?'

'I'm not quite sure, Mr Flynn. I didn't get that close to it.' (In fact I got very close, but I couldn't quite read the inscription as I was supporting Maria at the time and ineffectually rubbing her back. I suppose she didn't read it either, as she was too busy throwing up all over the pedestal.)

'Tadhg O'Donovan. That was his name. Poor fellow came to a very sticky end.'

'You're right. I think he did.' (That's for sure. Whatever did the poor guy do to deserve to be preserved in a draughty square with Maria vomiting beer and cheese-and-onion crisps at his feet?)

Theresa arrived into the staff room just then, giving me a brief respite. After a few seconds though, I found myself wishing she'd leave so I could go back to being innocently bored by Pat and Mr Flynn. Theresa was wearing a new scrunchy in her hair. It was a deep wine colour, like day-old blood. She was wearing matching wine-coloured tights, thick and woolly. Odd this, as it was only the first of September, and the sun was putting on its annual last-minute heat show to make us feel worse about being back at work.

With every passing year Theresa seems to be more gushy and more irritating. Her simpering smugness becomes almost unbearable, driving me to new levels of frustration. Or could it be that as I age, my already low tolerance level drops even further? Whichever, a good Christian should not entertain thoughts such as I entertain about Theresa.

Theresa and Michael spent the summer in the Gaeltacht, teaching Irish. (Lucky I didn't listen to Mr Flynn and go too. If I had to spend the summer with

Theresa and Michael, I'm not sure I'd ever recover.) Typical Theresa – her only two months of potential freedom, and she spent them teaching! She probably even enjoyed it. It also doubled their salaries, so their joint bank account is filling up nicely, and now they have enough for a deposit on a house.

'A nice semi-detached one. Something modest. Just to start us off. We wouldn't live there forever of course. It's just for the first few years. Until we can afford to build the home we really want.'

Theresa gave us her simpering little smile, and waited until we were all paying attention, for her big announcement. 'Michael and I have set the date for our wedding at last. The fifteenth of August. It's a Saturday. The year after next.'

Mr Flynn, Pat and I muttered our congratulations. It's hard to rustle up any real interest when you have a terrible feeling you are going to hear more on the subject. A lot more.

'We have everything booked. The church is booked for two o'clock. We didn't want it to be too late.'

Pat suddenly jumped to attention. 'God, Theresa. You're a bit ahead of yourself. I think you've made a terrible mistake.'

Theresa looked at him in shock. 'What do you mean, a mistake? Michael and I have been going out together since our second week in Mary Immaculate College.' She gave another little simper. 'We know we are right for each other.' She sighed. 'I knew the day I

286

met Michael that one day we'd be married. I just knew. Michael knew too. He didn't tell me until later though. He's a bit shy, you know. I do my best to bring him out of himself. He says he doesn't need anyone but me. He says I'm the centre of his universe.'

I was feeling sick in my stomach. Pat was looking bemused, when suddenly the penny dropped.

'Oh, no, Theresa. I don't mean that getting married is a mistake. I'm sure you and Michael will be very happy. It's just the date you've chosen is a mistake. It's all wrong. The Charity Shield could be on that day. Don't bother inviting me to your wedding if it's the day of the Charity Shield.'

Theresa dropped the simpering pretty fast, and spoke sarcastically. 'Sorry Pat, I forgot to check the soccer schedules when I was planning the best day of my life. It just slipped my mind.'

'Well Theresa. It's not just me. Don't say you weren't warned. If it's the day of the Charity Shield you'll be on your own. You wouldn't miss the big match either, would you, Maeve?'

It's true I'd sooner be in a smoky pub watching a match than in a church watching Theresa getting married, but that's not saying much. I'd also sooner be doing the ironing. Or having my bikini line waxed. Or getting my wisdom teeth extracted. Without an anaesthetic.

Theresa seemed to be waiting for an answer. I smiled a bright, false smile. 'Oh don't worry Theresa. I wouldn't miss your wedding for the world. No match could keep me away. And Pat will be there too. He could watch the highlights of the match that night.'

Pat looked at me in horror. 'I'm sorry Maeve. That's not funny. Highlights indeed. I haven't missed the Charity Shield since 1971. I even went to it once. Myself and two of the lads got tickets from my uncle, and we went over on the *Innisfallen*. 1980 it was. Liverpool versus West Ham. Great game. Liverpool won 1–0.'

Theresa wasn't pleased at the way the conversation was developing. 'Well, Pat, I'm glad to know that you have such a good memory. Maybe this year you won't forget every second occasion when it's your turn for yard duty.'

Wow. That was a bit below the belt. Especially in front of Mr Flynn, who was technically on yard duty as she spoke but was in fact sitting at the window keeping half an eye on the children happily playing in the sunshine.

Pat missed the barb though. '1980 was a funny old year. The FA Cup final wasn't on RTE for some reason. A strike or something.'

Theresa looked at him in exaggerated mock horror. 'Oh, Pat. Whatever did you do? How did you cope without seeing the FA cup final?'

It was Pat's turn to look horrified. 'God, Theresa don't be mad. Of course I didn't miss it. A few of us borrowed my friend's Dad's car, and we drove to

Portlaoise to watch the match in a pub there. They had the BBC there then of course. Poor old Arsenal. It was their third consecutive final. West Ham beat them. 1–0.'

'Tell me more.' Unfortunately Theresa's sarcasm was lost on our Pat.

'OK so, Theresa. Will I tell you about the second semi-final replay? That was a good one. Arsenal against Liverpool. Alan Sunderland scored after thirteen seconds.'

How does he remember these things? The situation was looking dangerous. From Pat's corner there loomed the danger of an in-depth report of a match that had been played over twenty years before, but I knew if I interrupted him, I could be unleashing an unstoppable torrent of gushy wedding plans. I looked to Mr Flynn in desperation. Maybe he'd like a little chat about Irish grammar. Or maybe we could discourse on statues in Skibbereen.

Poor Mr Flynn. Sometimes his role in the staffroom is that of a benevolent parent resignedly settling the squabbles of his fractious children. 'Pat, leave Theresa alone. And don't worry Theresa. I'll get Maureen to say a few novenas, and maybe they'll arrange the match for another day. And look on the bright side. At least your wedding won't be clashing with the All-Ireland. Wouldn't that be a disaster altogether?'

Theresa replied with bad grace. 'I suppose so.'

Mr Flynn wasn't giving up that easily. He was going to restore harmony if it killed him. What a pity he has no idea that most of the time he unwittingly adds to the disharmony in our midst.

'Now Theresa, have you got your wedding frock yet? Tell Maeve about your frock. Aren't you just dying to hear about Theresa's frock, Maeve.'

I was too weary to object. 'OK, then, Theresa. Let's have it. Tell me about your frock.'

Theresa knew well that I didn't want to hear about her 'frock', but she didn't let that stop her. 'Well Maeve, I haven't bought it yet, but I know what I want. It'll be white of course. I don't like those cream ones. You know what they say about cream wedding dresses.'

I didn't actually, but didn't want to know either so I let it pass.

'Snow white. Michael insists on that. And full length of course. And I'll have a veil. A short one.'

Pat interrupted. 'You know, Theresa, you might be in luck. I've just remembered. The Charity Shield was on a Sunday last year and the year before.'

Theresa cast her grey eyes heavenwards and continued. 'I'll have a small bouquet. Red rosebuds.'

Mr Flynn beamed. 'Now, Maeve. There's a job for you. Haven't you got roses in your garden? Couldn't you do a bouquet for Theresa?'

Theresa looked at him in horror. She was right too. My roses are always rather scabby, infested with greenfly and terribly afflicted with blackspot. If Theresa had a bouquet made of them her snow white dress would need a good dose of the Ariel biological before she was halfway up the aisle.

'No. Thanks anyway, Maeve. My mother is friends with a florist in Douglas. She will be doing all the flowers. We're having red roses in the church too. With small sprays of gypsophila. The arrangements for the tables in the hotel will be the same. Everything will be co-ordinated.'

I sat there listening to her droning on and on. What a penance!

I sat back in my seat, and closed my eyes as much as I dared. How I wished I was on a golden beach in Vancouver with Wes licking my shoulder.

Or in a bar with Charlie, sipping a beer and sharing a joke.

Or on a bike, whizzing through Stanley Park with Maria.

Or in a shady wood, on my own, on a warm summer's day.

Oh to be anywhere but in that dreary staffroom with Theresa!

How will I stick two years of Theresa's wedding plans? I'll be in a home for the bewildered by Christmas if she keeps this up.

One of the very many things I hate about Theresa, is something, which, I admit, is a good character trait in some ways. I could probably do with a touch of it myself. It's just that she's always so certain of what she wants. She makes up her mind, and then plans accordingly; no wavering; no dithering. What she wants now, much as I despise it, is exactly what she wanted last year and the year before. She'd probably wanted it when she was seven. And, what's even more annoying, I know she's going to get it, she's that sort of girl. I know that she will buy her wedding dress very soon, and even though it will be hideous, she will love it, and she will still love it the year after next, when the time comes to wear it. In twenty years time she will take it out of her wardrobe, and even though it will still be hideous and also yellowing, she will love it as much as ever.

Theresa will buy her pretty house, and decorate it with pretty pastel florals. She will keep it clean and organised, never running out of milk or sugar or vacuum cleaner bags. She will wash her net curtains every two weeks. Her skirting boards will always gleam. She'll have three perfect children, and die a peaceful death, at a suitably advanced age, surrounded by her weeping family, who won't even argue about her will.

My life is so higgledy piggledy. I'm all over the place, and she, the hated one, follows an even and clear course, straight and true, never wavering, never losing the plot.

Despite all of my plans to be the perfect teacher this year, by lunchtime I was wondering how to occupy my class until home time. But was Theresa similarly afflicted? Fat chance! After she told us of her life plans, she made it clear that she has her lesson notes for the year already written. She waved her folder in front of our eyes, so we know it's true. Her notes were beautifully typed on a word processor, with cute little graphics at the beginning of each subject section. Theresa knows what her class will be doing in June. It will be well-structured, and fun, and they will love it. I will have to suffer for another year, listening to the gushing praise of the parents outside my window, as they wait to collect their little darlings from her class.

'He's so lucky to have Miss Hourigan teaching him. She's so kind and gentle, and does great things with them.'

'Oh, yes. Jennifer just loves her. She can't wait to get to school in the mornings.'

'Yes, and Niall talks about her all the time. He wants to be a teacher when he grows up, and it's all because of Miss Hourigan.'

They go on and on, distracting me with their endless eulogies, making me feel sick and jealous and cross and mean, all at the same time.

I suppose I should look on the bright side. If I didn't hate Theresa so much, I'd have even more hatred to lavish on myself.

Oh, I forgot to mention. There is some major news from the Castlelough staffroom. Theresa has given up knitting for a while. 'Michael has enough jumpers for the moment.' I could have told her that. He had enough nine creations ago. When she presented him with her most recent work of art, a thick, cream-and-brown striped concoction, he must have reached breaking point, and begged her to stop.

Unfortunately, she hasn't decided to give her flying fingers a rest. She's taken up tapestry instead, and she's working on a set of cushion covers for the unbought chairs, to go in the unpurchased house, in the as yet undeveloped field, in which she will one day live. Cows still roam freely, munching lush green grass, in the space where these cushions will finally rest.

I watch Theresa selecting the colours, painstakingly measuring out the lengths of wool, and squinting slightly as she threads the blunt tapestry needle. She makes perfect little stitches, and each time she carefully pulls the needle through, I can see another few seconds of my life passing me by. In my worst nightmares, I see myself here in thirty years time, still listening to the same people, still wishing I were elsewhere, still watching Theresa's works of art unfolding before my ageing, sickened eyes.

Chapter Thirty-one

It's now half-way through October. Time and my life are passing me by.

Thirteen shopping days left until Halloween. I'm serious. A disc jockey announced that on the radio this morning. And he wasn't even trying to be funny. Halloween isn't like it used to be in the olden days. Long ago when I was a child it involved ten minutes trick or treating at the neighbours' houses, half an hour of snap apple, and then off to bed. Very happy we were too. We were easily pleased back then.

Now it's a different kettle of fish. Now houses have to be decorated. People buy Halloween lights and hang them in their windows for a week before the big night. Lines of fat orange pumpkins festoon every doorway. Glow-in-the-dark skeletons and witches dangle from every bush and tree in suburbia.

Get real guys. It's Halloween, not Christmas.

Then there's the dressing up. When I was a child you got to be a witch or a cat. If you didn't want to be one of those, you stayed at home. And the witches were just dressed in torn binbags, with the cats resplendent in black polo necks and leggings. We had no face paint, but soot worked very well, thank you very much. Now the talk in the schoolyard is all, 'What are you dressing up as for Halloween?' People go out and buy costumes. Every year the streets are awash with Barbies and Action Men and fairies. Last year a tiny purple Barney came to my door looking for sweets. What's Barney got to do with Halloween, for God's sake?

Then there's the rough element. Everyone has to have bangers and smoke bombs. I found a child in the schoolyard last week with an aerosol. It was labelled, 'Fart Spray'. Who thinks of these things? He was quite aggrieved when I relieved him of it.

'But Miss. I need it. It was for Halloween.'

'Sorry Shane, you'll just have to try to have a happy Halloween without your can of fart spray.'

'But Miss.'

I ignored his pleas, but next day he arrived at my classroom door with a cheeky grin and a note from his Dad:

> Dear Miss Hurley,
> Could you please give Shane back his can of fart spray? It is only a bit of fun. Were you never young yourself?

I didn't feel like taking on this particular, belligerent dad, so I reluctantly returned the offending item. I despair of humanity though. I truly do.

Long ago when I was a child, 'egg' wasn't a verb. Now it appears that it is. Children boast, 'Last year I egged nine people.' 'Yah. That's nothing. I egged ten people, four houses, six cars and a bus.' Halloween doesn't seem to be complete without this 'egging' lark.

Have I got a sense of humour failure?

Or is it just not funny?

But then maybe the poor kids are driven to new extremes in an effort to get thrills. I overheard a mother in the school yard the other day. After she had told the world her secret recipe for barmbrack, she shared her other secret. Apparently she puts four rings in it, and engineers things so that each of her children gets one. Where's the fun in that? Surely the whole point of getting the ring is that no one else has one?

Am I the only one who feels that the world has gone mad?

I could moan on for hours about Halloween, and its evils. But you're in luck. I won't.

I am almost certain that Maria is pregnant, or trying to be, though she's said nothing. We still go to the pub once a week, and have a great time, but now Maria drives, and doesn't drink. She says it's because Joe is busy at his new job, and she doesn't like to ask him to collect us. Somehow that doesn't ring true, and whenever I offer to drive, so she can have a few jars, she refuses, politely, but very firmly. I'm a little bit hurt about this. I know there are all kinds of reasons that people don't announce their pregnancies too early, but I feel that as her best friend, she might just have told me, knowing I could keep it secret if that's what she wished. After all, I knew her before Joe did. I knew her when she was madly in love with a hairy, spaced-out 'poet', who put her down at every opportunity. I knew her when she thought that lycra leggings were suitable attire for people over the age of five. I knew her when watching Dallas was the highlight of her week. Surely all that should count for something.

We talk a lot about our trip to Vancouver and the great times we had there, but Charlie doesn't get mentioned much. Last week though, he slipped into our conversation.

Maria had been moaning about our damp weather, and then she casually mentioned, 'It's been very warm in Vancouver recently. A late Indian summer.'

'How do you know, Maria? Do you still log on to the Vancouver websites?'

I could see in her transparent face her struggle between a simple convenient lie and a more complicated truth. As usual with Maria, truth won.

'Well no, actually. Charlie told me.'

'You've been talking to Charlie?'

'No, of course not talking. He wrote to me.'

I was still amazed. 'You write to Charlie?'

'No, not really. He just sent me a little note, and he mentioned the weather.'

I still couldn't quite understand. 'Why would Charlie be writing you a note?'

She shrugged. 'I wrote to him when I got back from Texas. Just to thank him for the swap, and to say how much I had enjoyed it. A few weeks ago he replied. Don't worry, it's not a big deal. He just sent me a polite little note.' She smiled. 'You thought I fancied him, didn't you?'

I didn't know that she had copped on to this aberrant little thought of mine. I blushed slightly. 'Well, you kept going on about how nice he was. What was I supposed to think?'

'Well. . .' She stopped. We both knew where this line of conversation could lead. This was the road to nowhere. Then she laughed. 'At least I made it clear I didn't fancy Wes.'

I laughed too. 'Yes, Maria, you're right. I was always quite clear about your feelings towards Wes. He wasn't that bad though.'

'Yeah, but would you smother your mother for him?'

Poor Mum. She wouldn't find that very funny. I pretended to consider. 'Mmm. Maybe. He was a fine thing. He had sexy, sharp little teeth.'

Maria gave a small shudder of revulsion. 'Don't start me about Wes, Maeve. Just don't start me. Another beer?'

Maria went up to the bar, and I was free to think about Wes. God I know he was a waster, but he was so good-looking. He said all the right things. I still remember his innocent little touches and caresses. He once stroked my cheek as if it were the most delicate surface in the entire world. He brushed sand from my belly button with gentle strokes. He kissed my shoulder, and the delicate skin on the inside of my elbow.

Some nights I wake up and think how nice it would be if Wes were there to hug and hold me.

Some nights I dream that he arrives at my door, declaring undying love.

Some nights I wake up and think what a fool I was to fall for his easy charms.

*

I think about Charlie too sometimes. About that night when he told me he loved me. I wonder if he's sorry he said it. I wonder if Todd is with him, and if he's sad about Melinda. I wonder if he thinks fondly of his holiday in my home. And the few days we spent together. He was a nice guy. Such a pity that things turned out the way they did. Such a pity I didn't love him. If he lived closer to here, we'd probably be friends, go for the odd drink, or a meal, perhaps to the pictures or the theatre. We could walk on the beach, and we could sit together on my veranda, chatting companionably, watching the sun set over the grey sea.

It was too dramatic, though, the way things happened. I'd have liked a few more days with him, but I didn't want to take the big step of cancelling my flight, which would have turned it into an issue, rather than a casual arrangement. After what he'd said, the pressure of being with him, and without Maria, would have been too much. I'd have been embarrassed. I hate being embarrassed.

If he hadn't said he'd loved me, would I have stayed and been his friend?

Could he ever have been more than a friend to me?

Should I have kissed him, that night when his lips were so close to mine?

Anyway, it's all over now. Charlie and I will probably exchange Christmas cards this year, and perhaps even next year a jolly, meaningless greeting will cross the ocean, to gather dust on a festive yuletide mantelpiece. Then we'll never see each other, or hear from one another again. We are like satellites that briefly came together, and then spun off into different orbits, different worlds. Ships passing in the night. All that old cliché stuff.

I went to my cousin Pauline's wedding last Saturday. The invitation had been on my kitchen shelf for weeks, haunting me. Long ago, wedding invitations used to be addressed to 'Maeve and Partner' but I suppose after so many years of me showing up partnerless, this was becoming a bit of a charade. Pauline only wrote 'Maeve' on the invitation line, making the word look bigger than it was by giving it a few extra swirls with her calligraphy pen. She's a nice girl though, and she did ring me up to say that if I wanted to bring a friend, that would be fine by her, but I had to decline.

Who was I supposed to bring?

The postman?

The plumber?

(Well definitely not him. He ripped me off when he came to repair my central heating. Ninety-five euro, and he was only there for five minutes! And in that time he had a cup of tea, a fag and six Fig Rolls. And the central heating still isn't that great.)

Could I possibly invite some handsome stranger from the supermarket, tempting him with the prospect of a meal of dried-up beef, promising him a night of sweaty dancing to 'Tie a Yellow Ribbon' and 'Que Sera'?

I think not.

Anyway I didn't have to go entirely on my own. I had Mum and Dad. And Sean and Eimear. And Niamh and her husband Brian. And countless cousins whose weddings I've been to, the names of whose spouses I've managed to forget.

It was awful. I travelled to the church with Mum and Dad, all of us in our finery, most unsuitably dressed for the driving wind and rain that persisted for the entire day. We shivered in the unheated church, and Mum passed the time by whispering nasty comments about Pauline's intended in-laws. When Pauline finally arrived, we gave the appropriate sighs as she sailed up the aisle. As usual, the organist could have been playing 'Three Blind Mice' for all the attention anyone paid. Pauline looked predictably radiant, hardly recognisable as the plain girl she really is. The four bridesmaids were resplendent in toilet-paper-coloured peach, though the colour did nothing to flatter the bulging waistline of the youngest girl. The men in the party really scrubbed up quite well.

But maybe I'm being too hard. I know I'm jealous. I can't even do the 'always the bridesmaid' lament, as I've never been one. My big chance was when Niamh got married, but she blew it by going to Rome. Her witnesses were two strangers, who beam out of Niamh's only wedding photograph. I don't think Mum has ever forgiven her for that. And the worst thing is, Niamh wasn't even pregnant.

Pauline's wedding reception was like a hundred I've been to before. Sweet sherry before the meal. Dried-up, overcooked food. Dried-up, overcooked wedding cake. Cringingly not funny speeches. Tasteless jokes to shock the maiden aunts in the company. Too much wine. A tuneless band playing songs that were played to death many years ago. Need I say more?

I chatted dutifully with friends and relations. I danced dutifully with all the men who dutifully asked me, smiling and nodding whenever they spoke, as the music was far too loud for conversation.

I sneaked away for a stroll around the hotel, trying to clear my throbbing head. I gave in semi-gracefully when my mum pushed me on to the floor for a Paul

Jones dance. I joined the large group of enthusiastic participants and we arranged ourselves into two circles, men on the outside, women on the inside. Each circle then turned in opposite directions as the band launched into a rousing rendition of 'I Only Wanna Be With You.'

When the music stopped, I tried to look pleased when I was faced with a red-faced, drunken man who lunged at me to avoid dancing with Pauline's spry eighty-year-old granny. He then proceeded to drag me unceremoniously around the dance floor, stepping on my toes, and staining the back of my best dress with his sweaty palms.

I even stayed for the undercooked cocktail sausages (why overcook the beef, and then undercook the sausages which could end up killing us all?) and the egg sandwiches that were served at ten o'clock. I stayed while the grumpy middle-aged waitresses gathered the broken-up cocktail sticks and the crusts from the sandwiches.

When the music started again, and I heard the first bars of 'The Birdie Song', I couldn't face any more. I wondered if I had died, unknown to myself, and if this were my own private hell. I pleaded a headache and got up to leave. Sean offered to drive me home, but I insisted on taking a taxi. Why should he get to leave too? He's married. He deserves to suffer.

I was very bold and left while Mum was gone to the toilet. I kissed Dad goodbye. He winked and gave me one of his friendly shoulder punches. (He definitely watches too many sitcoms.) I knew that at a later date I'd get grief from Mum for leaving early, but it was worth it. By the time she and two hundred others were crossing damp hands to sing 'Auld Lang Syne', I was tucked up in my bed with a hot water bottle and a cup of cocoa.

I'm worth it.

I met Walter last week. He was wheeling an overloaded trolley with dodgy wheels around the supermarket. I know writers have to eat, but nevertheless he seemed completely out of place, wandering around amongst the fruit and veg. He was still wearing his corduroy jacket, and his red hair was, as ever, uncombed and straggly. He seemed to be a bit embarrassed when he saw me. I don't know if that's because he didn't like to be seen in the supermarket, or if he didn't know how to greet me, the raving mad one who wrote all that drivel in his classes. He recovered well though, and gave me his puny, limp handshake. 'Maeve! How nice to see you again. How is your writing coming along? Are you writing something every day, just as you promised?'

I am actually, but I don't know if 'You must try harder' or 'I can't read this' or 'Capital letter please!!!!!!' count as writing to someone like Walter. When I nodded, he continued, pointing his bony finger into my face. 'Whatever happens, write from the heart. You must breathe it and feel it, let it come from inside you. Deep inside you. It must never be forced or strained. Don't forget to listen to your muse.' (I'm not making this up, I promise. That's what that crazy man said to me while I tried to weigh my carrots.) By the time my poor long-suffering muse got dragged into the picture, I was the one who was embarrassed. Terribly so. I had to stare threateningly at two teenaged past pupils of mine, who were leaning against a rack of cabbages, waving their hands in imitation of Walter, and skitting laughing. Walter was gone off into a speaking reverie, and showed no signs of an early recovery, so I caught one of his flailing hands, shook it very firmly, and set off determinedly.

I had to rush my shopping, and I forgot half of what I needed (no Hoover bags again) but it was worth it just to avoid the risk of encountering Walter in the frozen food aisle, with the attendant possibility of triggering another spectacular explosion of words and garlic-scented spittle.

When I got home I was in a state of nervous exhaustion. I turned on my grey plastic friend to find an e-mail from the home exchange company. Very uplifting. It informed me that the exchange year has just come to an end, and my home would be removed from the Internet listings within seven days, unless of course I were to part with eighty euro to renew my membership for another year. It seems the register free offer was valid for one year only. Smart trick, guys. The message proclaimed solemnly, 'If you renew now, your listing will be on the Internet for twelve months, thus enhancing your chances of securing a good exchange.'

This made perfect business sense, but I'm too fed up to do it. I could never imagine an exchange working as well as this year's one. For one, the apartment, and Vancouver itself, would be hard to beat. Also, it was great to have Maria with me this year, and I can't see that happening again. I can't see Joe going away for another summer. And they might well have a cuddly little baby by then. A sweet, baby-sized version of themselves. A slight impediment to a wild, girlie holiday.

Anyway, I am such a sad person these days that I can't even enjoy looking forward to next year's holidays. I just think that it might or might not be great, and then it will be over and I'll be back again, a year older, a year no wiser than before, a year no better prepared to answer Mum's annual question. An older, sun-tanned me will be condemned to another year in Theresa's company, watching her knit and sew and embroider my life away.

Thanks Walter. Beautiful, strong, healthy trees have been cut down in their prime, to make the paper I am soiling with these pathetic words. Little birds are homeless, with nowhere to lay their tiny blue eggs. Cows wander desperately, lowing pitifully, with nothing to shade them from the midday sun. Little boys stay home and watch television, getting fat and bored, because they have no trees to climb, no swaying branches to sit on, with the wind in their tousled hair.

One day, someone is going to have to go to the trouble of carrying a huge stack of self-pitying notebooks to a bonfire. They could put their back out, with the weight of them. Black, papery smuts will soil the freshly washed sheets that flap joyously in my neighbour's garden. Innocent, childish lungs will breathe in the smoke and soot from these pages. Pretty blonde children will cough and splutter.

It's all your fault, Walter.

Why did you start me off on this?

Why didn't you persuade me to write short stories? Two thousand words maximum.

Or brief snappy poems? Ten to a page?

It's not fair, Walter.

The world owes you one.

Big time.

Chapter Thirty-two

November is nearly over. One more month of me not being happy. I wonder is someone somewhere keeping a balance sheet? If they are I hope they have noticed that I'm due a happiness bonus. I'd like to redeem my points now, thank you very much. I'm not waiting for some afterlife scenario. I could live for years yet. I want to be happy now. This minute.

OK. I'll have a Mars bar. That will have to do for now. More ethereal pleasures will have to wait their turn.

Maria has finally come clean, and admitted that she's pregnant. What a surprise. Not. She told me on one of our drinking nights, if you can still call them that when one of the drinkers consumes nothing stronger than sparkling water. She had seemed a bit on edge all evening, and in the end, she just blurted it out, with no little opening sally. I am very pleased for her, but had to confess to not being surprised. She looked a little bit sheepish when I told her that I'd suspected for a while.

'I know, Maeve. Maybe I should have told you sooner, but I couldn't. For one thing, I didn't want to say anything until I'd gone past the dangerous time; I was too afraid that it wouldn't work out. And then. . .' She faltered for a moment, as if lost for words. I waited for her to continue, nervously sipping my beer, giving her a chance to find the words which were so slow to come.

Again she blurted out, 'I'm sorry, Mae. I was just afraid you'd resent it. I know you love children, and I didn't want to upset you. I didn't want to gloat, to throw it in your face, when you have none.' I could see that she was close to tears, and strangely, though of course it was I who should be upset, I felt that I ought to comfort her. I gave her a tentative little hug, and squeezed her shoulders.

How could I deny it though? What she said was true. Hundreds of magazine articles have been written about my sad plight. Stacks of self-help books have been written to console the likes of me. And what's worse, I've read most of them. Over and over. They don't help though. No amount of positive thinking can change the fact that the ticking of my biological clock is becoming ever louder. It doesn't help to know that my clock is ticking in unison with thousands of others. A little harmony of desperation.

I have the feeling that the final train to motherhood is pulling out of the station, and I'm not on it. I see the last few lucky women scrambling aboard the end carriage, and I'm still waiting in line for my ticket, fumbling helplessly in my purse for the right change.

I have to be honest to myself and admit that this is probably one of the causes of my recent bad spirits. There wouldn't be much point in finally meeting my one true love in ten years' time, when I'm past having children. It would be much too late by then.

Is it so wrong to wish for a husband and 2.4 children? It's the national average, and I only want to be average. I don't want to be the best and the brightest and the most successful. Plain old average would do me fine.

I don't believe in reincarnation. I wish I did. Then I'd have another chance to look forward to. (So what if I was reborn as a puppy? Puppies have fun.) Then maybe I wouldn't have this frightening sense that I've been given this one precious life to live, and that I'm squandering it; wasting it; letting it slip by me in a mess of discontentment and half-living. Spending my time on foolish, wasted dreams.

I have even, lately, begun to pay an unhealthy attention to magazine articles telling of single mothers who have made conscious decisions to become pregnant, without the benefit of a partner for life. Some of these women have benefited from IVF, using anonymously donated sperm. I've read of women who were impregnated by obliging male friends, who kindly offered their sperm as some might offer a cup of sugar to a neighbour in need. I even saw a bizarre television programme about a surrogate mother who had twins,

311

and she and the prospective biological parents agreed to keep one each, divvying up the proceeds. A very neat business transaction. Quite sensible really. Fortunately both babies were girls, so the viewer was spared an on-screen row about who would get which sex. Each mother took her precious little pink bundle in her arms, then the mums hugged briefly and set off into their new lives. The mothers drove the same make of car, in what may have been the most obscene version of product placement that I have yet witnessed. The worst thing is, I wasn't even shocked at all of this. I wasn't overwhelmed with waves of horror. I wasn't reaching for the phone to complain to some moral authority. My emotion was much simpler. I was jealous.

I've tried so hard not to view every passing male as a potential lover and soul mate. I've worked hard to this end, and I like to think that I have succeeded in this endeavour. But now I find myself looking at total strangers, wondering what their children would be like, and considering how well their genes might mix with mine. If they could only get the chance.

Sometimes I wonder if I should have slept with Wes. So what if I never saw him again? Would it have been so bad to have returned from Vancouver with more than a few dreams, a suntan and some cheap souvenirs? A child of his would surely be good-looking. And my careful parenting would surely overcome any light-fingered tendencies.

There was one guy in the video shop last week. He

was tall, handsome and healthy-looking. He had well-cut clothes, indicating some degree of success in the world (though I then decided this wasn't necessarily a plus, as he might just be good at drug-smuggling, or armed robbery). His choice of film clinched it. Just when I was afraid he was going to go for *Die-Hard,* Parts One to Twenty-seven, he won me over completely by selecting a really arty, intellectual film. You know the kind – black and white, made in some obscure eastern European language, with broody, smoky artwork on the cover. I'd been kind of thinking of IVF, but with a guy like that, I'd have been prepared to go for the natural way, and skipped the test tubes and the stirrups and the speculum.

I think I've mentioned before what a sad person I am. This man was innocently hiring a video, and before he knew it, he was being sized up as a possible sperm donor. He was counting out his change, and rooting in the pocket of his designer denims for his video card, and I was mentally raising his children. Poor guy. He paid for his video and left. A narrow escape, and he didn't even know it.

Anyway, Maria didn't have to go to these lengths to become pregnant. She has Joe, and they did it the easy way, the right way. In Texas by the sound of it, though I didn't like to ask. Probably on a beach. Are there beaches in Texas? I never did find out. I must find a way of asking her. Casually like, so she won't wonder why I want to know.

She was wrong to suggest that I might be jealous. I'm not. I'm very happy for them both, as I know that it's something they really want. It's not jealousy that I feel; it's just that I so much want to be like Maria. I want her life. I don't want Joe of course. Just some vague, faceless person I could love, who would love me like Joe loves Maria. I want to have someone to care just for me, someone to make me feel special, someone to keep me warm on cold nights, someone to escort me to my next cousin's wedding, someone to have a baby with. I know that's a string of clichés, but there you go. It's how I feel.

I'd hate for Maria not to have what she wants; it's just that I want it too. That's not jealousy. Is it?

Maria was relieved by my assurances that I am happy for her, and we stayed in the pub until closing time, though I couldn't relax fully. I know this is the easy part. It will get worse as her pregnancy progresses. I can't predict how I will react if Maria wants to show me grainy black and white scan pictures of her unborn child. What will I do if she wants me to put my hand on her swollen abdomen and feel the gentle kicking? Could I bear the sensation of the little arms and legs flexing their tiny muscles? I will have to stand by and watch as her perfect figure changes, becomes more round. I will look at my firm, flat stomach and hate it. I will see Maria and Joe get lost in the wonder of the new life they have jointly created. I know she won't gloat, but she will be rejoicing, and couldn't hide it if she tried. She will want to shout her joy from the rooftops. Print it in tall red letters on the cover of *The Examiner*. Write it on a banner and have a plane trail it across the sky on the day of the Munster final.

And what will I do then, in the face of all this joy that I cannot share?

A lighter note. Please. I need a lighter note.

I met two of the housewives yesterday. Unfortunately the Bad Poets Society is alive and well. They had a stall (well a small table actually) set up in one of the malls in the shopping centre. One euro will buy the fruits of their creativity. I was right – their works of art have been protected between the light green covers of a piece of A4 card, folded in half, and stapled, not quite in the middle. How did I guess?

One of the women, I don't know her name, had passed me in town some days previously, pretending not to know me, suddenly becoming very interested in the display of vitamins in the nearby chemist's window. That didn't happen here though – sales appeared to be slow, and my euro must be as valuable as everyone else's, so she waved and greeted me effusively. 'Maeve. How nice to see you again. How are you? How is the writing coming along? We were just talking about you yesterday. Weren't we, Annie?'

I bet.

The mean, nasty me was tempted to bark at her to forget the niceties, and just take my money, and be done with it. Luckily though, the nice me was dominant yesterday. I smiled and gushed out a few insincerities to match hers, and gave her my money. She put it carefully into a steel cashbox, which she then locked, a fairly pathetic act, as it was not exactly heaving with the weight of patrons' hard earned money. There were only three euro coins in it. And a few coppers. Did someone get a special deal? Then, once the box was safely locked, and the key tucked into her pocket, there was another bizarre little procedure to be followed. Annie (who must be the financial controller) took out a little spiral bound notebook, and neatly entered the amount, the time and the date. I sneaked a look, and found that there were very few entries, and I suspect that if family and friends were excluded, the sales would not be terribly high. I waved a chirpy goodbye, and left the two great writers to deal with a small boy who wanted a free copy of their book for his sick granny.

I went to get myself a nice strong coffee and a coffee cream slice and settled down for a good laugh. I was disappointed though. The work had reached that stage of awfulness that must be difficult to attain. There are many levels of bad poetry, ranging from just plain bad, to so bad it's nearly good, to dreadful, on to dreadfully funny, and then there's this level – even worse than funny, so bad that it's almost sad. I stirred my coffee, tucked in to my cake, and read the first few poems. Initially I wondered if they were really meant seriously; maybe they were just terribly tongue-in-cheek, sophisticated in their outlook with a quirky, smart humour that was lost on me, but I fear that's not the case. I read a few more, but they were no better. Luckily it was not possible for them to be worse.

I read to the end, and then back again, just to make sure.

My baby smiles at me.
I smile at her.
We smile at each other.
Daddy comes in.
We both smile at him.
He smiles at us.
Happy.

There must be laws against this type of thing. I can't sell rocks dug up from my back garden and call them diamonds. I can't take nettles from my vegetable patch, take them to market and sell them as lettuces. So how can they get away with selling this dross from a table that sports a sign with 'POETRY' painted in crooked capital letters on it?

This indescribable work that I have just quoted (do I need their permission?) is accompanied by a line drawing of a fat, badly proportioned, cross-eyed baby, with a big mop of unlikely curly hair. So they have notions about being artists too. I must warn my mother not to put me down for art this year; I don't want to be saddled with that mad lot again.

Come back, Walter, all is forgiven.

Chapter Thirty-three

First Week in December

By now my mum must be doing her annual homework. She'll be scouring the adult education brochures, planning some wonderful night class for me, trying to find something I haven't done yet, that isn't aromatherapy. She'll be picturing me, surrounded by twelve handsome, available, employed, heterosexual men, all keen to help me, all keen to date me, all vying over who will marry me. I'll just have to survey them all and choose the lucky one. Dream on, Mum.

She was very hopeful about her new neighbour, for a while, the alleged single guy. For weeks she begged me to call to his house on some pathetic pretext or other, so he'd have the chance to fall desperately in love with me. Then his beautiful golden-haired girlfriend appeared with a few leather suitcases, a toaster and a yucca plant. One look at her and my disloyal mum decided that perhaps this guy was out of her precious daughter's league, and he wasn't mentioned again.

Poor Mum. She's been shilly-shallying for the past few weeks, and it's been clear that she's trying to tell me something, and doesn't quite know how to start. Once or twice she nearly got going. 'Maeve, I was thinking. . .' She'd hesitate, and when I'd ask her what she was thinking it was always something really pathetic like, 'Oh, I was just thinking of getting a new kettle. The old one is very slow to boil. It takes me twenty minutes to make a cup of tea. I descaled it last week, but it's no better. And that old descaler is very strong. It can't be good for you. Mrs Murphy dropped her ring into a kettle full of descaler last year and it melted. The ring that is, not the kettle. Though the kettle must have been in a bad way too. That Mrs Murphy is as mean as dirt. The kettle was probably twenty years old. And the ring can't have been gold. Knowing her it was probably brass.'

Or, another time, when it looked like she was going to say something deeply significant, she stalled and said, 'I wonder should I buy your Dad some new shoes now, or wait for the sales.' One afternoon I knew she was almost there, almost ready to say what was really on her mind, but at the last minute she drew back and said, 'I was thinking of having scrambled eggs for tea.' I then had to listen to a recitation of everything they had for tea that week. And why they had it. And why they didn't have something else. And what was in the fridge. And how nutritious avocado pears are.

It's like Maria all over again. Suddenly the world is full of people worried about me, afraid to broach sensitive subjects, afraid of upsetting me. Do I seem so delicate, so easily offended? Unfortunately, I think I know the answer to that question.

Anyway, Mum got around to it eventually, after all the false starts. She usually starts planning for Christmas in September, so it's clear that she's been biting her tongue about this one for quite some time. It seems that both Niamh and Sean are going to spend Christmas with their in-laws this year. There seems to be some rule about who goes where each year. Some rule that only married people know. (Maybe they hand out a booklet when you go into the sacristy to sign your marriage vows.)

Do you go to the woman's family when there's an 'r' in the year? Or do you multiply the number of sandwich toasters you got for wedding presents, by the number of times your mother-in-law has interfered in your life, and come to a magical meaningful formula? I suppose I'll never know.

Anyway, with no Niamh and no Sean, and no kids to add some jollity to the occasion, that would leave just me and Mum and Dad together in their home. That wasn't a terribly exciting prospect, but it's happened before and we all lived to tell the tale. No one ever got stabbed over the turkey dinner, or burnt as the flaming pudding sailed through the air, thrown in a fit of uncontrollable anger and frustration. It would have been dull and predictable, but it would come to an end eventually, and before long another depressing January would roll along.

I was getting used to the idea of another Christmas for three when Mum got around to her big statement. Her proposal is even worse than the boring stay at home saga. It filled me with horror.

No wonder she had such trouble getting around to it.

It all came out when I went over for tea on Sunday. I had barely sat down at the tea table when she began. 'Maevie. You know Niamh and Sean are going to be spending Christmas with their in-laws, poor things?'

'Yes, Mum, they announced that weeks ago so you wouldn't be complaining that they didn't give you enough notice, and that you had included them when you were ordering your turkey.'

'There's no need to be like that, Maeve. I just like to be organised. You can never be too organised at Christmas. When I'm six feet under you'll realise that. But it will be too late then. Anyway I'm not ordering any turkey this year.' She gave a little girlish grin as she mentioned the turkey, and my heart briefly soared, as I felt sure she was going to say we'd be having goose for a change. Mum ruined our turkey each year, by cooking it for two hours extra. ('You wouldn't want salmonella, especially not at Christmas. You'd be admitted to hospital, and all the doctors and nurses would be tipsy. You know what they're like. Before you know it, they'd be operating and you'd never be the same again. Never.') Of course, Mum would ruin a goose too, but at least there would be less of it, and we might see the back of it before New Year's Eve. It wasn't as simple as that though. Mum's bombshell wasn't as tame as a change of menu.

'I'm not ordering turkey this year, because Daddy and I have decided to go to the Grand Hotel for Christmas this year. You'll come too, of course.'

'Well, Mum, actually. . .'

'Of course you'll come. They have a three-day package. It's only three hundred and fifty euro each. And that includes champagne on Christmas Eve, and wine with dinner on Christmas Day. And I won't drink the alcohol so you can have mine. Won't that be nice?'

'Mum, I don't fancy sitting in the Grand for three days, trying to sneak sly sips of your wine when the waiters aren't looking, for God's sake.'

'All right then, don't. Daddy can have mine, and then you'll be sorry. It's French wine too. Chateau something or other. There's a picture of it on the brochure.'

'That doesn't mean they'll be serving it, it's just to make the brochure look good.'

'Maeve, I'm telling you now. I plan to bring that brochure with me, and if they serve a different wine, I'll be having words with the somm. . ., with the wine waiter. They won't fob me off with any of that old cheap stuff. Full of anti-freeze it is. I read an article in

322

The Examiner last week, so I know all about it. Do you remember when Mrs Byrne had those gallstones? That was from the old cheap wine she drank on that foreign holiday. Kerry wasn't good enough for her, and she got her answer. Ten days in the Regional. Drips and everything. 'Twas like visiting a milking parlour with the tubes and the machines pumping things in and pumping things out. There were bags on one side of the bed emptying, and one on the other side filling up. I thought it was going to burst, and I had to call the nurse. And the nurse, a young slip of a thing, chattered away like there was no tomorrow. And for Mrs Byrne there nearly was no tomorrow. It was touch and go for a while. But at least it was September, and the doctors were sober, which was something.'

She rambled on, as she does, and I had time to think about the prospect of Christmas with Mum and Dad in the Grand Hotel.

I can't think of anything I would like less. Three days of being surrounded by old fogies. Three days of paper hats, in-house cabaret and enforced entertainment. There would be three days of treasure hunts and charades. I could act out a three-day-long charade of being happy. Three days of being pitied by everyone else. I can see people whispering and pointing.

'Look at her, the unmarried daughter, how lonely for her.'

'A bit plain, isn't she?'

'Sulky-looking too.'

Well, would you blame me? Wouldn't you sulk? Mum and Dad couldn't even chat in peace with the other old fogies. They'd have to include me in everything, whether I wanted to be included or not.

I don't fancy Christmas in my own house alone, but I think it would be just about preferable. I couldn't do that, though. Mum wouldn't hear of it. If I suggested it, I know she'd cancel her plans, and forget the hotel. She wouldn't allow me to spend Christmas alone, even if that was what I wanted. She'd find a reason not to go to the hotel. She'd pretend it was accidentally over-booked, or closed down for spreading salmonella. She'd sigh as if she were bitterly disappointed and then we would all go through the usual motions at home.

That wouldn't be fair though. Christmas has always meant a lot of work for her, with the preparations lasting for weeks beforehand. A simple roast dinner for the three of us would manage to take up days and days of her time. It is clear that Mum has at last reached the stage in her life when she likes the idea of letting someone else poke their hands up the turkey's greasy bottom. It's fine by her if someone else peels mountains of superfluous potatoes, and prepares an industrial-sized pot of brussels sprouts. She can obviously live with it if she doesn't get to make the melon into perfect little balls before drizzling it with the best port. She is ready for a rest and I couldn't spoil it for her.

324

I don't know what's best for me to do. The papers are carrying ads for singles Christmas functions in various hotels around the country. That, however, seems even worse. If I go on one of those, I will know I've become an official, card-carrying desperate person.

Once Mum came back from her scurrilous verbal tour of the medical establishments of Cork, I put her off for the moment, telling her that I'll decide about the Grand Hotel next week. She's not completely stupid though. I'm quite sure that it has dawned on her that I don't have hundreds of exciting options to consider. But she's humouring me, which is kind of her.

I'm wondering if I could book into the hotel with her and Dad, pretending to be all excited at the prospect of such organised festive fun. Then I could cancel at the last minute, pretending to be sick. I could pretend to have a vicious three-day tummy bug, which would make a stay in the hotel impossible. I could pretend to be terribly disappointed. I could then slink off home and spend the entire holiday tucked up in bed, swilling red wine, eating obscene amounts of white Toblerone, and reading trashy novels. Then when they called to see me, I'd really be sick, and I wouldn't have to lie any more.

Next week. I'll decide next week.

Theresa has every Christmas of her life planned. She doesn't know the official formula, as she's not married yet, so she's developed her own. This year, as it's to be her second-last Christmas as a single girl, she's going to spend it with her parents, going to Michael's house for St Stephen's Day, and he'll dine with her family on the 27th. Next year they'll do the same. Then, 'I know it's traditional for a bride to spend the first Christmas in her parents' home, but we're going to be a bit different. My sister will be home that year, so I'll go to Michael's, and the year after, we'll make up and go to my parents.' I kid you not. This girl has four Christmases planned, and what's worse, I know they'll go exactly as she says. Knowing her, she's probably got all the presents bought, and wrapped and labelled so she won't give the wrong present in the wrong year. She has probably already knitted sweet little pale green and yellow cardigans and romper suits for unborn nieces and nephews. I bet she has four Christmas cakes made and iced and stashed in her freezer.

Have I mentioned recently that I hate her?

As a child, like all children, I loved Christmas, it was the highlight of the year. The days were counted and ticked off on the calendar, starting in May if I could get away with it. As a teenager, I still loved Christmas, and this lasted until I was well into my twenties. Gradually, in the years since then, this gloss has vanished, leaving me as I am now, dreading it, wondering how I'll get through it, and already looking forward to it being over. I am one of the few people who really understands why people in January ask 'How did you get over Christmas?', as if Christmas were a terrible affliction that had to be endured and then 'got over'.

I must say, though, the excitement of the children at school is wonderful. They've written note after note to Santa Claus, no doubt each one more demanding than the one before, but what harm? For most of them, Christmas is the only time they're allowed to be so demanding. In a few weeks though, I'll hear the parents desperately trying to backtrack, wondering how they are possibly going to fulfil the long, expensive wish lists. Every year I hear the desperate pre-Christmas placating. 'You know, darling, I read in the paper that Santa is a bit low on Playstations this year, and he mightn't have one for you. He has already promised them to lots of boys and girls. Don't be too disappointed, I know he'll bring you something nice. I'm sure he's got lots of cool Lego sets. Or K'nex. You always liked K'nex, and he might bring you some of that.' Even those children who plainly know the score humour their parents, and go along with the little charade, politely declining to point out that 'cool' is their word and doesn't really suit their aged mums and dads.

Theresa's class is putting on a little play for the parents, and as the children are so young, and their concentration is so poor, they are already practising daily. I can hear the strains of 'Away in a Manger' and 'Jingle Bells' wafting along the corridor, almost deadening the dull monotones of Mr Flynn's class reciting their Irish irregular verbs.

I've caved in under the pressure of my fourth class, who remember that last year I allowed them to paint

Christmas scenes on the windows, with thick poster paint. They look very well at first, but I remember from last year how quickly they deteriorated. They soon became victims of poor glazing, and condensation, ending up in dribbly blobs, the remains of which adorned the window frames until Easter. We'll do it the day before the holidays, so I won't have to look at the mess.

I've promised the children two special Christmas art activities each week that they're good, but they're always good so I'd better think of some not too dirty ones quickly. If I don't, they will pick at me in my frequent weak moments, and I will find myself supervising mad, creative activities. These will be very fulfilling and very worthy, but also incredibly messy, leaving me terribly unpopular with everyone except the woman who runs the local dry cleaners where the school uniforms will have to be sent.

Maybe her children will get a PlayStation this year.

Chapter Thirty-four

I'm thirty-five years old.

How can that be?

How did that happen?

I can still clearly remember my Confirmation day.

My Communion day even.

I can remember my first day in secondary school. (I spent my bus money on crisps and had to walk home. Three miles. In the rain. And platform shoes were in fashion then. The blisters didn't heal for months.)

My twenty-first birthday seems as if it was only yesterday.

I checked my birth certificate just in case I'd skipped ahead by accident, but unfortunately I hadn't. I have to hold my wrinkled head high and face the truth – I'm half-way to seventy.

My birthday was on Sunday, and if it was up to me, I'd have let it go by unrecognised, but there was no chance of that. My nieces and nephews sent me sweet home-made cards. The aunties had to give me presents, revenge for the totem poles.

Mum and Dad had to drop over with a birthday cake, and go through the ritual of lighting candles. Luckily Mum could only find four, so there was no real danger of burning the house down. They sang a hearty 'Happy Birthday', and I dutifully blew out the candles. Dad punched me again. I wonder can you get therapy for that kind of thing? Mum hugged me.

'Well, Maeve, thirty-five. How does it feel?'

It feels absolutely awful, but I didn't want to admit it to my mum. 'Oh fine Mum. It's just another day older. No big deal.'

Dad disagreed. 'I don't know, Maeve. Thirty-five is old enough for a single girl.'

Mum glared at him. 'It is not. Maeve is still young. Luckily she has my skin. I always had good skin.'

Dad wanted an easy life, and he knew the required responses. 'Yes, dear, your skin was always lovely.'

'And I don't need fancy creams to keep it that way. Expensive rubbish. Full of chemicals. You shouldn't use them, Maeve. It would turn your stomach if you saw half of what goes into those fancy creams. Leftovers from the meat factories. Soap and water was good enough for my mother, and it's good enough for me.'

I couldn't stop myself. 'Soap has chemicals too, Mum.'

'Don't be ridiculous, Maeve. Soap is harmless. You

just wait and see. All those chemicals have to go somewhere. They soak into your skin. For all you know they could be gathering on the edges of your brain, waiting for their moment to attack. You could be fine for years and then – bang – your brain could turn to jelly overnight. You'd be sorry then.'

I couldn't resist. 'I wouldn't know though, would I? If my brain was turned to jelly.'

'OK, Maeve, be smart, but don't blame me when it happens.'

'OK, I promise. I won't. Anyway, I only use Body Shop moisturiser. That's hardly a "fancy cream".'

'That's even worse. Aren't they the shower that won't test their products on animals? Save the puppies and tough luck on the humans. Are we meant to admire them for that?'

'Actually we are.'

'Well that's rubbish. And even if those chemicals don't rot your brain, they could destroy your skin. It could peel right off. Like that Michael Jackson fella. Still, at least he was white in the end. How would you like it if your skin peeled off and you ended up black?'

'Mum, that's racist. There's nothing wrong with being black.'

'Maybe not. But you'd look a bit queer in the family photos.'

'Mum, you know you can't say queer any more.'

Mum gave a self-pitying sigh. 'I know, Maeve. I know. I can't say anything any more. I can't think anything any more. Life is too complicated nowadays. It was much easier long ago. I remember. . .'

Dad got to his feet. 'Now dear, remember Maeve is invited over to Maria's house. We'd better go so she can get ready.'

I flashed him a grateful smile, and ducked his punch. They set off and I knew Dad would have to endure a long lecture on the olden days. Still, at least he was there, so it mightn't be too bad.

And we hadn't eaten any of the birthday cake. Mum makes a mean chocolate cake and I got to eat it all myself.

Happy Birthday to me.

I can't write much tonight. I've got to do my Christmas cards. I'm very organised. I have a list of all the cards I sent last year, and there won't be many new additions this year. Though I'm glad to say I'm not mean enough to keep a list of cards I receive. I don't have two lists to survey in January, wickedly striking out those who forgot me. I have an aunt who used to do that. I lost my place on her list many years ago.

I must admit, though, every year I do think about abandoning a few of the old names. It would make sense really, when I realise that for ten years the only contact I've had, or wished to have, with some people on my list is an incredibly impersonal, shallow card, with a cutesy picture of a reindeer or a Christmas tree, and an insincere rhyming message. Or not rhyming if the cards are expensive and sophisticated enough. The correspondents might have climbed the Himalayas, opened a string of Vietnamese restaurants, or had both legs amputated since we were in touch, and still they write a breezy, 'Have a great Christmas. We should meet up next year.' A few of my old college friends send me one of these each year. I reply of course, and while I like to think that they get a different snow scene, or a slightly fatter robin on successive cards, my message never varies in any respect. How could it?

The ones they so dutifully send (poor Maeve is on her own, better not forget to send her a card) change from year to year. Often there's a new name, indicating the arrival of yet another baby, to join the others that I've never seen, fathered by the husband I've never met, and given birth to by a woman I probably wouldn't recognise if I met her in the street. I've already got a few like that this year, and no doubt I'll reply to them, just as I always do. I don't like to break with tradition, however insincere and meaningless.

Then there's been the three new ones. First came the one from Walter. Predictably over-decorated, with lots of glitter adorning Santa's beard and eyebrows, and a personal message in green ink: 'Have a wonderful Christmas. Don't drink too much, and don't forget to keep writing.' A bit cheeky really. He doesn't know me that well. For all he knows, I could be a recovering alcoholic and the mere mention of drink could be enough to set me off on a downward spiral. Anyway, he's probably just hoping I'll sign up for more classes, so I don't think I'll even reply.

The second new card came from Chuck and Darlene. Chuck's operation went very well, but he has to watch his diet and eat lots of roughage. It was painful, but he's very brave. He can sit down again. As long as he has his inflatable cushion. Sweetheart's half-sister is expecting pups and Chuck and Darlene are hoping to buy one when they get home. I hope the precious little puppy doesn't dig up his uncle by mistake when he's burying a particularly juicy bone. At the moment Chuck and Darlene are in Australia, and loving it. Their card had a picture of Santa lying on a beach in a red swimsuit trimmed with white fur. Rudolph and his pals are surfing in the background. Chuck and Darlene may be pathetic, but they're having a ball, and who am I to scoff? Naff and happy, is that so bad?

The third new card came from Charlie. I felt a little pang when I saw the postmark. I don't know what I was expecting, but I was disappointed when the message was brief and to the point: 'Happy Christmas from Vancouver. Hope you're having lots of crack. Regards, Charlie and Todd.' Like I said, what else could I want, or expect? Did I think he was going to declare undying love one more time? Beg me to fly out and marry him tomorrow? Say that he couldn't live without me, and that he'd be on the next plane? I've probably watched *An Officer and a Gentleman* more times than is good for me. Charlie wasn't a missed chance. He wasn't the potential love of my life, who I foolishly let escape. No. He just wanted someone to distract him for a few lonely weeks, and I might have done. He hardly knew me. How could he possibly have loved me? It's just a symptom of my empty life that I even think about him occasionally.

I'll send him an equally bland message, and that, as they say, will be that. I think I'll take him off my list next year. He was a nice guy, but a virtual stranger, and I have enough of those on my list as it is. If I go silent, I'm sure he'll reciprocate, and there will be an end to it. The environment will benefit too. None of that wasted cardboard, or extra weight on the mail planes. It's for the best.

I wonder should I send a card to Wes? If I addressed it to the beach where he hangs out would he get it? Probably not. The beach must be a bit cold this time of year. Beach Bum probably turns into Ski Bum for the winter.

Oh, I have some good news. Mustn't forget to write the good stuff. Maria and Joe have invited me to spend Christmas with them. They usually spend it with Maria's family, as Joe's parents are both dead, but this year Maria's parents are flying out to spend some time with her sister in Australia. (They might even run into Chuck and Darlene. I'll tell them to look out for a couple in matching purple shell suits.)

When Maria offered, I protested at first, though I was dying to accept. As usual I was afraid of being in the way, afraid that they were inviting me out of pity, hoping I'd refuse. Perhaps what they really wanted was a quiet few days together. Just Joe, Maria and the bump.

I began to regret all the whingeing I did about going to the hotel with Mum and Dad. Maybe Maria felt I was hinting that they should invite me. Then she played her trump card. She assures me that I'd be welcome anyway, but especially so as they weren't going to be alone anyway. Joe has had to invite his ancient old uncle, who otherwise would be spending the season of goodwill in a not very pleasant nursing home, cared for by cranky nurses who wished they were at home with their own families, not tending equally cranky old people who also wished to be elsewhere. Maria was unusually insistent. Perhaps she feared for my sanity if I was forced to do the hotel thing. 'Please say yes, Maeve. We'd love you to come. You can entertain us all, and you'll be more relaxed than in some stuffy hotel. You'd hate every moment if you went to the hotel. Come to us this year. It won't be so bad having the old man around if you're there too.'

That decided it. In the end Maria made me feel as if I would be doing them a favour by joining them. It would almost be mean of me to refuse. If they were stuck with this ancient uncle, they wouldn't be having lovey-dovey chats and leaping into bed at all times of the day anyway, so I wouldn't be a nuisance. I wouldn't be cramping their style. It would be cramped with or without me. I might even be able to help them. I've decided to be the perfect guest, and take the old uncle out for lots of afternoon drives by the sea. I'll play Monopoly with him. I'll push his wheelchair, and tenderly tuck a tartan rug around his wasted legs. (Maria says he's not wheelchair-bound, but he's very old, at his age he could deteriorate rapidly. Three days is a long time when you get to his age.) I won't yawn as he tells his repetitive tales of the good old days. I'll read aloud to him. I'll fetch his pipe and slippers. I'll fill his hot water bottle, and if he has a chamber pot, I'll even empty that, as I'm so grateful for the chance to spend Christmas with Maria and Joe. When I said that to Maria she got a fit of giggles, and assured me that their aged guest can use the toilet unaided. She even accused me of ageism, but that's not fair. After all, the poor old man is in his eighties, and it's a fact of life that men of his age often have waterwork problems. I watch ER, so I know these things. Anyway, chamber pot or no chamber pot, I'll make sure that Joe and Maria have lots of precious time to themselves. After all, this will be their last baby-free Christmas. Next year, if they are jumping into bed at odd times of the day, it won't be for mad, passionate sex. It will be to grab a few hours shut-eye, to make up for all the sleep they will have lost because of their squawking bundle of joy.

Strange, I've never heard Joe mention this uncle before. After I'd accepted their kind offer, and started to look forward to being with them, I began to worry that they'd invented him, just so I wouldn't feel bad about intruding on their Christmas. I'd be really embarrassed if I showed up on Christmas morning to find them alone, spouting lame excuses for the non-appearance of the old fogey. Maria has sworn, several times, that they were stuck with this visitor, and would love me to be there to keep the conversation going, so I've stopped arguing. And why deny it? Old fogey or no old fogey, I would ten million times prefer to spend Christmas with them, rather than endure the hotel scenario.

I was a bit nervous about telling Mum, though. You know, more of this over-sensitivity, afraid of unwittingly causing hurt. I needn't have worried though. She seemed almost relieved when I told her I'd be going to Maria's, making me feel a bit hurt instead.

'That's great, love, you'll enjoy that,' she said. 'You'll have much more fun in Maria's rather than being stuck with us. We got the menu for the hotel Christmas dinner, and there's no spiced beef. That's your favourite, isn't it?'

'Yes, Mum.' (Isn't shepherd's pie meant to be my favourite? Do I get a favourite for each season? Or do I get to nominate a new favourite after thirty-five years?)

'It would be a pity for you to have to do without it. Do you think Maria will have spiced beef? You could get her to ring Mullane's. They are taking orders. Why don't we run down now, and you can order a piece? Then you'll be sure. And you can't go to Maria's with your hands hanging, can you? A nice joint of spiced beef would be a lovely present.'

She rambled on about the spiced beef until I gave in and promised to order some on my way home.

And I don't even like it that much. Maybe the old uncle will eat it. If his teeth are up to it.

Like I said, I was a little bit hurt at the speed with which Mum accepted my absence from their Christmas. It's true, I didn't want to go with them, but they're my parents, they're supposed to want me more than I want them, that's their job. Mum didn't notice my hurt look though. I raised my head and found her exchanging a smirk with Dad, who'd just raised his eyes from the paper. That's very strange. What were they smirking about? Do they think that Maria, Joe and I have some sick love triangle going for us? They wouldn't find that smirkworthy, would they? Or am I on the wrong track altogether? Are they smirking about what they will do, on their first Christmas free of me since I screamed my way into their lives thirty-five years ago? Bizarre thoughts rampage through my mind. Maybe they are going to a naturist convention, and plan to eat their turkey wearing only tissue-paper hats, and plastic rings from crackers. Nude charades, and swimsuit-free jacuzzis. Or do they plan to live the misspent youth they never had, with the ladies giggling as they toss their bus passes into a pile, before having slow, creaky sex with whoever selects them? Maybe Maria is right. Maybe I am guilty of ageism. I shouldn't mock.

I'm not young enough for that privilege. Old age waits for me too, and it's not exactly a million miles away.

Thirty-five is very old.

One third of the way to a hundred and five.

I can't worry about all that now.

The Christmas cards await.

I wonder how many platitudes I can write in half an hour?

Chapter Thirty-five

Christmas Eve

School finished yesterday, it was late this year. Apparently we had extra days off in the autumn to make up, but I can't seem to account for them now. I never can once they are over. They slip into the murky past, and hide from me forever. Either I have a dreadful memory, or a most discriminating one, which refuses to strain itself to recall the unremarkable.

The children left at twelve o'clock, sick with excitement, barely able to contain themselves. I received the usual collection of presents from them, boring but well-intentioned. Why couldn't all the parents club together and buy me something useful? Like a car, for example. As it is, I had to struggle home with four carrier bags, bulging with gifts of varying degrees of uselessness. I could open my own branch of the Body Shop, with my collection of gift baskets, and I couldn't possibly eat all of the chocolates I've been given, even in weeks of my best piggish behaviour. I must be honest and admit that some of these gifts will find themselves reinvented, as presents to my aunts and uncles, and I fear that for some of these gems, it won't stop there, as they are condemned to a life of recycled kindness, until, betrayed by their sell-by dates, they will be either used or dumped.

The entire school was treated to the infant classes' version of the Nativity story. As it's the season of goodwill, I must admit that Theresa has done a great job, and her class did her proud, with just enough innocent slips to be cute, but not quite enough to spoil the story. The kiddies looked sweet in their sheets and tea-towel turbans. (I wonder what is being used to dry the dishes of Castlelough today?)

Baby Born had her usual starring role.

Everyone pretended not to notice the small yellow puddle that appeared under the feet of one tiny angel.

Perhaps her halo was melting.

Saint Joseph was very bold, and he pinched Our Lady twice, but she was impeccably behaved and didn't pinch back. She couldn't really. She was clinging on to Baby Born as if her life depended on it.

Poor Baby Born will be investigated by the child protection league. She must be bruised all over.

The doting parents clapped and cheered, charmed by the talent of their precious darlings.

I found myself picturing one more little darling, a vague, faceless one, in the back row with the other angels. In my dream, this child runs from the stage, and hugs me, throwing her small, thin arms around my waist, laughing and calling me Mummy.

Of course, this phantom child didn't materialise, so I had to be satisfied with a cacophony of childish voices shouting, 'Teacher. Is it time to go home yet?' ' When is the bell going to ring? ' 'I can't wait any more.' 'My Granny will be there when I get home.' The dream child vanished under the onslaught, and I led my restless charges back to the classroom to try to fill the last few minutes.

I have improved myself, and I made the supreme effort. I took down all the Christmas decorations before I left school yesterday. I removed every piece of second-hand tinsel, and every red cardboard creation. I even washed the remaining poster paint from the windows, and the frames are almost clean. January will be less bleak for my efforts, and maybe I won't hate Theresa quite as much as usual. Well, I need something to look forward to, so I'll have to hate her a bit.

Luckily we don't go through the motions of a drink with the staff before going home at Christmas, the way they do in some schools. If I am spending time with Mr Flynn and Pat and Theresa, I expect to be paid for it. I'm not doing it on my own time. I couldn't bear the false merriment, as we pretended to like each other, over hot whiskeys and glasses of Fanta. We would desperately scrabble for topics of conversation, a difficult task, without the props of the staff room to help us. Then without the school bell to save us, we'd wonder frantically how soon we could politely leave.

Instead Mrs Flynn always arrives at break time on the day of the holidays, with a plate of warm mince pies. She serves these on her best china, adorned with generous dollops of whipped cream. Mr Flynn beams at her and beams at us, and then runs out to do yard duty so the rest of us can enjoy his wife's cooking. I know that this tradition is important to him, one that he values, and one he will remember long after he retires. Mind you, I value it too, as Mrs Flynn is a marvellous cook, and her mince pies are the best I ever had. (Sorry, Walter. There's yet another reason my work can't be published. My mum would kill me if she ever read that.)

On Mince Pie Day Mrs Flynn sits and has a cup of tea with us while we eat, though I don't know why as she always appears rather ill at ease. Perhaps she sees it as her duty as the principal's wife. First Lady of the staffroom. Poor lady isn't very suited to her job though. Yesterday she was her usual bashful self.

I wiped the last crumbs from my lips. 'Those mince pies are wonderful, Mrs Flynn. Just wonderful.'

'Ah Maeve. Go on out of that. They're nothing special.'

'Really, Mrs Flynn. They are the nicest I've ever eaten. You're very kind to think of us.'

Mrs Flynn blushed at such praise. 'Don't mention it Maeve. 'Tis only a few old pies. But thanks anyway.'

Theresa couldn't be left out. She's very clever. Her questions never spring from a desire to know more on the subject at hand, instead they are intended to display her superior knowledge. 'Tell me Mrs Flynn. Do you use muscatels in the mincemeat?'

Mrs Flynn beamed at her. 'Oh you noticed, Theresa. I did, love. They're much more expensive, but well worth it in the end. The flavour is far superior.'

Muscatels. What on earth are they? How does Theresa know about them? Can you make mincemeat? I thought it came in jars with nice Christmassy pictures on the labels.

Theresa was enjoying being so clever. 'You're right, Mrs Flynn. You can't beat the muscatels. And do you know what too? I always think your shortcrust pastry is so light. Do you keep everything very cold while you are making it?'

'Yes Theresa I do. I even put the rolling pin in the fridge for an hour before I start.'

I gave a snort of laughter, but Mrs Flynn's bewildered smile made me realise that this wasn't a joke.

Theresa gave me a superior look, and directed her conversation towards Mrs Flynn. 'Michael is buying me a rolling pin and a weighing scales for Christmas. We're asking everyone for practical presents.'

Typical. Her house isn't yet built, and she is already kitting out the kitchen.

Mrs Flynn was impressed though. 'Aren't you the sensible girl? The world could do with a few more like you.'

Theresa adjusted her scrunchy and looked coy.

Pat leaned towards me holding out the newspaper. Apparently there was something there that should interest me. Hard to see what. It was the football page of course, but each headline was equally boring to me. I didn't like to encourage Pat by asking him what exactly I was meant to be looking at, so I gazed at the page trying hard to look as if it were the most interesting piece of paper I'd ever seen.

'Well, Maeve. What do you think of that then?'

'Er, great, Pat.'

'Great! You think it's great that he's injured. Whose side are you on at all?'

Oops. Wrong answer. 'What I mean is, it's great that they've discovered it now so he can have a rest over Christmas.'

Wrong again, it seems. 'Rest! All the biggest matches are on over the holidays. The team will be lost without him.'

'Well at least he'll get to spend some time with his family.'

Nope, that wasn't the right thing to say either. Three wrongs in a row. 'Family! What good are family to him? His team needs him. Do you know how much he cost? And he's only played five matches. He's got priorities, you know.'

Theresa had wrapped up her homemaking conversation with Mrs Flynn, and I could see her shrewd grey eyes observing me. She's no fool. She knew I was in trouble and she was enjoying the spectacle of my discomfort. I jumped up looking at my watch.

'Oh dear. Is that the time? We'd better go and let the kids in.'

I headed briskly for the door to the playground where I was met by a smiling Mr Flynn.

'Maeve, go back in and have another cup of tea. I'm enjoying the fresh air, and I've told the children they can play for another while. It is Christmas after all.'

I smiled weakly. 'Thanks, Mr Flynn. That's very kind of you.'

Thanks a million. I had to endure another twenty-five minutes of tedious chatter before I could return to the relative peace of my classroom.

Today I went to town to finish off my Christmas shopping. None of Theresa's 'I like to be finished by Halloween' for me. I shop better under pressure anyway, no time for dithering. If I had more time, I might spend ten minutes trying to decide between a blue or a pink shirt for Niamh, only to find that she never wears it anyway. I suspect that many of the presents I give her go in the first charity bag in January, Niamh not being a hoarder like me.

I invited all of my family over at six, for warm mince pies and mulled wine. The mince pies were from the supermarket of course, but as my family have all tried my own home-made version at various stages over the years, no one argued. This is the easy kind of entertaining that I like best. No fuss and no flap. Everything ready in ten minutes.

This occasion also gave me an excuse to put up a little Christmas tree for my nephews and nieces, which would otherwise have been a sad gesture. Mind you it was a fairly sad gesture anyway, as the tree is a rather puny artificial one. I bought a full box of decorations, but when they were spread out on the tinsel branches, they looked a bit pathetic. And I couldn't find my extension lead so the one string of lights ended up mostly on the floor behind the couch, intermittently illuminating the couch springs and my grubby skirting boards. In one nice touch though, I found a can of pine-scented Christmas tree spray, and as a result, my tinsel creation confusingly smelled like the real thing.

I was unusually organised by the time the family arrived. The house was as tidy as it ever is, the fire was flickering nicely, and I had all the presents wrapped and under the tree. The children pounced on these excitedly, and I let them open them, defying their disapproving parents. As a teacher, I am privy to the current trends in toy fads, so my gifts are generally well received by the children, and I enjoy indulging them. The children played happily, once they had checked out everyone's toys, and were convinced that no one had done better than anyone else. The adults relaxed too, knowing that there was no point in worrying about further panic shopping, as the shops were closed anyway, for the paltry twenty-four hours that now constitutes Christmas holidays for some unfortunate workers.

We get on quite well as a family, in a stilted kind of way, and we had a pleasant hour, reminiscing about childhood Christmases, before people had to leave for their various holiday destinations.

Sean, I could see, didn't like to leave me alone.

'Are you sure you're OK, Maeve?'

'Yes, Sean, I'm fine.'

'Why don't you go to Maria's tonight? I'm sure she wouldn't mind.'

'Of course she wouldn't. She invited me actually.'

'Why didn't you go then? Why are you spending the night of Christmas Eve here on your own? It's a bit bleak.'

'Honestly Sean, I'm fine. I don't want to overstay my welcome with Joe and Maria. I'll sleep there tomorrow night, and come home on Stephen's Day. That's the way I want it.'

He didn't look convinced, but as his children were impatiently pulling at his sleeve, and Eimear was pointedly looking at her watch, there wasn't much he could do. He gave me a quick hug and they left.

Mum and Dad left last. Once again I was prepared and managed to duck Dad's playful punch. (They hurt actually, when he makes contact. He's stronger than he realises. I must have a word with Mum about it.) Mum and Dad didn't seem to mind leaving me on my own, and were oddly skittish as they set off for their first night at the hotel. I hope I wasn't right about the bus pass sex. Dad's back isn't the best, and Mum gets a bit wheezy whenever she's excited.

Still, on the plus side, I suppose the AIDS rate among pensioners can't be that high.

I've tidied away the wine glasses and the plates. I've vacuumed up the pie crumbs, and I've folded the wrapping paper and put it away for next year. (Eat your heart out, Theresa.) My bin is now full with the packaging from the children's toys. I've cleaned up the wee with which Darragh adorned my bathroom tiles. I've scraped the half pint of liquid soap from the sides of the sink.

Sean and Eimear brought me a half bottle of expensive red wine, so I am going to sit by my fire, and sip this, and eat the microwaveable Thai green curry from the freezer. I have a full box of coal, a good book and an undemanding video. I'm going to have an early night, and in the morning I'll get up late. After breakfast (chocolate muffins, as it's Christmas), I'm going to go for a brisk walk on the beach. After that, I'm going to visit my two very dear friends, and their doddery old uncle.

Maybe Christmas isn't so bad after all.

Chapter Thirty-six

27 December

Another Christmas over. Predictable as ever. Time to tidy away the trees and the tinsel. Bring the cards into Boots to be recycled. Eat the last few ageing mince pies. Make the remains of the turkey into curry, and feed what's left of the ham to the cat. Roll on next year.

Well actually, it wasn't quite as predictable as all that. I'm just teasing, in the unlikely event that someone takes a sly look at this writing before tossing it on the bonfire. I'm dragging out the pleasure of the unexpected. I'm also savouring it for myself. Making it last. Enjoying every little moment in anticipation of committing my happiness to paper. I'm looking forward to writing this bit, and I don't want to rush it. And if no one else ever cares, it doesn't matter. I'm going to re-read this bit often. I'm happy today and I don't want to forget how that feels.

I'll go back to Christmas morning and explain.

I woke late, and lay in bed for a while, enjoying the comfortable feeling that when I did get up, I'd have somewhere to go. Somewhere I actually wanted to be, rather than somewhere I had to be. I had a leisurely breakfast of warm croissants, from the cardboard cylinder that explodes when you peel off the outside and press it with the end of a spoon. (I had forgotten to pick up the promised chocolate muffins. I went to the larder, and there they were – in Tesco's.) I ate the croissants with real butter and some of Mum's home-made raspberry jam. All this was washed down with strong coffee, freshly ground in the fancy gadget that Niamh gave me for Christmas.

I dressed in my new straight black trousers, and the mauve silk shirt Mum and Dad gave me. I polished my old black ankle boots in a failed attempt to make them look less old. I really splashed out, and sprayed on some of the expensive perfume that one of my pupils, son of the local chemist, gave me last week. (His presents never get recycled.) For me, this counts as serious dressing up, but I had no choice. Even I, the queen of scruffs, couldn't show up for Christmas dinner wearing denims and a sweatshirt.

I packed up the car with my overnight bag, two bottles of red wine, a large box of mince pies and presents for Joe and Maria. The spiced beef, upon which Mum insisted, which she mentioned every day for the month of December, had been delivered on Christmas Eve. I packed a recycled box of chocolates for the doddery uncle, so he wouldn't feel left out. Just in case he is in his senses, I even checked to see that they weren't too far out of date. Three months isn't too bad for chocolates. They surely couldn't become poisonous that quickly.

After the car was packed, I went for a walk on the beach. It was a cold, bright day, perfect for a walk. Perfect for laughing at the die-hards who seem to get pleasure from swimming on Christmas day. I don't get much pleasure from swimming in the sea, even in August, but each to his own I suppose. There was a large group of swimmers this year, loudly supported by fully clothed bystanders, who shivered in hats and gloves and scarves and fleeces. These warmly dressed ones manfully swigged hot whiskies from flasks while shouting encouragement, as their blue friends battled with the cold grey waves.

After my walk I drove to Maria's house, and the front door burst open as I pulled up outside. Before I had time to get out of the car, Maria and Joe rushed out to greet me with hugs and laughter. They seemed very glad to see me, and I found myself thinking that the uncle must be more doddery than they had remembered. I thought they must be happy at the prospect of talking to someone with more than half a functioning brain, and I was glad to be there. Glad to be of service. They made me feel very welcome, as they always do, but I got the strange feeling that they had been anxiously awaiting my arrival for hours. Maybe I

353

shouldn't have had that second cup of coffee. Perhaps I shouldn't have lingered quite so long on the beach. I began to worry at the prospect of spending time with the old uncle, but I consoled myself with the thought that the more difficult he was, the more help I would be to Maria and Joe.

Maria ushered me inside, and Joe chivalrously carried my bag upstairs, which was totally unnecessary, as it contained only my night things, my toilet bag and one change of clothes, and was very light. Maria took my mince pies towards the kitchen and I went to follow her, half-afraid to go into the living room, where no doubt the dreaded uncle slouched in wait. She stopped me at the kitchen door and whispered.

'Please, Maeve. Go in and chat to Uncle Danny, he's half deaf and I'm worn to a frazzle from trying to make conversation. I think he's a bit senile too, and he keeps repeating himself. If he tells me about the Emergency again, I'll go crazy.'

'Wonderful,' I replied as she propelled me through the door, smiling her sweetest smile as she did so.

Then she all but deafened me as she shouted at the top of her voice, 'Danny, wake up, Maeve is here.'

Maria's living room is very large, and he was at the furthest end from where I stood. I could see that he was sitting by the fire, with his back to the door, though most of his body was hidden by the high wing-backed chair. All that was visible, as I advanced the few steps towards him, were his outstretched legs, oddly clad, for a doddery uncle, in blue denim. In the next few seconds it began to dawn on me that old men don't usually wear trendy brown suede boots either, and I wondered if the poor senile man had lost all his clothes, and was now dressed in things belonging to Joe. I donned a patronising little smile, and braced myself for a shouted introduction.

I must have made a marvellous sight for Maria and Joe, who, though I didn't realise it at the time, were delightedly peeping around the door. There I stood, arm outstretched offering the recycled Quality Street (with the expiry date rubbed off), ready to bellow a polite greeting, when up from the chair in front of me, freezing me in my tracks, rose Charlie. Yes, that Charlie, the one from Vancouver.

He looked like a little boy, unsure of whether he'd done the right thing, unsure of how he'd be received. At the corners of his mouth was a little lurking smile ready to break out if things went well. (He told me afterwards that when he saw my stunned expression, he couldn't decipher it, unsure of whether it meant his appearance was a wonderful surprise, or a dreadful shock.) He extended a hand to shake mine, which was still outstretched, gripping the chocolates in their shiny red wrapping. Quickly he thought better of it, and stepped forward to hug me, a big old friendly kind of hug, a nice hug. Then he stepped back again, and what could have been a slightly awkward moment was relieved by Maria and Joe rushing in, laughing.

'Well, Maeve, how do you like my dear old Uncle Danny?'

'You rotten things. Why didn't you tell me?'

'And miss that look of stupefaction on your face? No chance.'

'And, Charlie, what on earth are you doing here? Where did you come from all of a sudden? I thought you were in Vancouver. How come you're in Cork?'

Charlie had difficulty in answering my rush of questions, as he was busy wiping tears of laughter from his eyes. Eventually he composed himself a little. 'Oh, Maeve, you were a picture. We should have had a video camera set up to record your reaction. I've never seen such a look of surprise.' He hesitated.

'It's so good to see you again. It's just great.'

My reply was spontaneous and genuine. 'Well, Charlie, it's wonderful to see you too. I'm delighted that you're here.'

I felt a mixture of feelings. I was surprised of course. And embarrassed too, in the light of our conversation that last night in Vancouver. Mostly I was just pleased. It was great to see him again, and it looked, by the way he was beaming at me, that he was glad to see me too. Joe, the perfect host, ran to the kitchen and returned with a silver tray, four glasses and a bottle of champagne. He opened the champagne, denting the ceiling when the cork unexpectedly went into orbit. Then he poured what hadn't spilt onto the carpet, and we drank to Christmas, world peace, old friends and new friends.

Charlie buzzed with a kind of nervous energy, which soon transmitted itself to the rest of us, as we talked and laughed and joked. Occasionally, one of us would address Charlie as 'Uncle Danny' and we'd all fall around laughing, giddy from excitement and champagne bubbles. Maria and Joe were clearly delighted at the success of their plotting. I was delighted to be there, and Charlie. . . Well I'd have to say that Charlie looked fairly pleased with himself too.

And so the day continued, like one long party. It was the kind of Christmas day I hadn't had for years, one like I'd had as a child. You know a child's Christmas day. You never want it to end, savouring every single moment, clinging on to each little event, trying to make it last longer than other days, though no matter what you did, it still whizzed by, ending all too soon.

There was a sad moment, when Charlie returned to the room after speaking to Todd on the telephone. It must have been difficult for him, hearing Todd's enthusiastic voice describing the presents Toby and Melinda had given him, and thanking Charlie for the ones he'd sent. We voiced our sympathy, and gradually Charlie brightened, not being one for brooding or melodrama. Not like someone I know well.

The story of his visit came out gradually. It seems that Maria and Charlie had maintained a busy little correspondence over the months, beginning as soon as Maria arrived home. Then, some time ago, when Charlie mentioned that Todd was spending Christmas with 'Melinda and Toby' and that he himself had to spend a week in London in January on a research project, Maria began to plot and plan. She invited him to stay, but didn't tell me, as she thought it would be a great surprise. This is a first for her, as she's such an open and honest person. Scheming doesn't come easily to her. Fortunately, she met my mum in the supermarket, and ran the idea by her. Mum, who is one of life's born schemers (in the nicest possible way), loved the idea, and then there was no going back. Charlie was happy to accept Maria's invitation to spend some time with herself and Joe. And with me of course.

It wasn't hard to get me to agree either. Even though I never suspected about Charlie, I was quite happy to pass on the hotel, and the geriatrics charades fest. Maria grinned guiltily as she filled me in. 'We wanted to surprise you, but we knew you'd go on about being in the way, and us needing our privacy. We were afraid at first that you would say no. Then your mother had the great idea of inventing Uncle Danny. Once he was invented, you were a pushover.' I blushed at the thought of how transparent I am, but was too happy to care much about it.

The dinner was perfect, though it wasn't on the table at one o'clock sharp, like it would have been at home. The roast potatoes might not have been quite as crisp as I was used to, and I found a small lump in my gravy, but that wasn't the point. There was no fussing and foostering, no nervous tension, and no minor heart failure when Maria realised that there was no cranberry sauce. We forgot to eat the stuffing, finding it in a dried-up lump in the oven hours later. But who cares? The icing on the cake was when Maria admitted to putting the spiced beef in the freezer, as she felt we couldn't manage to do justice to it.

After dinner, Charlie did the washing up, and I served coffee to Maria and Joe who took the opportunity to recline on the sofa, in lazy, post-dinner mood.

The day slid past, as we revelled in the easy companionship, and I noticed with great pleasure that Joe and Charlie got on famously, chatting and slagging each other like old friends. We didn't even find time to listen to the Queen's speech. And for the first Christmas Day of my life, I didn't watch a James Bond film or *Charlie and the Chocolate Factory*.

Finally, in the early hours, after sipping one last drink, we headed for bed. Charlie escorted me to the door of my room, and gave me a chaste kiss on the cheek before retiring to his own room next door. All his talk of love seemed to be forgotten, and that suited me fine. Being friends was just fine with me.

I had a storybook awakening next morning. I rubbed my eyes and looked around the unfamiliar room, before realising where I was, and why I had a nice warm feeling inside. I could hear muffled voices from downstairs, three of them, so I tiptoed to the shower, and had a luxurious five minutes, enjoying Maria's strawberry shower gel, her tea tree shampoo, and then her warm, fluffy towels. I dressed in my only change of clothes, and rather shyly went to join the others, who were sitting around the kitchen table enjoying a cup of coffee. Maria jumped up and got me the plate of sausages and rashers that she'd been keeping warm. I enjoyed a leisurely, companionable breakfast, as we sipped cup after cup of strong black coffee.

After that the four of us went for a long, bracing walk, and then, feeling suitably virtuous, we retired to the nearest pub, where a few hours passed by without our noticing. In the evening, Maria worked wonders with the leftovers, and produced a great, tasty meal. After another late night, I found myself sleeping in Maria's again, reluctant to leave the companionship of her home, and glad to accept her invitation to stay. The perfect guest I planned to be has vanished, but no one seems to mind.

I rose late this morning, had another great chatty breakfast, before packing my small bag and coming home. Joe and Maria are doing all their duty visiting this afternoon (to geriatric aunts and uncles that actually exist), and Charlie has to spend a few hours on his research, so I've come home to gather my senses, and change my clothes.

It's a great feeling. I've nothing particular to do, all afternoon to do it. I'm going to do some washing and ironing and then I'll potter around the house for a while. At around six, I'll shower, wash my hair, and put on my best gear for a night on the town. Joe, Maria and I plan to show Charlie the bright lights of Cork tonight, starting with a meal, and then, energy permitting, we'll check out one of the night clubs.

Charlie is like a breath of fresh air in my life. We get on great. I could talk to him all day and all night and never get bored. We laugh together, and mess about, but we also find time for more serious chat – books, films, the meaning of life, all that old deep type of stuff.

Still, though, we need to be very, very clear about one thing. Charlie is not the answer to my mother's novenas and first Friday Masses. He's not the love of my life, the subject of my waking dreams. I don't fancy him. I like him and that's very different. He's a friend, a very nice friend and that's all. I don't go all trembly when I meet him, my knees don't quiver and my heart doesn't leap. For a long time now, I have a limited (very limited, actually) circle of friends, and now I have one more. That can't be a bad thing. I'm very glad that Charlie is my friend. He will probably be on my Christmas card list for a few more years, now that we've met again and got on so well together. Some day perhaps, if he invites me, I might even visit him in Vancouver. He might come back here in a few years time, and spend some time with me. However, I am not, certainly not going to be stupid. I'm not going to mistake companionship for love. I am not going to tell myself I love him, just because I'm desperate, and because he's there. And because he's nice.

I've had a happy, happy Christmas. I feel wonderful today (as Eric Clapton nearly said).

The reason I feel so wonderful today, is that I've made a great new friend.

Charlie is my friend.

Full stop.

Chapter Thirty-seven

1 January

I think I picked the wrong medium for this record. A nice, old-fashioned, spiral-bound notebook would have been good. If I had used one of those, then I could discreetly remove pages that I didn't like, or pages that show how I was raving when I wrote them. There would be no tell-tale, torn edges to show that those particular, aberrant scribblings had ever existed.

Take the last few pages for instance. They could go.

That old 'he's just a friend' crap.

'I don't fancy him.'

'He's not the love of my life.'

Hah! Did I really write those words?

Did I mean them?

Did I think I meant them?

Am I a pathetic eejit or what?

I'm going to skip the suspense this time, Walter. It's too much trouble to construct the teasing passages, laced with little hints and pointers to help the reader to pick up the message. I'd never be able to weave the tangled threads. I'd surely lose track of where I was going. I couldn't work it so the truth would only gradually dawn, poking its sly little head out from under intricate layers of deep meaning.

This time it's the blunt approach, with no possibility of misunderstanding or understatement. I will leave no safety net, no chance of later backtracking. No opportunity for deceit. No saying, 'well. . ., that's not really what I meant'.

So here goes – I love Charlie.

Phew! Now, that's off my chest, and I can relax and tell how I came to this strange and wonderful realisation.

The few days after St Stephen's Day were wonderful. We enjoyed lots of fine food and drink. We went to bed late every night, and we rose late every morning. Mostly Charlie and I socialised with Joe and Maria, but occasionally we went out without them. Either option was fine by me. Some nights I slept at Maria's and some nights I went home. Each day was much the same, but they were all great. As the time went by, a nice easy companionship developed between Charlie and me. No romance, no sex, no heartfelt sighs and meaningful glances. No declarations of endless love. No violins. No embarrassing misunderstandings. There was nothing between us except friendship, plain, simple and uncomplicated.

Then came New Year's Eve.

Joe knew somebody, who knew somebody, who was having a party, and as none of us had any special plans to mark the occasion, we wangled invitations. The four of us went to the pub first, and arrived at the party house a little after ten. Joe rang the bell, and the door was opened by a giggling guest, who wore a blue and pink tissue-paper hat over a sparkly, silver-foil wig. This young man waved us in, quite unconcerned about who we were, or whether we had any right to be there. We edged our way in, past a large, noisy crowd gathered in the hall. Joe didn't recognise anyone, but that wasn't really a problem. It never became clear whose party it was. There was no obvious divide between those who were invited, those like us who were sort of invited, and those who had just wandered in on their way past, enticed by the laughter, the music, and the balloons that adorned the scraggly bushes in the front garden.

It was like a time-warp party. Everyone brought drink, mostly six-packs, none of them chilled, some of them almost warm. There was food laid out on the kitchen table, on floppy white paper plates. There were thin, anaemic-looking sandwiches (egg or cheese), and Ritz crackers with bright orange cheese spread. I had the funny feeling that if someone were to turn off the lights, the cheese spread would glow in the dark. It was that sort of colour. And I feared that anyone who had eaten it would glow from within, like a reversed X-ray.

Bizarrely, since this is not 1972, there were cocktail sticks with cubes of cheese and pineapple, neatly stuck into a half orange. All very avant-garde – twenty years ago that is.

The music came from an ancient music centre, and was made up of long-playing, black plastic records, many of which appeared to be scratched, which wasn't surprising really, since they must all have been at least twenty years old. 'Rumours'. 'Bat Out of Hell'. 'Dark Side of the Moon'. I don't think I need to say more. There was even a morose-looking girl, just like there always used to be, who seemed to be completely alone, unable to mix. This girl spent the entire night examining the record sleeves, as if they might contain within their ancient cardboard covers the secrets of the universe, or at least the formula for Diet Coke. Every few minutes she'd shake her lank locks dismissively, and switch records in the middle of a track, just when people were getting to like the one that was already playing.

Another sad soul, a sorry-looking article, clad in grey trousers like my dad wears, a striped shirt, a tie and V-neck jumper (yuck), had obviously brought no drink. Instead of just asking someone for a can or a bottle, or nicking one when no one was looking, he was wandering around to groups of people, holding out a saucepan and asking everyone to pour in some of their drink. In the few minutes that I observed him, he mixed together beer, vodka, gin, red wine and something from an unmarked bottle that may have been poteen. It must have been incredibly toxic, and I watched in horror as he proceeded to drink it in huge gulps, straight from the saucepan. I sincerely hoped I wouldn't be within spewing distance when his stomach realised what had been inflicted on it.

The rest of the guests, the relatively normal-looking ones, stood around in groups, chatting and tapping their feet in time to the music, slightly put out whenever the self-appointed disc jockey changed the beat.

There was plenty of drink, which oiled everyone's tongues, so the conversation was animated, though in most cases totally pointless. You know what party conversation is like. It is usually deep and meaningful, wandering around in endless circles, going nowhere, taking half the night to get there.

The party was strange enough for us, the locals, but completely incomprehensible to Charlie. He looked around in wonder, like a man in shock, and repeated over and over, 'I had a party just like this once, in my friend's dad's garage. It was in 1974.'

Maria and Joe disappeared, and Charlie and I found ourselves in a little corner of the kitchen (clichéd, I know), sipping our warm beer and chatting. Time whizzed by, as it tends to do when I'm with Charlie, and someone belatedly announced, 'It's the New Year, it's ten past twelve'. This prompted a flurry of kissing and hugging and well-wishing, followed by several out of tune choruses of 'Auld Lang Syne'. Charlie and I got sucked into a dangerously swaying circle, arms crossed over in front of us, singing loudly with the rest of them.

Charlie, though slightly dazed-looking, seemed to be enjoying himself. However, after the fourth stranger had given me a beery, slobbery kiss, I'd had more than enough. This must have showed, so Charlie, grinning at my discomfiture, suggested going somewhere less hectic. He thoughtfully grabbed our jackets from where we'd left them on a chair and led me out the open back door. We closed the door behind us, and stood outside like two escaped convicts, pleased with our freedom, but not quite sure where to go next. As our eyes got used to the half-darkness, we could see a little wooden bench, halfway down the small, untidy garden. Charlie led the way towards it, and he gallantly used his coat sleeve to brush off the accumulated leaves and assorted dodgy-looking debris. We sat down next to each other, but not touching. We were just good friends, remember? A comfortable, easy silence settled down between us, punctuated by occasional bursts of song or laughter from inside. Every now and then, in the far distance, I could hear the tooting of car horns, and once or twice an illegal firework spluttered into the sky over the city. It was a cold night, and there was a smoky, wintry smell in the air. I sat there, quite happy and relaxed, wanting nothing, expecting nothing.

After a while, Charlie spoke my name softly. I turned towards him, but he was staring silently in front of him, making me wonder if he had said anything at all. I looked at his face, half-lit by the light from the glass kitchen door. He wore a sad, resigned expression, and unsure of what to say or do, I turned away, facing down the concrete path again. Minutes passed and then he spoke once more, in the same soft, sad tone. 'Happy New Year, Maeve.' I turned to face him again, and this time he leaned ever so slightly towards me, and kissed me on the mouth. His lips were dry and cold, and after the barest touch, he removed them from mine. We looked at each other, and then, prompted by whom, I do not know, we kissed again. Another chaste kiss, just like the first. Since no one was objecting, it seemed prudent to continue, and we sat like that, tentatively kissing, mouths closed, still sitting slightly apart from each other. We both had our hands in our jacket pockets, against the cold, so the touch of skin was confined to our lips, concentrated there.

We drew apart again, and gazed at each other. I tried to read what he was thinking, but found I couldn't think straight myself. My thoughts galloped crazily around my head, out of my control. I felt slightly dizzy. Charlie took my head ever so gently in his hands and kissed me once more a different kiss this time, a probing one. It was a strange, unfamiliar feeling – I found myself responding to his kiss with something other than a panicky worry at how I would be able to disentangle myself without too much embarrassment.

Loins is a funny word. I always feel only biblical writers, or butchers describing their cuts of meat, should use it. I have to use it now though, because I can find no other. As I sat in that cold, untidy garden, licking Charlie's teeth, a feeling rose in a place deep inside me, a place that could only be described as my loins. It was a strange and wonderful feeling, unfamiliar, but so nice.

The door from the house swung open, and a drunken man stood in the doorway. He stood swaying on the threshold for a moment. Then he unbuttoned his fly with great difficulty and urinated at length on the dead plant which stood on the doorstep, before lurching back inside, slamming the door behind him, making the cheap glass rattle. Charlie looked on in wonder, shaking his head. I feared that our wonderful moment was spoiled, sullied by the intrusion. I looked towards Charlie, hoping for more of those stirring kisses, but this time he took me in his arms and we held each other tightly. I buried my head in the little warm space where his jacket was slightly unzipped. I could smell Maria's washing powder and the faint scent of Charlie's soap.

The door opened once more, and a couple swayed out, his hand searching up the back of her jumper, hers edging down the waistband of his trousers. I couldn't bear to move, to break our moment, but even more, I couldn't bear to watch the groping of the couple a few feet away. I dithered for only a moment before I did something that, for me, was very bold and quite out of character. I looked Charlie in the eye, and brazenly I suggested that we go back to my place.

It was only a short drive, and we didn't speak. I wondered in a mounting panic what I should say and do when we got to my house. All this was so new to me. I didn't know how to act. I was embarrassed. I was so aware of Charlie in the seat next to me, but I didn't dare to turn my head to look at him. Should I swan in, and suggest in a husky voice that I slip into something more comfortable? Should I boldly take his hand and drag him towards my bedroom, trailing socks and knickers as we went? I knew my knickers were clean, but were they old and stretched and grey? I tried frantically to remember what bra I'd put on before coming out. I hoped it wasn't the one with the frayed straps and the large hole in the left cup.

Or was this just a dreadful, humiliating mistake? Maybe Charlie just wanted a little innocent, uncomplicated snog in the garden. Did the tenth chorus of 'Auld Lang Syne' make him get slightly carried away?

I had a sudden irrational fear that maybe he was gay. When he said he loved me, all those months ago in Vancouver, did he mean it in a friendly kind of way? How could I have been so stupid? Could that be why Melinda left him? Was he now sitting in the passenger seat wondering desperately how to escape without offending me?

Or did he think I was inviting him back so that we could share some ham sandwiches and reheated turkey vol au vents?

I was nearly sick from desire and fear as we drove in through the gate. We climbed out of the car, and I went up the path first, opening the door and stepping inside. Charlie followed meekly, and as I closed the front door, he pressed his body against mine and we kissed again. He stopped for a moment and drew back. No one, ever, has looked at me like he did. When he spoke, his voice was unnaturally hoarse. 'Please Maeve. Please. Can we go to bed?'

Luckily he didn't look tired.

I nodded, and we went towards my room.

Sorry. Just in case I predecease my parents, and they look at this before tossing it on the bonfire, I'm not going to give the gory details. Saying Mrs Flynn's mince pies are nicer than my Mum's is one thing. Saying what Charlie and I did next is an entirely different matter. I am not comfortable about writing down rude words anyway; thinking them is OK, but writing them is not for me. And anyway, if I start writing about sex, there's no telling where it will all end. I might start drinking Chardonnay, and wearing Prada shoes, and shopping in Harvey Nick's, even though it's on a different island. I might accidentally write a bestseller, with raised silver lettering on the cover. (Now that I think of it though, the silver lettering seems to be a bit passé. A bit last year. Nowadays the trend seems to be for book covers to be bright yellow or lime green with writing in scarlet or orange.)

But why do I care? No, none of that is my style. I'm Catholic, and a teacher, for God's sake. I'm not writing down the sweaty, writhing bits. That would be quite beyond my limited capabilities.

Suffice to say that in the next half-hour I did things that I've never done before, and felt things I've never felt before. Unlike a certain celebrity, I think everything I did was legal, but that didn't spoil the fun. I liked it. A lot. I hope to do it again, very soon and very often. I plan to make up for lost time.

And, judging by the serene smirk on Charlie's face as he slept beside me last night, I think he might help.

Chapter Thirty-eight

It's still 1 January. It's still the morning after the night before. I just have to write more, before I forget. In case I change my mind and deny what happened.

I woke this morning and remembered at once what had happened last night. Now I admit I did have a few hints, pointers to put me on the right track. Instead of my usual pink brushed-cotton pyjamas with the sensible buttons down the front, I was wearing nothing but the silver chain I put on before going to that strange party, and a silly, self-satisfied smile. My body ached in the nicest possible way, reminding me. I turned to where Charlie should be, desperate for more of what I'd had last night, all that nice stuff I didn't describe earlier, and don't plan to describe now either.

Charlie wasn't there though, and a moment of cold despair grabbed at my bare shoulders. It must have been a mistake after all. He must have had a dreadful shock when he woke up next to a naked me. Obviously he had been too embarrassed to face me, so he'd slunk off to Maria's to hide. No doubt he was already packing his bags, hoping to be out of the country before I arrived to wear him down with my pathetic emotional needs and my sad passion. What a fool I was. How could I have thought it was any more than a drunken fling?

Before I could sink too low, though, I became aware of a soft whistling coming from the kitchen. It was 'Auld Lang Syne', slightly out of tune. I cast my eyes around the room, searching for something to put on (I'm not enough of a noughties woman to be able to stroll naked into the kitchen to join the man I slept with for the first time last night). Unusually, my room was fairly tidy, but I found my long fleecy jacket which lay in a heap on the floor. I put it on and wrapped it over my front. It just about covered all the rude bits.

Shyly I entered the kitchen. Charlie didn't see me at first. He looked quite at home, as he pottered around, making toast, and filling the cafetiere with hot water. I went to him and we embraced. I was at a bit of a disadvantage, as my jacket had fallen open, and he was fully dressed. Things were soon evened out though, as he led me back to the bedroom, removed all of his clothes, and we shared another half-hour of blissful cavorting. I've discovered my loins, and I like them.

Afterwards (as they say in the best romantic novels), we lay in each other's arms. I felt like all the lucky girls in all the romantic movies I'd ever watched. Imaginary violins played in my head. Charlie's arms were hairy and slightly freckled, and warm against my shoulders. The skin on his face was rough and stubbly where it rested against my cheek. His right hand held my left, and I noticed that his nails were perfect, as he carefully, gently traced the prominent blue veins on the back of my hand. I lay there, loving every single thing about this beautiful man who lay beside me, and wondered how I could possibly have thought that he was just my friend. How could I have denied my feelings? How could I have been so wrong? For an intelligent girl, I certainly have some weak points.

The phone rang, and being one of those helpless people who cannot ignore it, I picked it up. It was Maria, giggling. 'Just checking to see that you got home OK.' She paused, 'Charlie didn't come home last night. I wonder where he is.' Charlie leaned over, kissed my hair, and took the phone from my hand. He spoke with authority. 'Hi, Maria. Don't grill any bacon for me. When Maeve and I get up we'll get breakfast here.' There was no audible response from the other side, so he spoke again, 'We'll call you later. Thanks Maria.' He hung up without waiting for a reply. We giggled together, enjoying the fact that we would certainly be the source of animated conversation at Maria and Joe's breakfast table.

I could have stayed there forever, in bed with him, not speaking, just feeling him next to me, listening to his breathing, snuggled against his warmth. I felt moved to write soppy love poetry, like that produced by the housewives, all hearts and music and smiles and love. My bedroom, an ordinary enough square room, with its magnolia painted walls, suddenly seemed to be the most magical, beautiful place I'd ever been. It had become a wonderland with Dunnes Stores curtains and Marks and Spencer sheets.

Eventually, I had to get up, desperate to use the toilet. (Why doesn't that ever happen in romantic movies?) I went to shower, and Charlie joined me. He shampooed my hair and washed my back; a personal act, something no one besides my mother has ever done. When we had finished, I saw that he had placed a large towel on the radiator to warm, and this he wrapped around the two of us, drying us both. He wriggled out, and I followed him to the bedroom, still wrapped in the towel. I sat on the rumpled bed and watched him as he dressed. I saw him button his shirt, zip up his trousers, put on his socks and tie his leather shoelaces. I enjoyed the movements of his hands, and the glimpses of his body, healthy and strong. I gazed in wonder as he snapped his watch on to his freckled wrist and straightened it over a slightly prominent bone. He combed his hair and slipped his comb into the back pocket of his trousers. I took pleasure in all these mundane sights, as if they were part of the most marvellous scene ever enacted.

Charlie went towards the kitchen, turning back at the last moment, resting one hand on the door. 'You know what Maeve? I slept in this bed alone, for twenty nights in July. I lay between your sheets, and wondered what you were like. I wondered if you were lonely in this house. I opened your drapes every morning, and looked out, trying to figure out where all the boats that sail along the horizon out there could be headed. I looked at that badly plastered patch of your ceiling, and asked myself why you didn't get it mended. I thought a lot of things, but I never, ever thought that one day I would sleep here with you, and love you so much.' Then, closing the door gently behind him, he went back to the kitchen. I could hear the wheeze of the kettle and the clatter of utensils as he made fresh coffee and toast. The soft whistling began again. Still not in tune.

I sat on the bed for a while longer, luxuriating in the warmth of his open affection. 'I love you, Charlie,' I whispered towards the closed door.

Yes, Walter. Remember how you always told us to find our genre and stick with it? I've found mine at last. It's soppy romance, and I love it.

Chapter Thirty-nine

4 January

I've just got back from the airport.

I've watched hundreds of emigrants parting from tearful parents and siblings, before flying back to their real lives in the smoke and bustle of London. Toddlers with strong English accents were prised from the arms of Irish grannies they hardly knew. Tears were hurriedly wiped away, and brave faces plastered into place, as the final farewells were uttered. Promises to visit in the summer were made, though no doubt villas in Tuscany, and gîtes in Provence will intervene, leaving the ageing parents to lead another long, lonely year, waiting for the next bittersweet Christmas to arrive. Grey-haired, worn-down pensioners, with slouched shoulders and bent heads made their way slowly back to their small cars in the short-term car park. The still-twinkling festive lights were like a sick, cruel joke, though they must have been so wonderful on Christmas Eve, when these parents came to meet their precious sons and daughters, so full of hope for the joyous season that seemed to stretch forever ahead. As I climbed into my car, tinny Christmas carols still poured out from the external airport speakers, as if in final insult.

Charlie has gone to London to meet some people and work on his project. I lived without him for thirty-five years, and managed fine, but now a few days away from him seems like a very long time. He'll be coming back when he's finished, to spend a short time here with me, and then he'll have to return to Vancouver. Suddenly I hate Vancouver, the city I thought I'd always love. He's going back there, and I can't bear to think about that. I don't want to think about it, really. I've decided that I'm going to look forward to seeing him next week, and anything beyond that will have to wait for my attention, along with the dusting, the Sunday papers and the '50c off' vouchers for Sunny Delight that expire next month.

We've had a lovely few days. Charlie quickly gave up the pretence of staying with Joe and Maria, and moved his things over here. His jacket fits in ever so nicely on the hook on the back door, and his toothbrush soon found its place next to mine in the chipped blue mug over the sink in the bathroom. We've had wild nights and lazy mornings, and each day I looked at him in wonder, not knowing how I came to love him so much, so soon. We did real boyfriendy girlfriendy kind of things. We walked arm in arm on the beach, we went to the pictures and snogged in the back row, I gave him my last Rolo, and he gave me his last Star Burst. I go around humming, and thinking happy thoughts. It's a bit pathetic, but I don't care.

Maria is thrilled with the way things have developed, fully approving of our liaison. She's kind enough not to say, 'I told you so', though no doubt she's sorely tempted. Of course, Joe and I don't discuss relationships, but I can see that he likes Charlie, and that Charlie likes him. Sometimes, as they argue in a friendly way over the particular merits of soccer and American football, I feel a bit left out, so I retire in a mock sulk, knowing full well that Charlie won't exclude me for long. Anyway, I need the little respite so I can bore Maria by telling her at length how wonderful Charlie is, and how foolish I was not to have noticed it sooner.

Mum and Dad came back from their hotel, where it seems there was no bondage or group sex, well, not that they're telling me about anyway. It seems that it was all charades and bingo and table quizzes, and ham and turkey and sherry, and they loved every moment. Even without the spiced beef. I think that their funny manner before they left was in anticipation of me meeting Charlie. As I said before, my mother loves plotting, and I'd say it broke her heart that she couldn't witness my surprise when he appeared in Maria's on Christmas day. Mum doesn't find it at all strange that we have 'hit it off,' as she so quaintly puts it. I asked her why, and she just laughed, 'I'm your mum. I'm meant to know you better than you know yourself. I knew by the way you talked about him, the way his name kept cropping up. Then Maria confirmed it for me. She said you were cracked about him, and I could see it too. You might be able to fool yourself, but you'll never fool your dear old Mammy, who's known and loved you for thirty-five long years.'

Mum seemed to think that just because we 'hit it off', then everything was rosy and perfect, and that we would all live happily ever after. I protested at once. 'But he lives in Canada, thousands of miles away.' That wasn't a problem to Mum. It seems she's dropped her standards a bit over the years, moved the goalposts, so to speak. When Paddy and I first broke up, she talked about me meeting someone else, 'a nice doctor, or an accountant perhaps.' This revealed both her innate social snobbery, and the fact that she viewed getting a man as a sort of jukebox operation, where you press the right buttons and make your selection. Even then though, she rejected one vaguely possible suitor who appeared very briefly on the horizon of my romantic world, as he lived in Dublin. 'You wouldn't want to live in Dublin. It's too big, and far away, and we'd never see you.' Now though, her priorities have changed, and Vancouver was no problem. She hadn't yet met Charlie, and she approved already, even managing to ignore the few thousand miles of ocean that would soon heave and roll between us.

I began to feel the hot angry feeling I always felt when I knew she was desperate for me to get a man, compromising, as I saw it, my freedom and my individuality. 'You've never met him,' I burst out. 'He could be a pig. He could be Jack the Ripper's first cousin, or Bob the Robber's nephew. You just want to marry me off. You just want to tell your stupid narrow-minded friends that I've finally managed to get a man. You just want to get them off your back, so they will have to find someone else to gossip about and look down on. And, anyway, Charlie lives on the other side of the world, so what good is he to me?'

This I know is what was really upsetting me. I know he's a great guy, I know how strong my feelings for him are. I don't need my mum to affirm those. I just don't know what's going to happen when the time comes for him to leave.

Mum spoke soothingly, kindly ignoring the mean things I said about her friends. She calmed me as easily as she used to when I was a small child. She rambled on at length as she always did, with a few insightful comments lurking around within the mindless waffle. 'Look Maeve. I know we haven't met him, but Maria has told me that he's a fine person, and that's good enough for me. She has an excellent man in Joe, so I know her judgement is sound. I know I never liked that Peter chappie she used to hang around with, but at least she was smart enough to give him his walking papers. And I know Vancouver is a long way away, but think of your cousin Carol. She fell in love with that dark-skinned chap from Venezuela, and she hasn't looked back since. She got used to that foreign food in the end, and Auntie Nuala gets a few packs of Galtee rashers out to her every couple of months. If Carol can do it, surely you can work something out. That's if you really want to. And you were never that gone on Galtee rashers anyway, were you? You always preferred the ones from Mullane's. I bet Tom Mullane would vacuum-pack some if we asked him. He's got all kinds of fancy machines in his shop lately. I heard he got a grant from the EEC. He's dead right, getting the money before all those poor countries join up, with their hands out looking for grants of our money. Now, can you bring Charlie for tea tomorrow night?'

Really, if I had a pound for every time my mum has tried to get me to invite a male friend for tea, I'd be a very wealthy woman by now. (Well I suppose I shouldn't exaggerate so much; I'd have about thirteen pounds anyway). That was her ploy, years ago when I was younger, and still lived at home. Whenever Niamh or I mentioned going on a date, Mum would pounce in, 'Bring him home to tea first.' She loved to see our suitors properly, never content with just a fleeting glimpse as they called to collect us. She'd lay on a big spread, with the best dishes and a clean white tablecloth, despite our protestations that the young gentleman in question probably wouldn't notice, or care. Then the whole family would have to sit around

384

and listen, squirming with embarrassment, to her deceptively gentle, probing questions. She was well warned not to ask her favourite question, 'What does your father do?' but she still managed to glean this vital information in some kind of roundabout way. Soon, to avoid this ordeal, I didn't mention if I was meeting someone; I'd just skip off on the quiet.

For some reason though, Niamh regularly asked boys home, subjecting them to what I considered to be an outrageous grilling. Niamh always did what Mum wanted. I can't think why. She never read the book that said teenagers should be rebellious. She was never in trouble, and Mum always approved of her friends and her clothes. Niamh and I get on fine now, though I suspect we'd be closer if she hadn't always been such a goody goody, leaving me to rebel all on my own.

Where was Sean while all this was going on, I hear you ask? Well, that's the way things were back then. There was one rule for the boys and a different one for the girls. I protested, loudly and often, but I may as well have saved my breath. There was no backslipping on that particular one. Now, many years later, I can see why we were treated differently; the big difference was that Niamh or I might have got pregnant, while the fear that Sean might impregnate someone didn't seem to be an issue. Mum needn't have worried about me on that count though; look at me now, twenty years later, still childless. And Mum is obviously so desperate on my behalf that she'd probably even welcome an unplanned pregnancy, a baby fathered by a man who hadn't quite got around to adorning the second finger of my left hand with diamonds and gold.

I digress. Walter is losing his grip on me, and my work is becoming sloppy. It was the mention of bringing Charlie home for tea that did it; it just brought back so many teenage memories. I'm not a teenager any more though, and I knew sulking wouldn't save me, so I gave in, almost graciously.

After lengthy warnings to Charlie, letting him know what to expect, we arrived for tea. Mum had pulled out all the stops. I could see that the usually clean house had been scrubbed half to death. I could smell freshly baked bread, and her speciality, Chelsea buns. Dad was uncomfortable in his best suit and tie, and it became clear that he had been instructed not to read the paper, as unusually there were none in sight, and he didn't produce one during the meal.

Charlie was the perfect guest. He brought flowers for Mum and a bottle of wine. He admired the house, the garden, the food, the wallpaper and the cat. He asked Dad about his golf and Mum about her bridge. He praised me to the skies, insisting that 'you must both walk with your heads high, proud of raising such a wonderful daughter'. When he announced this, poor Mum flushed, unsure of how to respond to such a blatant effort to bombard her with charm.

Charlie responded to Mum's questioning in a chatty,

open manner. When inevitably the questions began to slide over the invisible line that divides healthy interest from rude personal inquisition, he ever so subtly avoided them, even fooling Mum to the extent that she didn't realise he was skirting some of the issues.

He coped so well that I began to relax a little, even enjoying myself, watching how he charmed them, knowing that he was sincere, knowing that they liked him. In the end I had to suggest that we leave as we had arranged to go out with Maria and Joe. Mum came out to the hall, and as we put on our coats, she smiled her approval behind Charlie's back. She formally shook his hand, and as she hugged me she whispered, 'He's nice, Maeve.'

I left feeling very pleased with myself and with Charlie. He had quite enjoyed himself, and berated me for implying that it would be an ordeal. I had to agree with him, conceding that it hadn't been that bad. I explained, shocking myself with the calculation, that it was seventeen years since I'd brought a boyfriend to tea with my parents, and that he had only been eighteen, not quite the worldly-wise, well-travelled gentleman that Charlie is. Also, though I couldn't mention this to Charlie, Mum was probably behaving better than she did on those earlier occasions. Back then she probably thought that Cork was full of men, all queuing up to court me, and her role was that of sifter of suitors. Now she knows better. She wasn't taking any chances, and wasn't going to risk scaring Charlie away.

I had no such fears. I was so happy and relaxed when I was with him, that I never felt the need to pretend to feel more or less than I did. I was myself, he was himself and we doodled along together just fine. I miss him now, but can live with it, as I know I'll see him soon.

Roll on 15 January.

Chapter Forty

14 January

You know the funny thing about clichés? They are pathetic and unoriginal, and used to death, but they are true. I always figured there had to be a reason for their popularity. The one I have in mind is, 'seeing the world through rose-tinted glasses'. That's exactly how I feel. Everything around me has taken on a wonderful new hue. I've gone back to work, and loved it. I sail in every morning on light, carefree feet. My class is basking in the joy of having a happy, slightly distracted teacher. We are flying through work, and when it's done, the children find many ways of persuading me to let them play games, paint or read their favourite Roald Dahl books. I rarely raise my voice, and the children have reduced their volume control accordingly, so the loudest noise is a busy hum as they read and work and learn.

I can even enjoy the staffroom, no longer seeing it as my own private purgatory. I have listened to Pat (three times actually), as he told the story of a great refereeing injustice perpetrated on Man. United on St Stephen's Day. I have listened to the rehashed opinions of every soccer pundit in the western world on the topic of this grievous wrong. I have joined in lengthy conversation with Mr Flynn, about the level of Irish required in the new curriculum. Wonder of wonders, though, I can now bear to be in the company of the great Theresa for more than two and a half minutes. I have listened to the account of her Christmas holidays without feeling nauseous. I didn't retch when she described every one of the ten presents she received from Michael, and the fifteen she gave to him. (She presented him with a gift-wrapped sod of grass, to represent the site of the house they will one day share.) I have endured the recitation of her teaching plan for the term. I know where her Auntie Mabel is going to sit on the day of the wedding. I have even asked Theresa how her tapestry cushions are progressing, and, what's more, I listened to the answer.

Pat and Mr Flynn are so caught up in their own worlds that they don't really notice me, they just use me as a convenient listening service, so they aren't aware of the rosy glow that surrounds me.

I think I could come to school with my head shaved and my nose pierced ten times, and it would take them weeks to notice. Theresa though, is different. I have caught her giving me strange looks, as she selects a new piece of coloured wool, and pauses to thread her needle, squinting slightly, and pursing her thin lips. Yesterday, after some moments studying two pieces of wool in ever so slightly different shades of green, she asked me outright, the most personal question she has ever asked. 'Isn't there something changed about you, Maeve? I'm not sure what it is, but since the holidays, you're different somehow.' I could think of plenty of smart answers to this, but enunciated none of them. I just smiled a dreamy smile, shrugged my shoulders and denied any knowledge of a change. I felt a (thankfully brief) moment of girlie closeness with her, as she shook her head, and insisted, 'There's definitely something. Give me time and I'll figure it out.' She will too. She's not one to give up easily. She will worry at the issue until she has it sorted to her satisfaction. She likes to be in control of her world, and won't rest until she finds the cause of my new benign personality. I know she will discover why the vibes of hatred have vanished, leaving behind a distracted, benevolent air. And I don't care at all. She can find out whatever she likes, and think whatever she likes. It's nothing to me. The rosy, happy me is immune to her petty ways.

There was a spring in my step as I left school today. I chatted briefly with some of the parents in the school yard, said farewell to my young charges, and waved cheerily at Theresa and Michael, as they set off together for another few days of happy mediocrity. It's Friday, and tomorrow morning at nine I'm going to the airport to meet Charlie, who's coming back from his

London trip. I've scrubbed the house, not because I feel the need to impress him, but because I have lots of excited, nervous energy and have to get rid of it somehow.

When it was no longer possible to clean the house any further, I tried to sit down and read, but I found it impossible to concentrate. I went for a long walk on the beach, but when I got back, I still found myself jigging around, unsure of how to occupy myself. I walked around the garden a few times, which was quite pointless, as there's nothing alive out there except for armies of hibernating slugs. (Do slugs hibernate?) The ground was a sodden mess, so I had to wash the kitchen floor again as I had covered it with muddy footprints. Then I paced the living room a few times, and rearranged the newspapers on the shelf under the coffee table. I paced some more.

Now I know how my poor past pupil Paul must feel all the time.

I forced down some food, which tasted of nothing, and then decided it was time to beautify myself.

I lathered a daring red colour into my hair, and half-read last week's newspapers, as I waited for the dye to soak in and transform me. I timed it carefully, and showered it off after the required forty-five minutes. I created my own private *Psycho* scene, as rivulets of red water flowed over my body and down the shower drain. Loath to abandon the pampering, I piled my silky, but redder than I would have liked, locks into a shower cap, and relaxed in a long luxurious bath. I treated my face to a soothing mud mask. Up to now, I never shaved in the wintertime. I figured that no one would see my hairy skin, unless I were involved in an accident and rushed to hospital. In that event, I reasoned, I'd have more to worry about than hairy underarms, so I've always spent six months of the year in slovenly hairy splendour, shaving only when it was warm enough again to wear shorts and sleeveless tops. I've shaved my legs and my underarms now though, confident that someone besides me or a kindly ambulance man in a fluorescent yellow vest will see them. I've plucked my eyebrows, and even (sorry Maria for the betrayal of our values) painted my nails a subtle shade of pearly pink. I don't think I'll ever be a scarlet woman, pale pink is the height of my daring.

I don't want to make too much of a fuss about tomorrow by dressing in my fanciest clothes, but I have taken care to iron the best of the casual trousers I bought in Vancouver all those long months ago. They are laid out on the chair in my bedroom, ready for the morning, along with the blouse I wore on Christmas day. On top of these lies the new lacy underwear I bought on Wednesday in Brown Thomas's January sale. Oh dear. Maybe I am turning into a scarlet woman after all. Isn't it great?

And if I'm buying lacy underwear in Brown Thomas, does that mean I am losing it completely? Is it time to put the Chardonnay on ice?

I'm relaxing in bed, listening to easy, romantic, tinkly piano music.

I'm admiring my painted nails, and running them through the soft red hair that no longer feels like my own.

I'm hoping that when Charlie steps through the customs area, he will recognise me.

I'm hoping that the mud mask hasn't released lots of hidden toxins which will hit my face tomorrow in a wild onslaught of pimples and blemishes.

I'm hoping that when I'm here again I won't be relaxing too much.

I'm as excited as any child on Christmas Eve; far too excited to sleep, full of joyful anticipation, willing time to fly by, so morning will dawn, and I can get what I dream of.

Isn't soppy romance a marvellous thing?

Isn't being happy so much nicer than being sad?

And so what if it doesn't make as good a story?

Chapter Forty-one

22 January

I'm just grabbing a few minutes to scribble some words. I haven't written since Charlie got back. I've been too busy, loving and being loved. I'm beginning to discover that it takes up a lot of time, this love business. Actually, it's very time-consuming indeed. You'd never think it.

Charlie came back last Saturday, and we had a joyful, romantic reunion: hugs, kisses and flowers, just like in the movies. I'd had a brief moment of doubt, as I waited in the airport, wondering if I'd just imagined how much I liked him and how good he made me feel. A moment of panic flicked towards me, as I wondered if I'd made a dreadful mistake. (After all, for a brief time last year, Wes was the man of my dreams.) Then the automatic, frosted-glass doors slid open, and I could see my beloved, walking behind a spotty teenager who was heavily laden with very dodgy-looking, overflowing canvas bags. Charlie stepped towards me, and tired of waiting for the teenager to manoeuvre his way around the railings, leaned across the waist-high barrier and hugged me. The pink roses he carried were squashed, but it was worth it, as all the good feelings returned, pushing my doubts beyond reach, back to the farthest edges of my mind, where I hope they will wither gracefully and die a painful death.

We strolled back to the car, and Charlie packed his bags into the boot, while I tried to reshape the crushed blooms. As I leaned against the car, in the cold winter sunshine, I found that my face was wearing that silly smile that seems to lurk around my lips a lot of the time lately, leaping into place at the oddest moments.

We mooched around for the weekend. It's great to be so at ease in someone's company. There was no need to go out, or do anything special; no agenda. We just pottered around the house, chatting; being together, washing socks and doing the crossword. The cryptic one. He's smart, this Charlie guy. (I've a funny feeling that if it had worked out with Wes there would have been no cryptic crosswords. Word searches would be more his thing. I could see Wes liking word searches. Or Spot the Ball, perhaps.)

Yesterday afternoon I found myself making a confession to Charlie. I revealed the fears I'd had when we first agreed the house swap.

'I thought you might be a great dirty slob.'

Charlie laughed. 'Whatever could have put that notion into your head?'

'I have no idea. I just had this crazy picture of you and Todd thrown on my couch, scoffing endless takeaways and downing gallons of Coke. I thought I'd come home to find my precious house infested with vermin, gorging on the greasy crumbs you left behind.'

He put on a mock offended air. 'Thanks a bunch, Maeve. Thanks for your faith in me.'

I sniffed. 'You're welcome. Anyway, Mr goody goody. I bet you had doubts about me.'

He looked horrified at the very thought. 'I was quite sure you would be perfectly nice.'

I snuggled closer to him and kissed his ear. 'Come on Charlie. Tell the truth.'

He twiddled my still soft red hair. 'OK, OK, I did have certain doubts. That's true.'

'Like. . .?'

He smiled at the recollection. 'Well, I had this crazy fear that you and Maria would be shameless maneaters.'

Now it was my turn to look horrified. 'How could you?'

'I don't know why, really. I just thought you would be having wild parties, and that every man in Vancouver would end up in my apartment, dancing and shouting and upsetting the neighbours.'

(He wasn't entirely wrong of course. I did entertain Wes in Charlie's apartment, but he no longer seemed relevant. I had half told Charlie about Wes, but underplayed his role in my life. I must be honest and admit to myself that I am now more than a little ashamed at my adolescent feelings for the golden-haired waster. Falling for Wes was like falling for Brad Pitt – rather sad, and a complete waste of time.)

I spoke teasingly. 'Well you are sort of right. We did have one regular male visitor. He came every second day at least. He was quite cute. The neighbours must have noticed him. Did they not tell you?'

Charlie was trying unsuccessfully to look disinterested in this news. He spoke in a false casual manner. 'Who was this guy?'

'The pizza delivery boy.'

'Very funny. And you thought I was a dirty slob.'

'I'm so glad I was wrong.'

Charlie gave me a fierce kiss. 'Me too, Maeve. Me too.'

Joe and Maria called over one night, raising their eyebrows when they heard how we have stayed at home, shunning the rest of the world. Maria knew the ultimate jibe. She knew how to prod me out of this exclusivity. She said it quietly, waiting for the desired effect. 'You know what, Maeve, you're turning out just like Theresa and Michael.' Now, no one in the room except for me had ever met these two individuals, but everyone had heard about them, and knew what Maria meant. There was a moment of exaggerated panic, as Charlie and I rushed around, looking for shoes and jackets and car keys, readying ourselves to go out.

When we breathlessly presented ourselves at the front door, ready to leave, Maria laughed, 'It's OK, guys. You've just met, you get a few months' grace, to get the soppy stuff over with. You get a dispensation in the beginning. Just don't make a long-term habit of it. OK?'

We went to the local, and enjoyed a few sociable drinks, alcohol for three of us, orange juice for the ever-careful Maria. I half-heartedly contributed to the conversation, but I couldn't get Maria's phrase out of my head. It rolled around my brain distracting me from the long funny story with which Joe was entertaining the others. Tears rolled down Charlie's cheeks, and Maria giggled helplessly, but I sat straight-faced, listening to the mean-minded echo in my head. 'Long-term habit.' How could I make a long-term habit of anything where Charlie was concerned? I love him, he'd be a great habit to have, one I could indulge at will, one I wouldn't have to resolve to give up every New Year. Small problem though. Vancouver. I don't think I could survive on phone calls and letters and e-mails and annual reunions. Twice-yearly stolen extravagant weekends would not be enough to get me through the lonely months of winter. A week of glorious concentrated passion would not be enough to compensate me for endless cold desolate weeks of being alone.

Once or twice I've mentioned his departure, but Charlie doesn't want to discuss it. 'Please, Maeve,' he always replies. 'Let's not talk about me leaving. We'll face up to that when the time comes, but now our time is precious, and I don't want to waste it.' I've been quite happy to agree, but deep down, I know this is wrong. I feel I'm in a runaway car, heading for a brick wall. I know the wall is there, but I'm doing nothing about it. I'm not braking, and I'm not trying to jump out. I'm just sitting back, hoping that the inevitable won't happen after all. I'm like one of those crash test dummies, with those funny little electrodes on their heads, and the skinny little arms. I know there's a big bang coming, but I'm unable to do anything except sit there, passively. Then I'll lurch forward, arms flailing, and split my head when the inevitable impact comes. And I bet I'm in the test car without the airbag. No doubt my seat belt isn't even fastened.

It's foolish really, but I don't care. *Carpe Diem*. I must enjoy today, and worry about tomorrow, tomorrow. To add yet another unnecessary metaphor, I do a good line in ostrich behaviour.

On Monday, I had to go to work of course. It was hard to get up, leaving Charlie, warm and sleepy, curled up in the bed. I was sort of tempted to phone in sick. It would have been my first time to do this, and no one need ever know. I would easily have got away with it. Something made me drag myself up, though. I knew I had to do it. I had to face work, as next week I'll be very glad of work to distract me. Next week, work will be the highlight of my existence.

I did my best to ignore Theresa, who still looks at me in a quizzical fashion whenever we meet. Even though the rosy hue is fading, she knows there's something going on. The day dragged by, and as soon as the children left, I followed them, just waiting discreetly for the last straggles of parents to leave the school yard. It wouldn't have been the done thing to be seen to be leaving before them.

I brought home some work that just had to be done for the next day, wondering if I'd be disciplined enough to do it. Of course I should have done it at my desk before leaving school, but I couldn't wait to get back home. I couldn't stay in that stuffy classroom, breathing in whiffs of chalk dust and sweat and cheese and onion crisps, when I could be with Charlie.

A beautiful hot, spicy smell greeted me as I opened the front door. Charlie, looking really ridiculous in a flowery plastic apron, given to me by my mother, was busy in the kitchen. He kissed me, and asked how my day was, before turning back to the bubbling pot he was stirring, the perfect househusband.

'Dinner's all set for later. I thought we might go for a walk.' Then he noticed the bag of copies I was trying to discreetly slide under the kitchen table. 'I could leave them until later,' I suggested. Charlie wouldn't hear of it though. He sat me at the kitchen table, served me coffee, and waited patiently until I was finished. His presence was a terrible distraction though. I couldn't give my full attention to the Irish essays I was supposed to be marking, and many scrawly, rushed offerings survived with a noncommital red tick, and a scribbled date, instead of the detailed correction they called for.

Eventually, with the job barely done, I packed up my work, and we went for a long, long walk, returning to eat the delicious curry that Charlie had prepared earlier.

The days fell into an easy, regular pattern. Charlie stayed at home and cooked and cleaned quite contentedly while I went out to earn a crust. I found myself thinking that I could live very happily like this.

I won't get the chance though, will I?

We went out with Joe and Maria a few times as the week went on, for casual drinks and meals, and we went through another tea at Mum and Dad's. I was less uptight on this occasion, and nearly enjoyed it. Mum was still on her best behaviour, though slightly more relaxed, and Dad got to have a sly look at the newspaper when Mum wasn't looking.

We also went to eat at Sean and Eimear's. This was a bit more of an ordeal, as I value Sean's opinion so much, and was afraid he wouldn't approve of Charlie. I needn't have worried though. It was clear, as the meal progressed, that Sean liked him, and even better, the feeling seemed to be mutual. Charlie has that wonderful quality, hard to describe, of fitting in well, whatever the company. I could see Eimear, normally quiet, almost withdrawn sometimes, enjoying the chat, appreciating his interest in what she was saying. The children thought Charlie was 'wicked', a great compliment it seems. (It's strange, isn't it? I know language evolves over time, but I don't quite understand how a word we used to use as an insult is now considered to be the highest praise.) He brought the children each a comic, and even better, sat down to read to them, and help them with the quizzes and puzzles. I could see Eimear and Sean smiling approvingly, as Charlie urged the children to find an atlas, so he could show them where he lived. He traced with his finger, showing them the route his flight had taken, winking at us while he explained how he thought he'd seen a family of polar bears as he flew over Greenland. I found myself thinking, not for the first time, how lucky Todd was to have such a father, even if only on a part-time basis.

The perfect guest, Charlie went into the kitchen to help Eimear to clear up. I could hear the murmur of their chat, above the clink of glasses, and the dull whirr of the dishwasher. Sean went upstairs to tuck the children into bed, returning unusually quickly. He poured us each a glass of wine, and sat next to me on the couch.

'He's very nice, Maeve. I like him a lot.'

I nodded my agreement.

He continued, 'What's going to happen when he goes back to Canada?'

I didn't reply.

'Is that it? Another one bites the dust?'

I shrugged my shoulders. I had no answers, and didn't really want to get involved in this discussion.

Anyway, I knew the washing up couldn't take that long, and that Charlie and Eimear would be back with us soon. Sean looked towards the kitchen, understanding my thoughts.

'Look, Maeve. I've never seen you so happy. You don't want to slip back into that lonely life, in your lonely home. Don't give up on this guy. He's nice. He's good to you. Why don't you go back to Canada with him? Give him a chance. If it doesn't work out, you can live with that. The worst that could happen is that you'd have to come home again. Big deal. You could put it down to experience. Go away with him. Don't leave yourself open to a long old age full of regrets and tales of what might have been.'

That was a long speech for Sean, and it was delivered at speed, as he kept one eye on the kitchen door.

Charlie and Eimear emerged just as Sean stopped speaking, sparing me the trouble of finding answers. Sean served them a last drink, and we talked small talk until it was time to go home.

As we said our goodbyes, I avoided Sean's eyes, but as he gave me a hug, he whispered one word.

'Think.'

That's it then, everyone who's met him thinks Charlie's great. I've hit the jackpot at last. I've met the perfect guy. Everything should be easy from now on. I should just pack my bags, turn out the lights, and go. The first day of the rest of my life beckons. So why am I waiting?

Small problem. Charlie hasn't asked me to go back with him. He's declared his love, many times, and in many ways. He's been perfect. But he hasn't asked me to go back with him. The best he's said has been a little on the vague side. 'We'll work something out. I don't want to lose you again.' That's all very well, but I can't respond to it. I can't pretend that the future isn't out there, lurking around every shadowy corner, waiting to get me. Even this sad crash test dummy can only pretend for so long. I can't act as if the distance between Cork and Vancouver isn't a problem. I've never been very good at pretending anyway, and I can't pretend now, when it means so much to me.

There's another problem too. Even if Charlie were to get on bended knee to ask me to return with him, I don't know if I'd go. I love him, I have no doubt about that any more. (Thanks, Wes. You taught me the important difference between love and infatuation.) Still though, I don't know if I'm able to commit myself to this love. I don't know if I could up and leave this life I know so well, for some unknown prospect far away. I like familiarity. There's nothing wrong in being comfortable. Who decreed that change is such a great thing? What's so great about it? Maybe my life alone here isn't so bad. I could do a lot worse than to stay here, out of trouble. Where I'm safe.

Yes, I know. I've read enough self-help books in my life. I know the problem is that I'm afraid of commitment. It's a common problem, apparently. I'm probably a textbook case. Psychiatry professors could base their lectures around me. Students could listen, shaking their heads in pity. I know all this, but knowing it doesn't help. I'm still afraid.

Charlie has gone to town to buy some presents for Todd. He'll be gone for a few hours. When he returns, we are going to Maria's house to eat. She wondered if perhaps Charlie and I would prefer to spend his last night here alone, but I didn't want to. It's all too sad.

Did I start this chapter by saying how wonderful love is? Forget it. Rod Stewart misled us for all those years. His hoarse voice was crooning out a pack of lies. OK, so the first cut might be the deepest, but the second one, the reopening of the half-healed wound, is much, much more painful.

Love isn't happy and wonderful. Love was invented by the singers of romantic songs, by the people with a financial interest in St Valentine's day, by the makers of tissues. Love is for suckers, and I'm a sad, sad sucker. I'm as sad as they come.

I hope the local shop has plenty of Kleenex in stock. It's going to do a roaring trade in the next few days.

And I haven't even got a cold.

Chapter Forty-two

January 23

He's gone.

Last night was terrible. Joe and Maria did their best, but it was no good. It was probably mean of us to involve them, as it was never going to be a happy occasion. It's sometimes possible to ask too much of one's friends. Even of good friends like Maria and Joe. Charlie and I should have stayed at home, being miserable on our own.

Maria and Joe talked brightly of how time flies, and how it would be great for me to go to Vancouver for the entire summer. Joe casually mentioned how little time there was left until the end of the financial year, and Easter, which followed on its heels. He mentioned a new budget airline that is investigating North American routes. They laughed and joked, but it was all empty, hollow. I tried, but couldn't respond, and Charlie was even worse. We're not rude, but neither of us could engage in sparkling dinner conversation, as if everything were rosy. Our two cross faces successfully dampened whatever false cheer Maria and Joe tried to create.

Charlie and I left early, apologising for our bad spirits. Maria hugged me at the door, and made me promise to call over on my way home from the airport.

Charlie and I went straight to bed when we got home, though not for a night of passionate lovemaking.

Last night there was no passion, no sex. He wrapped his strong, safe arms around me, and we lay together, not speaking, wallowing in our joint loneliness. I lay there hardly sleeping, watching the red numbers on my digital clock flash slowly onwards.

In the morning, after a restless night, we got up early. There was no romantic shared shower. Charlie showered first, and dressed in the bathroom. Then he went in to the kitchen, leaving me to my own devices. When I joined him, we both pushed pieces of toast and marmalade around our plates, and drank strong coffee. I tasted nothing at all, though. I just felt a gritty warmth in my dry mouth.

I washed our cups, plates, knives and spoons. I lined them on the draining board, and wondered if I would ever again wash up after breakfast for two. I dried the cups and put them away as I knew I could not face them on my return. I wiped the table, and even swept the floor, while Charlie packed up the last of his things. I could see through the open bathroom door to where my toothbrush reigned supreme again, alone once more in its chipped, blue china kingdom.

The drive to the airport was short, but dreadful. I knew one of us should speak. I was literally driving this man away, not knowing how or when I'd see him again. Most likely I would never see him again. Something had to be said, but I could say nothing, and he sat beside me, silent and grim.

We got to the boarding area, and all of a sudden it reminded me of Vancouver; of the time I'd left him before, though he had asked me to stay. Now he said nothing. This time I wasn't getting a chance to choose. Charlie seemed to be lost in a private world, out of my reach. I found myself wondering if we were going to part leaving everything up in the air; a wonderful relationship, not ended, not continuing, just suspended forever.

We hugged. A close, desperate hug. Then Charlie released me, and looked at me, with those eyes I love so much. I surveyed his face, his unremarkable nose, the lips I'd kissed and sucked, the eyebrows I'd stroked, the ears I'd whispered my deepest feelings to. He produced a folded page from his jacket pocket. Not a fancy vellum sheet, pink and scented, but a lined page, torn, I suspect, from the notepad I used for my yearly lesson plans. 'You had no envelopes,' he commented, and smiled a cold smile. 'I couldn't trust myself to say what I want to say. It might come out wrong. Please read this. It explains everything.'

He thrust the page into my hand, briefly brushed my lips with his, turned and left. He rounded the first corner without faltering, without looking back. I stood for a few moments, in the faint and unfulfilled hope that he'd run back, declaring how foolish he'd been and that he'd never leave me. The uniformed man at the desk studied the air in front of him. I found myself wondering if he were embarrassed or just bored of these tearful farewells, enacted daily as he counted the minutes, waiting for his shift to come to an end. Was he thinking how sad it was that we had to part, or was he wondering whether the interior of his car needed vacuuming?

I returned to my car, scowling at a family who were unloading suitcases from the car next to me. They were laughing and excited, obviously looking forward to a holiday, full of high spirits and anticipation. At least it had finally dawned on the airport authorities that Christmas was over, so I was spared the tinny 'Tis the season to be jolly.' That would surely have finished me altogether.

I put Charlie's page on the seat next to me, and drove home automatically, trusting my body to steer the car in the right direction, without conscious help from me.

I let myself in, horribly aware of how empty the house was, now that Charlie was gone. The door to my bedroom stood open, so I could see the rumpled sheets, and the print of Charlie's head on my spare pillow. I sat in my favourite window seat, with my back to the sea. How could I look at the sea?

I tossed Charlie's letter onto the small table nearby. Strange really. I'm the one who always wanted to open presents on Christmas Eve, the one who read the crossword answers before the clues, the one who got excited about opening junk mail. I couldn't bring myself to open this page though. I looked at it, lying there, taunting me. I felt sure that once I opened it, the dream would be over. Charlie didn't want to complicate his nice life in Vancouver by making promises to me. He wanted to give me the brush-off, and didn't know how. He couldn't tell me to my face. How could he be so cowardly? As long as I didn't read his note, I was fine, but once it was read, there would be no going back. I'd be officially dumped. I'd be the old Maeve again, the lonely one, the one who had no one special, the Maeve I didn't want to be.

It seems crazy now, a bit unhinged, but then it seemed perfectly logical. I sat there, in the unheated house, wallowing in self-pity, putting off the dreadful rejection. I half heard the car pulling up, the click of a handbrake being engaged, and the slam of a door. Footsteps crunched on the gravel, and then I heard the duller thud of soft shoes hurrying along the path. There was a light tap on the window, and I turned.

No, don't get excited, this isn't a film, it's real life, my life. It wasn't Charlie, back to reclaim his lost love.

This was no lover leaping from a taxi. There was no complicit taxi-driver adjusting his position on his beaded seat cover and smiling at the happy scene. It was Maria.

She's a good friend. When I didn't call to her on my way back from the airport, instead of finding an excuse and then forgetting me, she worried, and decided to see how I was. She shivered as she came into the room, which must have been much colder than her car. She looked at my face, grim and tearless. 'How about if I light a fire, and then we'll talk?' I didn't respond, so she set to work. It was vaguely comforting to sit there watching her bustle around, with no need for conversation. Within minutes, the first flames, not warm but promising, were licking around the generous chunk of firelighters Maria had used. She made coffee, and poured us each a cup. I circled mine with my hands, aware for the first time how cold I was.

Coffee. My first step into being a teenager, when I finally developed a taste for it, after months of trying. I must have been sixteen by the time I learned to like it and triumphantly I turned my back on tea, the drink of my childhood. Coffee was witness to all my girlish traumas and disappointments. Every melodramatic scene of my teenage years was re-enacted for my friends over a cup of strong, instant coffee. As a student, coffee revived me after night-time excesses, and sustained me in later months as I studied all night in an effort to make up for those same excesses. Coffee was my friend, and I needed it now. Sad really. My real, flesh and blood friend and lover had just flown out of my life, and the best I could do was replace him with a cup of ground beans and hot water.

Maria, tired of waiting I suppose, looked me in the eye.

'Well?' One short word, by which I could see she meant me to tell her everything, to unburden my soul.

I answered dully. 'Well what? He's gone.'

She spoke brightly, probably afraid of being sucked into my pit of listless despair, never to surface again. 'I know he's gone. Lousy isn't it? You must feel rotten. When are you going to see him again? Can he come over at Easter? Are you going there for the summer? What have you decided?'

'Nothing.'

Maria shook her head in wonder. 'Well, it's no wonder you look so grim. You should have arranged something. You'd feel better if you had a fixed date for your next meeting. Why don't you ring him tonight and fix up something for the Easter holidays?'

How could she be so obtuse? 'It's not like that, Maria.'

She spoke brightly. 'You can't arrange things for Easter? That's a pity. Still, summer won't be long coming. Then you'll have two months to look forward to.'

I spoke rather sharply. 'He's just gone, Maria. Gone for good. There are no plans and there won't be any plans. Charlie doesn't want to see me any more. It's finished between us.'

She looked at me in disbelief. Clearly Charlie hadn't confided in her. He hadn't discussed his plans with her. He mustn't have told her he was going to abandon me. They were nice and pally before Christmas but evidently he felt he couldn't share this particular little gem with her. Maria spoke softly.

'He can't just be gone. He couldn't. He wouldn't just go.'

The fire was beginning to give off its first heat, with a few crackly spurts. I pulled a low stool towards it and sat down, stretching out my hands to feel the warmth. We sat for a while in silence. I had nothing to say, and while Maria probably had plenty to say, she wasn't saying it. I studied the fire as if the secrets of the universe were contained in its yellowish flames. Maria waited patiently.

Eventually I broke the silence, speaking in disgust. I pointed at the letter.

'He's given me the brush-off.'

Maria rubbed my arm sympathetically. 'Oh, Maeve, you poor thing. I'm so sorry.'

'He couldn't even do it to my face. Don't you think dumping me by letter is a bit chicken?'

'You're right, it is. I'm surprised at Charlie. I'd have expected more of him.'

'Me too. I expected a lot more of him. What a fool I was.'

'Everything seemed to be going so well. You were getting on great. I can't understand it. What happened?'

I couldn't answer. I could feel the first tears gathering. Maria rubbed my arm some more.

She spoke tentatively. 'Maeve. . . would you mind if I read the letter?'

I shrugged. I didn't care. Someone may as well read it after all Charlie's trouble writing it. I believe in protecting the environment, and I don't like to see paper wasted.

I passed her the paper, hating its smooth, cool touch against my skin. Maria unfolded it carefully, and read. After a few seconds, she raised her head and looked at me in puzzlement.

'This is the brush-off?'

I shrugged again. It was that kind of conversation, lots of despair, lots of silences, lots of shrugs.

Suddenly realisation dawned on Maria. 'You big eejit! You spend your time putting yourself down, and now you've got used to disappointment, and expect it everywhere you turn. You haven't even read this letter, have you?' A faint glimmer of something like hope stirred, and I reached for the letter.

Briefly Maria taunted me, holding it out of my reach, but she quickly relented, and handed it over, shaking her head. 'You big, big eejit.' She wasn't lost for words; she just seemed stuck in a groove, repeating the same ones again.

She discreetly picked up the cups and went towards the kitchen, closing the door behind her. With hope and fear jumbled together in equal measure, I read.

> Dear Maeve,
> I love you. I loved you when I met you in Vancouver. I love you now.
>
> You left me last summer, and I learned to live with it. I can't bear to lose you again. I am afraid to discuss the future with you, afraid of what you will say. I feel I can't reach you, and that's why I'm writing this. I couldn't look you in the eye, and be rejected again. Please, please consider giving me a chance. I have to get back to Todd, otherwise you'd find me loitering in your house, in hope. As it is, I must leave, and it breaks my heart. Could you find a way to come here, soon? I miss you already and I haven't even left. If you want me, I'll come back at Easter. I'll come back in the summer. I'll do anything. Just please say you want me. Please call me. I love you.
> Charlie.

Charlie, my North-American lover. My new man, unafraid to express his emotions. How I love the fact that he could write such sweet, dear words. Words like the lovers in the movies write.

Years ago, the few missives I got from Paddy

consisted of cartoon postcards, or notes on my books in the library: 'I can't meet you tonight. I've got soccer training.' 'I'm in the bar. Can you drop over and lend me a fiver?' That kind of thing. Now Charlie was laying bare his soul with no real hope of acceptance. I didn't deserve him. I didn't believe in him. Oh Hell. I do deserve him, I love him, and I'm not going to mess it up.

I could see Maria peeping around the kitchen door, grinning. She was still stuck in the same old groove, 'You huge big eejit.' I forgave her though.

We opened a bottle of wine, and drank to the new, open me. (The new, pregnant Maria only had half a glass.) We discussed the options – ways that I could pursue the relationship, with Maria encouraging me, knowing she had the perfect opportunity to get me to override my cautious approach to affairs of the heart. I think she was afraid to leave me to my own devices, afraid that even at this stage I'd find an excuse to backtrack.

'Charlie says he'll come over at Easter. You should let him.'

'Why?'

'So then it will be your turn, and you can go over to Vancouver for the summer.'

'Wow. I'd love another summer in Vancouver. And with Charlie. I'd just love it.' I smiled a dreamy smile.

'Maybe Charlie could transfer to UCC for a year. Maybe his research could be done here.'

'No, Maria, I don't think so. He needs to be in Vancouver. And anyway, what about Todd? Charlie wouldn't leave Todd for a year.'

'Yes, I suppose you're right.'

I spoke tentatively. 'I could take a career break. I could go there for a year.'

Maria laughed. 'A year to start with, you mean. Come on Maeve, I've seen you two together. I don't think you will be finished with each other in a year.'

She's right. I can see a long, soppy forever stretching in front of me. What a lovely feeling!

'Ring him now,' she urged.

'How can I? He won't even be home yet.'

'Ever hear of answering machines? You can call and leave him a message.'

Clever move, Maria. I couldn't find a way to unleave a message once it was left. And it would make a nice full circle. The first time I heard Charlie's voice it was on his answering machine, so it was fitting that he should hear this important message on the same piece of clever technology.

It took ten minutes of frantic rummaging for me to find Charlie's number. I eventually discovered it on an e-mail he'd sent me before I went to Vancouver. I dialled and waited impatiently for electronic permission to speak. I left a brief and hardly original message: 'It's Maeve. I love you Charlie. Please ring, sorry, call me back. Soon.'

I emptied the bottle of wine, and it magnified my

good spirits, leaving me grinning, and sure that the world was a marvellous place. Maria sipped her half glass, and left for home.

So here I am, all tucked up in my bed, alone, but far from lonely. I am writing these few words because I never want to forget how wonderful I feel tonight. Also, to be honest, I don't want to be able to backtrack in the morning, telling myself I'm overreacting, that it's just a holiday romance that's got a bit carried away with itself, you know the kind of thing.

Though no one will ever read it, I'm putting it in writing, for myself – I love Charlie, he loves me, and I am going to do my very best to make this work, to make it last.

Goodnight.

Chapter Forty-three

12 February

This is it. I have made the arrangements. I am going. I have taken a big leap, and become one of those people who actually do things, instead of finding pathetic reasons not to. Think what my life could have been if I'd always been like this!

I could be a high-flying executive.

I could be running a huge organic farm.

I could be President.

I could have died in a skydiving accident when I was twenty.

Things happened very quickly in the end. Charlie rang me as soon as he got back to Vancouver, and we said all the silly romantic things about forever that we'd never got around to before. The dialogue for fifty trashy novels whizzed over and back across the Atlantic as we gushed forth. I undid ten years of desperate cynicism in one phone call. We finally rang off after lots of failed attempts ('Bye. . . Are you still there?' 'Yes. I love you. Bye so.' 'Maeve?' 'You hang up, I can't.' 'OK. Bye.' 'Charlie?'). I gently replaced the receiver, and sat looking at it for some time. Gradually I became aware of the silly smile that was plastered all over my face, and though I tried, I couldn't quite remove it. I was tempted to leap on the next plane, and hang the consequences, but that would have been too much, even for the new me. Instead I rang Maria, and she patiently listened while I waffled on for ages about how wonderful I felt. She's such a good friend; she didn't even snigger once.

A few days later, I made my first move. Egged on by Maria, my mother and Sean, all afraid I suppose that the old me would reappear, and I'd change my mind, I approached Mr Flynn, cap in hand, and told him the truth. The truth being that I want some time off so I can go to Vancouver to see if I can make myself a happy life with my boyfriend. Soft-hearted man that he is, Mr Flynn thought it was a great idea, and helped me to concoct an acceptable story for the board of management. Persuaded by him, the board agreed to grant me six months exceptional, unpaid leave, which can be extended if I wish. I try not to be cynical any more but I expect I was helped by the fact that the parish priest's nephew has just returned from voluntary work in Rwanda, and needs a job, and would be only too happy to fill in for me, for as long as necessary. Maybe he'll like soccer, and Pat will at last have a soul mate. He might hold Theresa's wool for her while she knits, or help her to count out her tapestry stitches. He could turn around the entire dynamics of the staff room. Lucky him.

Theresa hugged me when she heard the news, and confessed that she'd always secretly envied me and wished she could be more like me. Not. She hasn't undergone a personality transplant either. What really happened was that she grudgingly wished me well, but I heard her muttering to Pat later on. 'It's going to be very disruptive for her class you know, changing teacher in the middle of the year. But Maeve always puts herself first. Remember last year when. . .' She halted abruptly, when she saw that I was standing at the photocopier, partly shielded by a mound of dusty old reading books. I just smiled sweetly, too happy to be offended, as she reddened and slunk off to her class. However badly things go in Vancouver, I will always be able to console myself with the idea that things could be worse — I could be in the staff room watching Theresa knitting.

After work was sorted out, there were only minor details to consider. It's funny how simple it is to walk away. Sean will arrange for my house to be let out while I'm gone, and I've given my car to Maria for the duration. Of course, she didn't want to accept at first, but I managed to persuade her, and I sincerely hope I won't be back in a hurry to reclaim it. She swears she will be selling it in six months, and sending me the proceeds.

Mum and Dad, though I know they'll miss me, are delighted to see me go, glad to see me so happy. (Imagine a good Catholic Irish mother glad to see her daughter going thousands of miles away, to live in sin with a divorced foreigner. How times have changed!)

Charlie has sorted things out in Canada for me. He will enrol me in some kind of course in the university, so I can get a student visa, and we think this will allow me to do some paid work. I think I might try my hand at teaching English as a second language. (Thanks Mum. That TEFL course was one of the many you persuaded me to take, one of the few that looks as if it might be useful. I don't think, somehow, I could make my living by origami demonstrations or car maintenance, or indeed, creative writing.)

Charlie said he would love me to live with him, but offered to find a flat for me to rent if I wished. I was tempted, cautious to the last, but then figured I could prevaricate forever, and never do anything, so I agreed to take the plunge, and stay with him. It will be strange going back to his apartment again, now that things are so different. I'll sit on the balcony with a beer, and look out over English Bay. And he'll be sitting next to me. I'll drop my toothbrush into the Bart Simpson mug over the bathroom sink, and Charlie's brush will be there too. I'll be sleeping in his bed again, wrapped up in his sheets, but this time he'll be there. It's going to be very strange. Strange, but nice.

I'm a bit worried about Todd, as I don't want to fall into the wicked stepmother role — I've read too many fairytales, and they can't all be wrong. Charlie assures me that Todd spends his life trying to fix him up with his friends' mothers, so as he won't feel too bad about all the time he spends with Melinda and Toby. Therefore, he says, Todd will love the idea of me being around. I've decided to believe him, and if he's wrong, well, I'll cross that bridge when I come to it.

That's about it then. I leave tomorrow, the first day of my new life. My house is strangely empty. I've gone through cupboards and shelves, bravely following the clear-out rule and dumping things I haven't used in the past year. Some stuff made it to the charity shop, but most of it was only fit for the bin. I've packed away all my most personal stuff, the stuff I cannot persuade myself to part with, and stashed it in the attic. I packed it in large cardboard boxes and sealed them with Sellotape. There was something strangely reassuring in the sharp noise of the Sellotape unwinding, as I put layer over layer over layer, all totally unnecessary.

I wonder when, if ever, I'll open those boxes again.

In my rummaging, I found a bundle of photographs, taken many years ago. These ones never made it into my photo albums. They're the ones of Paddy and me. My youthful, trusting eyes dance out from the pictures, as I drape myself across him. I noticed that in each one he's standing a little aloof, detached, often leaning slightly away from me. In most he has a strange half-smile, and he seems to be scanning the horizon, as if he's looking for something. Funny how I never noticed that before.

I was going to burn them. Then I decided not to

bother. I had too much to do. It would be bad for the environment. And it doesn't matter any more.

I'm sitting here in my favourite window seat, gazing out at the moon on the sea – the view I love. The view that can calm my soul even on my darkest days. I am so very happy that I won't be here gazing at it tomorrow. Or the next day.

Soon I'll pack away this journal, and hide it in the far reaches of the attic, behind my First Communion cards, my college lecture notes and the certificate I won for gas cookery when I was in fifth class. The new me will have no time for writing.

Sorry, Walter, this would never have made a good novel. This won't be your big chance of a mention in the dedication of a bestseller. There won't be any, 'To Dear Walter. I couldn't have done it without you.' You drummed it into us, many times, and we repeated it back to you, like obedient eight-year-olds reciting their tables, 'A good novel needs a strong plot and dramatic tension.' This fails on both counts. I have failed you Walter, even more than those sad housewives have failed you. (Incidentally, those housewives can still be found hawking their domestic dramas around the shopping centres of Cork, picking on unsuspecting passers-by, and making them part with precious euro.) At least I am realistic about my work. I don't expect anyone to pay money for it.

Can't you just imagine the reviews, in the unlikely

event of it ever being published? 'Sad Irish teacher whinges on at length, before convenient Canadian takes pity on her, and whisks her off to predictable married bliss.'

I know I'm getting a bit carried away, but I can even picture the scene in cinemas, during the great premiere of the movie of my life. I see bored viewers fumbling at their obscenely large, striped cartons of popcorn, burping loudly after swigging their Coke too quickly, and muttering to each other at the beginning of the second reel, 'Bet you any money the beardy guy gets his leg over. It's dead obvious.' Next I see a stampede from the cinema, with showers of popcorn cascading through the half-dark, to be trampled unceremoniously into the sticky red carpet. By the time the escaped viewers are happily knocking back their third pints in the pub next door, the projectionist and the usherette are slumbering peacefully, as the closing credits roll slowly over the great moments of my life.

I have to face up to the truth. I know now that I'll never be a writer. Great books aren't made from the pettiness of lives such as mine.

No, I'm afraid my work will surely, as I first predicted, be tossed unread on an environmentally unfriendly bonfire, and the wisps of smoke it produces will spiral gracefully upwards, into the blue, blue sky, before vanishing forever, like my lonely, self-indulgent words.

And do you know what?

I really don't care.

Sorry, Walter

*Win two free flights to Canada!**

Have you enjoyed your trip to Canada with Maeve? Fallen in love with the gorgeous scenery and fabulous food? Would you love to go, to sample the sights and enjoy the nightlife?

Now's your chance! Tivoli is delighted to offer you two free flights to Canada, and the adventure of a lifetime.

From oceans to mountains, from cowboy chic to urban élan, from dreamy landscapes to timeless cultures, Canada is a tapestry of captivating pursuits. Laced with natural marvels, woven with fascinating history, dotted with stylish cities, this is a land of limitless possibilities...

All you have to do is answer the following question:

What is the name of Maeve's best friend?

(Direct flights from Dublin to Toronto)

INSTRUCTIONS

1. To enter the competition, answer the question.
2. Detach and post this page, along with your name, address and telephone number to:

    Sorry, Walter Competition
    Gill & Macmillan
    Hume Avenue
    Park West
    Dublin 12
    Ireland

3. The entry form does not give rise to any contract between Gill & Macmillan Ltd. ('Gill & Macmillan') and the entrant.
4. The competition will be run and determined in accordance with the Rules below.

RULES

1. The instructions above form part of the Rules.

2. Only entries on an original entry form contained at the end of a copy of *Sorry, Walter* will be considered.

3. Multiple entries will be accepted, but each such entry must be on an original entry form.

4. No cash will be offered in lieu of the prizes available in the competition.

5. Gill & Macmillan will in its absolute discretion decide any matter or question concerning the running of the competition, these Rules, their interpretation or any ancilliary matter and any such decision or necessary opinion of Gill & Macmillan will be final and no correspondence will be entered into concerning such a decision.

6. Gill & Macmillan will have no responsibility for, and is not obliged to take into account, any entry lost, damaged or delayed in the post or otherwise.

7. All entries must be sent and received by Gill & Macmillan, by ordinary post. No entries received by any means other than ordinary post such as by hand, courier, facsimile, etc., will be accepted or considered.

8. All entries must be received by Gill & Macmillan prior to or not later than 31 September 2003 ('the Closing Date')

9. Gill & Macmillan reserves the right to extend the Closing Date if necessary.

10. All entries properly received by Gill & Macmillan prior to the Closing Date will be stamped with the date and time of receipt.

11. Gill & Macmillan will notify the winner within two weeks of the Closing Date that he/she has been successful.

12. The competition is open to residents of the Republic of Ireland and the United Kingdom, except the author, employees of Gill & Macmillan and their families, and employees and/or administration of *Sorry, Walter* and this competition.

13. The winner's name may, at Gill & Macmillan's discretion, be published in the press.